Engl.

D0991040

"Where shall I begin, please your Majesty?" he asked.
"Begin at the beginning," the king said gravely, "and go on till
you come to the end: then stop."

LEWIS CARROLL, *Alice in Wonderland*

Melinda by

TRANSLATED BY L. K. CONRAD

Gaia Servadio

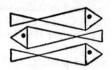

Farrar, Straus and Giroux · *New York*

Copyright © 1968 by Gaia Servadio
Published in Italian under the title
Tanto Gentile e Tanto Onesta,
© Copyright 1967 by Gaia Servadio Mostyn-Owen
All rights reserved
Second printing, 1968
Library of Congress catalog card number: 68–14913
Printed in the United States of America
Designed by Kay Eaglin

853
S591.E

Harriet Irving Library
217767
Universit... ...runswick
9/68

TO PUCCI

Melinda

✦

At the age of thirteen, after having seduced her father, Melinda was placed under the care of the best analyst in the world, Professor Hochtensteil. Hochtensteil had been Freud's favorite pupil but later quarreled violently with the Master, and rumor now had it that among his patients were the Queen Mother of England, Malraux, and Goldwater. The victim of the seduction, Melinda's father, was a serious and highly respected publisher with considerable financial backing. Abraham Publishing had arrived in England in 1934, leaving behind him in Eastern Europe a small fortune and a beautiful but insufferable wife. Instead he brought with him his two children, Melinda and Medoro.

Hochtensteil had always admired Abraham Publishing. He admired his literary salon, his distinguished dinners, his placid, discreet way of removing himself when he was tired or bored—which he often was. Hochtensteil had learned to recognize this condition by the wearied flutter of Abraham's eyelid that barely affected the rest of his otherwise attentive face.

The women invited to Publishing's were elegant and intense. Which of them was his favorite at any particular time, no one quite knew. Hochtensteil, in fact, had come to the conclusion that Abraham found a great deal more fascination in his work than in beautiful women.

With the exception of Melinda. In her increasingly frequent appearances at her father's gatherings she charmed guests and

Melinda

family alike. The product of many nationalities, she spoke a number of languages fluently and very badly, each with a strong accent, translating idioms freely from one to another. Perhaps the language she knew best was Czech, which her nursemaid had taught her.

To look at, Melinda was not quite as striking as people said. She was tall, she had long legs, long hair, and a variety of faces, for she had discovered the importance of being able to draw on a vast stock of expressions at will. She had made a study of eyes wide open with amazement, mouth pursed in consternation, eyebrows pathetically knit. She had perfected the aware face, the malicious face, the face loaded with suggestion. She learned at her father's parties that it took her fifteen minutes at the outside to fascinate the most difficult, restless person in the room.

After this discovery and after hearing the hundreds of phrases her father's friends used to describe her to herself (about her body, her role as girl-woman, her role as woman-girl, her hair, her way of wearing her hair, her fluently inaccurate language), Melinda set out to conquer the most unattainable of all the men around her, her father. Abraham resisted for a few days, then a blissful relationship began. There were no complications about rooms or hotels, no excuses to be invented. They slept in the same house; it was natural that father and daughter retire early together, as soon as Abraham's eyelids began to flutter.

Melinda therefore did not understand why her father wanted to end their happy intercourse so rudely and pack her off to Hochtensteil to be cured.

The sessions with the professor were tedious, almost social. Hochtensteil—school of Freud—asked no questions, he let her talk. Melinda didn't know what to say to the man. Several dull weeks passed before she put her sad eyebrows and wide eyes into operation, and not even Hochtensteil could withstand these for long. Once she had established physical intimacy with him, Melinda was able to become friends and tell Hochtensteil about the affair with her father, her occasional absent-minded visits to her brother Medoro's room, and some tepid affairs with writers. In short, she became the ideal patient. Hochtensteil didn't believe her and convinced himself that Melinda was having adolescent incest fantasies, until Melinda (not that she was offended at being called a liar, but she did want to help the professor) verified her stories with a series of photographs taken by automatic camera. At that point Hochtensteil felt that Melinda, since she suffered no guilt complexes, was successfully through her analysis. He then had Melinda analyze him, and she soon cured him once and for all of his Calvinistic complexes.

"Now that you've been analyzed and have analyzed someone else," Hochtensteil said, "you can practice." But Melinda, tired of spending months at a school in the country and wasting energy on pretexts to get to London or sneak out of school, announced that she would continue her education taking lessons from life. Which she did, until she learned that boarding school hadn't taught her how to ward off Nature and that she was expecting a baby.

But all this happened later. "It was such a chaotic week," Melinda explained to Hochtensteil.

Nobody could put a finger on the paternity of the child, whether Medoro, the professor, or Abraham himself, so they palmed it off on a man named Jacques. Not without some embarrassment, Melinda's first-born saw the light of day, a beautiful boy named Jove.

In a way it was Abraham's fault. After Melinda had her analyst's license, Abraham decided to send her away with Medoro to Italy. Melinda found herself in Liguria, a guest at the villa of old Spencer, a blind octogenarian writer. The villa was immense, marble inside and out, with a panoramic view of Portovenere and the Gulf of La Spezia; and there were all the latest memorials to the usual English poets who had merely tried to swim across the Gulf and had naturally ended up by drowning. There was a plaque where Shelley had lived, one where Keats had stayed, and one marking Byron's Grotto, which was used as a public lavatory

because of the lack of other facilities for holidaymakers' conveni-
ence. Even D. H. Lawrence had a plaque, in spite of his letters
from Italy being so rude about the Italians. But then probably
nobody in Liguria had read them.

The villa had a garden, an olive grove, and great rocks and
beaches nearby. This gave Melinda some freedom; she could sneak
off to the local bar and listen to the jukebox whenever she was
able to evade the chaperoning of the old man's niece, Lily Spencer.
Lily, whose sole topic of conversation was her oozing gums, occupied herself with complaining. Any occasion was appropriate for
her to fly down to the town hall and complain in an English accent
which twenty years in Italy had not erased.

Lily Spencer was one of those people who invite disaster. If
she went for a stroll through the woods, she was mistaken for a
bird and shot at. If important people were invited to dine, dinner
was served punctually, burnt to a crisp. And there was the time
she wished her husband a good trip: the end of their only car
and her only husband.

Once the villa had been quite beautiful. Lady Volumnia Spencer, the very rich dead wife of the aged writer—whom Abraham
published—had furnished the house with tapestries, rugs, damask
draperies, and varicolored marble flooring. The draperies were now
in shreds, the sofas saturated with dogs' urine; the rest of the
furniture looked like pop sculpture. On the great terrace were
Spencer's wheelchair, his many little tables covered with obscure
brands of Vermouth, his fans, his bandages, his bottles of medi-
cine. The aged writer was always complaining of the heat and
listened to music from a tape recorder. He hated records—they
were mechanical devices. Tape recorders, on the other hand, he
could tolerate: indeed he made his nephew Eros slave whole evenings at the piano while he taped his wobbly performances.

Every once in a while Melinda would visit the writer. Old
Spencer had never liked women but decided that Melinda had a
masculine voice, full of harpsichordal notes. Even so, conversation
was not easy. After they had exhausted literary subject matter

("How *is* Henry James? and Eton? and England?"), long silences would ensue, during which Melinda was enthralled by the old man's bare paunch spreading out of the folds of his dressing gown. Spencer was quiet only when that same paunch contained a fair amount of liquor, forbidden by his niece and his doctor. His and Melinda's friendship was based primarily on the amount of alcohol she was able to smuggle to him.

Literary topics exhausted, they had little to say to each other. The panorama over Spencer's shoulders was unbroken blue; there were the islands, the perfume of the junipers. And Melinda would escape to the beach.

The first mistake was to put Melinda and Medoro in the same bedroom. ("Melinda's a mere child," said Lily Spencer.) Two large fourposters, one large mosquito net. From Medoro's canopy hung no mosquito net at all. So, to prevent his being eaten alive by the mosquitoes, poor Medoro was forced to sleep in his sister's bed.

The second mistake was to invite another teenage girl, Lily's daughter. She was a dear, and had gone to Marymount, but between her and Melinda there were abysses of all kinds. She bored Melinda to distraction.

One day, descending the long stairway carved in the rock cliff that led to the beach, Melinda stopped for a moment to examine a structure overgrown with weeds. Lady Spencer had dreamed it up after seeing the Gloriette in Vienna, and Melinda was amused at the rapid destruction of time and ideas. She left her clothes under the Gloriette. Going down toward the sea she spotted a couple embracing. The fine brown body of the boy belonged unquestionably to her brother, and the girl . . . three more steps and she could see it was that tiresome, whining girl, Lily's daughter. It was then she decided that the nights spent under the mosquito net with her brother would cease to be innocent. This elated her, and the consequence was that both Melinda and Medoro appeared in the mornings with great bags under their eyes, exhausted but happy.

Melinda

Medoro's sudden lack of interest in Lily's daughter, the new way brother and sister exchanged glances, their obvious continual desire to touch each other, to be together alone, their long solitary swims removed all doubt from Lily's expert eye. She decided to send them both back to their father. Melinda returned to London.

Actually she stopped off a few days in Paris.

Paris is a city of much overblown reputation. Melinda had been there before, only for a few days, when Abraham had taken her with him on a business trip. This time as soon as she arrived she rang up Jacques, whom she had met some months earlier while skiing in Pontresina. Abraham had gone to Saint-Moritz, but he got it into his head that he ought to keep his daughter well away from his cosmopolitan friends. And so, at Pontresina, she had to make do with Jacques, Jacques of the enormous cashmere and vicuña pullovers, of all the wrong colors, Jacques of the enormous blue eyes and suntanned face. Jacques had accosted her in the street. Melinda was put off by the approach, but those blue eyes decided her to follow him. He took her for a Campari at a bar, where they chatted; then he bought her an excellent dinner. After dinner they went to Jacques's hotel.

"Do you know where we're going?"

"We're going to your room."

"Why?"

"Why not?"

Possibly Jacques, who after all was only nineteen, was a little shocked at Melinda's ease at grasping certain facts of life.

He undressed her. Off with her long lace stockings, her pretty panties—off with everything. Afterward they bathed together, made love again, then a shower.

Melinda went home at two or three in the morning. After lunch she and Jacques skied together, and the governess who had been sent with Melinda watched them with a tinge of envy. "Lucky young things." Jacques took her to good restaurants, and once or twice they ran into Abraham and his friends. Still more baths, more long evenings with Jacques. Then Jacques left, so did she . . .

What a good idea to see him again in Paris. He came to pick her up at the airport. They drove off in a car stuffed with gadgets and loudspeakers, music spilling out everywhere. "Jacques, I'm so happy." Melinda was always happy. At three in the afternoon they were on the wide highway to Poissy, so that poor Melinda had no chance this time to see the city.

From the house, surrounded by a garden full of ferns and furnished in precisely the wrong way (huge modern chandeliers, horrid combination of wrought iron and tinted plastic), Melinda could see the sun between the trees and ferns. It was all so poetic, including the absence of Jacques's parents. In the few hours they didn't spend in bed or at a country restaurant, Melinda and Jacques went riding, which she didn't enjoy at all because he was much better at it than she was.

The bedroom: fake Swedish modern, some African masks and modern paintings by unknown artists of dubious talent. But it was comfortable. There was a bar and ice came out automatically, brought by phantom servants. The record player poured out waves of stereophonic concerts. On those waves of music the two made love.

A chauffeur drove her back to the airport where she caught the first plane to London.

Hochtensteil was a little perturbed about Melinda's pregnancy. Melinda was proud of it and happy. She wanted a handsome, intelligent son. Which of course she had. On reflection, Hochtensteil decided to speak to Abraham. The episodes concerning Medoro and himself were left out. They would talk only of a romantic affair in France with a boy named Jacques.

Melinda balked. She had no desire at all to marry. But Abraham reluctantly decided that was the way it had to be. He went with her to Paris, where he met in person his future son-in-law's family and the young man himself. Abraham was appalled.

Melinda threw an engagement ball, to which she didn't invite her in-laws to be or even Jacques. The party went over so well that nobody went home until seven in the morning and everybody talked about it for months. But nobody managed to find out who the fiancé was.

With the help of a lawyer, Melinda drafted a letter to a mutual friend a few hours before the wedding ceremony. "I'm being married against my will." So after Jove's birth there was no problem about the divorce.

Jacques was furious. He loved his wife. Melinda explained to him that it was utterly absurd for them to tie themselves down so early in life and, if at all, they would remarry in a few years' time. Meanwhile it was important to keep in touch.

Instead they never saw each other again. The young divorcée and her son returned to London.

Some months later, at a debutante ball, something she didn't attend as a rule and to which generally she wasn't invited, not merely because she already was divorced but she was still under eighteen, Melinda met Lord Lawrence Inchball.

Lord Lawrence had one defect: he was the second son of the Duke of Brighton. His elder brother, alas, was happily married. His wife Loelia, a robust English rose, would doubtless produce heirs. If Melinda were to consider Lord Lawrence Inchball a step up, there had to be at least a possibility of her becoming Duchess of Brighton. But things moved faster than Melinda could ever have imagined.

Lawrence Inchball, who already was thirty and longed to marry into a more enlightened circle, or at least one different from his family's, was not only immediately touched by the situation of this adolescent divorcée, but fell madly in love with her. Their relationship, which could not have been purer, more delicate, or more boring, developed through parties and lunches, clubs and meetings. The greatest intimacy they achieved was an occasional breakfast at the Ritz before Lawrence went off to the City in a dark gray suit. This happened very seldom because Lawrence didn't often go to the City, having no need to work. He also preferred to stay in the country.

By the time Lawrence took Melinda to Saltlake to meet his ancient father in the famous castle on the Sussex coast, everybody considered her Inchball's future wife. Saltlake was a vast edifice. A series of castles, the oldest Norman. Bedrooms and towers had been added in the eighteenth century. In the nineteenth century Victorian ancestors had of course thought to fill in the gaps with a series of turrets and buttresses and went so far as to add a hundred-room wing.

The old Duke lived in the original southwest wing, as far as possible from his wife's apartment.

Not even the Duke could resist Melinda's charms; he admired the way she moved, the assured way she talked and operated, and he was pleased to hear the girl already had a son. At least she won't be sterile, he thought. His only hesitation was that Melinda wasn't English. A foreigner, he thought, what would my father have said? And probably Jewish blood, I'll wager, with that father called Abraham.

With the help of the butler, who propped him up, the old Duke took Melinda to see his great collection of paintings—the fine Tintoretto, the two Reynolds, the series of Canalettos. Melinda was full of comments and observations. The Duke admired her vague preparation, her feigned timidity, her courtesy to the old Duchess when she appeared for luncheon covered with jewels.

"Miss Publishing," the Duchess said while she ate her veal cutlet, "I hear you would like to marry my son Lawrence."

"You're mistaken, Your Grace," replied Melinda. "It's your son Lawrence who wants to marry me."

This retort to the wife he hated persuaded the old Duke to give the marriage his blessing—in fact to hasten it. He felt very tired and didn't want to miss seeing his young daughter-in-law enter the chapel at Saltlake wearing his grandmother's grand-

Melinda

mother's lace gown. A privilege he'd denied his own wife, who was accepted into the Brighton family solely because of the vast fortune she had brought with her.

As usual, it was raining. But it was a radiant day for the Duke of Brighton. Melinda looked marvelous and her guests were so unusual and amusing. He even liked the bride's father. Abraham Publishing was happy with this marriage: he had always dreamed of marrying into the English aristocracy. And it would benefit his professional activities. The Duke sent for Melinda. He had already gone to bed and he was exhausted. He gathered the family around him, including his wife and elder son. "My dears," he said to Lawrence and Melinda, "you two have married for love, and how lucky you are. You, Melinda my dear, are by far the best-looking member of our family. Try to produce some handsome children for the ugly Brighton clan, and do see to it that they inherit the title." And slipping a lapis lazuli ring on his daughter-in-law's finger, he drew his last breath.

Lawrence and Melinda spent their honeymoon at Taormina. "I'm so happy," Lawrence kept telling her. And Melinda began to realize how dangerous and easy it was to make everybody happy. However, the mere existence of her mother-in-law, of the new Duke of Brighton (the fourteenth) and of his wife, the Duchess, caused her to be profoundly unhappy.

Lawrence had political ambitions, fomented by the Conservative Party, who were conscious of the Brightons' popularity in the district. Melinda, not a bit happy to live in the country, was delighted with the idea and tried to help her husband. For a time she was forced to abandon short skirts and gay blouses, and instead wore pastel flowered hats and embroidered woolen dresses she bought at Harrod's.

She followed with some interest her husband's political preparation. "Labour are stupid. This country needs a certain percentage of unemployed. Nationalization is ridiculous. All the civilized countries have come to realize that. Don't you think so, my dear?"

Lawrence in the House of Commons: it would be exhilarating, a marvelous joke.

"I don't know what these Communists want . . . It's a scandal that in a country like Britain we should have trade unions . . . The stuff they show at the cinema today and that the censor lets pass—but when I get in . . ." Lawrence's acceptance speech was a great success. Abraham wrote it, but because it was judged too bold, Lawrence's brother Oswald had rewritten it. The sudden death of the Member for Brighton and Melinda's increasingly obvious pregnancy caused Lawrence, feeling awkward and very shy, to take his seat in the House of Commons long before he'd expected to.

Lawrence found Parliament an uncivilized place. This House, where half the Members slept, some wandered back and forth to the bar, others scratched themselves and passed around funny notes, and one or two rose to torment the Opposition, seemed most unattractive to him. But then nobody had ever suggested to him that the House of Commons was very pretty. The two galleries above, one for the public and the other for the press, terrified Lawrence. There was an atmosphere that took him back to his days at Eton, a school he had particularly loathed, given his scant prowess at sports and studies. The only triumphant moments of the day were those in the morning when Melinda accompanied him, elegant with her hat smartly placed and in her full maternity dress. He saw on the faces of the other Members a distinct admiration, an emotion he was unable to arouse in them during the latter part of the day. Lawrence was seated on the back benches with the other new arrivals and insignificant Members, and day after day he sat there in agony. Parliament was waiting for his maiden speech.

He had already written twenty-three and recited them in front of Melinda and the butler, but he had never had the courage to stand up and deliver them in the House. Even the subjects were too difficult for him. Foreign policy, disarmament, airline strikes, the economic situation. No matter how hard he listened, he could never follow what the other Members said. Melinda attended every day and devoured the debates, so much so that she had written Lawrence's last few speeches herself. Lawrence was discouraged and thought about abandoning his new activity.

When their first child was born, Melinda was much photographed. She spent a week in the country to relax. She detested the country and that particular kind of relaxation. One wakes up feeling heavy, there's nothing better to do than eat and afterwards drink and after that go back to sleep. Taking walks wasn't her idea of amusement. She went hunting a little, with a double-barreled shotgun and a pocketful of cartridges. Hares all over the place. And partridge and pheasant. Melinda shot at anything in any season. Her mother-in-law's company was particularly disagreeable to her. Uninvited and already drunk, she would arrive at the wing of Saltlake where Melinda had installed herself with the child, for hours she would repeat the same stories about the good old days when she was young and beautiful, about fox hunting, about the novels she was reading. Usually there was the same set of characters, an evil couple, one good man, a victim, and the usual devious Italian who enamors the romantic, wide-eyed maiden and carries her off.

Evenings with her sister-in-law were not less tedious. Loelia got on her nerves. She had the flaccid flesh of someone who's never been properly fed. Her fragile bones carried an overload of pallid skin. Her dresses were all alike: she sent away for them from a catalogue. A string of pearls during the day and pink brocade in the evening. The bare flesh above her large sagging breasts was adorned with jewels. The Brighton Jewels. The big emerald set, tiara, necklace, and bracelet, were wasted on that skin and almost emphasized her ugliness. When she went to a ball she spoke to no one, or rather no one spoke to her. If anybody was attracted by her august name, Loelia ungraciously put on her glasses and glared through them at the speaker. Oswald was always far away, dancing with some debutante or playing roulette. Melinda couldn't understand why the old Duke had allowed an idiot like her into the family, aside from her money, of course, but then the Brightons didn't need that any more. Thinking of Loelia, down in the Saltlake cellars tending her mushroom cultures that grew on clumps of manure, terrified her. Loelia was in fact happy whenever she could be alone with her horses, even more so with her mushrooms. She picked them in baskets decorated with the Brighton coat of arms and a little design reproduced from one of her own shaky sketches of Saltlake Castle. The mushrooms sold very well, not because they were any better than others but because housewives were wild about the baskets. Those with Loelia's signature naturally cost more.

Loelia's passion for mushrooms, her evident disgust with the marriage bed and with Oswald's increasingly blatant infidelities gave Melinda something to think about: whole evenings of thought. The temptation was great. Scotland Yard would have no doubts. Oswald, the new Duke, didn't have much to do, in spite of being president or member of some thirty committees and societies in the City. From time to time he opened the park and gardens of Saltlake to the public, who paid their five shillings to have a look. The proceeds went into the coffers of the local Conservative Party. Melinda decided to study secretly which of the many grades of mushrooms growing on the damp Saltlake soil were edible and which on the other hand were mortally poisonous. Reference book in hand, she hiked around the estate and collected forty-four varieties. Some were exquisite, fungi and toadstools. One had to pay attention, however. Some were only slightly poisonous. They produced stomach upset and headaches for a few days. "The last group—mortally poisonous fungi," said the book, "—contains only a few species. Unfortunately there is no way to ascertain their poison content. These fungi occur in open country as well as in woods, both in spring and in autumn. Nearly ninety percent of fatal fungus poisoning has been attributed to *Amanita phalloides* (Death Cup). *Amanita virosa* (Exterminating Angel) and *Amanita verna* are also deadly but distinctly rare. In the Death Cup the toxic principle is a complex mixture of A and B amani-

Melinda

toxin and phalloidin—both relatively simple polypeptides containing sulfur. The toxin is not destroyed by cooking and is unaffected by human digestive juices. Symptoms do not occur until two to three days after ingestion, by which time so much of the toxin has been absorbed into the body that neither vomiting nor the use of a stomach pump is effective. Symptoms include acute stomach pains, vomiting, and nervous disorders. The patient remains conscious and may even go through a period when the symptoms diminish, only to return more acutely. A single cup of *Amanita phalloides* in a dish of mushrooms is sufficient to cause death."

The solution to Lawrence's problems as well as her own was all too obvious. Poor Lawrence could not remain in the House of Commons. He would never be able to make a speech. Besides, leaving without a good reason would be undignified. What he needed very soon was to inherit a title that would require him to give up his seat in Parliament.* For Melinda's part, she would have the splendid title she longed for.

Melinda studied *Amanita virosa* carefully: it was all white and faintly slimy. *Amanita phalloides* was also slimy but it had an attractive greenish-yellow tint and white gills. The flesh was white too. It looked slightly more edible. She picked that one.

Before she returned to London, her new wardrobe ready and a Swiss governess for the infant, Melinda mixed a tiny piece of *Amanita phalloides* in with Loelia's mushrooms that went with the roast liver. Then she caught the ten o'clock evening train. That night Oswald dined alone.

Melinda felt nothing toward her brother-in-law, she had never thought about him. Was he nice? Shy? What was he like? Deep down, he was already dead. So she thought while a steward poured her a whisky.

* The title of duke in England gives the right to sit in the House of Lords. The title of lord that Lawrence would have until the death of his brother is considered a courtesy title, that is, used for sons or brothers of dukes, and does not carry with it the right to sit in the House of Lords. However, the wife of a duke may sit in the English Parliament.

Anthony paid for the drink. He had been watching her. Anthony, whom she had known for some months, had come to take her back to London. He had been kind. He saw that she was in a pensive mood and didn't dare ask her why. Anthony, so sure of himself in Parliament, perfectly at ease at Cabinet meetings, moving remorselessly to power, was suddenly intimidated. She's got something on her mind. She's going back to London. What does she expect me to do? Perhaps I should go and sit next to her.

He got up. Melinda went on looking out the window. What if someone saw me cooking the mushrooms? And collecting all those different varieties? They're sure to do an autopsy.

"My dear, what are you thinking about?"

Melinda suddenly realized that she looked worried.

"What were you thinking about?"

It was always difficult to invent a thought extemporaneously.

"I was thinking about my husband."

There you are, thought Anthony, she was thinking about us. And about what's going to happen between us.

"About his career," continued Melinda, seeing doubts in Anthony's tired eyes.

"We could help him," Anthony said, "no doubt about that. But first he must make a speech."

"To tell the truth, I don't think he's cut out for Parliament." Perhaps he thinks I want something from him?

A pity, Anthony thought, it would please her if I gave Lawrence a hand. "You'd be a perfect MP."

"Good. Then you can help me become one."

They looked at each other. Anthony had moist eyes, a bit like a dog's, a ruddy face and a good smooth head of hair. He was an excellent minister. Melinda leaned her head against his tweed jacket and stopped thinking about mushrooms.

"We must be careful," Anthony said, looking around. Just then the ticket inspector came along.

"When can we see each other, Melinda?"

"Tonight."

Melinda

"No—I mean alone."

"So do I."

"You can leave Lawrence tonight? How long has it been since you last saw him?"

"Only a week."

"Haven't you ever loved your husband?"

She had never thought about it. Had she ever loved her husband? What did it mean? Oh well, he was pathetic and sweet, kind, polite. What boring questions. Why did Anthony say such ridiculous things?

"To be honest, I don't fall in love easily."

"But with your husband?"

"Really, I don't believe I've ever been in love."

Before I become Prime Minister, thought Anthony, Melinda must fall in love with me.

"Could you spend a weekend with me?"

"Maybe."

"We could go to my house in the country."

It mustn't coincide with my brother-in-law's illness, thought Melinda.

Lawrence was at the station and Anthony, who prudently descended from another carriage, came up and said how sorry he was that he hadn't realized Melinda was on the same train. They could have done the journey together.

"My dear, how are you? And how's the baby?"

"We're both very well. What shall we call him?"

"Haven't you thought of a name? Perhaps we should name him after my father, poor father."

"How did it go in the House? Did you make your speech?"

A shade of pain passed over Lawrence's face.

19

✦

After the weekend that Melinda spent at Anthony's beautiful house in Wiltshire, everybody in London considered her his official mistress. Her social standing shot up and she received so many invitations that she had to ignore three quarters of them. She had to get a secretary.

On the steps in front of Anthony's house grew clumps of wild flowers, and sprigs of thyme sprouted between the stones. As one walked up, the air was filled with their perfume. To her amazement, Melinda found there were six other guests in the house that weekend. Anthony took her hand in both of his and gazed tenderly at her. They spent the weekend like that. At night, they separated. Melinda went to the large room with a double bed he had given her. She also had a bathroom and a little sitting room, with windows looking on to the garden and the heated swimming pool. In the morning Anthony, in a blue dressing gown and embroidered slippers, came to breakfast with her. He brought the newspapers and together they discussed politics. Later on Melinda went downstairs, got herself a whisky with ice and had a swim in the pool. A famous journalist and the wife of a press lord sat discussing the affair. The young and beautiful Lady Inchball, the famous Minister . . . how romantic! What luck to witness a passion that defied convention. What courage to go and stay with her lover, flouting all the rules. At lunch and dinner Melinda sat at the head of the table, mistress of the house. What an odd situation, she thought. Here's Anthony passing me off as his mistress, while privately we have only the most chaste conversations and an occasional kiss on the cheek. But what an enjoyable weekend. The conversations were agile and brilliant, she liked the people.

On Sunday morning Anthony came to her room at about ten o'clock, loaded down with the Sunday papers. "You really should take up politics, Melinda. We need some aesthetic pleasure in Parliament."

"If you'll help me, Anthony. I'd like to very much. I'm not very clever, but the speeches I wrote for Lawrence aren't bad. Besides, I know the House by now."

"We shall have to find you a seat. Of course Lawrence's would be perfect. It's so safe—whoever stands is sure to win. Lawrence may not stand at the next election. He's not cut out for the job and it bores him. By the way, the papers say he's gone to Saltlake because his brother's not well. It would be best if you left today to join him."

So soon, thought Melinda. Those scientific handbooks never give you exact information.

Oswald, fourteenth Duke of Brighton, duly died. The agony was long and painful.

The new Duchess, grief-stricken, had to take to her bed, but she was obliged to talk with a Scotland Yard inspector.

"Your Grace," he said, "did you know your late brother-in-law well?"

"I couldn't say I knew him well. Or really at all," and a shadow of sorrow passed across Melinda's brow, "intimately. He wasn't particularly fond of the country. We didn't see much of him at Saltlake. Oswald often went to London, he had his own—how can I put it?—private life."

"Did he have any enemies, as far as you know?"

"Enemies?"

"I must inform you that we have reason to suspect that your brother-in-law's death was due to poisoning. We haven't talked to your husband yet—we don't want to distress him any further."

Lawrence had just sent in his resignation from Parliament,

which would of course have happened automatically, since he had become the fifteenth Duke of Brighton.

"A man like Oswald couldn't have had enemies. So sweet and kind—he'd never hurt a soul."

"We know that the Duke had love affairs. What about jealous husbands?"

"I would ask you to show more respect. I know nothing of that side of Oswald's life."

"Forgive me, Duchess, but it's my duty. How were relations between His Grace and his wife?"

Here Melinda had to proceed very carefully.

"They seemed excellent. Not particularly close, but good. They rather went their own ways. Loelia is a *fine* person—she understood her husband and there's no doubt she was a great comfort to him."

"So far as you know, was the Duchess jealous of the Duke?"

"Really we never spoke of personal matters. Loelia was quite taken up with her own interests, she is a woman who knows how to live alone."

"What are your sister-in-law's interests?"

"Well now, this house is so big that we see very little of each other. There certainly isn't much social life, and what there is doesn't interest her much. She's happy with her horses. She breeds race horses. And she spends a lot of time in the cellar—that's where she grows mushrooms. She's very clever. She's made quite a commercial success of them."

"Tell us more about these mushrooms?"

"I don't really know any more. If you like, I can show you the cellar."

"We've already been there."

"Why?"

"Your Grace, we suspect your brother-in-law died from mushroom poisoning."

Melinda couldn't believe it would be as easy as this. She stood up, her face pale, and said with great dignity, "I can't allow such

Melinda

monstrous suggestions. I would ask you to leave this room and this house immediately." The interview ended in embarrassment.

The police and the new Duke decided to save the Brightons' reputation by avoiding a trial, and Loelia was shut away in an asylum, where she settled down very well. She went on growing mushrooms, although the baskets now fetched far lower prices. Something leaked into the papers, but with their influential connections the new Duke and Duchess kept even the tabloids quiet.

Lawrence had been deeply upset by his brother's death, though the situation also had its cheerful side. To have got out of that accursed House of Commons so easily seemed to him a gift from heaven.

When Anthony phoned to ask him if he could come and lunch at his club and talk some things over, Lawrence was afraid he was going to offer him a political appointment. I don't want to set foot in the House of Lords, he thought.

Anthony and Lawrence met at White's, where they were both members. The young Duke and the old Parliamentarian, who was now recognized as the new Duchess's lover, excited a certain interest. As they walked in, heavy eyelids were raised and sleepy faces came to life.

It was over the first glass of port that Anthony broached the subject that weighed so heavily on his mind.

"Your seat's vacant, Lawrence. We've got lots of chaps who would jump at the chance. But there's one person the party particularly has in mind for it."

It had taken many hours and several dinners to persuade the Cabinet that it would be a wise move to elect Melinda.

"Do as you please. If I can be elected, then anyone can. I leave it to the party to decide."

"Completely?"

"Yes. As you'll have realized, I'm not very interested in politics."

"My dear Lawrence, to tell you the truth it's your wife we were thinking of."

"Melinda?"

"Melinda."

"As an MP?"

"And why not?"

"Have you talked to her about it?"

"Vaguely."

"Melinda never said anything to me."

"She's young, of course, but she's very capable and she's got a good political brain."

"But she's also got two children and two houses. And now quite a few social duties."

"Melinda's not the sort to be content with charity balls and afternoons with the children. She would be unhappy. This new responsibility will tie her more closely to her family and to her country."

"To her country? Really, I've never considered my wife English."

"But she is. And she's also a very fascinating person, with an infallible political intuition."

Anthony almost hoped Lawrence would refuse.

"Let's leave it to Melinda to decide," Lawrence said, lighting a fat cigar for the third time. "I wouldn't want to run her life for her."

So it was that Melinda found herself in Parliament. Her election attracted a great deal of attention, but Anthony's influence was such that all criticism was silenced. The arrival of the beautiful Member in a very short black dress, her hair blowing in the wind, was much photographed and her maiden speech was carried by all the papers. It was short, lively, and clear. This Brighton girl, said the other MP's, has brought a breath of fresh air into Parliament, apart from the scandal of being the Minister's mistress. Abraham was extremely pleased. This was more than he had ever hoped. Jacques, too, wrote her a letter overflowing with compliments, but when he came to look her up, Melinda was too busy to see him. Later on she heard that he had married, but unfortunately every time Jacques came to see Jove, Melinda was either abroad or busy.

Melinda

Melinda's third pregnancy was immediately attributed to Anthony, who in the meantime had become Prime Minister. Melinda was to be seen in the House until a few days before the birth of her baby girl, who, in spite of a striking resemblance to Anthony, was in fact Lawrence's daughter: this time there was no doubt. The christening was a great social-political occasion, and the fact that Anthony was asked to be godfather seemed to confirm the rumors.

It was some months after the birth of the baby when Anthony asked Melinda to lunch. By now they were meeting so often in public that they almost avoided each other in private. He took her to his house in the country, where they found a cold lunch laid in the dining room. No one served them, but one could feel the presence of several shadows in the kitchen.

"Aren't you pleased with me?" said Melinda.

"I'm very pleased."

"Are you frightened by the rumors?"

"I couldn't care less."

"What's wrong then?"

"Curiosity."

"What sort?"

"The morbid sort."

"What do you mean?"

"Sometimes one has suspicions and wants to know the truth even if it would be better not to know."

"Do you want to know the truth about us? Is there any need?"

"Melinda. I'm much too old for discussions about us. And there is no need. You and I understand each other very well. But there's one episode in your life that intrigues me."

"What's that?"

"I can't ask you."

"Then I can't help you."

"Really?"

My father and I? The analyst? My brother? My first marriage? My son? My ambitions? . . . Oswald?

"Melinda, you know perfectly well what I'm talking about. I'm talking about a situation that didn't suit you but there was a solution. And in fact you found the solution. Nobody else could have done it."

"There are certain things, Anthony, that you and I know but we shall never mention them either to other people or to each other. It's the whole secret of our relationship. Isn't that so?"

It was the first time she had ever talked about a relationship. Usually it was other people who described to her their imaginary relationships with her. Melinda would nod and gush with admiring phrases. How clever of you to have guessed . . . but really she never thought about her own actions or their consequences. Analyzing things was a pastime for which she had no inclination. It didn't even amuse her. The fact that she had been the one to speak of a "relationship" with Anthony seemed to her a sign she was aging.

Anthony was sitting opposite her. In spite of his tired face, so often in the newspapers, his graying hair, and his shoulders round from years on the benches of the House, Anthony was physically attractive to her.

"I haven't liked any of the publicity you've had, in the last analysis . . . the automobile accidents . . ."

He had her in his grasp at last.

"How did you know?"

"Are you serious? Don't you read the papers?"

"To tell the truth, never."

"How do you manage in Parliament?"

"I listen to other people in the evenings. That's all anybody talks about over drinks. The only thing you have to know is what paper they read."

"But you'll never know what's in the gossip columns."

"What do you mean, I won't know? People talk of nothing else."

"But not the gossip about you."

"It doesn't really interest me."

"You're irresponsible. You ought to read the papers."

"But look here, why should I? And if you think I'm irresponsible, you should have thought about it before."

"I did know it before. Or maybe I only suspected it."

Silence. Anthony didn't approve of her. She was disappointing him. She didn't like this atmosphere. It displeased her to be disappointing. It was the first time.

"Well then?"

"You absolutely must get yourself a driver's license."

"I don't feel like it."

"You can't afford a scandal."

"I'm not making any scandal. I drive perfectly well without a license."

"I repeat: have you seen the newspapers?"

"What do they say?"

"That you've had two accidents and put an old woman in the hospital. With no license."

"So?"

"So if you'd been just anybody, you'd have gone to jail."

"But I'm not just anybody."

"I've got a headache. As if I hadn't enough problems . . ."

Anthony had never suffered from headaches before. At least he would never have admitted it. He too was losing his vigor.

"You're causing a scandal. Get yourself a chauffeur."

"He'd know all my secrets."

"Have you many?"

"A few."

"Like the one we were talking about?"

"The one we *weren't* talking about."

"That's the one."

"But why this sudden interest in my affairs?"

Anthony looked through her. All his years were suddenly etched on his tired face.

"You scare me."

I scare him. Why? I scare him. "Just now or before as well?"

"Just now. You're capable of anything."

"How? In what sense?"

"In the sense that you feel no remorse. You don't feel anything."

"I don't understand you at all. What is it that you want from me?"

Now she was embarrassing him. Now he was the one who didn't understand. "I don't know. You'll go a long way, Melinda."

Admiration. She hadn't expected that.

"Shall I see you on Friday?" he asked.

"When?"

"For dinner?"

"I can't."

"What are you doing?"

"I'm going to France."

"What for?"

"A ball."

"Will you see your husband?"

"Not at all. I'm going with my husband."

"I mean the first one."

"No, I never see my first husband."

"Did you quarrel?"

"Never."

"And when will you get a divorce?"

"Why, do you want to marry me?"

"My dear, I wouldn't dream of it."

"Then why should I get a divorce?"

"Because you don't care a damn about Lawrence."

"I care about all the rest."

"You don't need all the rest."

"And what *do* I need?"

Melinda

"To fall in love."

"Why don't I fall in love with you?"

"You couldn't do that. You should have done it before."

"And why aren't you in love with me?"

"I'm not, that's all. Anyway, get yourself a better secretary. The one you've got now leaks things to the press."

"What sort of things?"

"Gossip."

"I don't care."

"I've told you. Find another secretary."

"And do you think it's easy? They all leave."

"Do you treat them badly?"

"No. And I pay them well. But they disapprove of the way I live. My appointments. And they always think the worst. Most of the letters I get are obscene. It's embarrassing for them."

"What's in these obscene letters?"

"Sussex farmers that voted for me for their own particular reasons. They start off 'Dear Duchess, Last night I dreamed I wanted to fuck you.' I must confess that these letters cease to amuse me."

"You should develop a more dignified public image."

"How?"

"A really good secretary, a chauffeur, a Rolls-Royce, a publicity agent."

"It would cost too much."

"You've got the money, and if you need any more, I'll give it to you."

"I'll find something else to do."

"I wish you would."

What an unpleasant conversation, thought Melinda on her way out (she was immediately photographed as she got into the taxi, legs exposed and mouth half open). What a dull lunch. Anthony's getting old and becoming a real Prime Minister. He wants me to quit politics. He's horrified at the thought that I might have done away with Oswald. It was stupid of me to let him think that. The best thing to do is pretend I thought he meant something else.

She went to do some errands; she liked to window-shop, at jewelers, bookstores, in pubs, as long as she wasn't recognized. She went into Christie's and looked around for one of the directors, who gave her a rose. In his office there was a portfolio of Tiepolo drawings: cherubs among clouds lightly sketched in sepia, the foggy whorls of flesh mingling with the clouds. Perfectly darling. Charlie left the office for a moment; Melinda shoved six into her bag; Charlie came back. Four seconds had passed.

Melinda took a walk through Christie's and left a couple of bids: one for a Chinese porcelain dish which didn't interest her at all, the other for a silver tureen made for Elizabeth of Russia. The dish would make a Christmas present for Abraham. Not the tureen; it was too nice. She would keep it for herself.

Before the ball she had to go to the conference. Melinda was to act as her father's ambassadress; Abraham couldn't come for who knows what mysterious reasons. Melinda was seeing him less and less and getting to like him more and more. They met in Paris.

He didn't come to the airport to meet her, as he usually did, but Melinda found a nice passenger who took her to the hotel; Abraham was anxious and impatient.

"You're late."

"The plane was late."

"I never know whether to believe you."

The porter stood at attention. Her new title made a big impression. The English are so clever at putting their titles on documents.

"I do hope you're not going to do anything stupid at the conference. You represent me and in a sense the nation. Pretend you've read the books. It'll be easy enough. Nobody else will have read them either."

Abraham had booked her on a flight at eight in the morning. He took her to a restaurant off the Boulevard Saint-Germain.

"My friends generally take me to the Grand Vefour."

"But I am your father."

They ate well and talked a lot. Abraham wasn't particularly interested in his daughter's private life, although he was vaguely curious. "When are you going to fall in love?" he always asked. People were always nagging her about that. Why should one fall in love? Is it so obvious that I haven't? What do they expect?

Abraham had so much to tell. He had seen the General. He adored the General. "Don't you understand? He's the only one we've got. Look what he's done. Algeria. Could the others have done it? And he's the only one who realizes we need to break up the Arab coalition."

"Papa, you ought to take my place in Parliament. You're so much better at it than I am."

"I know that; but you're a joke."

One day she would show Abraham what sort of joke.

"And why aren't you coming to the conference?" she asked. "Tell the truth."

With some difficulty: because of the usual love affairs. His authoress was to be queen of the conference ("apart from you, my dear, but for different reasons"). His affair with her had gone badly; in other words, it was better that they not see each other.

Melinda met the woman who frightened her father the next day at the airport. Abraham, who had gone to see his daughter off, fled in terror when he saw the corner of Helen's ravenous mouth appear under a flowered straw hat. The last time Helen had seen Melinda was when in school uniform she had come running to greet her father with tears in her eyes. Helen remembered her very well. During the flight they had a long talk. They read the papers. Helen marveled at the view of the Côte d'Azur.

She had never been there and had never believed it could be beautiful: Helen hated touristy places.

Helen rather intimidated Melinda, the way she talked. She never referred to herself, never began a sentence with "I've seen" or "I heard" or "I think." She seemed to digest words without chewing them, devouring entire sentences.

One night, three days after the conference began, Melinda decided she was lonely, very lonely at night. She had a big room, a balcony with a view of the tops of some pine trees, a double bed; the furniture was full of drawers, so everything could be put out of sight in a few minutes and the room quickly made neat and tidy. Ideal for love-making. Melinda didn't like the dark. She didn't like being alone, either. Above all, she wasn't used to it.

He was an American writer. "Jacob was wondering who you were," Helen told her at the bar. Melinda and Jacob had dinner together. He was sure of himself and had that syrupy American accent. Then they went for a romantic walk and spent part of the night together. He didn't stay till morning because he was afraid of falling in love. He admitted that later.

The conference interested her less and less. Jacob took her hand after breakfast. Before lunch. After lunch. On the stairs. After dinner. In the lift. They spent most of the day making love. Every once in a while they spoke. "Come with me." "Where?" "Away with me. Forever." Perhaps because he wasn't English Jacob lavished so much attention on Melinda's body and on an act, love-making, that had always seemed to her, in the last analysis, rather incomplete. He had been married. They had divorced. Two kids. He talked about his ex-wife all the time. Kissing. All saliva and teeth, too much sucking and noise. Like dogs. Perhaps Melinda had fallen in love with him . . . "But you must kiss me one day, darling." "No, please, I think it's revolting." They went back to Paris and lived together for a day. Paris seemed quite new to her for the moment. Jacob made her walk miles, taking her to squalid, rather affected places. He took her round and showed her off to his friends. He was also quite stingy and never gave her anything.

Then Melinda took a plane to London to pick up her jewels and ball gown. She said goodbye to Jacob, perhaps they would meet again.

The police at the airport looked everywhere for the tiara. Luckily they didn't find it. It was illegal to take it out of the country without special permission. And there was no telling how difficult that would have been. Bureaucratic machines gave Melinda a feeling of claustrophobia. One day, she said to herself, I'll probably commit suicide over the loss of a couple of irreplaceable documents.

Melinda didn't like to fly. She loathed being cooped up. Every time she had to go to the loo meant crawling over bodies. There wasn't even room to read a newspaper. Not that she wanted to read; only if her two seatmates spread out their papers, there wasn't room for her face. If I go to the loo I'll throw the plane off balance, Jacob. What are you doing? Jacob's legs, his heavy body. He had worried she would be bored. She was, most of the time. Sometimes he asked her. He sensed everything. It wouldn't have lasted anyway. But they wrote each other and phoned every day. She even called him up one day from Parliament. Jacob was afraid of Lawrence and of spending money. This time they wouldn't see each other in Paris. Jacob, who would have to leave for the U.S. in a few days, didn't even know her phone number and would have thought it monstrous that she was in the same city and hadn't looked him up.

Lawrence was tired. He didn't want to go out before the ball. There were some eggs in the kitchen. Melinda looked at them. There was some butter too. "Let's stay home for supper." How does one mix eggs with butter and butter with eggs harmoniously? It was the first time she had ever found herself in front of a stove. "It's chemistry," Abraham used to say. He was an excellent cook. "A rational science women don't grasp. Some of them do it by nose. But there's no such thing as a really good woman cook." Melinda vaguely remembered scenes between her mother and Abraham, who always wanted to do the cooking. Out with cook, out with his wife. In with the king of scrambled eggs. Why hadn't he ever taught her anything?

"Do you boil Nescafé before or after? I mean, do you boil the powder with the water?"

Lawrence cooked.

Jacob. Is that what it's like? A nervous stomach when you were away from each other and indifference when you were together? Is that how it is, falling in love? Was this another of the laws of society? Jacob, in that little hotel, all alone. Perhaps not alone. But he thought of her. And that was the important thing. Important for whom?

Some hundred cars at a gate garlanded with flowers. Statues on either side of the entrance bearing stone bowls brimming with pink hydrangeas. Guests had to show their invitation cards. Several cars were turned away. It was the ball of the year. No doubt about it. After half an hour in line, they got in.

"Who are they?" asked an onlooker.

How marvelous to be a star.

The garden was lit with hidden spotlights. Chandeliers hung from the branches of the highest trees. A series of identical marble blackies supporting atop their heads heavy bowls of flowers, hydrangeas and wistaria. The lake, too, was illuminated. And finally the castle. It was decorated in white tulle, yard after yard of it

Melinda

cascading down the façade. Tiers of candelabra corbeled up the columns, which had been painted silvery white. Candles everywhere. The house sagged. Even the boat on the lake was a phantom shipwreck. At the entrance, more cars. Ladies in phosphorescent dresses and immense jewels. They mounted the stairs. The gypsy orchestra that greeted the guests embarrassed even Melinda. Another queue: presentation and greetings to the host and hostess. The Marquise in a silver dress almost covered with emeralds. Now that she was here, Melinda thought no more of Jacob. In a moment of lucidity it occurred to her that she would never in her life think of Jacob again. And so the possibility of falling in love vanished forever. She went over to greet the famous soprano.

"How nice that we'll be hearing you in London in a few days."

"Actually, I've no intention of going."

"But . . . do people know? The papers haven't said so."

"No, nobody knows yet. But I'll tell them, I'll tell them."

Buffets everywhere. Vast tables, decorated with flowers and ducks stuffed with goose liver, festooned with lobsters and orchids.

"Tonight I'm going to eat, and that's all," Melinda announced to Lawrence, and she moved off.

She walked around the garden, greeting people here and there. She saw Mark Van Der Belt sitting in a corner with his beautiful wife. Melinda knew nearly everything about him. He was rich, the richest. He was handsome, the handsomest, even though fifty years of too much wine and too many cigars made his face and hands ruddy. He came from a family famous for its economic and political power. Invitations for the weekend at his country house were much sought after.

Mark Van Der Belt moved away from his wife. Melinda came up behind him while he was being served champagne. "What are you drinking, darling?" asked Van Der Belt over his shoulder, automatically handing her a glass of champagne. "I'd prefer whisky—ice, no water," she replied. Mark Van Der Belt suddenly turned around.

"No, it's not your wife."

"Do forgive me."

He turned, fled, vanished. English, thought Melinda. What can you do? She ordered her whisky and went up the steps toward the ballroom. Here too the decoration simulated ruins. Tulle colonnades and stalactites. She found Abraham.

"The only intellectual here!" Melinda said, embracing him.

"You mean the only person to talk to? Look, I've no intention of dancing with you."

"I was hoping you would. I shall go upstairs then."

"Make sure you see the hostess's bathroom. It's solid gold."

"Who can I talk to?"

"You've nearly eight hundred people to choose from."

"Who's going to introduce me?"

"But you know far more people here than I do."

"Not here."

"Really?"

"You're the cosmopolitan in the family."

"Look, there's the golden boy of London."

"Van Der Belt?"

I must get a bit drunk, thought Melinda.

"Don't get drunk." He stopped her as she picked up another glass.

"It's only my second."

"You look famished for alcohol."

"I'm famished for Van Der Belt."

"For God's sake, don't make him another of your husbands. Stay away from him."

"Why?"

"He's absolutely wrong for you. Weak, weak."

"But all my . . ."

"Yes, but this is a different sort of weakness. He's too vague, he destroys everything."

"What an obscene thing to say."

"Well, you're the only one he might not destroy. I've even done business with him. Disastrous."

Melinda

"How?"

"It would take too long. Besides, here he comes. Look how hesitant. No wonder, he ought to be embarrassed."

"By what?"

"For instance, he rings up. An appointment to come and talk about the great book he wants to write. Lunch at one o'clock at the Ritz. He rings again an hour before to postpone. He's done it several times. As if everybody had hours to waste on him."

"Obviously he's spoiled."

"Worse than you."

"I'm not spoiled."

"I never know what you are, Melinda. No, you're not spoiled. You're as fresh as a rose, a rose in a refrigerator, and for now it's all right. Until you get bored with it all. Then, you're capable of changing your whole life, husband included, once you feel a niggle of boredom."

"I'd never thought about it. Do you really think so?"

"You're a creature of instinct. But you've managed to have a genuine conversation with me."

"This isn't a conversation. It's a father-daughter exchange. We never talk . . ."

"You never ring me up."

"But you're the father. You should ring me up. Well, are you going to introduce me to him?"

"Listen, if he doesn't come over here, I can't go over to him."

"Show him you're a superior being."

"But I'm not."

"You can always pretend."

"I've no intention of being a superior being, or of pretending to be."

"Now look, if you don't introduce me to Van Der Belt I'll stick to you all evening."

"I'll dance."

"All evening I'll stick to you."

"Melinda, stop it."

"Introduce me."

"Can't you do it yourself?"

"He's English. He wouldn't approve."

"But can't you see he's hanging around you?"

"But I tried before. It doesn't work."

"Mark." Abraham has raised his voice. Mark Van Der Belt was coming over. "He's coming. Satisfied now?"

"Good evening, Abraham."

"If it's impossible to meet for lunch, one can have the pleasure of seeing you in the evening, Mr. Van Der Belt."

Trust him to bring his little quarrels into it. What a bore.

"I'm sorry. It's been a hectic week."

"For me too."

"Really a great deal to do."

"Lots of guests? Dinners to arrange?"

If he goes on like this, he'll go away.

"Have you met my daughter?"

"Almost. Is this your famous daughter?"

"The only one I have."

Abraham moved off.

"What have you done to my father, Mr. Van Der Belt?"

"I hope you won't be as stern as he is."

"I've no reason to be. Not the slightest intention."

"What's your name?"

It was the first time. Was it possible he had said "your famous daughter" and not even known what her name was?

"Melinda Brighton."

"That's it. Sorry. How's it going in Parliament?"

"I see you find it amusing too."

"Not at all. I used to be an MP."

"I know. I also know your name. Why did you give up politics?"

"You keep up with things better than I do, Melinda." He spoke with a fatherly manner that Abraham had never had. He put his arm round her waist, patting her with the palm of his hand. "I

Melinda

had no intention of being a back-bench MP. Besides, I wanted to write. Have you read my book?"

"I will. What's it about?"

"You'll see." Suddenly very confidential, he said, "I'll ring you up when you've read it."

"So you left Parliament to write. Or was it boredom?"

"No, actually I went into Parliament because I'd married a boring woman. But after I divorced her and married Aglaia I didn't need to stay away from home all day. Do you know Aglaia?"

"No. Perhaps I also . . ."

"I also what?"

"I've had an idea . . ."

"Do you enjoy Parliament?"

"Oh yes."

"What a beautiful woman! Really marvelous."

"Me?"

"Melinda, why haven't we met before?"

"Why, indeed?"

"I don't meet many people. I never go to balls."

"And tonight?"

"Aglaia wanted to come. And then I wanted to see my brother who's in France."

"Where?"

"Do you know my brother?"

"Yes. And one of your sisters too."

"What do you think of my family?"

"Every analyst's dream."

"Now that's unkind."

"But you asked for it."

"I like talking to you."

Once again the fatherly manner, an arm round her shoulders. Mark's hair was brushed down flat, Scott Fitzgerald style. He had an elegant vagueness about him, a dreamy way of talking, impossible to understand. Pretend to adore him—that was it. After all, he was the Dick, and Melinda the Rosemary, of the situation.

Nicole was bound to come along, it was only a question of waiting; and the atmosphere was just right. Besides, somebody was leaving the house and the ball: he was fed up, had his aeroplane waiting and would go for a swim on the Côte d'Azur. But Melinda didn't know anything about him, and, what was worse, he didn't know anything about her. So Melinda, bold in her ignorance, smiled adoringly at Mark.

"Why haven't we met before?" *(Mark)*
"I tried." *(Melinda)*
"Where?" *(Mark)*
"At the bar." *(Melinda)*
"Where?" *(Mark)*
"Here, half an hour ago." *(Melinda)*
He hadn't even looked at her *(thinks Melinda)*. How rude of him *(thinks Melinda)*. Or genuinely absent-minded?
"Tell me about my family." *(Mark)*
"But really I don't have that much to say about them. Your sister, so-so; your brother, poor fellow, has dreadful taste . . ."
But she shouldn't seduce him just by talking about his family.
"And my other brother?"
"More interesting. Another analyst's joy."
"In what sense?"
"You ought to know. Why do you ask? I've only seen him once in my life. At dinner."
Mark's hand pressed firmer round her waist. Suddenly he removed it. "Ah, here's my wife. Ag, have you met Melinda Brighton?"
Delicious creature. Little girl's face, wan voice, hair to her shoulders.
"How is it we've never met before?"
She asked the same questions as her husband.
"See you soon," Mark said, moving off with Aglaia.
What? See you soon, and then he disappears with his wife? How dare he? And such a horrid expression. He certainly *won't*

Melinda

see me soon. Pretending to have an intimate conversation, all about his family, as if anybody could care less, and he leaves me in the lurch.

She was alone again. She made her way towards the second buffet (there were twelve, she had made up her mind to visit them all). The phantom shipwreck was still being maneuvered up and down the lake, lights following it everywhere. The brilliant splashes of tulle seemed to sink into the lake.

A cavernous voice behind her. "Would you care for something to eat?"

Graying hair, tall, elegant, pearl tie pin and cuff links. He didn't appeal to her at all.

"And what's your name?"

"I cannot pose the selfsame question to you, Duchess." He bowed.

Not the trace of an accent in his archaicisms.

"Yes, I would like something to eat . . ."

"Archibald Ostrovsky."

"Polish?"

"Almost. Russian."

"Usually it's the other way round."

"What do you mean?"

"Russian? Almost. Polish."

"Not in bygone days, Duchess."

"Look, I won't be one very much longer."

"What?"

"A duchess."

"How not?"

"Because I want to get a divorce."

"Really? And why are you telling me? These things are private . . . And you mustn't get a divorce. A position like yours, envied by all the world."

"What do you know about it?"

"Duchess, I must tell you that I have agonized for months in anticipation of this meeting."

"How cheerful."

"Do not jest."

"I'm not in the slightest. I've just met . . . never mind, it doesn't matter."

"Why don't you confide in me? Do you not trust me? Even a modicum?"

"Let's eat."

"What would you like? Stuffed duck?"

"Stuffed duck? Are all the buffets alike?"

"Oh, you're used to Buckingham Palace?"

"If that's anything to go by, I can tell you that you only get cucumber and tomato sandwiches there."

"Are you wont to visit the Royal Palace"

Am I *what*? Is it possible? Are there still people who talk like that? "Yes, since I've been in Parliament. I don't think they invite me very willingly. Only when it can't be avoided."

"And when can it not be avoided? When the Prime Minister goes to dinner?" The little smile of one who knows, is well informed.

"I take it you read the tabloids, my dear Ostrovsky, though you don't live in our country. Where do you live?"

"I, Duchess? Everywhere. France, America, Poland, Italy."

"Poland?"

"I have a castle in Poland."

"And it's still yours?"

"Certainly, and why not?"

"Sorry, sorry. And what do you do?"

"Nothing, my beautiful lady. Nothing. I rejoice in beautiful things. In beautiful creatures like you."

"Shall we eat this duck?"

"And when will you receive your divorce?"

"I was joking."

"Quite to the contrary."

"It just came into my head on the spur of the moment. I said it because I was bored."

Melinda

"But if you are to be divorced you will need money. Have you given thought to that?"

"No, I haven't. But money always comes to people like me."

"Your father?"

"Yes, there's my father too."

"He doesn't make that much, and you've become accustomed to a certain style of life . . ."

"Listen, I'm rather tired of discussing my private affairs with you, my dear Mr. Ostrovsky. Either we eat this duck or we go our separate ways."

"How would you like fifty thousand pounds?"

"How would you like it?"

"I have it."

"And if I . . . with you . . . Fifty thousand to share with you for the rest of my life . . . Is that it?"

"No."

"How then?"

"We'll talk about it later."

And Ostrovsky disappeared too. A depressing evening, this. Am I so unattractive? They all run away. Maybe her mascara was smeared or her nose was shiny or her powder was smudged. Better check. Opportunity to see what a gold bathtub looked like.

She entered the castle again. Splendid girls, superbly dressed. Everybody was there. Big money, principalities, and recalcitrant pretenders well represented. The Marquise's bedroom was done in blue, an enormous canopy with nineteenth-century blue silk hangings falling from very joint. Little blue armchairs, blue opalines. All in cobalt. Where was this famous bathroom? She opened a door.

"I hoped you'd already peed." It was Mark's voice.

"I don't want to pee. I'm looking for the gold bathroom."

"Let's look for it together."

"Where have you been?"

"Dancing. And you?"

"I met a strange man."

"You must have incredible success with men. They never leave you alone."

"They did just now."

"But for other reasons."

"Am I ugly?"

"You're so beautiful . . ."

"Did you come here after me?"

"I followed you."

"I'm very glad. Very glad. A phrase like 'See you soon' doesn't generally mean a thing."

"So you haven't read my book?"

"I told a lie. Yours is one of the few I have read."

"Did you like it? Obviously not."

"Not much. But I didn't know you. I've forgotten it a bit."

"But you knew my family?"

"Yes, but don't let's talk about your family."

"But my book's about the Van Der Belts."

"Yes, but try not to talk about it."

"You didn't like it, then?" The fatherly hand. "You're so beautiful."

"You're so handsome."

A kiss on the neck. Good. A nice kiss on the neck. And a kiss on the cheek. Good. No kiss on the mouth. Good.

"Shall we get undressed?"

"We aren't in our own house."

"Shall we meet at one of our houses?"

"I expect so."

"Now I'd better go and see what Aglaia is doing."

And away again, walking with a slight stoop, in that awkward way men have when they begin to age.

Later Mark saw her pass near him. Melinda didn't see him. She was as tall as he, and he liked that disarrayed hair of hers. He would never have imagined her like that. Heaven knows where she had left her husband. These girls, today, never take their husbands anywhere with them. He noted that she drank a lot of

Melinda

whisky, danced with a tall man who had the look of a Latin lover. Mark began a discussion with a friend. They talked about the Van Der Belts. Then Mark danced with Aglaia. Melinda looked bored. But perhaps she always looked bored. And her eyes, what were they like? He must have a long talk with her. He would read her the things he had written. He would write a poem for her. Melinda would understand it. He had an urge to dance with her and touch her. Why hadn't he thought of it before?

Melinda was looking around for him. She saw him talking, and now and then it seemed as if Mark glanced her way, but more by chance than by design. Ostrovsky continued in his flowery language to promise her immense sums of money. She couldn't understand why he was being so long-winded. After all, she knew perfectly well what he wanted.

"And what sort of information would you want from me?"

"Information? I don't understand. Me? From you? Why?" She should have gone on pretending she didn't understand.

"Excuse me. I must have made a mistake. I take it all back. Just imagine, I was thinking you were a spy and wanted information from me. A pity, because I'd have been interested."

(That'll teach him.)

"Duchess, your gracious way—your beauty—your perspicacity . . . shall we go out into the garden for a moment?"

(They move out together on to the terrace.)

"Melinda."

"Mark?"

"I wanted to dance with you."

"And Aglaia?"

"She's talking to a friend. I don't know where she is, anyway. Shall we dance?"

"You don't mind," Melinda said to Ostrovsky with no hint of a question in her voice. "I'll see you later."

(Poor spy. He thought he could pull it off so easily, and now he's terrified. He'll be afraid I've been making a fool of him. Or that I'll tell Mark all about him. Or maybe he had hoped to sew things up as soon as possible so he could run home to bed: mission accomplished. What fun being a spy. I might try it— just for a while.)

"You're dreaming. Don't you like me any more? What are you thinking about? Your husband? Your lover? Is he in love with you?"

Mark's hand slid round Melinda's waist: this time, at least, there was the excuse of the dance. He put his cheek close to hers. It was warm. I love him. I love him. I've fallen in love. How marvelous. At last. All in one evening.

"I've written a poem for you."

"Mentally?"

"No, on a scrap of paper."

"When?"

"While you were dancing with that man who can't keep his eyes off you."

"Isn't it proper to look at one's partner while dancing?"

"He seems particularly interested. Aren't you aware of it? You must be very successful with men, Melinda. Melinda. What a lovely name."

So clever. So young.

"You know you're clever?"

Her hand on his neck.

"Your husband's watching you."

"How can you tell when you don't know what he looks like?"

"I can feel it. I'm sure he's watching us."

"Maybe it's your wife."

"No, but she's watching us too. I can sense it."

"Let's get out of here. Let me read your poem."

She took him by the hand. He was hers.

"Where shall we go?"

"To the garden."

"It's a bit damp."

"Never mind. We'll go to the covered garden."

"I didn't know there was one."

Melinda

"I went there with—"

"—Aglaia."

"No, a friend. We talked politics."

"And aren't you going to talk politics with me?"

"We shall have time for that, too. You will spend next weekend with us, won't you?"

"Do I bring my husband?"

"Certainly."

"I'll have to think about it."

Once again the tall graying man was coming over. He had been eyeing them all the time.

"Your Grace?"

"Ostrovsky?"

"Might I ask again for the honor of a dance?"

"Later, my dear Ostrovsky, later . . ."

A someone who cries to the night
Someone who calls for the light
Crying because she cannot see.

"Do you like it?"

"What is it?"

"Poetry."

"And where do I come into it?"

"It's about you."

"If you say so. But it's not true, you know. I'm not like that. Is this all of it?"

"Don't you like it?"

"Not much."

"I wrote it with great affection."

He bent towards her, kissed her hands and eyes, and took hold of her arms.

"Let's go upstairs."

"But where?"

"We'll find somewhere."

They went up. Ostrovsky passed by, pretending not to see them. They went through various bedrooms. Many of the guests were staying for the weekend. Suitcases and jewels and hairbrushes on the floor: disorder. From the darkness they could see the chandeliers and tulle flapping in the wind.

There was nobody about.

"Here."

Mark stretched out on the bed and took her in his arms.

"Let's not make love, shall we?"

"No, let's rest."

"From what?"

"From ourselves."

Mark was undressing.

"Why are you undressing?"

"You undress too."

"So that I can rest?"

"Quite."

"And if somebody comes in?"

"Nobody will. Who's likely to? Apart from that monster with a Slav name who's fallen in love with you."

He helped her undress.

"You're beautiful. Do you know you're really beautiful?"

He gazed at her.

"Your skin . . . what lovely soft skin."

He kissed her and she closed her eyes. I love him. I love him. Abraham will be furious. I love him.

"When was it you met William?"

"William?"

"My brother."

Now I'm going to get up and leave, thought Melinda. "A couple of months ago. At dinner."

"Darling, darling."

He buried his face in her hair.

"No, I'm not going to make love."

"All right, we won't make love."

Melinda

They did, though.

"My sister is the only member of the family I like seeing," Mark said. "She's ill, you know, very weak."

"Do you see each other often?" She loved him, one had to suffer. She would talk about his family, always.

"A couple of times a year. When she comes to London, of course I invite her to lunch. But generally we meet in France."

"Have you ever been to her house?"

"Yes, but it was a long time ago. I don't remember the house. I don't go about much. This year I've even forgotten to arrange my summer holidays. What are you doing?"

"I'm going to the coast, work permitting. Coming with me?"

"I can't of course. But we must meet, alone."

"That's what I meant."

"But not so conspicuously. What do I tell my wife? She depends on me. She couldn't stand it if I left her. If she suspected I was being unfaithful . . . She wouldn't tolerate it, you know. If I left her . . . But why do we always talk about me? I know nothing about you, Melinda. Melinda?"

Footsteps outside the door.

"Oh no," said Mark. "I wouldn't like to be found in a bedroom, undressed like this."

They dressed hurriedly. Still the footsteps outside the door. That nightmare of an Ostrovsky.

"Shall we go out together?"

"No, separately. Meet you at the bottom of the stairs."

Mark went down first; Ostrovsky stopped Melinda.

"Really, Ostrovsky, if you're going to keep spying on me, you can go to hell."

"Duchess, it is my duty."

"Listen, I can't now. We'll meet in about an hour at the buffet in the velvet room."

"Too many people."

"We'll meet there. Then we can go out."

"I would like to discourse with you a few minutes."

She ran down the stairs. Had she kept Mark waiting? She couldn't wait to touch his hands, look at his face. Where could Lawrence be? Mark's voice . . . He would talk to her about his family . . . Patience. What did he want from her? Mark . . . How dull her life had been till now. Down the stairs, quick but not too quick, mustn't make it obvious. Mark wasn't there. She began looking for him, walking slowly, exchanging a word here and there. Then she danced, to see if Mark was in the ballroom. Could he be in the loo? Or perhaps he went back upstairs and couldn't find her. She rushed out of the ballroom. No sign of him. Impossible to examine all the rooms. There were too many. She spotted Lawrence dancing. She greeted him with exaggerated warmth.

"Enjoying yourself, Lawrence darling?"

"And you, Melinda?"

"Very much." She was glancing right and left.

"You seem agitated."

"I've had a lot to drink."

Obvious where he'd be. With his wife. Chatting. And Ostrovsky too, only a few feet away from them.

"Ostrovsky. We'd better talk now."

"It is pointless, Duchess, to lose your temper and your charm. It doesn't become you."

"Listen, Ostrovsky . . ."

"And it doesn't become you to visit bedrooms in strange houses . . ."

"If you think you can blackmail me, you're mistaken. For one thing, I couldn't care less, since I'm about to get a divorce—in fact it would only speed up the ridiculous formalities. And secondly, it would make me less inclined to collaborate with you."

"Whereas now . . ."

"Whereas now, probably I would. But let's go and talk."

"With a little lobster?"

"Fine."

They served themselves. There were all kinds of divine mayonnaise: with brandy, with parsley, with oil and sugar.

Melinda

"Melinda."

His hand suddenly on her back.

"Mark?"

"Let's dance."

"I can't now, darling, I must talk to my friend Ostrovsky for a moment."

"Duchess, I thank you."

Mark left them, frustrated.

Melinda and Ostrovsky walked across the damp grass and white cushions. There were candles in the garden and boughs of wistaria.

"Where would you like me to begin?"

"For one thing you can tell me who you work for."

"For myself, my dear Duchess. Might I call you Melinda?"

"You may call me Melinda. And you don't want to tell me who you work for?"

"No."

"But there's no fun in spying if you don't know who it's for. Anyway, you're a Russian spy—that's obvious."

"You'll know in good time. For the moment, what is required of you is very simple. You know a lot of people, some of them very intimately. There's one group that we're particularly concerned with. Katerina Nubytch is an agent of ours, but we suspect that she's passing information."

"To whom?"

"Let me finish. Madame Katerina Nubytch is a masseuse and she has some highly placed clients. Two of them are friends of yours, Melinda. One is the Prime Minister, the other the Leader of the Opposition."

"You don't suspect Anthony, by any chance?"

"There's no knowing what a man might say under a soothing massage."

"Is she beautiful, Madame Nubytch?"

"Sixtyish, very fat, hennaed hair kinky with permanents. There's another person who worries us. Another client of Madame

Nubytch. All we know about her is that she works in a Sexyboy Club as a Pussygirl."

"Is she an agent of yours too?"

"Perhaps. But we know for certain that information is being leaked from this little group."

"And I've got to find out who's talking?"

"Exactly. Nobody will ever suspect you, Lady Melinda. After this assignment, you can help with others if you like; if not, we'll leave you in peace."

"How long will you give me?"

"We're in rather a hurry. A couple of months. Everything calm, mind you; make it look natural. But I know you'll be brilliant and do a magnificent job. You will communicate through your maid, Nora."

"My maid?"

"She's one of our agents, too."

"Since when?"

"She's always been."

"Planted in my house by your lot?"

"Of course."

"But I don't want to lose Nora. She's the only good maid I've ever had."

"Unfortunately, once our agent has completed her mission, she'll be sent elsewhere. That's how we work."

"And when will I get in touch with you, Ostrovsky?"

"You won't. We shall never see each other again."

"Never?"

"No."

"I'm sorry."

"Tonight I shall go on pretending to court you, and you will be rather rude to me. I shall pretend to be offended. It will be very easy to fool Mr. Van Der Belt. The money will be paid to you tomorrow. You will find it in locker A015 at the Gare Saint-Lazare."

"But I don't want to go all the way over there."

"I'm sorry, it's already in the locker and only you can collect it."

"So you were quite sure I . . ."

"Yes."

"Do you know much about me?" (The mushrooms?)

"A great deal. Nothing, unfortunately, that's really damaging. But our agent had described to us your adventuresome character, and when I saw you . . ."

"Your agent-maid?"

"Precisely she."

"I shan't be able to look her in the face when I go home."

"Melinda. I must insist. Normal relations with the maid, just as before. The briefest possible exchanges of information. Possibly when you are alone together, and not at home."

"And will she continue to spy on me?"

"Certainly. As she has done until now."

"So I can't sell myself as a counterspy."

"Please don't try to be funny. By the way, there's also an osteopath. The director of a health farm. His name's Dief. Piotr Dief. You may hear his name. He's one of us. Take no notice of him."

"You'll have to write these names down for me."

"No. Not a word. Memorize everything."

"But I've no memory."

"You'll find you'll remember everything very well." He bit into the lobster that had lain untouched in his plate. "Well, that's all. Go back inside now. Look rather cross. Dance with your Van Der Belt. I won't bother you any further."

"My, my, how we've changed our tone of voice. For one thing I'm going to finish my lobster, and for another I do what I like. If I choose, I'll dance with you all night, Ostrovsky. And let's have fewer comments on Van Der Belt."

"This is no joke, Melinda, it's not a game. It can be amusing but it's also dangerous. Obedience is essential. And in this business I'm your superior."

Melinda was slightly drunk. She slipped away to the terrace, grabbed a glass of whisky, and gulped it down. Now she'd look for Mark. He was talking to two men. They were all sitting on a sofa and Aglaia was talking to a man with smoky eyes. Mark threw a casual glance towards Melinda. It took her in. Then flashed back a second time.

"Melinda, shall we dance?"

His hand on her back guiding her towards the band. He danced, of course, in a rather old-fashioned way.

"I thought you'd disappeared for good. I've met your husband. He asked me if I'd seen you. I'm sure he saw us together."

"Don't worry, I shall get a divorce one day."

"Don't do that. It's awful. My own divorce was traumatic. My children will never forgive me. She was such a dull woman. I was so bored with her. A conventional woman. My family has always been on her side. She's happy now. I'm glad she's happy. Once you've been married, in a sense you stay that way."

"Really? I never think of my first husband."

"You've been married twice, then?"

"Yes, didn't you know?"

"You're so young . . ."

"I was when I married my first husband. I never see him. Since we got divorced I haven't set eyes on him." (She shouldn't be talking about herself, she was boring him.)

"Was it painful?"

"What?"

"The divorce."

"No, to tell you the truth, it wasn't. In my opinion a divorce is a happy event. I'd be bored if I thought I should have to spend the rest of my life with Lawrence."

"Do you really mean that?" He was terrified.

"Certainly I do."

"But why? Aren't you all right the way you are?"

"Things could be better. Or at least different. I was thinking tonight that I really need a change. Change of people, way of life.

Melinda

That's what a husband means, after all. Then I met you and fell in love."

"But you can't have fallen in love with me this evening."

"Why not? Don't be so frightened. I already know who I'm going to marry." (Untrue. She didn't know at all.)

"Who will you marry?"

Now what could she say?

"I don't want to live in England any more, for a start. I'm fed up with it. I'll probably marry an American writer." Jacob? What a thought. And why tell this lie to Mark? It was the first time she'd thought of Jacob since she'd decided not to think of him any more.

"You're such an unpredictable person and yet, in a sense, so sure of yourself. What were you and Ostrovsky talking about?"

"Various things."

"He's in love with you."

She remembered what Ostrovsky had told her. Another lie to tell Mark.

"Yes, but I can't stand him any more. I gave him a rough time."

"And so?"

"I told him to keep away from me."

"How cruel of you." (What satisfaction in Mark's eyes.)

"He told me to be careful. He said that you . . ."

"Did you talk about me?"

"Of course."

"Why?"

"Because I'm in love with you."

"Melinda, please."

"Why not? Aren't you in love with me?"

"I don't want to be and I would treat you terribly."

"But maybe tomorrow I won't love you any more."

"How's that?"

"At dawn we'll both look hideous, I'll see you clearly and your affected languor will have lost its charm for me."

It was a cruel thing to say. The sky was getting lighter and

Melinda noted the wrinkles and red blotches that were exposed on Mark's face.

Ostrovsky appeared. There was a desperate look in his eye.

"Will you save the next for me, Duchess? Please?"

"Ostrovsky, I asked you to disappear. Go to bed, it's late."

Precisely what she wanted to say to him.

"Mark. When will we go away together?"

"Aglaia's watching us. I'm afraid she suspects that I'm . . . Before, when I was married to my boring wife, I didn't care, but since I've been living with Aglaia, I've never had an—"

"The time has come."

"Will you come and hear me read my novel?"

"Of course."

"To my place in the country?"

"Of course."

She felt like Susanna with Count Almaviva. Mark was drifting again. He hardly glanced at her. And yet they had been in bed together just over an hour ago. He was looking around. Who was there to talk to? There were plenty of people who interested him. She had better talk to him and arouse his interest. Politics? Family? His family.

"There's only one of your brothers I've never seen."

"Which one's that?"

"I think the youngest."

Their eyes met. New interest in Mark's voice. "Please, not while we're dancing. Didn't you have enough of him in the book?"

"Are you really happy?"

"But why must you be so serious while we're dancing?" He squeezed her tight and bit her shoulder.

"We'd better separate."

"Separate?"

"Aglaia's watching us."

"I'm sure she's delighted you're enjoying yourself."

"I can see her. She's not at all delighted. I'm going."

"Don't go, please. Don't always go away."

Melinda

"We mustn't talk any more this evening. I'm going home."

But two hours later he was still there, while Melinda wandered around lamenting to herself the loss of her loved one and the only time she'd ever fallen in love. It seemed absurd to meet, love, and be abandoned all in one evening. Ostrovsky had left. That put an end to the possibility of insulting him. And she was too lazy to strike up new friendships. It was morning: there wasn't going to be another chance of falling in love. Then she felt something thrust into her hand. A piece of what? Of paper, of course. Another poem.

No, Mark wouldn't be right for her. His family . . . his wife . . . his poems . . . She'd have to marry somebody else.

Melinda's divorce caused a tremendous stir. Everybody was surprised. Above all, Lawrence himself. Abraham strongly disapproved, and so did the gossip columns. Melinda would lose her title and the prestige that went with it. But everybody was convinced her next husband would be Anthony, and rumor confirmed that the Prime Minister was about to divorce. But Anthony steered clear of her and Melinda married Jacob. But since they were married secretly in Paris before her divorce from Lawrence was final, Melinda had the vague suspicion that this was only a transitional marriage, a temporary alliance, in between Lawrence and some future, real husband. Jacob, on the other hand, had no suspicion and seemed happy. He didn't want to live in England. How could she explain to him that it was essential, after all the money she had had from Ostrovsky? And she still had to go to the House of Commons. But Jacob, like any good American writer, pretended to be leftist, so Melinda went over to sit with Opposition, an event that aroused a great deal of comment. But then the British electorate, snobbish as it was, would never reelect her now that she had lost her title. In any case she was fed up with being an MP and in the long run she felt being a spy was a much more appealing occupation.

With her new income she bought a house in the country, where she never went; instead she installed her children there, as well as Jacob's, who adored her. Too much so, because Melinda didn't actually like children. She found them ugly and boring. And she detested everything that went with them—parties, nannies, doting mothers, fathers who lionized their own offspring, nappies, toys, untidiness, innocent faces, whims condoned by analysts. But social custom called for having a child by a new husband, so she immediately brought one into the world for Jacob; after all, there would be time enough for spying.

When she learned she was expecting—it turned out to be a girl who looked just like Abraham (but this time she was almost sure it was Jacob's)—she telephoned Madame Nubytch. It had taken some time to find somebody who went to Madame Nubytch. Melinda had casually asked several of her friends if they knew a good masseuse. She hadn't said anything to Anthony so as not to arouse suspicion. After her divorce, remarriage, and political defection, Anthony avoided her. Phone number: Earls Court 7500.

"You don't know me. I'm Mrs. Johnson." (It was her new name, Jacob's name.)

"This is Madame Nubytch speaking."

"Yes, Madame Nubytch, I'm . . ."

"This is Madame Nubytch speaking."

"I would like to have a massage . . ."

"What did you say your name was?"

"Mrs. Johnson."

"Ah my dear. How nice to hear from you."

"Would it be possible to make an appointment for this week? I'm a bit flabby . . ."

"But très chère madame, of course."

Having made the appointment, Melinda had almost forgotten the object of her mission and didn't have the nerve to ask Nora.

Melinda

Ostrovsky had not been in touch again. She had even looked for his name in the telephone directories of Paris, London, and Amsterdam to refresh her memory. She had called one Ostrovsky on a number given to her by the Madrid operator. The voice of Ostrovsky himself had told her that "Mr. Ostrovsky is not at home and in any case, as his private secretary, I can assure you that he has no Melinda Johnson-Brighton among his acquaintances. Obviously you've got the wrong Ostrovsky."

Three flights of stairs, an elderly lady on the ground floor who grumbled when Melinda slammed the door, a smell of cabbage and frying, the stair carpet riddled with holes, a pay telephone.

"But chère madame, what a pleasure to meet you."

"Good morning, Madame Nubytch. I need a massage badly. You can see the condition I'm in."

"But you're beautiful . . . what a marvelous body. Please undress."

Melinda obeyed. Everybody was always telling her to undress. Madame Nubytch handed her a dressing gown that had touched many clients' bodies and extremely rarely in the meantime soap and water.

"Madame, what aristocratic breasts, magnificent, stupendous. Now lie down."

Even the couch was a bit dubious. To tell the truth, Madame Nubytch wasn't a very good masseuse. She chattered too much; she didn't set the circulation flowing before she began massaging. Melinda would continue to use the excellent blind masseuse who would come at any hour of the night or day, accompanied by an Alsatian and a white stick. Madame Nubytch, as described briefly but accurately by Ostrovsky, was stout, with kinky, hennaed hair and tiny brown eyes. The cubicle where she gave massages was full of copies of *Elle*, from which she got a friend to make up her clothes. She put on display a French that even Melinda thought was funny; she spoke of clients who were "très aristocratique, n'est-ce pas?" On a little table stood photographs of her most illustrious clients (not the men, Madame Nubytch told

Melinda: male vanity was different from the female sort). There were women in various poses; their slimmed-down hips swathed in evening gowns; or in a narrow wedding gown: no hint of the struggle to squeeze in the fat. Soon she had added a photograph of Melinda, Brighton Castle in the background. She'd clipped it out of some magazine. She confessed to Melinda that she had always hoped to have her as a client, and she asked her to sign the photograph as the Duchess of Brighton. Melinda pictured the dozens of hopeful Duchesses of Brighton who would have married poor Lawrence for a title which owed its mere existence to her.

"Madame, a friend of yours has spoken to me so often of you, told me you were so beautiful . . ." She maintained a tea-party tone throughout. "Ah, madame, I detest the English—they're so cold, n'est-ce pas? I can understand you marrying an American. Like Lady Sympson, only that marriage didn't turn out well, n'est-ce pas?"

Madame Nubytch said she would like to meet "monsieur."

"I'll bring him along one day, Madame Nubytch. He needs massages too. The incredible thing is that men are, in a way, modest . . ."

"Ah, madame, vous dites bien, vous dites bien. However, I have many gentlemen, even some very important ones. Naturally they come in the evening after work, or in the morning if they work in the afternoons."

Who works afternoons only? wondered Melinda. An MP. A Prime Minister who goes to the House.

So Melinda scheduled her appointments for morning only every day for two weeks, putting up with the inane autopsies on social functions that the other clients performed for Madame Nubytch, as well as her unending "n'est-ce pas?" and commentary on hips, thighs, aristocratic breasts—and the odor of cabbage cooking.

"Ah, madame, quel corps! Quel corps aristocratique, n'est-ce pas?"

And yet she must have been making a lot of money, Madame Nubytch. Certainly she had been a spy for many years. From massage to massage she told Melinda she had been a partisan in Poland during the war. When it was over she found herself in Grenoble in a displaced persons' camp and there she had met her third husband. "Oh, madame, I adored him. Je l'adorais. He died some years ago, you can imagine, madame, you can imagine my grief. N'est-ce pas? A woman alone in the world, with no means of her own. What can you do. Ma chère madame, a masseuse. And in England, too . . . Ma chère, ma très chère madame." Who had approached her first? At Grenoble? Or even before? The Russians, of course. Or the counter-espionage people? How could Melinda find out? And why had she chosen to live in that squalor, amid the stenches of Earls Court, the cage of canaries, and those filthy dressing gowns? If Melinda could earn so much money for a single mission, Madame Nubytch had to be rolling in money.

Perhaps the jewelry that Madame Nubytch sported on her vast bosom was all genuine. Melinda looked more closely and could see that it probably was.

One afternoon, Melinda went to the House of Commons and sent a note to Anthony. "It's absurd your being cross with me and sulking. Let's meet in the bar in a quarter of an hour." Anthony reacted cautiously. She saw him come in perfectly suited to the background of neo-Gothic arches. She was pleased to see him. He a spy too. For whom? And why? Because he was bored. Like her. No doubt about it.

One day they would marry.

"Melinda, our dear Melinda. How many changes we've made these last few months."

"You don't mean to say you're angry with me?"

"What do you think? We get you elected, we give you a position, and you make fools of us."

"But it's not quite like that, Anthony."

He had aged. His hands were knotted with veins and his manicured nails picked at a shiny, delicate wood pipe.

"I've never seen you smoke before."

"I've changed a bit too. Even we poor mortals do, you know."

"I've something to tell you."

"First let me tell you something: I suppose you know that you won't be adopted again for the next election?"

"Of course I know. Anyway, I'm fed up with all that. It gets boring after a bit. I'll make a good speech one of these days. Besides, nobody's ever taken me seriously. Not even the tabloids, from what I hear."

"And what will you do afterwards?"

"After what?"

"Instead of coming to the House."

"I come so seldom as it is."

I wonder if Anthony knows . . . The time she trailed him from Madame Nubytch's to his house. Friday she even followed him as far as his club.

"What were you up to at my house the day before yesterday, Melinda?"

"I was looking for you."

"You know very well that I'm always in the House in the afternoon."

"I still hoped to find you."

"Why did you tell my maid you were looking for a letter in my study?"

"Because I'm keeping a watch on you."

It was best to be open with him. The two of them were vaguely alike . . .

"Yes, I know. You do it so badly. You've shadowed me a couple of times. What did you expect to find out at that hour of the day? I always do the same things."

"I'd better improve. Will you teach me?"

There was no need for explanations or stories, Anthony knew all about it.

"One or two wigs. One black and one red, short curls, a different kind of dress, sunglasses, a head scarf. In other words, change your whole appearance when you shadow people, otherwise get somebody else to do it for you. Why are you watching me?"

"I'm jealous."

"It's not true."

"Then you must know, but I can't remember very well what it is I'm supposed to find out. You knew that I . . ."

"From the moment I saw you coming out of Nubytch's place."

"So you followed me?"

"Certainly. You weren't aware of it, I imagine."

"What shall I do now?"

"You ought to know."

"Help me. Otherwise I'll have to give back the money, and I've already spent it. We could work together."

"First get a divorce."

"Why?"

"I can't stand the idea of you married to that lout."

"All right."

"We've got to find the Pussygirl." (How did he know?) "I've taken photographs of all the girls that go to Nubytch who might be Pussies. Anyway, I'll show you the photos. You have a look around the club. You must go there."

"On what pretext?"

"An article."

"Have you already?"

"Only once. As Prime Minister I can't go any more. It would give the photographers a field day."

"Did you see the girl?"

"None of them. Perhaps she's hiding, perhaps she's not there."

"But who is this girl?"

"We don't know. She's dangerous and very cunning. She knows everything about everybody."

"And how do you know this? That she knows everything about everybody?"

"Because I know even more than she does."

"Was it you who told Ostrovsky to come and find me?"

"What do you think?"

"I think you did. But are you higher up than Ostrovsky?"

"You don't need to know, Melinda. In any case you'll find out everything by yourself. What would you like to drink?"

He ordered a whisky. As usual, there was no ice.

"Anthony?" Melinda's face, close to his, her eyes wide open, delicious, full of attention. "Who are we working for? I mean, which country? You know which one . . ."

"And don't you?"

"No."

"Patience, Melinda, patience. In the meantime, drink up your whisky and get a divorce . . ."

"You treat me the way Ostrovsky does."

"Did you enjoy yourself at the ball?"

"Not at all. I met somebody and fell in love."

"Yes, I know. What ghastly taste. Van Der Belt."

"So you're the chief of this spying outfit."

"Don't say such things."

"Why? Isn't it true?"

"Even if it were true, it's something I don't want to hear, especially in the House."

Now that her days had become so hectic (people to see, dinners to attend, houses to visit), Melinda had given up the idea of keeping engagement books. For instance: breakfast at the Ritz, tea at 11:00 with a lawyer, bed at 12:00 with an undergraduate, lunch with an ex-husband. Afterwards, a business meeting from 3:00 to 3:35 (she had invested money on the Stock Exchange and was also vice-president of two committees: one for the prevention of child deafness—the Queen was president; the other for the protection of aristocratic animals, horses, pedigreed dogs, and dolphins. She had to organize countless balls and charity lotteries). How would all those dates fit on a skimpy half page?

Melinda

She had also invested money in Lloyd's, which gave her a good return. Her lawyer was always telling her that everything she touched turned to gold. He was right.

Her problem now was that she couldn't find a private secretary. They all quit. They changed by the dozen and she was sure she'd been through all the secretarial agencies in London. The trouble was that the perfect secretary had to know all her employer's secrets, not only of her daytime life, but sometimes of her night life too. Melinda's secretaries left because they disapproved of her intensely. The final scenes were dramatic: Melinda would be accused of being amoral, treacherous, cold, of having no affection for anybody, of constantly being unfaithful. As if it really mattered. What did these tiresome women expect, after all? What business was it of theirs if she was sometimes unfaithful to her husbands, when they were so happy with her?

Male secretaries cost more and they tended to get more involved in their employer's life. Often they were rude on the phone because they were jealous. They would forget to note appointments so they could spend an hour alone with her. There were other unpleasant episodes which always ended in arguments, and Melinda detested arguments. It was Smith who'd had photocopies made of all her compromising letters. When Melinda complained to Smith about his behavior, Smith had accused her of being immoral just as all her other secretaries had, and then quit. As for her personal maid, now that Melinda knew she was one of Ostrovsky's spies she didn't trust her any more.

So Melinda's appointments came to be jotted down on scraps of paper, instead of in a notebook. However, as bits of paper tend to disappear, she'd landed in some glorious messes: two appointments, same time, same place. To her right, for example, at a café table behind a column covered with gold leaf and Edwardian cherubs, she could see Jacob waiting for her. She had to tell him she wanted a divorce. It gave her a feeling of tenderness to be able to watch him unseen, this man she didn't know at all who'd been her husband for such a short time. In Room 302 on the third floor in a suite full of candelabra and stucco that had a view of

St. James's Park, her future husband, David Llewellyn-Jones, was
waiting for her. How negligent to make dates with both of them
at the same hotel. The lawyers had said that it would be very
easy to get a divorce from Jacob: the marriage in a sense had never
really existed. But Melinda had felt an urge to see him and had
rung him up. How could she tell him over the phone that he
couldn't come to her house any more? Jacob said he would come
right away and asked her to meet him at the Ritz in the lounge.

This had been her shortest marriage. And the happiest . . . But
then all her marriages had been infinitely happy, and all her affairs,
even those very brief ones of only a few hours. Excepting maybe
the one on the night of the ball. It was Anthony who had persuaded her to get a divorce. And, Melinda knew it was inevitable,
the judge would again give her custody of the children. She
couldn't understand why judges were always so unfair: they always
had it in for the women. Every time they had awarded her the
children, so already she had several in the house, in addition to
the ones belonging to her husbands or her current boy friends.
Even Jacob's two, nearly grown, fourteen and eleven, lived with
her. And here, too, she was unlucky. It's custom, it's as much as
a law, a veritable law of nature, that children hate their stepmother;
they run away from home, they don't want to live with her. Instead, all these children, as well as Anthony's, who spent most
of their vacations at her house, not to mention Jacques's new
children and Daniel's and David's, all adored her. Some of them
had chosen to live with her after the divorce or end of the affair,
or else they kept coming to the house to see her.

Not to speak of the dozens of goddaughters that mothers had
entrusted her with because of her title and her money. From time
to time she had to give some demonstration of good will or some
justification for having accepted the honor of holding another
infant at a christening. Thus she found herself taking awkward,
bad-tempered little girls to lunch at the Connaught, and the
bigger children to the Mirabelle in the evening. Then she would
send gifts of air tickets to romantic islands. One-way tickets, to
be sure, whether to spite the parents or to get rid of another

godchild. In any event, how was she going to get through the hotel lobby without Jacob seeing her? If, on the other hand, she stopped to talk to him, it would be a question of hours, discussions, and upstairs David would decide to come down and there was the strong possibility that in leaving he would see her.

Melinda had been to one of David's lectures at Cambridge. They were introduced afterwards and David had taken her to see a couple of writers who were Fellows. Then to his room. Despite his fragile appearance and long elegant hands, it was David who made all the decisions.

Probably she would marry him. Without saying anything to Anthony, who would surely have disapproved, out of sheer prejudice.

She plastered herself up against the columns, and one by one she managed to scuttle past Jacob. She reached David's room. She held out her hands to him, rang down to the porter, and dictated a note for Jacob. "Forgive me, darling. A dreadful inconvenience, I know. See you in three quarters of an hour."

"But aren't we lunching together?"

"I thought you'd want to come to bed."

"I do. But what about afterwards?"

"Afterwards what?"

"Afterwards you know damn well. Afterwards we have lunch at a restaurant. I've booked a table."

"Where?"

"Prunier's."

She preferred Wilton's, where she didn't like the food but where she saw all her friends and, more important, her friends saw her. For some reason she thought about the restaurant while David was kissing her. And she had no news of Mark . . .

Jacob never had been considerate enough to bring her as much as a flower or the smallest gift. He had always promised to but nothing ever materialized—only innumerable copies of his novels in various languages. When it came to repaying debts, he would write her a check for little more than half the amount, affecting an innocent vagueness about figures. He was mean—something Melinda couldn't forgive, least of all in a husband.

"Shall we have some lunch? Let's go to one of those nice English pubs, where it won't be crowded."

"And where they poison you and you drink warm beer? No, thanks. You go, if you like. We can eat here. Don't worry: my treat."

"You seem excessively rude."

"I only wanted to simplify matters. I know it bothers you to have to get your money out."

"I'd like to go somewhere quiet where you won't meet all your friends. I wanted to talk to you. We never see each other. We live in two separate houses with the Atlantic in between. Our children live apart. I write to you, you seldom reply, you can't tear yourself away from this country and . . ."

"So you've decided to ask for a divorce."

"A divorce?" He looked at her with desperation. "I demand that you live in New York and that you come away today."

"Darling, I wouldn't dream of it. But your first idea seems a good one."

"What was that?"

"The one about a divorce."

"I never mentioned divorce."

"Never mind, Jacob, never mind. After all, we've been happy. Come and eat. What would you like? To start with, there's a nice prawn cocktail or vichyssoise, no, better not, your breath will smell of chives. How about smoked trout?"

"I'll never give you a divorce."

"The sad truth is . . . now don't get angry, a divorce isn't necessary, it wasn't a proper marriage . . . in fact we can say goodbye to each other right now."

"What about the child?"

Melinda

"Do you want her?"

"Certainly."

"She's yours." Wouldn't you know he'd start to cry! I don't want to watch . . . it's horrible. Not in a restaurant, not at the Ritz.

Somebody else was going out of her life, with a flutter of purple wings and art nouveau murals in the Ritz Grill. What in the world was he thinking of! Why complicate life with romantic notions?

"Do you want to come home with me?" They went out into the rain. "Let's take a taxi to my car." Jacob wanted to walk all the way to the house. Melinda detested romantic walks, especially along Piccadilly, past the bus stops. As for rain being romantic, that was something she had never understood. It soaked her hair and dribbled down into her eyes. "I'd rather take a cab."

"Let's walk as far as the white houses."

"I suppose you mean Belgravia." Suddenly Jacob irritated her. She began mentally criticizing his sneakers, the mass-produced gabardine trousers on his stumpy legs. Even the gray light of the London afternoon didn't hide the blackheads on his nose and forehead.

"Listen, Jacob. Would you mind if we said goodbye here?" (After all, she had bought him lunch. And his daughters were still on vacation at her house.)

"I've dedicated my latest book to you."

"Thanks."

"When shall we meet again?"

"Life's long . . . paths cross . . . we'll meet one day . . ."

"But don't we want to see each other, you know, tomorrow? To decide about, you know, the children? the house? the food?"

"No, we don't want to see each other. The lawyers will take care of it all."

Melinda knew she'd unerringly chosen the right moment for her speech going over to Labour in Parliament. And the right dress. A day of bad tempers and unbearable heat. Heat has a strange effect on English Parliamentarians: their skin, unused to sweat, sticks to their trousers and a muggy atmosphere weighs on the Chamber. Her flowered dress radiated freshness. Result: the Leader of the Opposition saw in her the symbol of the conscience of the electorate, which was moving Left and repenting its earlier choice of rulers. But Melinda, who had hoped to cross over almost unobserved ("I owe my colleagues an explanation. I'll be brief, since this is of little importance . . ."), became the center of a debate that raged for hours. Anthony looked daggers at her. "It seems to me absurd," said he, "my esteemed colleagues, to elevate the caprice of a young woman whom one cannot justly describe as one of the more dedicated Members and treat it as a manifestation of ideology or political thought . . . And it seems to me rather tiresome of the Opposition to take advantage of an arbitrary reversal of this sort . . ." How right Anthony was; he knew her so well.

The Opposition fought back, defending Melinda and her courageous decision. They also decided that once they were elected they would make Melinda a Peeress so that she could take part in the Lords' debates. All this furore, the noisy headlines, Anthony's acid comments hadn't pleased her at all. Anthony always gave her the disagreeable sensation that she had made some tactical blunder. One more blunder. Too many, one after the other.

Abraham: "You haven't done anything right for some time." (How infuriating!) "The less you say in Parliament, the better.

Melinda

You can't speak English properly, you know nothing about politics, and you pile up one stupidity after another."

Anthony: "The most imbecile speech you could possibly have put together."

(But you wouldn't even let me speak, instead you all let fly the most nauseating pile of rubbish. What should I have said?)

Anthony: "You should have said something like this: Gentlemen, I shan't even attempt to justify my action in going over to the Opposition. I ask only that my new party, my ex-party, and the country take note of the fact."

Even Medoro, normally in a world of his own, was faintly worried about his sister. But Medoro didn't matter and Melinda was beginning to be ashamed of him. He had become an interior decorator as well as a photographer of minor members of the royal family. Since he was a homosexual, sooner or later he was bound to marry into it.

And Nora, her maid.

After what Ostrovsky had told her, Melinda realized that a maid, even on excellent wages, could not afford the luxuries which that monster with a square face around a mouthful of gold teeth allowed herself. Nora had a mania for very hard leather shoes, made to order for her in a shop in Jermyn Street. Her short hair was set weekly and retinted fortnightly by Michelange, the best hairdresser in Mayfair. Everything indicated a career as a clever and highly professional spy. By now Melinda was terrified of her presence in the house. She knew that she poked into everything. On one of her days off (Nora had taken a taxi to Michelange), Melinda went to have a look in her room. She found two revolvers, one minuscule, both with silencers, a knife with a blade longer than necessary for the normal uses of a knife, no license to bear arms, invisible inks, a portable receiving and transmitting radio, a memorandum left on a table but written in code, and Melinda didn't feel like spending hours trying to make out what was in it: her name appeared in Cyrillic characters (as if she couldn't read them!). An open Bible (obviously the cipher key—typical, they never seemed to choose anything more subtle). Nora was so used to her mistress's lack of curiosity that she no longer took precautions to hide her paraphernalia. The gadget that delighted Melinda most was a tape recorder built into a stiletto heel. What a fantastic plaything for her. What she wouldn't have done to have it! What she wouldn't have done . . .

Royal Chinchilla, the silver-gray dye which the hands of a new assistant at Michelange massaged into Nora's scalp the following week, produced strange symptoms. Nora tried to call a doctor. Melinda said she would look after her. There was no need for a doctor. Nora needed a rest and complete isolation.

Alone, suffering indescribable tortures, Nora died, cursing Melinda and wishing on her a death racked with the same dreadful agonies or if possible worse. Melinda, delighted with the nice toys she had inherited, decided to do without a personal maid. She was very curious to know how Ostrovsky's messages and orders to Nora would arrive, and how Ostrovsky would react to the silence of the excellent and, alas, deceased agent-maid. Finally Ostrovsky turned up in *The Times* want ads: "Madame Nora: David's daughter is on the warpath. The giant Goliath." She wasn't sure who David's daughter was, but Melinda decided that it was time to go see Madame Nubytch and interrogate her at gunpoint. She wanted to find out a few things.

She had lunch with David and they visited a number of galleries. The revolver was heavy in her bag (she had with her the larger model because the other was hard to see and wouldn't have made any impression on Madame Nubytch, who would have taken it for a "très aristocratique" trinket). The shoe-*cum*-tape recorder, a little dated in style, weighed a ton. Melinda meant to find out all about the intrigues of Ostrovsky and Nora, who the Sexyboy Pussy was, and where Anthony fitted into the plot.

To David, she said nothing. Even if she had explained everything, she doubted that he would have had the patience to listen. David's perpetual absent-mindedness was often manifested in a complete lack of expression in his dear face. Sometimes he would

Melinda

listen to people at the next table in a restaurant or a lounge. It was almost an instinct for him to listen to other people's conversations rather than to what came at him from his own companion. David was not interested in people or in being close to anyone. Perhaps he was right. What point was there in listening to what people concocted for their listeners' ears? Much more interesting to listen to what people didn't mean to say.

They had decided to marry very soon. Melinda was proud of this man with his slim neck, delicate profile, and finely etched features. She seized his hand: she wanted five minutes' attention. "Shall we meet in an hour?"

"Are you tired already? Do you want to rest? How would you like a room at Claridge's for the afternoon—then you needn't go all the way back home?"

Would they meet later in the domestic appliances department of the store in Tottenham Court Road? No, at the hotel. She was so tired . . .

David was picking out gadgets for the house. He had a passion for them. He had already bought an enormous quantity of things. They hadn't found a house in London yet, but they had decided to live in a hotel for the first months. A couple of vacuum cleaners, spin dryers, steam irons, an automatic dishwasher, a machine to make the hard London water soft as a mountain stream, a machine that chewed garbage up into a pulp. The metal nest that David was going to build around his new family was also to be adorned with pictures, sculptures, and knickknacks. A solid, lasting nest of stainless steel. A true marriage.

This time it would be for good.

It was true. Melinda was in love with this strange astral being.

A room at Claridge's. A curly wig (of real hair), spectacles (not obtrusive.) Taxi. Destination: Sloane Square tube station. She buys her ticket (not from the machine. At the ticket office. You never know.) She drops her black leather glove (checks the revolver). That man sitting opposite—has he recognized her? No, he's reading an evening newspaper: the city edition of the *Evening Standard*). Is the tape recorder working? (Gentle pressure on the toe of her shoe.) The tape's running. The train stops (Earls Court). Up the escalator. (The Inspector checks her ticket.) The front of the hotel where Abraham lived when he first arrived in London. Then the house where Katerina Nubytch lived. Typical doorway, gray, square, just like all the other houses on the street. Four steps, several doorbells. (Cracking paintwork, worn soapstone steps, transparent curtains at the windows.) The street door ajar. Melinda pushed it a little way open and was struck by the reek of cabbage and mutton grease. In the half light inside, the pay phone, the tattered red carpet, snatches of the voices of irascible old ladies. Dark. The shadow of the stairs. (Everything all right.) One more flight to go. A shadow flits by. (The eyes in the dim light move. They watch her for a moment.) The man (the shadow) makes to stop. A door opens on the floor below. The man (Not tall. Fifty? Dark eyes. Crew cut.) moves, disappears down the stairs. Who was he? Suspicious type. Concentrate on the essential: Madame Nubytch. The door of her flat open (copies of *Elle* on the coffee table). Madame Nubytch? Silence in the massage room. A round table covered with a cloth embroidered by machine. A vase of faded geraniums, some Renoir reproductions (girls in a theater), the canary clucking in its cage (no, dear, not clucking, canaries don't cluck), the usual roll-away cot. Madame Nubytch on the cot, eyes staring open, mouth gaping, throat blue. Horrible to look at. God, they've knocked her off! I'm not touching her. I must get out. If they find me, disguised, a revolver in my bag . . . The man-shadow was afraid. He was really flying down the stairs. He looked at me oddly . . . Down the stairs, quickly and silently. She would ring Scotland Yard (anonymously). Careful not to get killed by that man. Down the stairs in a second, off with the wig, into her bag, down with her long hair. A quick comb through. Her reversible coat back on with the plaid side showing. Off with the sunglasses and into her bag. Now walk steadily, as if nothing had happened. It's beginning to get dark. It's raining. It's turned out badly. Very badly. Don't get a taxi here. Never. Walk slowly. Yes, there he is. Behind a pillar. He's waiting. There's nobody on the street. Shall I run? Steady, steady. Move slowly. Maybe look at him. No, he hasn't recognized me. He's waiting. Obviously he's waiting for that girl he saw going up the stairs. Perhaps he's going back to the flat now. Poor Madame Nubytch. What wretched luck! Back to the tube station again. A ticket to Sloane Square. Into the phone booth: 999. "Hello. Police? I want to report a murder. Cullingham Gardens, number 7. A woman strangled. If you're quick you might find the murderer there. No, I can't give you my name. Where from? From a public call box. You can't trace it." Away. A taxi. To Claridge's. Half an hour had gone by. A little more. Ready to go in, the wig back on and the reversible coat turned back again.

David came in and found her still asleep. Lying there like that, with her hair wound into the folds of the sheet and her long legs curled up, Melinda was the loveliest creature David had ever seen. His beautiful wife, so pure asleep. So anxious to begin a family, some permanent ties.

"Melinda . . ."

A hand in her hair. Fingers lightly on her face. She sleeps on. "Melinda?"

She opens her eyes. Sleepy eyes, bleary from deep sleep . . .

"I've bought something nice for the house, darling."

Did he mean a picture? A machine? The light on his eyelids, so transparent. How contented she was. He hadn't noticed her disappearance from the hotel or her hurried return.

David was saying something about an automatic mixer. Better than the one he'd bought the week before. A mixer that does everything, peels vegetables, drops them into a container, and tips them into a plastic cup, all ready to drink. The same thing to fruit, meat . . .

"I'd like to ask you to do something for me . . . oh yes, darling, a favor . . . but now's not the time, I can see that . . . yes, really . . . a pleasure, I mean a favor . . . darling, my dearest . . . a pleasure, pleasure, pleasure. My God, what pleasure! Nearly pain."

So they had dinner at the new Sexyboy Club. David had never heard of the Sexyboy Club or seen photographs of the club's branches in various capitals throughout the world. Melinda's numerous explanations meant nothing to him. "Why don't they use waiters, then, seeing as you can't lay the girls?" At the club entrance, a flight of steps and marble and lots of neon. A Pussygirl asked David and Melinda their names and wrote them up on a board. "Now when they come in, your friends can see that you and this beautiful girl are already here."

"But none of my friends come here."

"But perhaps some of your girl friends do."

"She's my fiancée. And my fiancée's friends wouldn't dream of coming here either. Dreadful idea of yours, Melinda."

There were several lounges and dining rooms to choose from. On the second floor: taped music. Dancing. Wearisome cold-cut plates spread out on a buffet: the mayonnaise separating and oily. The third floor: a cabaret, a burning log fire, the British version of Frank Sinatra crooning old-timey ballads. On the fifth floor, the plushest, reserved for the "luxury Sexyboy" (as the manager explained), there were tablecloths, one pussy per person, pink telephones at every table.

"What's the telephone for? To ring up the girls?"

"Your own personal telephone," the manager explained rather haughtily, "is not to call the Pussygirls (unless you're dissatisfied with the service, in which case you call the manager), but your friends who have come to the club."

"None of my friends come here, as I've repeated several times since I came in."

"Well, you can ring one of the girls to ask her to change a record, or the orchestra for your favorite tune, or the latest dance."

"I don't dance and I don't know any songs."

"Or you can ring your friends outside and tell them where you are and perhaps ask them to come and join you and your pretty companion on the fifth floor of the Sexyboy . . ."

"I never heard such nonsense . . . I don't want the telephone. Take it away immediately."

"But it's included in the price."

"Just so it's not included in my table."

Melinda was looking round, searching among the Pussygirls for one of the faces that Anthony had photographed outside Madame Nubytch's house. The girls walked with some difficulty on very high heels. Their flesh, which the English sun could not tan, bulged in more or less abundant rolls from their tight bodices. And the whalebone stays made red chafe marks under their shoulder blades and around their groins. Their smiles were smeared with garish shades of lipstick, their eyes clogged with make-up and false lashes. Their faces, even if disfigured, all looked alike and not like those in the photographs. She looked at the screen of the closed-circuit television. It was coming from a floor below, the one where the cabaret was. At a table alone, there he was. It was impossible to mistake him. The man Melinda ran into at Madame Nubytch's. She couldn't be wrong. She had passed him on the stairs only a few hours before. She musn't let him see her. The man would realize why she was there. Perhaps he, too, was looking for the Pussy . . . but no, he had found her. Melinda recognized her immediately on the TV screen.

"Do you want a drink?"

"Yes, please." Her eyes were glued to the TV.

"What will you have?"

"The usual."

She had spotted two of Madame Nubytch's other clients dressed as Pussies. Three of them in all. She must tell Anthony immediately and get out of this place.

"Shall we go after our drink? Would you like to?"

"I would, I certainly would."

"Then let's leave right now."

"I'd like that even better."

"We'll be back some other time," Melinda told the manager, who had sprung up to bar their way. "No, no. Excellent service. Yes, really, I assure you. Just a bit of a headache . . ."

David was suddenly very cheerful.

How could she get in touch with Ostrovsky? In *The Times?* But then he would realize that she was responsible for Nora's demise.

David lit her cigarette.

"I'm so disorganized," Melinda said. "I haven't done anything about the papers or the witnesses. Do excuse me, darling."

But he had seen to it all. Was she terrified by the prospect of another go at matrimony after so many painful adventures? (Painful? Adventures?) Her eyes were moist, as they had been on the stairs. The same feeling of fear. Fear? Had she been afraid then? It surprised her to be thinking about herself and considering her own feelings. Not worth the trouble.

"I've taken care of everything," David said. "I'll come and pick you up tomorrow morning at ten, even if it's not done for the bridegroom to arrive with his bride."

"Ten o'clock? It's a bit early. Have we got any witnesses?"

"We'll find somebody, anybody. One's enough, at a registry office. And tomorrow do get up in time."

Melinda

That throat of Madame Nubytch's. Tomorrow it will be in all the papers. She would have to send flowers. And those Pussies, all three of them went for massages at Madame Nubytch's. The Sexyboy Club. She would have to become a Pussygirl, otherwise she'd never find out anything. There was no need to talk to David about it. Anyway, he wouldn't listen.

City Hall looked horrible. The room where marriages were celebrated was small, triangular, outfitted with twenty or so red movie-house chairs, a red rug, and a pulpit behind which sat Mr. Wedding. Mr. Wedding was soon to retire, after uniting in matrimony eighty thousand couples. How many was that per day? He didn't know. Ceremony: six minutes; signing and smiling for photographs: three minutes; a little speech: a minute and a half. He had insisted on David's having the room decorated with some bouquets of flowers. It was still dismal.

"You can give me a check."

"Ten pounds?"

"Make it twenty, will you."

So: eight marriages a day, each with the same bouquets: twenty pounds multiplied by eight? Doubtless the flowers lasted two or three days.

He had to be very rich.

"I wasn't able to keep it quiet," Mr. Wedding whispered in Melinda's ear. "There are several reporters and photographers waiting outside."

. . . Plus gratuities from the papers every time a celebrity got married . . . What would his annual income be?

The little speech: "Now united in matrimony, David and Melinda, think of this link between you as indissoluble. For you,

David, it is your first marriage, and for you, Melinda, still so young, it is your fourth. Let it be the last. May you be happy."

A handshake. The bride and groom embrace. Photographers.

"Is this your third husband?"

"What does your new husband do?"

"Where did you meet?"

"Has he a title?"

"Is he rich?"

"What does he do?"

Into a Rolls-Royce. Home.

"Where are we going?"

"Shall we have some lunch?"

"Let's catch a plane."

"Where do you want to go? I've got to be in London tomorrow."

"Let's go somewhere nice, any place, and then come back tomorrow."

"A waste of money."

(No, he wasn't the type to do this sort of thing. That's why he was rich.)

"I was thinking we could go and see my mother for the weekend, so that you could meet her."

"What's she like, your mother?"

"Mad. Like all mothers of respectable people."

"What does she look like?"

"Ugly."

"What's the house like?"

"Beautiful."

"Is it yours?"

"When she dies."

"Where shall we live?"

"I'd say in London and the country. I have another house."

"I'm not very fond of the country, but I could send all my children down there."

"That too, maybe. Anyway, I hope we shall have children of

our own, though there's no hurry. First there are things we must buy."

"Machines?"

"Lots of machines."

Melinda went to the House of Commons that afternoon. Her latest marriage was in the evening papers.

A bouquet of orchids:

"Hope it works out this time. Hugs and blessings." Signed, A. *"P.S. I'd like to talk to you."*

What a gentleman. He wants to know about Madame Nubytch. The evening papers also carried this story: *Polish Society Masseuse Strangled—Clients To Be Questioned.*

"Will you do me a favor and get me the name of the manager of the London Sexyboy Club," Melinda asked her new secretary, "and make an appointment for me to see him during the week."

The secretary, an odd woman who certainly couldn't be one of Ostrovsky's spies, went to work.

Melinda had tea in the Members Bar with Anthony.

"Did you know about it?"

"About my marriage?"

"You know very well what I mean."

"Yes, I knew all about it. I was the one who found her and rang Scotland Yard."

"That was a mistake. Did you give your name?"

"Of course not."

"That's why they want to question her clients."

"I've nothing to hide."

"Really?"

"It wasn't me, anyway."

"Who was it?"

"How am I to know?"

"In my opinion it was Ostrovsky paying her back for killing Nora."

"Do you think so?" (And how did he know all this?) "I saw a man on the stairs. Obviously he had come from her flat. I suspect he would have liked to kill me, too. Dark eyes, small. He frightened me a bit."

"Dark hair?"

"Yes, very short. Then I saw him again at the Sexyboy Club last night with the three girls. Not one but all three of them at that Sexyboy Club."

"I think I know who this man is."

"Who?"

"A friend of Ostrovsky's who lives in Corsica, Count de Blamonche."

"What makes you so sure?"

"I know more than you do."

"Listen, Anthony, are you the head of it? Tell me. Seriously."

"Don't be ridiculous and stop acting like such an idiot. What do you want to do now?"

"I want to become a Pussy so that I can find out some things."

"But there's nothing to find out, Melinda. It's all a colossal mess. If it amuses you, go on and be a Pussy, but don't poke around in the spy game. There are no more secrets left to steal in the world, so how do you expect there to be any real spies?"

This patronizing sort of talk got on her nerves. Why did he spy himself?

"And Mark? Have you seen him again? Why didn't you marry him?"

"No, I never saw him again."

"He'll be very upset about your getting married."

"Do you really think so?"

"Hah, look at you, you're interested."

"You know I like you all to think of me. Besides, you and Abraham make me cross. That frightfully superior manner you have all the time, as if I didn't know a thing . . . Come and talk to me after I've seen the boss of the Sexyboy Club."

"Just as you say, madam."

They kissed on the cheek. Outside, the Thames. Inside, various extremely curious MP's.

Her secretary had made an appointment with the director of the European Sexyboy Clubs, Anthony G. Gambaino III. They were to meet in New York, because he was in America. The trip and all expenses paid by the firm, of course. It was worth their while: an ex-duchess for a Pussy. They would make her the Superpussy of the Month.

Abraham was on the same plane. As usual, when they met, it was purely coincidence. He was with one of his mysterious ladies and Melinda didn't want to disturb him.

"Congratulations, my girl," he said during a moment when his companion was in the loo. Obviously he didn't want the woman to know he had a grown-up daughter, or that this grown-up daughter was traveling on the same plane. Propped up reading Jacob's latest novel, Melinda fell asleep and awoke to find herself above a New York whose expanse of little houses was so different from what she had expected that she decided to go back to sleep. Where were all those skyscrapers you saw in wide-screen Technicolor?

At Kennedy Airport she was met by a little man holding a big placard with bold letters: DUCHESS PUBLISHING. Melinda followed him, casting a faint smile at Abraham, who was very patiently answering the questions of the notoriously difficult American customs officials. The little man took her passport and whisked her through customs. It was Anthony who had laid on this reception: his influence stretched across the Atlantic. Me-

linda's bags weren't even opened and the porter had been paid
in advance.

Gambaino had sent a car to pick her up. Melinda looked with
interest at the neighborhoods they went through. A jungle of de-
caying tenements and hovels. Not one skyscraper.

"This is Queens, lady," said the driver. "Then we come to
Brooklyn. That's where the World's Fair was, over there. They're
tearing it down now." But they had already passed it. Melinda
noticed only a cluster of crazy-looking structures shaped like atoms
or shoes, and round buildings, nothing that looked like a pavilion.
Brooklyn Bridge, then a few skyscrapers . . . "This is the East
Side." The news didn't impress Melinda. On the other side was
the West, clearly. The west side of Manhattan, Melinda knew,
wasn't in, unless one lived very near the park on Fifty-fifth, Fifty-
sixth, or Fifty-seventh Street, or in the Dakota, with its stucco
lacework and high ceilings. "Lexington Avenue, lady." She peered
upwards and was stunned. Park Avenue she liked, because it had
lots of glass skyscrapers, and she even liked the Pan American
Building, planted in the middle of the street.

"The Plaza, lady. Here you are. Fifth Avenue—the best street
in the world." A host of skyscrapers and the Park with a few
spindly trees and a fine sky, but that was no credit to the street.
"In New York, lady, we have the best climate in the world." He
had to be exaggerating. The lights of the city were beautiful. But
what a disappointment: only a few skyscrapers, far fewer than she
had expected.

And this evening. What was Melinda going to do this evening?

In the lift at the Plaza there were notices advising where to
take refuge in case of atomic attack. The same notices in her
room, as well as two bottles of whisky, some flowers, and a television. There was also a cable from Mark: PLEASE WRITE STOP
WHERE ARE YOU.

How had he found out where she was staying? And what was
he up to?

But how marvelous anyway, Mark wanted her.

And tonight she would have to sleep alone, something she hated.

She had heard so much about the buses of New York. She got on one.

"Greenwich Village," she said to the ferocious driver, who took money, made change, and put it through a machine which digested it loudly. A grunt for a reply.

She gave up the bus and took a taxi. The taxi driver was equally rude. "You got me on the wrong side of the street, lady. I'd have to turn around. Catch another one across the street."

They argued. Melinda got into the cab and tried to placate the driver.

"I've just arrived in New York and I don't know my way around."

"Ah."

"I see from your name that you're of Italian origin."

"Hum."

"Where do you live?"

"Brooklyn."

In a few minutes the driver was launched and there was no stopping him: the war, the Vietniks, his twenty grandchildren, the cost of living in New York, Communism.

Greenwich Village seemed an ugly copy of Saint-Germain-des-Prés, which wasn't much of a place anyway. Phony little restaurants, shops selling Op art clothes, little houses. Everything was The Corner This and Ye Olde That in a city where there should have been no Ye Olde or The Corner anythings.

She walked a block over to Marshal's office. A grimy elevator, a rather squalid waiting room, an inefficient receptionist. What were all these tales about New York?

Marshal was the publisher of a literary magazine; Melinda had met him several times at Abraham's house. He was an old man who had launched all the American writers from Bellow to Mary McCarthy.

"The publisher, please."

Through one big room after another. Newspapers and magazines everywhere, dust, editors, everything strewn around in disorder.

"Melinda Publishing! How nice to see you."

"My dear Marshal. Glad to see me? I'm here for the day. I didn't know where to go. I don't know the city, or the country for that matter. It's the idea of not knowing the whole country that scares me. But how well you look. What are you doing? No, I've never seen your magazine. Weekly? How do you manage it? What do you print? A drink? But of course, I already had some at the hotel . . ."

"It seems ages. Ah yes, I knew you when you were a child. Well, a child in a manner of speaking. You were always quite a girl. Still are now. It's as if time stood still for you. And you've already had three husbands. Even one of our authors . . . an American. Good for you. I know Jacob, you know. A very nice boy."

"Really . . ."

"Are you divorced already?"

"Yes."

"But how sweet. You're a great girl, just like Abraham. No ties. Watch out you don't make the same mistake and get married again. Or have you remarried already?"

"Remarried already . . ."

"She's great this Publishing girl. And who have you married?"

"An Englishman."

"Too many Englishmen. You marry too many of them, they're so dull. Marry me. You'll see how much better we Americans are. Listen, my dear, right now I've got a few things to do. I'll introduce you to one of our editors. A good girl, very sweet. She's not clever like you, but she's a good girl."

Instead of the girl editor, Melinda met the Italian writer Amerigo Vespucci, who was writing a series of articles on American literary magazines. Dark eyes and curly eyelashes, Amerigo came over to her.

"I know your husband."

"Which one?"

"Jacob, of course."

"Actually, I've got another one now."

"And here you are, dressed up like a daisy. Where do you want to go? What do you want to do? Who do you want to see?"

To the Empire State Building to see New York through the smog, away for a Chinese meal in Chinatown and a stop for incense sticks. Half hour at the Cheetah. A snack at Maxwell's Plum. A drink at the Four Seasons. A visit to Robert Lowell and a minute to see Bob Silvers.

Cablegram: YOU NO LONGER EXIST FOR ME STOP TRY TO UNDERSTAND STOP YOU ARE IN PURDAH MARK.

What did Mark want, the idiot? It was he, of course, who no longer existed for her. He should have realized this after that ball, which hadn't been *fin de saison* so much as *fin de siècle*.

Anthony G. Gambaino III was tall, dressed in leather and rubber, certainly impotent, and moved like a great black snail. He had drinks served in a study of shiny leather and painted plastic. Pretty little girls came and went. Another Sexyboy director and a journalist joined them. Lunch was served by a butler, something very rare in the U.S., in a room frescoed by a painter who must have seen reproductions of some eighteenth-century Venetian frescoes and a lot of Leonor Finis. The dreariest food: boiled ham, salad with no dressing, and for dessert some tinned pineapple.

"So, my dear Duchess, you'd like to be one of our Pussies? I applaud your modern woman's initiative. You've caught the tenor of the times. The experience will be useful and most fascinating to a woman of the world like yourself. We're very honored. Naturally we'll put on a big publicity campaign."

"But I'm not a duchess any more."

"But you have been. And you're a Member of Parliament. We're honored by your request. We would be even happier if you could start here in New York."

"Impossible, I've only just married in London and I've got Parliament."

"However you want to do it. We'd like you to visit one of our clubs this evening and we'll give you a few lessons, although I'm sure you'll know how to behave."

"I'd rather stay away from the club. All you need to do is explain the rules."

"The manual of rules is ready in the special kit we've prepared for you. The uniform is so famous that I don't have to describe it. But it must be impeccable. You'll have to wear lipstick."

"That I never do."

"It's one of our rules. Now you needn't worry about an outfit. The Motherpussy will look after that. No Pussy is allowed to date customers. And she can't drink or smoke. I must tell you that we have our own detectives and there's one on duty in the club every night. It's usually a good-looking man and he may ask for dates and promise you large sums of money . . ."

"You don't think that . . ."

"It's my duty to warn you of the rules and the precautions we must take to protect the name of the Sexyboy and the Pussies. Because our organization is morally pure, it has the approval of all American housewives and the blessing of people of the highest principles. We're one big happy family. Our customers become members of this big happy family—one where men and women are companions to each other."

"Good, fine."

Melinda

The speech had been learnt by heart, but Anthony G. Gambaino uttered it with conviction.

"Any questions?"

"No. I'll read the manual. When do I start?"

"When would you like to?"

"As soon as I get back to London."

"And when's that?"

"As soon as possible, tomorrow even."

"You'll have to give us time to prepare some publicity for you."

"Look, I'd rather we skipped the publicity."

"That, I'm afraid, will be impossible."

"I think it would be in your interest to avoid it. It will come anyway. If you're going to mount a publicity campaign on me, I'll have to back out."

"A. C. K. Ffeifer wants to meet you."

"Who's he?"

"Really . . . he's our founder. It was he who invented the Pussygirl. He's made millions, he's founded clubs all across the country. It's a great honor to meet him. Forgive me, but I want you to understand that. He doesn't meet everybody. There isn't an artist or man of influence he hasn't entertained. Being received by him, well, it's like being crowned."

"I'd be delighted to meet him."

"Then we'll go right now. As soon as you've changed."

"Look, I feel perfectly ready to meet . . . what did you say his name was? . . ."

"Ffeifer."

". . . just as I am now."

"I'd like to surprise him. You'll be dressed Pussy-style, in your little satin outfit. You'll have to do something about your hair, though—it's too messy."

"I'm sorry. Mr. Ffeifer will see me dressed up as a Pussy, if he wants to, in his London club."

"You're being difficult."

"So are you, Mr. Gambaino III."

The ground floor of the Ffeifer house had been converted into a large swimming pool where several guests were swimming. Upstairs Pussygirls and other guests were drinking non-alcoholic beverages. Melinda was received in private audience in Ffeifer's large bed-sitting room. It was all in pink. Ffeifer was also in pink. The bed was perfectly round and occupied most of the room. On one side was the bathroom, without a door, the tub sunken into its pink marble floor and the walls covered in tiger skin.

Ffeifer left Melinda almost immediately and she found herself surrounded by a group of women wearing mink stoles. They were mostly wives of Republican candidates. They had been to Europe. "Where did you say you came from?" "I live in London now." "My husband and I have been to Europe. London's a very beautiful city. But Paris is very beautiful too, and so is Rome and Madrid. Spain, olé, it's so cute and picturesque. Do you know Vienna? A taste of the Old World, the Golden Days. Opera, operetta, officers on horseback. We only spent a few hours in Vienna, unfortunately, but I know we'll go back. Switzerland, of course, is the most beautiful country in Europe. What scenery. What manners. And they're clean." "I've been to Europe too. We go every year. My girl friends and I. We're widows so we get together and go on a cruise every year. When our husbands were working, we couldn't do it. Now we go to a different country each year. We haven't decided yet on next year's country. Russia we don't want to see, not for political reasons, you know, but they say it's exactly like the States. So it's not worth it. We can't go to China, as I'm sure you know. But all the other countries . . . You should see Bolivia, it's so picturesque. The colors, the sunsets . . ."

"Milady, you're wanted on the phone."

It was one of the few times she had heard her title used in public.

"But are you really an English Lady?" asked the mink stoles.

Who could it be? Amerigo . . . David?

It was Mark.

He had tracked her down after a number of calls, or so he said

Melinda

(maybe he was in touch with Ostrovsky, too?). "Just a minute, please," the operator's voice, "I'll put you through to Mr. Van Der Belt."

I absolutely should not talk to him.

"Hello. Yes. Aren't you ashamed of yourself?"

"Melinda, I need you."

"What for? To escape from purdah?"

"Are you angry with me?"

"You change your mind too often."

"What did you say? It's a bad connection. I'd like to see you. I'm going to Spain tomorrow. Will you come?"

"Unlikely, because I'm going to Venice."

"What are you going there for?"

"It's my honeymoon."

"But that's crazy. All on your own?"

"Obviously David is meeting me."

"I spoke to him on the phone."

"Good for you."

"You seem a bit distant."

"I am."

"No, I mean cool towards me. Why's that? Anyway, why don't you spend your honeymoon in Spain? It would be more original."

"Honeymoons should be spent in Venice or nowhere at all."

"Stop joking."

"I'm not joking in the slightest."

"Come to Spain."

"No. Besides, there's already another friend coming to Venice."

"A honeymoon à trois?"

"Why not? Let's meet somewhere else."

"Where?"

"In Milan."

She knew it. She shouldn't have spoken to him.

"What day?"

"Either Saturday or Sunday, two weeks from now. At the airport."

"Let me think about it for a minute."

"Don't you care what this call is costing?"

"I've already spent plenty to find you. Saturday would be all right. I'll cable you my arrival time tomorrow. No, I'll phone. At your hotel?"

"All right, but early. I'll be leaving for the airport."

"So soon? How many hours' difference is there between you and London? Is it morning or afternoon where you are?"

"It's almost dinnertime."

"Not here."

"I know that."

"You won't mention this to anyone?"

"What?"

"That we're meeting in Milan."

"Whom do you expect me to tell?"

"People."

"Right now at a cocktail party? Why do you always want to play the woman's role?"

"Are you angry again? I only said that because there's already been some gossip . . ."

"That's your fault."

"Who's this other friend of yours?"

"This call's costing you too much."

"Who is he?"

"A writer, as usual."

"Do I know him?"

"No."

"And does he know me?"

"What difference does it make? And anyway, why should he know you?"

"I mean, have you told him about us?"

"It may seem strange to you, but I haven't told him a thing." (Which wasn't true.)

"I'm glad we'll be seeing each other soon."

"So am I, I think. But you'll change your mind."

"No, believe me."

"Bye."

"What are you wearing?"

"Feathers."

"No, seriously?"

"I am being serious. Black feathers."

"And your hair?"

"It's all down, except for a bit on top with a ribbon."

"What color's the ribbon?"

"You know this call's costing an awful lot of money?"

"Don't worry about that. What color is it?"

"That's a pointless question."

"Not for me. I want to imagine you as you are now. Please describe yourself."

"I'm surrounded by chattering women drinking fruit juice. They're talking about their travels, plastic surgery with scars behind the ears, and dead husbands. There are lots of pink rooms, except for the one where I am now. It has a brass floor and zebra walls. I'm sitting on a sofa, also zebra, with a cigarette and the only whisky on the premises. The walls are covered with paintings, all atrocious."

"Where are you going tomorrow?"

"I've told you. Venice."

"Who with?"

"The writer."

"But are you fond of this writer of yours? And what about me? Where do I fit in?"

A question he should have asked before sending that ridiculous cable.

"Do you still want to see me?"

"Certainly."

"And will David be in Venice too?"

"Everybody will be there."

And away: lunch and a film and hand in hand with Amerigo

on the plane. And her lips on Amerigo's cheeks, Melinda snuggling on his lap. Everything so fast, too fast.

Venice, there was no doubt about it, was incomparably the most beautiful city in the world. A pity the people spoke Venetian and were Venetian.

David seemed glad to see her.

"Melinda, I missed you."

"So soon? You miss me already?"

Melinda explained that she had to go back to London. She didn't explain what she would be doing at the Sexyboy Club, but she didn't know how she could keep it a secret from him. In Milan she had to meet people on business. She did not explain what sort of business. David would have liked a long holiday with his wife but said nothing and resolved once again to change her way of life.

The Gualdini-Tebaldi motor launch was waiting to take them to their palazzo. On the Grand Canal, of course.

"Now I'll have a nice bath and then a nice little rest with you. Yes?"

But instead there was Count Alessandro, who had to show her the house. No shower, no nice little rest with embraces. "And these are the carpets, the only ones of their kind in the world, that my grandmother acquired" (he never said "bought") "ten years ago, and this is a portrait of my great-grandmother, she was born a Guendolazzi, Genoese family. Fascinating woman. I spend hours looking at her face. You see these candelabra? All Canova. These pictures are by Longhi. He was an ancestor of mine. He married a Teodoluzzi, Salerno family, and this is another ancestor. You see him here just after his beautiful wife died at the age of twenty-seven (of Catanian family). This is a watercolor of our

Melinda

castle, we have two more in Tuscany. Empty, mind you, completely empty, and the Italian government doesn't give us a lira towards restoring them. Do you know how much they gave us to restore this palazzo? Sixty rooms, mark you, sixty rooms. Just a few hundred thousand lire. Fortunately we've let part of the house. Now we're getting back on our feet. We've got to build a kitchen. First our rooms, Alessandra and I decided, then a baby and then the kitchen . . ."

Alessandro was a decorator. He designed furniture of colored Plasticine that changed shape every time it was used.

Finally Melinda was able to go to her room. A shower. Her head resting on the pillow. Hands caressed her body and suddenly she felt her lungs begin to heave. Her hand became the only object of any importance. With experience she touched the curves of her body, the warmth, the hidden recess of her pleasure. Electric reactions steered her hand and urged it on, banishing the ignorant violence and lack of insight with which strangers touched her. Alone it was possible to achieve a pure sensuality. Beads of sweat came with the increasing pulses of her sex. She stopped at intervals to breathe with her eyes closed. "Coming. I'm coming." Nothing but that hand existed for her, with its way of touching her, nervous, delicate circles that spiraled downward. Her throat trapped the air in her lungs and her eyes gaped fixedly at the ceiling. Gasping, she called her own name, any name.

She could do it a number of times consecutively. After the first the pleasure became less intense, the sensation briefer, close to pain. Three. Four. If there was a fifth it was born of nerves. Afterward she would have to drink a glass of whisky or take an Alka-Seltzer.

She remembered as a child she could stay in bed for hours making love to herself, never having to fantasize images of men, never murmuring any names. Pleasure was an end in itself. Once in a while she would masturbate in front of a man: to be watched gave her another kind of pleasure.

Farther, deeper.

Again quickly, before David comes in. She heard David move in the bathroom.

The lightning shudders strengthened. She was nullifying herself in that hand. Then her breath broke loose and with it flew all thought. A fruit sliced open, juice dripping, held out in offering to itself. Her hands' veins bulged and her legs trembled in a last, overpowering spasm.

"Melinda, are you ready?"

"Darling, I've been making love to myself. Get undressed immediately."

"I can't, really. You've got to be ready in five minutes—washed, dressed, combed, and not late."

"But we don't care about being late."

"I do."

And where was Mark? Where was Amerigo? Why wasn't anybody there? Anyway, Amerigo was at the Lido. And Mark? Sexually and socially distracted.

Mark's telegram wasn't even addressed to her. Alessandra Gualdini-Tebaldi announced that he would be arriving the next day. He was spurning the Milan plan. How to punish him?

Alessandra got all her clothes from *Choses*, at least so she said; as if that were anything to be very proud of. "This garment," she would say (she didn't say "dress" or "trousers"), "I acquired" (neither would she say "bought" or "got," which would have been better) "from *Choses*, that little shop in Saint-Trop. A vulgar little place, Saint-Trop, since the tourists moved in. Still, the French know how to keep up their tourist resorts . . ." How could people still talk like that?

The sky was overcast. David had decided to visit a couple of

Melinda

electrical-appliance shops, both of them on the corner of the Mercerie. He had heard good things about them.

"Good morning, everybody!" It was Amerigo in blue silk trousers. Introductions, chitchat. "Where shall we lunch? Coming to the Excelsior?" "We're lunching here, thanks. We're expecting Mark Van Der Belt. He should be arriving this morning." "Well, let him come, let him come, and you come with me in the meantime. Let's go for a drink. Yes?"

Mark arrived almost at the same moment as David.

"Alessandra."

Needless to say, he didn't speak a word of Italian.

"Darling, here I am. I lost my cases at Rome airport. Good morning, Melinda." A chaste kiss on the cheek. "I had dinner with my brother William before I left. Have you heard the latest gaffe?"

"No, Mark."

Glances full of questions. And why had he ever come to Venice? Were they going to meet each other in Milan? How would he straighten things out now?

Melinda followed Amerigo into the water as far as the Excelsior. At the bar there were some people she knew vaguely. And suddenly through the pearls and Dubonnet of a woman who was pretending to stare at the water, there was Mark. An arm round her waist. And his dear face. He rested a hand on her hip.

"Let's go to Glorian's for a minute, we can sit down and have coffee."

He meant Florian's, of course. Florian's was where Abraham had always taken her when they came to Venice together. Abraham used to say they shouldn't go to the Quadri because it was the café of the Austrian hordes in the nineteenth century and it was still a place for barbarians. He would always leave her sitting at a table with her governess and a big ice cream while he went off to Harry's Bar. And now Mark had chosen the same place to tell her something unpleasant, of course.

Aglaia . . . a terrible feeling of guilt . . . they couldn't meet in Milan. But she understood. She did understand, didn't she?

How disgraceful, confessing such things to her in an operetta café like Florian's. Things to say in bed, if at all. She would never listen to Mark again.

The waiter brought the coffees. In spite of the gray hair and thick glasses, she could see perfectly well that it was Ostrovsky.

"Ostrovsky. At last."

"I beg your pardon, madam?"

"Mark, doesn't it seem to you that this gentleman and the man the night of . . ."

"What, Melinda?"

Vague as he was, there wasn't a prayer of his remembering a face.

"Sorry. I must have made a mistake. You resemble a servant my father had in Czechoslovakia, when I was a little girl . . . many years ago . . . you really look very like him."

Of course it was Ostrovsky. And he wouldn't even acknowledge he'd been recognized.

"Mark, would you get me some cigarettes?"

"You've got a full packet."

"They're old and moldy."

"Let's send the waiter who looks like your Hungarian friend to the tobacconist's."

"That's not what I said, but never mind."

"Tell me, Melinda, you've never said anything about your childhood or your family. One day I'd like to hear all about you, where you were born, your friends. I saw my brother William before I left. He came to dinner. Do you know my brother?"

How many times had he asked her that question?

"Yes, I met him once. Look, it'll be quicker if you go and get those cigarettes."

Ostrovsky came straight over.

"Very unprofessional. I've received no information from you, my dear Melinda."

Melinda

"But I never know where to contact you, and Nora's disappeared. Do you know where she's gone?"

"No, I thought you knew. Anyway, I'm the one who contacts you—and keeps an eye on you."

"How?"

"That's no business of yours."

"Anthony spies on me, doesn't he?"

"The Prime Minister? Don't talk nonsense . . ."

"But . . ." (No, she'd better not say they sometimes talked about Ostrovsky.) "How did you find out I was in Venice?"

"Quickly, or your friend will be back with the cigarettes. What news of Madame Nubytch?"

"Haven't you read the papers? She was strangled. I was the first to see her, after she was murdered. I know who it was. A man with black eyes and black crew-cut hair. I saw him on the stairs outside her flat, after the murder. I saw him again that night at the Sexyboy Club with three of Madame Nubytch's clients, all three dressed as Pussies."

"The murderer must have been Blamonche. That was to be expected."

"Why? Explain."

"There isn't time and it's not necessary. But how do you intend to earn that money I gave you?"

(What a boor.)

"When I get back to London I'm going into the Sexyboy Club as a Pussy. I've arranged everything."

"Make sure they use you for publicity, otherwise you'll be killed immediately. And if you can do it, try to kill the three Pussies."

"All three? How about Blamonche?"

"Later you'll go to Corsica. You'll find him there. First, though, go to Moscow. You'll find a friend there. Maybe I'll be there. Go whenever you like. I'll find out and tell you what to do."

"Anything else?"

"That's all. May I bring you another coffee? . . . He's coming back. Naturally you'll arrange immediately to divorce this ridiculous new husband you've picked up. You can't be a spy and married, there isn't time. Another thing. The less you see of this Van Der Belt, the better. All right, he doesn't know what's going on, but I don't want him to get suspicious."

"That's my affair. And where shall I find the money?"

"This time it'll be delivered to your house."

"Where do you get your information?"

"Didn't you order another coffee?"

Mark was coming back with the cigarettes.

"I saw you chatting. So you *are* Yugoslav?" Mark said to Ostrovsky. "Here you are, darling, your cigarettes. Right brand, aren't they?"

They picked their way through the pigeons and tourists. Divorce David . . . he'll agree, I suppose. Go to Moscow. How marvelous. Three Pussies to kill, and Blamonche . . . Blamonche scared her.

Mark wrapped his rather heavy arm round her shoulders and kissed her outside the Hotel Luna. In the meantime, Aglaia, London, his friends, family, above all his family, were far away.

The guests lingered on after lunch. But their faces were drowsy. Mark had just disappeared from an armchair where he had been reclining with an enormous cigar and behaving as if he were in an English club, without a word to anybody. Presumably to the bedroom. He was waiting for her. Obviously. Melinda got up, trying to be inconspicuous.

Melinda

♦

SCENE I   *The setting is a Venetian drawing-room.*
Several guests, among them David Llewellyn-Jones, an English-
man, and his wife Melinda, dressed in white chiffon that suggests
transparency.

DAVID: Are you coming? Can you be ready in ten minutes?

MELINDA (*pretending to stifle a yawn with her hand*): I'm so sleepy. I'd love to have a little rest and then I could join you in a couple of hours in Piazza San Marco.

KATHERINE VAN BLISS, *another guest*: Can I come with you, David? I've nothing to do till this evening. Perhaps I could just brush up first. Can I come into your room for a minute, Melinda? *They exit, exchanging pleasantries with other guests.*

SCENE II   *The Llewellyn-Jones bedroom; adjoining*
it, Mark Van Der Belt's room, empty. Melinda is obviously trying
to be noisy to warn Mark that she isn't alone. Miss Van Bliss is in
the bathroom. This we know from the sound of the tap running.
David, on one side, is consulting a map of Venice.

MELINDA (*to the audience*): Let's hope Mark doesn't appear now.
Katherine Van Bliss reappears, with her hair combed.

KATHERINE VAN BLISS: Well then, shall we meet at five-thirty at Florian's?

DAVID (*to both women*): Let's make it six, otherwise it'll be too much of a rush.

MELINDA: If I don't wake up in time, give me a ring here.

DAVID: Bye, darling.

KATHERINE: Bye.

MELINDA: See you later.

Exit David and Katherine.

SCENE III   *Melinda, carefully combing her hair, then polishing her nails. She undresses. She puts on a short dressing gown. In her hurry and nervousness she drops a bottle of eau de cologne, which breaks.*

MELINDA: Damn it.

She looks in the mirror. Evidently she is ready. She exits the opposite direction from David and Katherine. We hear Melinda knocking at a door.

Damn it.

After a few moments, Melinda comes back on stage.

(*Talking to herself*) The idiot. He's obviously gone out. He's always making me feel like an ass. He's gone out. It was perfectly obvious he should wait for me.

She picks up the phone and sits on the bed. She lights a cigarette. She is plainly jumpy.

(*On the phone*) Hotel Excelsior? Mr. Vespucci, please. He should be in the lobby.

After a bit, she throws the receiver to the floor.

That imbecile Mark. He always ruins everything.

Melinda goes into the bathroom and emerges dressed, ready to go out. She puts various things into her bag.

(*Murmuring to herself*) Glasses . . . powder . . . where's my comb? . . . Hell, no money. And what can I do till six? Never mind, I deserve it. That idiot.

SCENE IV   *A door opens.*

MARK (*Dressed as at lunch*): Melinda? Are you going out?

MELINDA: Where have you been?

Melinda

MARK (*Holding out a little necklace of Murano glass*): I went for a little walk. Look what I brought. Can you do something for me?

MELINDA (*Tenderly*): What?

MARK: Could you ring the hall porter and tell him to wake me up at six and ask the driver if he can take me in the launch to the Gritti at half past?

Melinda picks up the house phone.

MELINDA: Hello? Mr. Van Der Belt would like to be woken at six o'clock. What? What's that? (*Puts her hand over the receiver.*) Can I come to bed with you? (*Takes her hand off the receiver.*) And he wants the launch for half past six.

MARK: Where's David?

MELINDA: He's gone out.

MARK: Weren't you on your way out?

MELINDA: Not any more.

MARK: What if David comes back?

MELINDA: We'll pretend we're talking about your brother William.

MARK: What?

Melinda takes him by the hand and leads him off.

SCENE V   *Mark's room. Moderate disorder. Plane tickets, money, books, and scraps of paper on the table, on the floor, and on the chairs. Melinda undresses again.*

MARK: I've changed my mind.

MELINDA: A miracle. I don't believe it. It's impossible.

MARK: Now stop joking. Please, let's meet in Milan.

MELINDA: No, no. You might turn up and say you've changed your mind again, or that you're stricken with remorse.

MARK: But don't you want to go?

MELINDA: Of course I do. Don't you remember? It was my idea.

Mark draws her on to the bed with him. The two of them disappear under the covers, from which emerges first a brassière and then a pair of panties which we saw Melinda put on before she got dressed again. They kiss.

MARK: What if your husband comes?

MELINDA: Please stop distracting me all the time.

MARK: Darling, darling. Really we could see each other in Milan. I've never seen the Pinacoteca. My sister was saying it's marvelous. I must tell you something, though: I'm a difficult man. To live with, I mean. Even for a couple of days. You'll notice that.

MELINDA: I've already noticed.

MARK: Don't make fun of me.

MELINDA: No, I mean it seriously.

Melinda turns over and Mark holds her close.

MARK: Have you got something on?

MELINDA: No, I'm naked.

MARK: No. I mean a contraceptive, or something.

MELINDA: Of course I have. But you shouldn't ask questions like that.

MARK: Why? *(We now see Mark drive into Melinda.)* Help me. I can never find the right spot.

MELINDA: As if there were more than one. Now I can't get my hand out.

MARK: I love you. I love you. I love you. Oh, how I love you. How I missed you. I couldn't have missed seeing you.

MELINDA: What do you feel?

MARK: You, all around me. And love for you. Did you like my letter?

MELINDA: Which letter? I didn't get it. But don't distract me, for heaven's sake.

MARK *(Raising himself a little)*: I'd like you to come first.

MELINDA: How can I if you keep on talking? Come back, please.

MARK: I'm afraid of coming too soon.

MELINDA: Oh well, never mind. It'll be my turn another time.

Melinda wipes something off Mark's forehead which the audience may assume to be sweat.

Melinda

MELINDA: And now what do you want to do?

MARK: I'd like a little sleep. Then we could go out together.

SCENE VI   *Footsteps in the corridor.*

THE PORTER'S VOICE: Mr. Van Der Belt, the launch is ready.

The door handle moves. Panic. Melinda gets up, wearing a sheet.

MARK (*In a frightened voice*): You can't. Don't come in.

MELINDA (*From behind the door and with her hand cupped over her mouth, speaking to the audience*): I bet he's forgotten to lock the door.

SCENE VII   *The porter has evidently gone away. Melinda embraces Mark as he lies on the bed, almost asleep.*

MELINDA: Bye.

MARK: I'll get the plane tickets later, so that we can meet in Milan.

MELINDA: We'll discuss it when you wake up.

Melinda goes off, dragging behind her a sheet, some clothes and underwear. In the silent bedroom there is the sound of regular breathing. The breathing gets louder and louder till it splutters into grumbling and snorting. From the other room comes Melinda's voice.

Damn it. He even snores.

Mark continues to snore as the curtain comes down.

Two things happened then. Melinda rejected Amerigo as an eventual future husband. And she decided to stop seeing Mark. Between one conversation about his brother and another about his wife, Mark had let his mind wander and had booked the wrong tickets for the wrong dates, leaving Melinda with the humiliating feeling that he had done it on purpose.

So it was that Melinda and David flew to London together. David saw a chance of saving their marriage by taking refuge in the country and trying to return to the ancestral way of life. His battle strategy was: a visit to the mother-in-law and then his estate. Save their marriage . . . when a decision like that is in the air, whatever is said or done comes out forced and wrong.

David never talked much when he was driving; but this time Melinda sat silent too. She only hummed a little. The country was a bore and of course there was nothing to say about the scenery. And it was raining.

She did try, though, to make conversation. "It's freezing," she said. "Yes. We know it's cold. There's no need to say it." "I just said it to say something." "Next time don't say something just for the sake of saying it." "But it's damp too." "Of course. It's raining." "But is it always damp when it rains?" It was no good. An impossible situation. Not even Melinda could get around it. She smoked one cigarette after another. She was getting a sore throat.

"I've got a sore throat." "You've been smoking too much." "Is your mother's house warm?" "It depends which part you're in." "You mean some parts are cold and others warm?" "Exactly. Well done." "Are there lots of fireplaces?" "If you go on asking questions like this, I'll go mad. Haven't you ever been in an English house? Haven't you, in fact, owned five or six yourself with all the husbands you've had? Now will you stop getting on my nerves." "But really, I was only making conversation. Not very brilliant, but not particularly . . ." "Enough, I said."

Silence. They came to a side road.

"This is where my mother's land begins." "Is it yours too?" "Only part of it. My own property is in Yorkshire. You'll see it later this week." "Any game?" "Excellent game." "What is there?" "Pheasant, mostly."

There were woods and parkland around the house. They passed

through several gates. David kept stopping to open them. Dusk was falling and blurred the silhouette of the house. Melinda could make out the outline of enormous rectangular windows from patches of light behind curtains. A colonnade flanked the entrance.

A butler emerged from the darkness. He greeted David with deference. He hardly glanced at Melinda, bestowing on her only a hurried nod. It wasn't lack of respect. Just the usual English shyness.

"How's my mother?" David asked.

"The same as usual, sir. We can't say she's in very good form."

An enormous figure had silently taken up position under the portico. Melinda looked at it with interest and saw two fiery eyes boring into her. The woman had on a felt hat adorned with a multitude of holes made by the various pins stuck in it during the course of the century. Her dress was artificial silk with a pattern of yellow and pink flowers, and she wore several colored scarves, some tied around her neck and others to her hat. Several bracelets, rings, brooches, and necklaces. Some glaringly paste. Others genuine. Her stockings were coming down, one almost to her ankle. Perhaps she didn't use garters, or the elastic had gone. On her feet were a pair of shapeless, tattered slippers. A carved walking stick supported the 320 pounds (which Melinda later verified) distributed over the six-foot-six-inch frame of David's mother.

It was an absolute shock. "Is that your mother?" Melinda asked weakly. But already David had thrown himself at the mountain of flesh.

"Mother."

"How are you? How was the trip? Are you tired? Come in and have a drink."

They went into the house, leaving Melinda gaping. When she tried to follow them in, three dogs she hadn't noticed before jumped at her and tried to stop her from entering the ancestral home of the Llewellyn-Joneses.

"So is this my daughter-in-law. My only daughter-in-law?"

"Yes, Mother."

"You can tell she's a foreigner."

"But she's lived a long time in England."

"She doesn't look in the least aristocratic."

"Please, Mother, not in front of the servants. Anyway, I won't permit you to say such things."

"If your father could hear you!"

The muddled ticking of six or seven clocks. Two in the drawing room, three in the vast hall, one, stopped, in the brown room. One in the study? She hadn't noticed. None of them had the same time, so there was a continual striking of quarter and half hours, with brief intervals between.

"Pour me some wine."

"You've drunk enough for tonight, Mother."

"I won't allow you to criticize your mother in front of strangers."

"Don't speak like that about Melinda."

"I shall be forced to ask the butler for the wine."

"Go ahead. You won't get it from me."

Tick-tick, tock-tock.

"Your father said you could marry any girl you wanted, but never a foreigner. And where do you come from?" (It was the first time she had spoken to Melinda.)

"In what sense, where do I come from?"

"From what country?"

"Czechoslovakia."

"Where's Czechoslovakia? Anywhere near India? I spent my honeymoon there. It's a country of nice people, not like here. Everybody gave me presents. Too hot, though. We had so many friends . . ."

"Now don't start your stories about India, Mother. In any case, all you saw of India were the Viceroy's receptions."

"What do you know about it? You weren't even born then. You don't look very Indian, Melinda."

"You have a point."

"And what's your name?"

"Publishing."

Melinda

"It sounds like an English name."

"My father changed his name when he came to England. It used to be Publikovsky."

"He certainly did the right thing to change his name. Is he still alive? What's his name? Is he good-looking? Why didn't he come to spend the weekend? David never thinks of these things. He always brings me some girl or other. But why did your father leave his own country?"

"It was before the war."

"Ah, I might have known. Your father didn't fight for England. He ran off, deserted. Was he in the war?"

"He wasn't, to tell the truth. But he fought in the First World War."

(Was that true? No, couldn't be. Abraham must have been too young.)

"Ah, that's all right then. Now that was a war! This last one was a joke. They were all heroes during the first war. I was in the Red Cross out here in the country and the soldiers came to me with a smile on their lips."

"Mother, don't start on the First World War."

"You shut up and pass me the Bordeaux."

"You've drunk too much already."

"Don't pass comments in front of strangers, I told you . . . And why did your father escape from India?"

"Because of the racial laws."

"What racial laws? I've never heard of such laws in India. The new generation have got a mania for blaming Britain. We behaved very well in India. My God, we did. You'll find out . . . You'll all go to your death."

"That's enough, Mother."

"There'll be an atomic war and you'll all die. I don't envy you a bit. I shall die before because I'm very ill. My children don't look after me. I shan't last long."

"Mother, no more of the old stories, please."

"You see? He doesn't want me to talk about it."

"But you're in good health."

"I've got a terrible disease. One that never lets you go. In my lungs. It's destroying me."

"Pleurisy?"

A deep sigh. The tick-tick of the clocks.

"You see? This wife of yours doesn't know a thing, David. Pleurisy! I've got consumption. Consumption, my dear friends. And you'll weep. No, you won't, you'll be glad. You'll laugh at my funeral. If there *is* a funeral."

"Not at all, Mother."

"What did you say?"

"I said, no—we won't be glad."

"What's that?"

"She's getting a bit deaf. It happens when she drinks too much."

"He thinks I can't hear. He thinks he can treat me like an old invalid. But I'm perfectly all right and healthier than he is. He can't wait for me to die and leave him the house and the furniture and the land. But I won't, I won't die at all."

"But, Mother, I have my own estate. I'm not interested in having yours."

"All right then, I'll leave it to somebody else."

"I suppose you mean Jeremy?"

"What did you say? Speak up. He always tries to leave me out of the conversation."

"I said Jeremy. He's her fancyboy," he added softly.

"What's a fancyboy? I can hear perfectly well, you know."

"By the way, Mother, I'd rather not talk about these things, but since we're on the subject I had better tell you that your bank is complaining about the debts you're running up. I know you gave five thousand pounds to Jeremy and you pay the school fees for his three children. You can't afford to spend money like that."

"There you are. A spy. That's what my son is: a spy. And if I can't do what I like with my own money, then I'll sell the land and furniture. Poor Jeremy, I know you hate him. You're jealous.

Melinda

I hope Melinda will take it to heart. He's my only real friend.
Married to a nice Catholic girl. They have lots of children. Do
you want a lot of children?"

"We shall see."

"What do you mean, we shall see? I had four. And you, as an
Indian, should be able to have many."

"I already have quite a few."

"Quite a few children? You've been married before? Are you
divorced? You aren't Catholic? So are the two of you living in
sin? You know, I suppose, that divorce isn't valid in the eyes of
God?"

"But I'm not Catholic."

"Not Catholic?"

Silence. Tick-tick. A long sigh. The wind. Tock-tock.

"Anyway you've no right to think only of Jeremy's children.
Think of your grandchildren. You never give them a thing."

"What do you say! It's all I ever do. Besides, your sister is rich,
richer than I am. She shouldn't keep a butler, a cook, and two
maids. Pass me the bottle."

"Mother, you've had enough."

"You see? He's always criticizing me. He comes to my house
just to criticize me. Ah, if only his father could see him!"

Suddenly she stood up, took two steps toward the door, and
plunged forward, tripping over the dumbwaiter.

Chutney in her hair, mint sauce on her dress, a bottle of
Tabasco in hand, she said, "Call the maid and the butler immediately. And God help you if you laugh."

Conversation after dinner was just as difficult. David
put a record on the ancient Victrola.

"Do call me mummy." An enormous hand squeezed Melinda's
arm. The chutney had been summarily cleaned up. All of them

had been required to get the old lady back on her feet. The butler and the maid could never have done it by themselves.

"If you don't mind, at least for now, I'd rather call you Molly."

"Well, all right, if you insist." She sighed again. "So few people understand music." She squeezed Melinda's arm once more. "But I know what music *means*." She began to cry.

David had entrenched himself in an armchair and was reading various newspapers. He wasn't listening and couldn't see anything. Melinda gave him the eye. What was she supposed to do? No reply from David to her glance. He was immersed in some weekly.

"Please don't cry, Molly. I *may* call you Molly?"

"You must understand—what did you say your name was?"

"Melinda."

"—you must understand, Melinda, how much I've suffered. I have a dreadful disease. My son ignores it. But the doctors are very worried."

"Why don't you have it treated?"

"Now you're interfering. You don't understand. It's an incurable disease. Always fatal. I imagine in your ignorance you don't even know what I'm talking about."

"But of course, about consumption. You already told me."

"What's that?"

"Consumption."

"You're beginning to mumble too. You young people ought to enunciate more clearly. Always trying to leave me out of the conversation."

"Not at all and besides the conversation's between us two. I have no intention of keeping you out. I said, consumption."

"Consumption? What about it?"

"That's your illness."

"Well done. You've guessed. How did you do it? You can tell, eh? A sensitive person, that's what you are, Melinda, an intelligent person. My dear daughter-in-law, my son did well to marry you. I should have realized. Yes, my dear, you've understood perfectly, I've got consumption. Anyway, for heaven's sake stop that Gramophone, it makes too much noise and you can't hear a thing. What was David saying?"

"He's reading. He didn't say a thing."

"How long are you two staying with me?"

"A couple of days, we thought."

"Why so few?"

"We're going on to Yorkshire, so that I can see David's house."

"Yorkshire? You don't tell me anything. I'll come too."

"But I think we rather wanted to be alone."

"What did you say? Speak up."

"I believe David wanted to be alone with me. We've never been left to ourselves since we got married."

"But I shan't disturb you. You know I'm not the sort to be a nuisance."

"Of course, but . . ."

"David."

His mother's voice tore him away from an article on a new grass-cutting machine.

"Yes, Mother?"

"When are we going to Yorkshire?"

"Who told you we were going to Yorkshire?"

"Your wife did."

"We're going alone."

"What did you say?"

"Mother, we want to be alone, just the two of us."

"But I shan't disturb you, as I was telling your wife. And anyway, it was Melinda who invited me. Wasn't it, Melinda?"

"Well really . . ."

"There you are, you see."

A clock struck midnight. Another, half past eleven. All the others just tick-tock. Melinda left the room. She climbed the great stairs alone, studying the faces of David's ancestors closely. The bedroom was huge and frigid, and on the floor lay hundreds of flies in their death throes. Was their demise caused by insecticide or the cold? Her guess was their deaths were attributable to the icy wind that was blowing in through the large number of cracks in the windows.

Melinda undressed slowly, keeping near the fire. She noticed the dust in the marble flutings and the handsome Adam-style marble panels. It was cold. David had stayed downstairs to read the papers and showed no signs of coming up. Melinda was too frightened to go to the bathroom alone; it was too far. She didn't know where the lights were and to go through those dark corridors full of clocks . . . who knew what ghosts might live in that house . . . And even if there weren't any now, Molly would someday provide one.

She got into bed. The heavy canopy gave her a feeling of claustrophobia and she couldn't read. She could only concentrate on the murmur of the agonizing flies, the clocks, the wind.

When she fell asleep an hour later, David still hadn't come up.

The maid woke them up with breakfast.

"Why are there so many flies?" were her first words that morning.

"Is it raining?"

It was.

They went out to have a look at the park, the garden, the rare flowers, the orchard and greenhouses, and the woods.

"Did you read late last night?"

"Till two. I also went over some of my mother's correspondence."

"Where is she now?"

"In bed. She stays there all morning. Why did you invite her to Yorkshire?"

"But I wouldn't have dreamed of inviting her. You might have warned me or at least listened to what was being said. She's not easy to get along with, your mother, you know. You ought to have put me on my guard."

"I warn you she's in a foul mood in the mornings."

"Why's that?"

"She drinks on an empty stomach, and it makes her very bad-tempered."

"How long are we staying here?"

"Another four days, I thought. It's so nice in the country. We could tour around this afternoon and see the farmers, and then the countryside. We could have a drink with the neighbors, maybe. We've got some nice neighbors."

"But what did you do when you lived here?"

"I read."

"And you'd like to read for four days on end?"

"Why not? It'll be a rest."

"A rest from what?"

"Don't you want to stay here?"

"No. Let's go to Yorkshire."

"Tomorrow, if you like. But aren't you enjoying it here?"

"Are you?"

"I am. I love it here."

"Are there any ghosts in this house?"

"I've never seen any. And even if there were, what harm would they do?"

"I'd be terrified."

"Why? If they're good ghosts, there's nothing to be afraid of."

"But wouldn't it scare you to walk along in the dark and suddenly, right in front of you, to see a ghost?"

"Not at all. I've seen some, a couple of times."

"Ghosts?"

"Yes."

"Here?"

"No, at some friends' in the country."

"And didn't you nearly die of fright?"

"Why should I? I told you, I saw them. That's all. They didn't do anything."

"And you're sure there aren't any here?"

"I've never seen any."

"Probably your mother, after she dies."

"Oh, absolutely, she'll infest the place."

They found her in the drawing room. She was pouring herself some sherry, but as soon as they came in she began humming and pretended to dust the bottles off.

"Sleep well, Mother?"

"As well as possible, considering my condition."

Nevertheless she eyed Melinda with horror.

She turned back to David. "Have you been out? You can feel the spring in the air already, can't you?"

"But it's only the beginning of autumn," said Melinda.

"These are things you either feel or you don't. I'm very sensitive and I feel them. Of course you, being a mere child who doesn't even know where she comes from, couldn't possibly understand. Springtime. Yes, a well-bred, sensitive person would already be able to smell it in the air. Especially a person who loves nature and knows everything about flowers. You know nothing, I suppose, about flowers?" (She gave Melinda no time to reply. In effect it was true, Melinda didn't know the first thing about plants.) "Nor about horses. You see, a girl with none of the qualities of a gentlewoman that your father so admired. What would he have said? This is for you."

She put a packet in her hand. "I tore that out of my heart. It's beautiful. Too good for you."

Melinda opened the packet: it contained a tiny brooch of diamond chips.

"Thank you."

She tried it on. It was lost on her blouse.

"Don't you think my dress is elegant?" Molly turned to David.

"Just think, I got it in 1944. And what about my hat? It's prewar. Don't you think yellow suits me? It's my color. So mind you are pink and periwinkle. I've still got lovely arms, don't you think? Everybody tells me so. They've kept their shape splendidly. I've always been known for my arms. I don't think you've thanked me enough. Obviously you don't like the brooch. I'll have it back."

"But it's beautiful. And I did thank you."

"Not enough, though. Lack of breeding. Stands out a mile. I could tell the minute I saw her at the door. From the way she looked at me. And she's not Catholic and she comes from India. The sort of girl that wouldn't have been accepted in English society in my day."

"That's enough, Mother."

"I'll say what I like in my own house."

Lunch proceeded in long silences between clocks striking and sudden gusts of wind which had arisen in the meantime. In the afternoon David and Melinda drove out into the country. Later they went to a cousin of David's for sherry. The evening was an exact repetition of the one before. David read and said nothing.

It was a long journey. Melinda looked at David's profile and then at the view: the hills, the identical villages, the people in the rain. Conversation was becoming increasingly difficult. She dictated several letters on her tape recorder.

Whatever had possessed her to agree to try and salvage this unsalvageable marriage? Molly was traveling by train. They would meet her in the ancestral castle, already settled in and full of drink.

"I took this road, Melinda, to show you Durham Cathedral."

"In the rain?"

"It won't be raining in the cathedral."

"But you've seen it before?"

"Many times."

"Well, let's not go then."

What had induced David to get married after years of solitude and blessed bachelor life? He glanced at Melinda and almost drove off the road. She was beautiful. But apart from that? David never knew what went on in his wife's head. What interests did she have? Herself? No, not even herself. She was often bored. There was no doubt she was often bored with him. But then why had she married him? Out of habit, probably. What had she thought of the days they had just spent in Wales? Had she been bored there? Had she liked the house? What did she think of his way of life? Perhaps she would like the house in Yorkshire. It would be nice to spend a few months in the country with her, to try and change her and give her new interests. After all, was it realistic to expect responsible conduct from Melinda after the disorderly life she used to lead? Had she been Mark's mistress? Was she still? Had she been the mistress of . . . But why bother wondering? And what point was there thinking about Melinda, when she obviously didn't think about him? What was her opinion of him? Why didn't she ever criticize him and why did she ask those point-blank questions and from his answers seem to want to judge him as if they were on a TV quiz program? He remembered the first time he saw a photo of her with that sexless child's face. She never spoke of her children, or of her other husbands. Yet surely she must think about them sometimes.

The tedium of a week in the country. I'll be all right if it goes quickly and I find something to do, a boy friend. I'll ring up Anthony. I'll write Amerigo. I wonder where he is? And what about Archibald Ostrovsky?

"Don't you think this is a nice spot for a picnic?"

"Charming."

"Let's stop then."

"What for?"

"To have our picnic."

"But I haven't brought anything."

"Cook's laid something on."

Melinda

"But think how damp the grass will be."

"We'll sit in the car."

"Well, let's find a restaurant and have our picnic sitting at a table."

"There won't be a restaurant open at this hour."

"What time is it?"

"Two o'clock."

"But in London I always . . ."

"We aren't in London. We're in the English provinces."

"What an uncivilized place."

"Maybe—but you *have* chosen to live here."

"I've chosen nothing of the sort."

"I don't think there's any point in arguing. Do you want to eat or don't you?"

"I'd rather not, if it means a picnic."

"All right, you can watch me."

David ate sitting in the car, after poking through the collection of packets done up in wax paper. The usual fare: hard-boiled eggs, tomatoes, ham.

They started off again.

"We're in Yorkshire now."

"Really?"

"Don't you find the scenery beautiful?"

"I've seen it before."

"But it's still beautiful country, don't you think?"

"It's raining."

Later on.

"We're nearly there."

"Yes, the countryside's lovely."

"We're nearly home."

"It's a long way. Couldn't we have come by plane?"

"From Wales?"

"Why not? You can hire one."

A divorce, quickly, a divorce. And when would this conversation end? It ended when they arrived.

"You see those hills?"

"Beautiful."

"They're mine."

This was more interesting. Melinda sat up in her seat to take a closer look. She combed her hair and powdered her nose. She wanted to feel beautiful when they arrived. Fresh as a rose. High gates supported by lions, griffins, peacocks. The park stretched towards the hills. Far ahead in the failing light the castle was dimly visible with smoke rising from the chimneys and lights at the windows.

"There's no electricity," David said.

"How nice! But there's a phone, I suppose?"

Shall I tell him I'm expecting a baby?

"Don't say anything." (How had he guessed?) "Just look at the view."

David, it was obvious, adored this house of his. And indeed it was a fine house, and very well run. An excellent cook and a multitude of women who polished all day long. A house, in fact, that had no need of a mistress.

Molly was waiting for them in the big stuccoed drawing room, sulky and with another little hat on her head, a lilac scarf at her throat, and a green one in her hand.

"I suppose this is the arrival of the lady of the castle."

"Yes, Mother, that's exactly what it is."

"In my dear old house. You can't know," she said to Melinda, "the joy of returning to one's old home."

"Oh yes, I can imagine."

"What do you mean, imagine. You need to be sensitive to understand these things. Which you're not."

David had gone to take the cases up to the bedrooms and to see how the old cook was getting on.

"Did you have a good journey?" Melinda asked.

"A witch, that's what you are. A witch. You're trying to take over my house. I won't let you."

"Is it necessary to be drunk all the time?"

Melinda

"What? What did you say?"

"Drunk. Drunk all the time."

The mountain got up and lurched towards her.

"Witch, whore, foreigner, Communist, Jew." She rained blows on her.

Melinda hid in a corner. The thunderbolt was upon her.

"Wretch. Bitch. Slut."

A maid had discreetly appeared behind a sofa.

"Madam. Control yourself."

"This witch is trying to hit me."

Melinda's eyes opened wide in amazement.

"Poor Madam is so tired," said the maid.

"The hell she's tired."

"You'll see, ma'am, tomorrow your daughter-in-law will apologize. She's only a young girl."

"I'll be damned if I'll apologize. I'm going. I've had enough."

Melinda picked up her handbag and was leaving the drawing room when she ran into David.

"Where are you going, darling?"

"I want a taxi. I'm going back to London."

"What's wrong? Don't you like it here?"

"A nice welcome."

"What's been going on?"

"Your mother's taken to hitting and insulting me."

"Well, she's drunk. Anyway, you're the one who invited her."

"But I didn't invite her. Send her away immediately."

"Who?"

"Your mother."

"Impossible."

"Then I'm going."

"No, you can't. You've just arrived. What will the staff and the village think? They want to get to know you. You're the new wife."

"The staff are so glad to see me that they immediately take sides with your mother."

"She's old. They're all very fond of her."

"Listen, I don't want a repetition of the Wales performance."

"Didn't you like it there?"

"I have told you, David, that I didn't like it at all."

"You'll see, Melinda, it'll be different here. We'll both make an effort. And in a few days we'll suggest to Mother that she leave. In the meantime, come and have some dinner."

The dining room wasn't as big as the one in Wales and was furnished with less taste. The food was excellent. Good wine, essential for warmth: Melinda felt good. She went up to the bedroom. The bed was full of hot-water bottles. She had left David in the drawing room immersed in agricultural machinery magazines. On her bedside table was a bunch of flowers, sent by the gardener. She looked around for a book to read. It was months since Melinda had had to resort to a book to combat boredom. She lit the gas lamp and blew out some of the multitude of candles. It scared her, having all those flames around. Molly was too nasty to ignore. If she made too much trouble she would have to kill her.

A shooting party. But how to make a convincing show of mistaking that great shapeless hulk who never left the beaten track for a deer or a pheasant? And David probably wouldn't be pleased.

Melinda spent the first day looking over the house. From time to time she ran across Molly, who would say, "Anyway it doesn't belong to you."

Melinda pretended not to notice and went from room to room taking mental notes.

She waited for David and his mother to go out hiking and then mobilized the entire staff. Farmworkers, maids, gardeners gathered to move furniture, take down curtains and canopies, put up pictures.

"Surprise, surprise."

Tea was served in the drawing room.

"What did you do this afternoon?" Molly asked. Astonished, Melinda pointed around the room.

Melinda

"Ah, good girl. You stayed in and rested. You were quiet for a bit. You need it. Let's hope it's a sign that you're expecting. You ought to be having a baby by now."

"Quite right, I am expecting."

A modest little smile, eyes to the floor.

"What did you say?"

David was reading a paper.

"Molly, I'm expecting . . ."

"All right, we've all been expecting in our lives. And if you mean we're a bit late for tea, it's your husband's fault for driving so slowly."

"But have you looked at the room?"

"Of course I have. For years and years. Ages before you came along, my dear. This is the house where I first saw the light of day . . . I've seen it all right."

"But the chairs. And those water colors, and the three tables I brought upstairs. And the sofa you're sitting on that wasn't there before."

"Wasn't here? Where the devil was it then? What? You've taken the liberty of touching my things? So you didn't like my house, eh? David. David, stop reading."

"What is it, Mother?"

"Your wife. Look what she's done."

"What's she done?"

"She's spoiled this house."

"In what way?"

"She's moved all the furniture around. Disastrous. I've never seen anything like it."

"Ah, so she has. It looks nice. Well done, Melinda. There's more space. More elegant, when you look closely. Yes, I like it."

"She could have waited till I was dead, at least. So painful for a poor sick old woman like me. She's killed me. Give me some sherry."

She got up and took the bottle from the tray.

"I rang up a decorator too," Melinda said nervously.

"I'm delighted, darling, that you're taking an interest in your new house. You've done well."

"I'd like to replace those curtains. Look, they're coming to pieces. And the armchairs need reupholstering. Do you mind?"

"Go ahead, darling, if it makes you happy."

And he sank back into his magazine.

The third day Melinda rang up Anthony.

"It's raining. I can't stand it. I've had all I can take."

"Poor lady in her castle! What do you expect me to do?"

"Help me."

"How?"

"Come up here."

"Is your husband inviting me?"

"Yes, and I am too. Please, come for the weekend."

"I've got to go to . . ."

"Please. And I've got an idea. I must talk to you."

"What about?"

"Not on the phone."

"A nice place you've got here, Melinda. Very nice indeed. Are you bored?"

"I told you. Bored to death. If I hadn't had this thing to think about . . . Have you got any money?"

"Do you mean capital?"

"No. I'll put it another way. Could you do with a very, very great deal of money and have you a little capital that you could invest in order to make this very, very, very great deal of money?"

"Have you?"

"Yes, I have. But I need your help."

"Now look, I've no wish to invest money in crazy schemes. Of course I could do with a very, very, very great deal of money. Or at least I'd like it. How much would it be?"

"Two and a half million pounds, about."

"What?"

"You heard."

"My dear Melinda, investments that yield that sort of money simply don't exist."

"Anthony, you know all about the Glasgow-London mail train. It regularly carries huge sums to London from the provincial banks."

"Melinda, how naïve you are. Everybody's thought of that. Just imagine: the train known to every criminal in the land, three or four wagons that are strong rooms on wheels. My dear, you've no idea of the minute precautions taken—the passwords, for instance, which they invent at the last minute. And it's watched every yard of the journey. Each station telephones the next, to check it's on schedule."

"But listen, nobody's managed it because nobody's studied the thing closely enough. And above all nobody with any capital behind him. It would take a lot of planning, but once we'd worked it out properly, with your contacts and my connections . . . And the two of us putting our minds to it. Listen, I've got a plan. But we'll have to work on it."

They spent the whole afternoon in Anthony's room. Old Molly was furious.

"How can you tolerate such a scandal in your house, David? So it's true they're lovers. You could see it. A slut. You go straight into that bedroom. If you don't, I will."

She went in and found Anthony and Melinda sitting at a little table with a bottle of whisky, the petrol lamp burning, some maps, pencils, and tracing paper.

"What are you doing?"

They hadn't reckoned on members of the family getting suspicious.

"We're planning a political campaign," Anthony said. "You

see, some parts of the country, like the industrial districts, need careful planning." Molly wouldn't remember that Melinda now belonged to the Opposition.

"But a fascinating man like you, an honor to have you here. I've already been on the phone to a friend of mine. You shouldn't stay in your room working. There are so many things I'd like to tell you. I realize an old woman like me would have no attraction for you, but everybody tells me I'm still sprightly . . . don't you think? My arms, now . . . I'd like to talk to you about the war. No doubt you fought in the war, and perhaps you knew my husband. It was a dreadful war. Certainly politics . . . you must be so very busy. The laws, and the corruption. And the delinquency among the younger generation. Would you like a sherry? And perhaps you'd like a bigger room to work in, rather than your bedroom. I could come and do my knitting. I wouldn't disturb you at all. I wouldn't say a word."

"Mrs. Jones, you're very kind. Could you leave us alone, though. We've got a great deal to do." Melinda admired the assurance of this man so used to dealing with people, to committee meetings, to handling nuisances.

"Let's go on."

He was interested. Very interested. And he was helping enormously with the first steps.

"So let's see. It would be three o'clock in the morning. It's a diesel train with lots of cars. Some of them are mail coaches and inside are the sacks of bank notes. Sometimes the banks will take the notes out of circulation. We shall have to find out about that. If the train goes through Leighton Buzzard—that's forty-five miles from Enston. You know what's at Enston?"

"What?"

"The health farm."

"What's that got to do with it?"

"Don't you know? It belongs to Ostrovsky. He's often there."

"You'd want him in on it?"

"Certainly. We shall need a lot of people, but especially ones with brains that can organize things. And, as you said, with quite a lot of capital. Five or six cars, a lorry, a good mechanic, two or three houses we can rent, one of them very near the spot we choose."

"And will Ostrovsky play along with us?"

"Certainly he will."

"How do we stop the train? In my opinion the red signal ought to do the trick. It's the one that means stop. No engineer driver would suspect anything if we chose a place where there are houses and a certain amount of traffic. The engineer, according to the regulations, must telephone. So there's one less to deal with. There are four guards on the train, or maybe five. But they're inside the armored cars, which are all barred and bolted, and they're obliged to stay inside at their stations. As for the others, they won't know a thing."

"So, according to you, we uncouple the engine and some of the coaches and take them on to a prearranged point, where we have a car waiting. We shall need a lorry, though."

"We shall have to rehearse it a few times. But fifteen minutes should be long enough to unload the sacks and put the guards out of action. Once we've got our hands on all that money, there's no police force in the world that could catch us. Let's go down now. We'll carry on after dinner."

"Or perhaps tomorrow morning would be better. Otherwise they'll get suspicious. Molly's already been in . . . thinks we're having an affair, that's all. But you like it, eh? A marvelous idea, don't you think?"

They spent most of the weekend working on the plans. Anthony showed himself a perfectionist. The statesman who would discuss every detail for hours. A man used to formulating plans, working them out detail by detail, weighing the pros

and cons. Mathematically. With precision. It might be an armed
holdup, but there mustn't be any killed or wounded. Anthony
and Melinda would be in London or possibly abroad. The difficulty lay in finding the right men, trustworthy and highly skilled.

"What we want are men who have already thought about rob-
bing the Glasgow train. It's enough to convince them that this
time it can be done; they'll never know we had a hand in it."

"In that case they mustn't talk to us."

"No."

"So could Ostrovsky be our intermediary?"

"In all probability, yes."

"And if it doesn't work out?"

"Nobody knows us. Ostrovsky has a thousand aliases. And anyway, nothing will go wrong. How can it fail, with you and me
in it?"

"And if anybody gets arrested?"

"We'll see that he escapes. With all that money, you can take
on any police force in the world."

"Bridgego Bridge, then."

"We'll drive by there one of these days."

"And when can we go into operation?"

"It depends how hard we work. In a couple of months, even,
if we find the men. It would be nice to do it in August when
there's a lot of traffic on the roads and the post is all disrupted."

It was still raining when Anthony left. He would speak to
Ostrovsky as soon as possible. He would collect all the information about the dispatching of the banknotes. He congratulated
Melinda. Though it had flaws, the idea was a good one and the
plan exhibited a precision and grasp that Anthony had never
suspected in Melinda.

Anthony even managed a round of golf in the rain, which attracted the attention of some local photographers. He and Melinda
kissed goodbye at the door. They were now friends for life. Melinda destroyed any scrap of paper that might have suggested the
scrutiny of maps of England and, having nothing better to do,

Melinda

went back to London. The next day a letter was delivered to her from David's lawyer. It asked for a divorce. Too bad, but never mind. She would be very, very rich.

Melinda held her press conference at the Savoy. Several papers carried the news on the front page, in preference to the Vietnam War, the Congo uprising, and the European economic crises. WOMAN MP IN BATHING COSTUME. EX-DUCHESS GOES INTO CABARET. (It wasn't quite true, but what wouldn't the English papers do to sell a few more copies?)

Ostrovsky's telegram said, PUBLICITY PERHAPS EXCESSIVE STOP GOOD LUCK STOP CONGRATULATIONS DIVORCE. Melinda decided to put off the decision whether to have the baby she was expecting or to fake the usual nervous breakdown and go to a good gynecologist. When she showed up at the Sexyboy Club, after an afternoon in the House of Commons, Melinda knew there was going to be a mob of photographers at the door. Interviews would be painful and extremely trying. She made up her mind not to give any. She made a few brief, obscure allusions to the emancipation of women and social conventions; after all, why couldn't an MP work too? Anyway, she needed the money. It would be an interesting experience. Then away in the lift, several photographers in hot pursuit.

Just as Anthony G. Gambaino III had told her, the Pussymother, an ex-hairdresser of German origin, immediately took her in hand. The satin top had to cling, her hair was stuffed into a wig with a fringe, her lips were smeared with pink goo.

"If anything goes wrong, if you split your seams or your wig slips, or your fingernails, eyelashes, or moles fall off, just come see Pussymother. That's what I'm here for. I'm always prepared."

Melinda looked at herself in the mirror. Not even her best disguises had made her so completely unrecognizable. "And if you've got a problem you want to talk over, I'm here for that too. I'm mother to all you girls. Always keep your collar clean and starched."

"Make sure you shave carefully. You know where I mean. With wax. Otherwise with a razor the skin is irritated and it shows." The Pussymother ran her hand down Melinda's neck. "Nice lines. Very natural. Good-looking girl, no doubt about that. This is your button with your name MELINDAPUSSY, to be worn on your right thigh."

It wasn't improbable that this Pussymother had been one of those who had once made lampshades out of human skin.

"The first two hours, Melindapussy, you will be assigned to the Souvenir Shop so that you can watch the other Pussies. The Souvenir Shop carries an exclusive Sexyboy line. Sells very well. Pussy dolls. Souvenir ashtrays. Souvenir cocktail glasses. Ideal presents. Any tips are yours. Be sure to read the Rule Book."

"I have."

"Read it again. We could read it together." The Pussymother moved closer and reverently she began leafing through the Pussy Rule Book.

"Let's go through the index together. Absences. Assemblies. Authority."

"What a long index."

"Then you didn't read it."

"To tell the truth, I didn't have time. But I know all these things."

"Oh no. You must read it. We'll do one chapter a night before work. Like mother and daughter, together. For a start, I'll read the introduction now.

" 'Our organization is based on friendship; we are proud of those who work for us, especially of our famous Pussies.' You see, you're not in any old job now. You're part of our organization. You should be proud of it. Pay attention to the next paragraph. 'As soon as a Pussy is ready for work, she will report to the Floor Manager. The Pussymother and the Floor Manager will check that her appearance and costume are perfect. When the Pussy speaks to a superior she will call him "Sir." ' Now you'd better go. Tomorrow come early and we will read together for half an hour."

She let her hands caress Melinda's bare shoulders. The Valkyrie's fingers were big and cold. Melinda decided she'd have to get it over with fast. She wanted to spend as little time as possible in this place. She wasn't used to walking on such high heels. She lit a cigarette and went up to the Floor Manager.

"So who do you think you are? A new one, eh? Haven't you read the rules? No smoking during work."

"Excuse me, sir. Yes, I'm new."

"And what's your name? My name's Metcalf. Mr. Metcalf to you, of course."

"I'm Melindapussy."

"Melindapussy. Oh, yes, the Duchess. How very nice to meet you. Come with me, then. And just call me Metcalf. I'll introduce you to the Pussies who will be working with you this evening. Beautiful girls, all of them, very willing and of good character. Not of course your class, my dear Duchess, but decent girls all the same. Very respectable."

All three of them were there. Annpussy, Sallypussy, and Robertapussy. They were introduced. The three girls didn't seem particularly keen on talking to her. I'll keep an eye on them, thought Melinda.

It was they who kept the eye on her. Melinda realized that immediately: one of them was always on her heels. After selling about a hundred useless objects (the demand for the Pussy MP was enormous), Melinda went off to redo her make-up.

Roberta came straight after her.

"You'll like it here, you'll see. We're all one big happy family."

"Oh yes, so they told me."

"You'll be feeling a bit lonely, especially now that your husband has left you. We read about it in the papers. But you're better off without men, don't you think? You save yourself a lot of worry."

"Doubtless. Have you been here long?"

"Only a few months. After all, the Sexyboy Club is quite new."

"I'd like to see you some time. Away from work, I mean. Then you can tell me some of the tricks of the trade. One never knows at first what to do."

"You'll soon learn. May I call you by your first name?"

"Certainly, Roberta."

"No, no. You must always say Robertapussy. And I'll call you Melindapussy. It's one of the rules."

"What's Pussymother like?"

"A bit Lesbian, but after a while you get used to it. A nice person. But you have to keep on the right side of her, otherwise she'll make things rough for you and give you demerits."

"Demerits?"

"Yes. Haven't you read the Rule Book?"

"You're the third person to ask me that. I suppose I shall have to read it."

"It'll help you get some Gold Stars. If you get a lot of demerits, they give you the sack."

"What about Gold Stars?"

"More money."

"Do you earn a lot?"

"Depends on the tips."

"Are there big ones?"

"Not often. It depends."

"Do you have any girl friends here?"

"No."

"What about Sallypussy?"

"She's only an acquaintance."

"Is she a friend of Ann's? Sorry—Annpussy's?"

"No, no. They barely know each other."

They separated. The Motherpussy told her that Roberta was

one of the most trusted and efficient Pussies, but she had nearly been thrown out because she had once been a Communist. Now, though, she had joined the National Socialist Party, and she looked lovely at the parades all dressed in black.

"She doesn't like men either. Maybe you noticed that."

Melinda had lunch with Anthony the next day. He was distraught. They went to the Ritz, and there were the usual curious looks. "You'll see this time they'll get married." "No, it seems she's about to marry the composer." "Not at all. She's been sleeping with the conductor."

At last the oyster season had come. They ordered several dozen. Anthony squirted six raw ones with a little Tabasco sauce and lemon, then sucked them out of their shells. Next he ordered a half-dozen oysters Mornay. To finish, oysters delicately fried with parsley.

"I hope you appreciate how brave I'm being."

"In what way, Anthony?"

"Taking you out to lunch."

"But you're wrong: I'm very popular and well loved."

"Very popular, no doubt. Listen, you've got to leave that Sexyboy Club. It's dangerous."

"Who told you?"

"I know. Did you see the Pussygirls you were looking for?"

"All three of them."

"And what do you intend to do?"

"I don't know."

Never tell Anthony the truth. Keep him guessing.

"Come and help me do some Christmas shopping," he said. "My secretary's run out of ideas."

"Mine's full of ideas. I'll ask her."

"No, no, I want *you* to come."

"I haven't time."

"I wish you did have time. Time for the things that other normal women do: shopping, looking after children, tending house. It's a pity David's asked for a divorce."

"Before, you didn't like him."

"It's not that I didn't like him. It's just that one's always a bit jealous with you, so one tends not to like your husbands."

"Darling Anthony, how nice of you to tell me such pleasant things."

"Shall we have lunch tomorrow?"

"Lovely."

"At the club. Ladies' entrance. One o'clock sharp."

The ladies' entrance. One o'clock sharp. No, she was late. Pale Melinda. Circles behind the big sunglasses. A childlike expression. Innocent little girl. But what nonsense—innocent. Just looked it. Woman without a wrinkle. Somehow ageless. Not a care in the world. Do you feel like talking? What happened? Some vegetable soup to start with. No, she didn't have much of an appetite. No, she wouldn't have anything else. Perhaps a steak, on second thought. And a nice potato salad. Didn't feel much like talking. Let's drink and to hell with it all. A third whisky, after the Campari. At the club they noticed these things. Women who drink too much before lunch. But who was this Pussy, Roberta? Was she one of the three? What should she tell him? If she said yes, he would be sure to know it had been she who killed her. But perhaps he realized anyway. If she said no . . . Anthony, after all, had already seen this Roberta at Madame Nubytch's place. There might also be some shots of her in the papers. What a stupid idea, this lunch. I don't know. What do you mean—you don't know? She looked vaguely like the one; I began to think she was when she took me out on the terrace. And what happened on the terrace? Now what was she to say to him? What did happen on the terrace? She kissed me. That's all? I rejected her. Rejected, rejected. Another obscene word from the

Melinda

love comics, or *True Confessions* or *Grand Hôtel*. In what way?
What do you mean, in what way? How does one reject a person?
With my hands. And then? She took me in her arms and was
pushing me towards the balustrade. Balustrade. Balustrade. Another odd word one never uses. It sounds nasty, ugly. Parapet?
That means something else. She wanted to push you over? Yes.
Why? Maybe because I had repulsed her advances. Let's say
that was the reason. Let's say that, yes, let's do say that. I defended myself, naturally. What else could I do? I could see Park
Lane below me and the cars, quite small. We were on the sixth
floor. It was no joking matter. And then? Then she fell. Did you
push her? What a question, damn him. No, she threw herself
off the balustrade. Here we are again with that balustrade. Heaven
knows if Anthony's noticed I'm talking differently. Oh God. I'm
a bit drunk. We understand each other so well, we two, why is
he making things so difficult? And who's going to believe you?
Everybody, except you. And Ostrovsky. And Ostrovsky. What will
you say at the inquest? That I refused her embraces and that she
was in love with me. Everybody knew she was a Lesbian. And
the other two girls, poor things? They tried to save Roberta. And
they fell over, too. That was more difficult to make people believe.
Nobody will believe you. It's a ridiculous story. The balustrade
gave way. Important, that balustrade. Witnesses? For what? I
wasn't on the terrace. I was inside selling souvenirs. Everybody
saw me there when the screams rang out. Piercing. Really, they
didn't sound human at all. Don't get carried away with your
poetic descriptions. Anyway, who did it? Did what? Killed them.
Come on, Melinda, let's be straight about this. You know that
I know. But what are you saying? What do you know? It's an
absurd story. Look, where were you? At first I was on the terrace
with Roberta. After she pushed me, I went back inside. Then the
other two girls tried to stop Roberta, who wanted to throw herself off that balustrade. What balustrade? The balustrade, that's
all. And the balustrade gave way and all three of them wound up
down below. But I was inside. Nice story. How did you manage it?

Manage what? To be inside. Did you pay somebody to do the job for you? But why don't you believe me? Never tell Anthony the truth—in any case he'd find out for himself. Certainly it had been her double with the same wig, lipstick, and costume at the souvenir counter when the drama occurred. How tiresome he was being. And Metcalf was certainly in with Ostrovsky, otherwise he wouldn't have helped her. He didn't believe her. But would they believe her at the inquest? Still, she had many witnesses, including the American couple, to whom she sold a souvenir tie. All right, let's say I believe you. It's been a shock. I'm convinced. So what are you going to do now? After the inquest I want to take a holiday. I'll probably go to Moscow. And of course I'll quit being a Pussy. Anyhow, the job is done. What job? Have it your way. Will you go on holiday alone? Why don't you come with me? I've no husband any more. I've too many children, all without a father. Abraham's always traveling about and if I take a lover with me it might bog down the divorce. Won't you feel a bit lonely? Feel lonely? Lonely, her? Never felt the sensation. Loneliness, what a joke. She didn't even know what the word meant. I don't suffer from loneliness. You always manage. Everybody adores you. You'll get away with this too. Even the inquest. Don't worry. Anyway, we'll help you, if you need us. But you won't need anything. (And won't you ever get married?) The steak had arrived. God, what an appetite, after all that whisky. Why, would you like to marry me? Wouldn't you like that? No. Why? We're better off as we are. We get on better like this. Besides, you'd leave me. What number husband would I be? Number five? And what about the train business? Don't breathe a word about that.

Melinda

The inquest was conducted in a most delicate and gentlemanly manner by the police. Melinda hardly realized it was happening. Public opinion was much moved that the poor MP had been driven to work there for a living after she had been abandoned by her husband. Doubly blameworthy, the husband, who had left her four months pregnant. There was just a suggestion of swelling, which the doctors confirmed. Melinda received a number of offers: to write her memoirs for a Sunday newspaper, to make a film about her life, to play the part of a young girl seduced and abandoned in a film that would start shooting after the birth of her child.

She announced instead that she was going to Russia and would have the baby in a Soviet hospital. She would prepare herself for a psychoprophylactic birth, following the Pavlovian method, which was properly taught only in Russia. Melinda gave a farewell party. Abraham put his arms round her.

"My little girl, my wonderful little girl."

And like that they were photographed. The rogue, he knew her well enough to know what a great joke that "wonderful little girl" was.

Melinda embarked at Tilbury on the ship that would take her to Leningrad.

She had only her chauffeur with her, and her arrival in a Rolls-Royce was much admired by the Russian sailors. The voyage went on and on. Stops at Copenhagen, Stockholm, Helsinki. Food immediately began to be a problem. Most of her fellow passengers were English. Of the sort that live in the country and play bridge, go to pubs, clap one another on the back in goodbye, later to find themselves at little supper parties for six, laid on by one of the wives. Bedrooms decorated with hunting pictures, pink chintz, dark red carpets. They all felt it was their duty to be friendly with the Russian barman, a swindler who would bring out the decent vodka only for a heavy tip. Otherwise it was oily rubbing alcohol. The waitresses were dressed in blue and couldn't understand English. It was their job not to understand. Melinda's Russian, spoken with her usual difficulty and the usual mysterious accent, aroused suspicion.

One morning she was woken at dawn by a plump woman. White hair planted in a neat flat bun on her neck; buck teeth and a black suit. Where she had appeared from was a mystery, for the ship hadn't berthed since Helsinki. She inspected Melinda's luggage and listed on a scrap of paper all Melinda's jewels, disapproving.

She was the customs officer. She meditated on the unmade bed and Melinda's body and her lacy nightdress with its plunging neckline.

"I'm expecting a baby," Melinda said, meeting her eye.

"It's six o'clock. Go upstairs, we're entering Leningrad Lagoon."

"Thank you."

"Cover yourself up well. It's cold."

A gray-white dawn on the lagoon. Leningrad in the distance. There were the palaces extolled by the poets, the turquoise cupolas, blue, greenish, and the golden bell towers.

It was five hours before they unloaded the luggage and the car.

"To the Astorial Hotel."

"Certainly, milady, but how do you get there?"

They tried to buy a map of Leningrad, but there were none on sale. By dint of asking directions several times, they reached the hotel, a solid pre-Revolutionary construction in period hotel architecture: volutes, marble stairs, little spires, red velvet. In her suit-

Melinda

case Melinda found a little packet. "With love from your Papa." The handwriting was that of her father's secretary, but inside was something very useful: a Baedeker dated 1905. "These are the only Russian maps you will find anywhere. Moscow hasn't changed much, apart from the names, and Leningrad's still the same. In cities like Kiev and Kharkov it's best not to look at maps. Novgorod is the same as it always was, that heavenly city where your mother and I went on honeymoon . . ."

(He was beginning to miss his wife. He should have thought about that before. Still, Abraham would have been lost with a wife to drag around.) "Good luck."

(The wretch, calling himself "Papa" as if there had ever been a relationship of the kind between them. "Abraham" maybe, or else "Your father.")

Melinda was a little tired. She had already had to do a lot of arguing. First because the bathroom she was promised turned out to be a yard-wide closet with no bidet. The second time over the sluggishness with which her lunch was served and because there wasn't a separate dining room for the staff. For her chauffeur to eat at the same table with her was unheard of. It was embarrassing even to have him eating in the same room. Then it proved impossible to have a Campari served with ice in her room. The floor waitress insisted she had never heard of the drink. Moreover, when Melinda tried to bribe her with some Coty lipstick and chewing gum, the maid had nearly thrown them at her.

Melinda had the constant impression that there were no men in Leningrad. She saw some bathing in the Neva, but they were huge, square-shouldered men with mouths full of metal teeth. Apart from Anatoly, a good-looking sailor from the Crimea, she had never had a love affair with a Russian. But that wasn't the real problem; it was having to sleep alone. But she did have a lot to do, places to see, the Hermitage Museum, which went on forever, people to call up, lunches, and the theater, which hadn't expired completely. Leningrad parties were rather boring and Melinda was counting the days until the birth of her child: there were too many. She consulted Nina. Nina was her new friend. Thick glasses, blotchy skin, something between an English governess and a German tourist. She hadn't been a Party member very long, she too was getting a divorce, and she was one of the bigshots of the Kirov Opera. Nina advised Melinda to rent a dacha on the shore of the lagoon or come to be her guest at her house in the country; she could do a little sailing and ski in the hills.

"I'm afraid I'd be dreadfully bored. I'd rather go and see things."

She decided to go to Asia.

"Are you a capitalist or a proletarian?" Nina asked her.

"A capitalist, of course."

"But wouldn't you like to be a proletarian?"

"You mean would I like to be a socialist?"

"Yes."

"But I am. I'm an MP in a leftist party." It was the thing that most horrified Melinda. The very idea of socialism. Those somber Socialist countries, everybody ugly, everybody equal, everybody throwing themselves out of windows. England, fortunately, was an oligarchy and members of the aristocracy always survived, as long as they were rich. Nina must have sensed something because she disapproved of Melinda's Rolls-Royce and plagued her with boring speeches.

"Don't imagine I'd jump to defend my country," Melinda would reply. "I don't even know which country I'd live in if I had to choose. But I think I'd be all right wherever they put me. Anyway, I find politics an exceedingly boring topic of conversation."

That night Nina took her to a gala. At the Leningrad Opera they were doing a new version of *Traviata* sung in Russian. The tenor was Rumanian. The tenor arias were sung in Italian. Recitatif: in Rumanian. Heaven knows what a sensation Melinda would have caused if she had worn all the Brighton jewels. It was the first time she had thought of her old family. She wondered what Lawrence was doing, if he had remarried. She sent him a postcard.

Melinda

She arrived at the theater with Nina; they were in a box with seven other people. They couldn't see very much; just as well, considering the mediocrity of the sets.

"Look over there," Nina said, pointing at the box in front of them.

It was dark and the curtain hadn't gone up on the first act.

"I can't see a thing."

"It's our Prime Minister and his wife."

"Do you know them?"

"Just barely. We're introduced every time they come to the Leningrad Opera."

"Does he come often?"

"Hardly ever. He goes to sleep at the opera. Sometimes we have to send somebody to talk to him during the performance, otherwise he snores too loud."

"Could I go?"

"What for?"

"To meet him, talk to him . . ."

"Impossible. It's hard to get anywhere near him. If it's necessary we send somebody who's worked here for years."

In the interval Nina took Melinda to the lobby. The audience was promenading in an orderly, rhythmic pattern. Impossible to break through.

The second act was about to start and Melinda still wasn't back to her seat. She would have to disturb everybody in the box, including some wives of important men. Nina almost regretted having invited Melinda. She was a fascinating creature but she did exactly what she pleased. Or rather, she had no discipline. Nina peered in front of her. Melinda was talking to the Prime Minister. They were both smiling and the conversation didn't look as if it were ever going to end, not even when Alfredo launched into "De' miei bollenti spiriti." By the "Ah! Dite alla giovine" the Prime Minister's party had disappeared.

Melinda left a note for Nina. She was going home with the Prime Minister and his wife, and since they were all leaving the next day for Moscow, she wouldn't see Nina before she left. She hoped to persuade the Prime Minister to visit some churches in Novgorod (after all, Abraham would be cross if she didn't go). Lots of people wondered whatever Melinda and the Prime Minister talked about. Politics? The arts? Travel? One such person was Archibald Ostrovsky, who had come in person to keep an eye on his protégée. He wanted to see how she was getting on. No doubt about it, arranging to be pregnant was a master stroke, worthy of a professional. She was made of the right stuff, this girl.

What was so striking was that Melinda was incapable of feeling. She was never frightened, she felt no affection, she was never lonely, she knew no remorse, had no need for friendship. She only felt sensations of heat or cold. She attempted the most extraordinary things because they were unattainable, like her pigheadedness over Van Der Belt. She had a spirit of adventure and a tendency to get bored if she wasn't continually after something new. She had no particular friends, because she accepted everybody. Her friendship with Anthony was a mystery. Ostrovsky couldn't explain it. If he asked her to kill Abraham, would she do it? For a lot of money. And Mark? Probably both of them, without thinking about it for one second.

Or perhaps Ostrovsky had misunderstood her. Perhaps Melinda needed her entourage round her, needed a father like Abraham as much as she needed a lover like Mark, or a lover like Abraham and a father like Mark. And would she manage to kill the chief? Would she kill him if she knew he was Blamonche? Or if she found out at the last minute, would she turn on Ostrovsky? There was no point even in threatening her children, which usually worked with mothers. That mass of people she'd brought into the world made absolutely no difference to her.

Meanwhile, Melinda had decided to take things calmly, otherwise what was she going to do with all those months in Moscow? She had been to Novgorod, where she spent a week looking at the long white churches and the Byzantine frescoes, and going for

Melinda

walks along the lakes, visiting monasteries. Novgorod was full of chattering swallows and Melinda complained about them to Intourist. The only thing that really annoyed her was that she did nothing but run into pairs of European tourists who felt they had to make conversation. The worst were a couple from Montreux. Like all the others she'd met whose conversation she'd tried to turn off in various restaurants, these Swiss were convinced they were being spied upon day and night. A garage owner and a schoolteacher. Microphones in every room . . . in the phone. In the garden. Under the bed. Above the lampshades. I've heard . . . I've seen . . .

"You won't believe it, but just this morning, on the road even. A car was following us."

They fled from hotel to hotel, trying to shake off the specter of the microphones.

Just in case, thought Melinda, I ought to hide my revolvers, cameras, microphones, and tape recorders.

From Novgorod she phoned Moscow.

Her arrival must have been announced. Anyway, she wanted a room at the Hotel National on Red Square, dinner at the Writers' Union, and she dictated a long list of people she wanted to meet. She gave Intourist the job of organizing her first fortnight; the rest she would manage herself. She would arrive by car and go straight to the hotel.

She found she was staying at the Leningradskaja Hotel. Horrible, full of chandeliers and delegations of Orthodox priests.

"I'd like to change hotels." "That's impossible." "In that case, I want to leave." "Where do you want to go?" "Anywhere, so long as I don't stay in this hotel." "I'll book you a seat on the plane next week." "To Tashkent, today." "We might be able to arrange it. Come back this afternoon." "No, I want to leave this afternoon." "Today's impossible." "It must be possible. Everything's possible, if you pay." "There aren't any seats." "Find some. You haven't even tried."

Melinda had already phoned the hospital and booked a series

of lessons in preparation for a painless birth by the psychoprophylactic method. She had sent a note to the Prime Minister, inform-
ing him of her arrival and immediate departure. She packed a
couple of suitcases and threw out the clothes that wouldn't do
for Asia or had grown too tight. Since there were no garages where
she could leave the car, she locked up the Rolls-Royce and left
it in Red Square. She put the rest of her luggage in the hotel
porter's custody.

Archibald Ostrovsky, who finally managed to track down
Melinda's name in the Leningradskaja register, had arrived only
to be told that the lady had just left for Central Asia.

Melinda was stunned at the sight of the airport: enormous
Ilyushins, crammed with passengers.

A tractor hauled the plane out onto the runway. Melinda drew
the flowered curtain to keep out the sun. At one point the hostess
sat down next to her. Did she like the Soviet Union? Very much.
Was it the first time she had been to the Soviet Union? Yes. And
did she find the Russians nice? Very. Was the Soviet Union all
she had expected?

Why did they always ask the same questions? As if she could
ever have answered them. This Amazon dressed up as a stewardess
irritated her.

She looked down at the Aral Sea, more like a vast lake dotted
with little islands which probably had never been trodden on by
human foot.

"Those are the caravan routes," the hostess told her. There were
also rivers, trying wearily to find their way through the dunes to
the sea. Some never made it and died in the sand. There wasn't
a single oasis to be seen.

Tashkent she didn't like: too flat, Odeon cinema sort of architecture too much like Manchester, too many Cuban delegations,
too many Americans who knew all about everything. Worst of
all was meeting American Communists. They took things as
seriously as the Germans. Even the Uzbekistanis made fun of
them. On the plane she met an Indian cotton merchant who was

going to Tashkent to cancel an order for some machinery ordered five years before.

When the passengers left the plane, they were ushered into a big waiting room. Melinda and the Indian waited for an hour. Through the window they could see the vast airport full of planes and, through a glass door, hundreds of passengers milling round the entrance. Some of them had obviously spent the night at the airport, with children, baskets, and cushions.

"There's no such thing as a booking," the Indian merchant told Melinda, "unless you're a tourist. And of course there are no trains across the desert."

The people queued up as they do in London at a bus stop. The women wore gaudy silk or nylon dresses that looked like bathrobes. Some of the men wore Asiatic clothes (others just the embroidered hats). Many were dressed in European style.

That evening they went to the Tashkent Opera. They were doing *Carmen* in Uzbekistani. The smugglers reappeared in the last act dressed as toreadors. The Indian enjoyed himself less than Melinda; for one thing, he had an attack of malaria. Melinda abandoned him in his sick state and left for Samarkand, where she posed for a poster *(The Soldier's Return)*, wandered about some oases, and had an affair with a Tamburlaine expert. She hardly saw Bukhara, because there was a sandstorm and it was burning hot. She tried several times to phone Anthony, without success.

She flew back to Samarkand. The plane landed in a plowed field. There were no safety belts in Russian planes and Melinda hoped for a miscarriage.

The Soviet Prime Minister had arrived in Samarkand to visit the agricultural collectives in the black deserts of Kabul. Melinda immediately tried to contact him. It was impossible to speak to him on the phone: it meant going through fifty people. And then in the end he was busy or not there. Had he taken a dislike to her?

Fortunately she found Irina, an Intourist official.

"Where's your husband?"

"Don't tell me you're divorced too?"

"That's why one gets married."

"But I'm not on my own."

"Neither am I, but I'm bored."

"The world's a small place. I'm sure even my grandmother used to say that."

"What are we doing today? Shall we have a swim in the river? Shall we go shopping?"

"Shall we go for a picnic in the forest?"

The forest consisted of dense brushwood around one of the oases closest to Samarkand. There were supposed to be lions there, but Melinda didn't see any.

"If they'd seen the Siberian forests, they wouldn't have had the face to call this a forest." All the same, she was excited because of the lions.

They picked a clearing near the river and started to cook.

"Watch out for snakes."

"You take it easy. You're pregnant."

"And you, Irina, would do well not to remind me of it."

When she woke up, there was the Prime Minister. He had eaten all the shish-kebab and was now munching some cucumber. Irina was taking pictures.

"I've been looking everywhere for you."

"What are you doing here? Nobody told me."

Never talk politics to a Prime Minister. She told him about England, about the countryside, about the Leningradskaja.

"Is it true that the food's bad in England?"

"I think it's a myth. The sausages are exquisite and so are the potatoes, and wherever you are in England you can always eat those. Or fish. The fish is very good. The English despise cod because they have so much of it, but you can have fried cod fillets in suburban cafés that you can't get anywhere else in the world. And sole: thick, enormous, marvelous . . ."

"Can you get oysters?"

"Plenty and very good. Much better than in France. Apparently the American ones are even better, but when I was over there they were out of season."

"They never served me any. Maybe they thought oysters weren't the right thing for a Communist, as if Communists didn't have a palate like everybody else. Do you like Russian food?"

"What you get in restaurants no, not much. But that dinner I had with you in Leningrad was stupendous. I'd never had eggplant cooked that way before."

"Do you know how they're done? You cut them in two and leave them in salt water for a day. Then cook with cream, cucumber, and onion (sometimes potatoes too, but there weren't any that evening) . . ."

"Wait a minute, I'm taking notes."

"Cook for half an hour. Then, while they're still boiling, add yoghurt, salt and pepper."

"They were marvelous. And the blinis with caviar inside and sour cream and salmon roe . . . Gorgeous."

They talked for a long time about food. There wasn't much difference after all between the Prime Minister and Cyril Connolly.

"I must confess I very much enjoy eating. And I'm very gluttonous."

"Are you here on your own?"

"No, I'm with the Iraqi Finance Minister. Don't you know him? He stayed in the car. Oh, of course, I didn't ask him to join us. They have the same problems of reclaiming land from the desert. Even if there's oil . . . We've got a couple of interpreters and secretaries . . . yes, they're all in the car."

In fact they were talking to Irina. The minister was short, wore an attractive medal in his buttonhole, was suffering from the heat and cursing himself for having smoked a cigarette.

"It's bad for me and yet I go on smoking."

He spoke good French. "A beautiful woman in the desert. What a surprise. Translate, translate for the Prime Minister. What

organization in the Soviet Union. Marvelous. If there's one thing
I can't resist, apart from a cigarette, it's a beautiful woman. I'm
old and ugly, but you with your beauty still please me. Woman
loves with the ears, man with the eyes. What are you doing here?
How can you stand this heat? Are you Russian? From the north?"

She had never told the Prime Minister that she was really Czech.
He might be annoyed if he knew Abraham hadn't gone back
to his country at the end of the war.

"Tell me—" It was the Prime Minister with his broad smile.
"—what about chicken Kiev—have you ever tried that? When it's
perfect, you can stick a knife in it and, pouf, out spurts the melted
butter and the marvelous aroma, and it's all golden-brown on the
outside. It must be served with those very very small new potatoes,
after some sturgeon. And what about smoked sturgeon?"

They were off again for hours.

The next day Melinda left for Moscow with the Iraqi Finance
Minister. She went straight to the Hotel National in Red Square.
There they told her she was booked in at the Hotel Ukraine. She
got her car back. At first they didn't want to let her have it because
she had lost her claim check. She also got her luggage back.

The Hotel Ukraine, one of Stalin's skyscrapers, had several
thousand rooms on more than twenty floors which were reached
by staircases and a couple of lifts. But to go up or down in the
lifts meant queuing and there was always a half-hour wait.

The Iraqi minister, who out of fondness for Melinda had moved
to the Ukraine from the National, never managed to get up to
Melinda's room. To forget something was fatal: half an hour to
go back up, another half hour to come down again.

"You'd be doing me a great kindness if you allowed me to take
over the room you vacated at the National."

How could the Iraqi minister say no?

Melinda began attending the prenatal exercise classes. Some
fifty mothers-to-be were instructed by Arcadievna, a plump woman
in her middle forties with gray hair, plaited in a bun behind, and
tiny earrings. Three afternoons a week. Tummies stretched out.

Melinda

"And now push. Breathe. Hold your breath. One two three. Count up to ten. Push again. Hold your legs firmly with your hands. Publishing, you haven't understood. There's nothing to laugh at. Concentrate on a tune."

Then there were long explanations of Pavlov's studies on conditioned reflex. Train the muscles to respond to a contraction.

"Let's pretend now that we've got a double contraction, which in birth will be produced by the muscles of the uterus. Now we shall train the right arm and leg to undergo a contraction. Relax the rest of your body. Publishing, stop laughing."

The National was a delightful hotel. An art nouveau dining room, wide wooden stairways, a cozy lobby.

Melinda invited to dinner the Iraqi minister, an American journalist and his wife, Irina, and a Hungarian writer. The American journalist's wife was Russian and talked continually of the war that the Soviet Union was going to unleash at any moment. The Hungarian was furious. The Iraqi minister flirted with Irina. The conversation switched to Pasternak. He was a great poet. Not a novelist, but a great poet. This made Irina cross. The Iraqi minister obviously couldn't care less. A disastrous evening.

A letter arrived from Anthony.

Dear Melinda,

I almost begin to miss you. I shall soon be leaving for my summer holidays. After all, it will soon be August. A lot of my friends are staying in England. Everything seems to be going well. I've never thanked you for the weekend in Yorkshire. I should love to come and see you, but it would be better if I went to the coast.

Yours,
Anthony

So the train robbery was going to take place, and soon. And the money? They hadn't discussed how to dispose of it or how they would divide it up. But Anthony would certainly have thought of that. And Anthony could be trusted. After all, he was an honest man, very respectable. He would make an excellent husband. A pity Melinda had never married him.

The Writers' Union had its headquarters in the old house of the Rostovs, a little way from the center, towards the road to Zagorsk. It was exactly like an English club. Leather sofas, rather worn carpets, wood paneling, a smell of cigars, alcohol, must. The Russian writers even seemed to dress on the model of the Anglo-Saxon gentleman, threadbare at the elbows, brown leather shoes, a feigned shabbiness. The food was equally similar to that served at the Travellers' or the Reform Club: boiled potatoes, overcooked chops, doughy puddings. The only difference was the wines, which in the Writers' Union were Georgian and syrupy, while in the London clubs they are exquisite and the port is the finest in the world.

"Several of our writers have asked whether you would be so kind as to make a speech."

"On what? I've nothing really to say. I haven't prepared anything. I didn't expect it."

"On English literature. Your father's a publisher, so you must know many English writers. We'd be very interested to hear about them."

"Perhaps it would be better if you asked me questions. A sort of interchange . . . all together . . ."

It was the most charming thing she could have suggested and the easiest for her.

"Your father is Czech and he has a successful publishing house in England. Was that easy? Why didn't he consider going back to Czechoslovakia?"

Melinda

"Why isn't poetry as popular in England as it is in the Soviet Union?"

"Do English writers take part in politics?"

"Are there any right-wing intellectuals in England?"

"Do English writers meet often?"

"C. P. Snow, is he well thought of?"

"Not very."

"Why?"

"He's not considered a serious writer."

"And as a politician?"

"The same applies, I think."

She was in excellent spirits, as always when she had eaten a lot. Later she would regret it: potatoes vinaigrette, fried potatoes, creamed potatoes, potato soup. For the time being, the sweet wine and starch had put her in a glowing mood and she was pleased to be there, to be pregnant, to be about to become one of the richest women in the world and to have no ties. By now the prenatal classes were part of Melinda's Moscow routine, just like shopping and visits to the GUM department store, where she never found anything and yet had to queue up for hours.

Arcadievna was pleased with her pupil, especially as Melinda's presence in her class had got her picture into *Izvestia*. The foreign girl was said to be a friend of the Soviet Prime Minister, though the rumor had never been confirmed.

"At this stage, if the pains are bad and control is difficult, massage your tummy with the fleshy tips of your fingers, using a circular movement. When you are tired of doing it, ask your husband to help. Publishing, your husband left a message: he says he's coming to pick you up after class and he will also be coming to the evening session for future fathers."

Melinda wondered who he could be. Certainly not David, who was convinced, probably rightly, that the child wasn't his. Perhaps Mark had tracked her down. Or Anthony? Impossible. He would never meet her, especially at such a dangerous moment for them both.

It was Ostrovsky.

Obviously, Archibald Ostrovsky had a penchant for sudden dramatic appearances.

"Darling."

They embraced affectionately. Arcadievna decided he was a little old to be the husband of her beautiful pupil, and she didn't like the bushy black mustache drooping across Ostrovsky's cheeks.

"Is it false?" Melinda asked.

"Of course."

"It looks it."

"That's the secret. It looks so false that people take it for real."

"What shall we do?"

"Let's go and have some dinner. I've booked a table at Seliene's."

"Nobody can book tables in a restaurant in this country."

"I can."

"And what about the fathers' class at the clinic?"

"You'll have to say I couldn't make it."

Archibald Ostrovsky was supremely elegant. He had had his suit copied from an old photograph of a Golitsyn prince. His overcoat was lined with bearskin and the lapels were of velvet. Marvelous chamois leather boots. "You needn't have dressed so conspicuously." "If I'd disguised myself as a Polish comrade over here with some delegation, I should have looked a lot more conspicuous. Dressed like this, I can't possibly be a spy."

It was already very cold outside. Melinda had changed into a coat she had bought at GUM. It was long and too wide across the hips. The restaurant was huge. The enormous wall at the far end was frescoed with a mass of badly painted icebergs. The icy atmosphere of a Fascist gymnasium hung over it even though the restaurant was packed with people.

Laboriously, as usual, they were able to order the meal.

"Could we have some red wine?"

"No red wine today," replied the waiter.

"You'd think we were living in a city under siege. Melinda, will you hurry up and have this baby. Let's talk about Corsica."

Melinda

"And how did things go at Tring?"

"The train? For heaven's sake, don't mention Tring. It's known as Operation Melinda."

"Ah, thanks very much, now I'm involved, whatever happens. Well then, how did it work out?"

"Stunningly well. Nobody arrested, so far. But we know Scotland Yard has some names. Four or five people will be arrested. They won't talk: for one thing, they know little or nothing. And for another, they've all been promised whatever happens they'll be able to escape from prison."

"Is it a serious promise?"

"We can buy anybody we like."

"Where's the money?"

"Some in Ireland, some in Switzerland. There was a fuss over a boat carrying part of the loot. One man was killed."

"How was that?"

"He wanted to make off with all of it. The others got rid of him. They knew that only we had a way to let the money dribble back into circulation without exciting suspicion or provoking needless killings."

"Did you make a lot out of it?"

"You'll have a detailed account in due course, if you're interested. What concerns you is that you now have a considerable sum in a Geneva bank, and that you're one of the richest women in Europe."

"Fine. We'll say no more about it. Now let's talk about Corsica. But first I want you to tell me a few things. Who are we working with, and who for? And who's the boss? And where do I come in? And who were those Pussygirls?"

"Don't worry about these details. There's only one thing you need to know: Count de Blamonche is the victim."

"Are you partners?"

"He was one of my agents."

"Till when?"

"Till he turned against us. Three of his female accomplices

were removed by you, Melinda, in a brilliant operation. You ought
to do the same with Blamonche."

"But he knows me."

"He's only seen you once very briefly. He was in a nervous
state just as much as you were. Then he's fond of women; he'll
be quite taken with the arrival of the beautiful, elegant Melinda.
You will be the guest of the Surrealist painter Millefiori Cucchi.
You must be at your very best: slim, no children, hair combed.
Nice clothes. You will spend some time in Paris or London or
Rome, wherever you like, to get back in shape."

"All right."

"Count de Blamonche is one of the best-known men in France.
He's immensely rich, owns a great deal of land. He has several
murders to his credit."

"I understand."

"He's an influential man, does a lot of entertaining, usually
three or four ministers. Years ago he was a personal friend of
Hitler and Göring. He has a passion—I'd say a mania—for women.
Any one of them will do, from seven-year-olds on up, very indis-
criminate. On Corsica he lives in a house built by an Englishman
who wanted to introduce fox-hunting. The trouble was that in
Corsica all the horses went lame and the foxes escaped in the
scrub. He lost a lot of money. Blamonche bought the house for
a song. It's fairly removed from civilization, but the castle Millefiori Cucchi rented is fairly close. You'll have to approach Blamonche."

"I understand."

"You should act as soon as possible, before Blamonche gets
to know about you. I know I'm being watched."

"Not for a couple of months, though. I've got to have the baby
and then pull myself together again."

"When you're ready, write to Cucchi and then set off. Don't
get in touch with me at all. How's your Van Der Belt getting on?"

"I haven't seen him in ages."

"I saw him a couple of nights ago in Corfu. Of course he didn't recognize me."

"What was Mark doing in Corfu?"

"He was with his wife and a couple of Greek shipowners. Nothing very exciting."

"Did he look nice?"

"Melinda, are you really interested in this Mr. Van Der Belt? Why don't you marry him then? I shouldn't ask you these questions, I know, but one of the things I admire in you is the way you never get fond of anybody. This Van Der Belt, if you married him, well, you'd leave him after a few days. You'd divorce him out of boredom, like all the others. A cretin. Sorry. I hate making personal comments, but he really does seem stupid."

"How do you manage to find time to bother about other people, Ostrovsky? I'd never thought about it, none of these things you've just said to me. Anyway, keep your place. You never give me any information about the work I'm supposed to do, and yet you want me to tell you all about myself. How much are you going to pay me for Blamonche?"

"You've already had a lot of money, and you're rich now from 'Melinda.' "

"In that case it's not worth it. Besides, I'm beginning to enjoy this business rather less."

"But you're bound to us, Melinda. And anyway, how would you use your spare time if you weren't spying? Think how bored you'd be."

"I'd be bored, yes I'd be bored. How much then?"

"If the operation is successful, we'll give you a reward of sixty thousand dollars."

"Which bank?"

"Where you like."

"The usual Swiss one, I suppose."

"I would advise you to pretend you're setting up a joint stock company."

"That's something I've never tried before."

"This is something I've never tried before." The voice was coming from the buffet itself. Melinda realized that the object stretched out, covered with several courses of food, was a live woman.

"I think Millefiori would be angry if she knew you were talking to the guests," said Melinda, lightly touching a naked hip that stuck out white from the sauce sprinkled over its skin.

"But it's terrible having to keep so still!" Yes, it must have been tiring with all that food on her body. Russian salad on her bosom, cutlets with gravy on her belly, strawberries and cream in her crotch.

"Millefiori, where are the plates and forks?"

"But, my dear sweet girl, all the fun's in eating straight off the body, just sink your mouth into the food."

Millefiori wore all lilac make-up: lipstick, powder, eye shadow. An infinite series of plastic-surgery jobs had preserved her face from total erosion, freezing it into an expression of beauty surprised. Even her shawl was lavender and her high leather boots were pink. The shawl covered a certain portion of her legs, and when she turned around, a corner of her belly. The other guests were completely naked, excepting the five boys that belonged to Millefiori. The oldest of them was well over forty but Millefiori insisted on calling them "her boys." "The boys" were playing with each other. "The boys" were incapable of doing anything that wasn't obscene; Millefiori usually helped them along. Of the five, the first was Armenian, the second Hungarian, the third Argentine (German mother), the fourth, Jori, American (Irish father), and the last, Jin, a Swede. One couldn't understand much of what they said to each other, but they had lived with Millefiori for five years and had made up an Esperanto they themselves understood perfectly.

Melinda

Melinda was wearing a long dress of transparent cellophane Millefiori had made for the evening. Melinda was her latest acquisition.

Everybody lived together in the dilapidated castle-monastery, which made one a little uncomfortable, to say the least. Too many cliffs and stairs, a soft stone that crumbled under one's feet, an insubstantial retaining wall that kept breaking off and dropping violently into the sea, a few graves in the garden, some crosses scattered among the rocks below. But there were Millefiori's soirees and amusements; there was even the sea. Melinda had a room whose only window opened out on a sheer drop down to the howling waves, but she never slept alone, so she was never afraid. And not even the wind shrieking past Cape Corse could keep her awake, so exhausted was she after these evenings at Millefiori's.

Blamonche wasn't among the guests that evening.

"You have to be careful whom you invite to orgies. Only beautiful, amusing creatures. I don't care for Blamonche and neither do my boys. You'll see him tomorrow anyway. We're going over there for lunch."

Millefiori could easily be seventy but seemed much younger. It was no secret that she'd been the mistress of Matisse, Gustave Moreau, Apollinaire, and Trotsky. When she let herself go in her sexual enthusiasms, her carefully constructed face came apart, and Millefiori purposely kept well in the shade. Millefiori couldn't help mentally thanking that rogue Ostrovsky who had obviously guessed how well Melinda would fit into her monastery and her evenings.

"Come on, let's see how you're doing."

Melinda sunk her mouth into the girl's breast, bit off some potato and licked mayonnaise from around the nipple. "I hope you had her bathe beforehand?"

"Of course, my dear. She's been completely disinfected."

The girl was gazing at the ceiling but Melinda had evidently given her a certain pleasure.

Millefiore gave her more by tiny nibbles and licks at the point and base of the breast. "Boys, boys, come here. There's something for you, too."

"The boys" enjoyed it less and the girl was almost embarrassed; she continued to look at the ceiling.

Wine was served in conch shells. "The conch is such an erotic thing. It's the very epitome of eroticism, don't you think? . . . This is true theater. A spectacular we put on for ourselves. It must be *forced* to be *real* theater. Darling, how that dress suits you and what a divine body you have!"

Millefiori had decorated the castle and the collapsing walls with enormous wax dolls she had made herself. Modeled hands gripped the walls. The veils dressing the huge puppets flapped in the wind, threatening to catch fire from the candles that lit up the ruins. Maurice came up to Melinda.

"Good?"

"Very good. Have you had any?"

"I'd rather eat off you."

"Later."

"The wine is stupendous. Millefiori's specialty. If it doesn't knock you out immediately, you can keep up five days of fucking without batting an eye."

"I wouldn't say anyone here much needed it."

"And Millefiori—how is she?"

"She's very nice."

"I know that. I've known her for years. I mean, in bed?"

"In what sense?"

"How do the two of you make love?"

"Be patient and you'll see."

"That doesn't seem the right attitude for an orgy."

"Oh, is this an orgy?"

"What would you call it?"

"A supper party."

Maurice plunged his mouth onto the girl's breast.

"Do you like it, Marion?" He stroked her thighs. The strawberries trembled; so did the steak.

Melinda

"Shall we eat these with our hands?"

"No, darling, can't you see I made them small on purpose, so that you can grab them with your teeth? Would you like me to take Marion's place? We could do it alone tomorrow, for supper, just you and the boys. With too many people I should feel humiliated, and besides, my body isn't as appetizing as it once was. But you, Melinda, I'd just love to eat you, covered with cream and oysters and shells and raspberries."

"What an odd menu!"

"Shall we try it? Tomorrow? Would you like it?"

"It's fine by me. It sounds rather amusing."

"Now I'm going to start."

Maurice bit into a piece of steak and in doing so gave Marion a bite. Marion let out a yell.

"Now that's not right. Poor girl! What's she done to you?"

"She's got a marvelous little belly. I had such an urge for it."

To make up for it, Maurice kissed Marion's arms and thighs and licked the small of her back, wiping his mouth on the cloth that lay under her.

Other guests began to gather round. There weren't many.

"In Corsica you always meet such strange people—you never know who's going to show up."

There was Nadine with the enormous blue eyes and a tiresome body and neurosis all over her face. Her husband was mixed up with "the boys" in every sense of the word. She was wearing a fishnet bathing suit from which she had obviously taken out the lining. Her husband had on a striped Indian shawl and gold sandals. A model with eyes like saucers, dressed quite demurely, was completely naked behind. Not beautiful to look at, but amusing.

"Isn't she lovely, our Ninelotte," exclaimed Millefiori, wrenching at her dress.

"My name's *not* Ninelotte and leave my dress alone!" They were the first words she had spoken. She had a cross, whining tone.

"Go on, eat up."

"I don't like eating off Marion."

"And what have you got against Marion?"

"The last time I saw her, she was nasty to me."

"All the more reason then—humiliate her, nibble her thoroughly, be naughty and close those eyes of yours for a minute."

"Somebody's already been at the dessert! Who was it?"

It was Maurice who had plunged his mouth into the cream.

"You could have waited for the rest of us!"

"Watch out for Marion: she gets excited when you eat the strawberries," said Maurice, laughing. "It'll be disastrous."

"Oh God. It doesn't sound very attractive."

"Melinda, do you like the idea?"

Melinda looked out on to the terrace. It was a fine terrace overlooking the sea, with lush grass and sweet-scented bushes. Everything possible had been decorated with conchs. Below, the sea fretted; it caught the brunt of the wind from Cape Corse.

"Certainly, darling."

Melinda came over and put her arms on the table and plunged her face into the cream. She felt the cream sticking to her forehead; she was breathing in strawberries. Marian quivered under her mountain of food; her breasts were soaking in mayonnaise and some cutlets jiggled on her belly.

"Good for you, Melinda!" She heard Millefiori's excited voice at her shoulders.

The cream was up to her hair. She could hardly breathe. She began to be truly aroused. She could feel everybody's eyes on her while Marion's body quivered and her pelvis arched. Melinda was seized with a desire to scrape away all the strawberries and drag the girl onto the terrace and sink down with her and hurt her. She leaned with all her strength on Marion's loins.

"You're hurting me," came Marion's spent voice.

"Don't you want me to go on?" A look of malicious joy.

Millefiori looked at Melinda and knew she would have to curb her. "You'd better leave her to us for a bit."

Millefiori took Melinda by the waist and dragged her into a

Melinda

corner. She let fall her shawl and squeezed Melinda's body, cold as the cellophane that enveloped it. "I adore your feeling of a dead body, frozen, sticky, like a newborn babe."

"Your cellophane, our cellophallus," said Maurice, laughing.

Millefiori tore the dress off Melinda. It came away easily; she had intentionally sewed it with loose stitches. She sank her face on to Melinda's. It gave her a feeling almost of panic: Millefiori's hungry, spectral face magnified by its nearness. But this devouring greed gave Melinda a novel sort of pleasure. Who would disapprove? Ostrovsky had obviously known what would happen. Abraham, no, he wouldn't have disapproved. Abraham was broadminded, very broad-minded, liberal without bounds. Mark? He would have watched absent-mindedly, thinking about one or another of his family. Jacob would have found it intolerable, Anthony degrading and deplorable, but he would be a little desperate with envy because he would have wanted to watch.

The last few months in Moscow had dragged for her. The letters from Helen had been a comfort, the painless birth had not been painless at all, but of course she had to tell the papers what a marvelous thing it was, a scientific discovery, and all children should be born via the psychoprophylactic method. The baby didn't look like anybody for the moment. She had left him in Moscow in a home. She'd have been delighted to have had the Soviet Prime Minister stand as godfather at the christening, but she forgot that baptism was out of fashion in Russia. In fact he had refused. She had called him Nikolai out of respect for his birthplace. Already the name was getting on her nerves. Eventually she'd find out whose he was when he began to get a face. Mark's? David's?

The Rolls-Royce had broken down in the Carpathians and she had to travel to Rome by train. Between beauty salons and masseuses that put poor Nubytch to shame, Rome pulled her together. She had briefly seen Amerigo, a couple of days, but otherwise she didn't see a soul. Amerigo had asked her, of course, to marry him. Perhaps it would have been an ideal marriage. But would she have been able to sleep alone at night?

Oh God, and here she was, thinking of all this while that poor Millefiori was exhausting herself in a frenzy over her body. To tell the truth, Melinda felt herself gripped with acute pleasure, but she had to watch what was happening. She put her arms round Millefiori's legs. They were well into the shade. Her tanned legs were still beautiful.

Millefiori chewed her gently.

This annoyed her a bit, but Millefiori went on with it until Melinda exploded into waves that made her eyes squeeze closed, her neck stretch taut. Her mouth fell open as she heaved to catch her breath.

Maurice threw himself on Melinda, who still lay on the ground. "Magnificent," he whispered in her ear. "I've never seen anything like it."

"You enjoyed watching?"

"You were beautiful. Millefiori a hyena, you a wicked angel." He took her breasts in his hands and penetrated her. He gave her no sensation of pleasure.

What a bore it must be to be Lesbian. Hiding behind drawing-room doors and making passes at little girls, lapping up their chatter and helping along in their careers. It would have been a stroke of genius to take Mark's wife off to bed and then tell him about it. But Mark wouldn't have listened. And Aglaia would never do it.

Not that.

A pity, because *sodomy* had always seemed an elegant word to Melinda.

Here was Jin, whose Swedish face was also repulsive.

Melinda spent the rest of the night and the morning with Marion, Millefiore, Jin.

More with Jin than with the girls.

Melinda

For this reason she flopped exhausted into the motorboat that Blamonche sent to the monastery and she woke up only when they reached his dock. She put on her sunglasses. Would he recognize her? They were all on the beach. All: about ten people. Unmistakable among them was Blamonche: his bright black eyes, wrinkled skin, and cropped black hair. She debarked and walked towards them.

Blamonche was trying to think where they had met, or was Melinda imagining the flashes in her host's tiny eyes?

Introductions.

"So you're the famous Honorable Publishing. Well, we too have our politicians."

He introduced her to three ministers. One was small and lively, with no hands, or nearly. The second was very big, with white hair and a red bathing suit. The third disappeared against the sand: he was the same color.

"I'm sure we've met before somewhere," Melinda said to Blamonche, hiding a feigned yawn with her hand.

"Tired, eh? Heaven knows what you're up to at the monastery. Why doesn't Millefiori ever invite me?" Blamonche touched her shoulder, fingering her skin. "Yes, I expect we've met somewhere. At a ball, maybe? Perhaps it was in Paris."

It went over. He hadn't recognized her at all.

Maurice came up to her with a glass.

"What is it?"

She hadn't noticed him on the beach. She was exhausted.

"A cocktail, it will pull you round. You must be very tired."

"Yes, I'm dead."

"And you have your work cut out for you, if you're going to keep Blamonche off."

What did he mean?

"He attacks immediately."

And indeed he was all over her.

"Under that little costume, so sweet and dainty, I see two delicious little things . . . How I'd love to take off that little costume."

"But we've just met, my dear Blamonche."

"You mustn't waste time in these things. Besides, they tell me you don't beat around the bush. Eight husbands, no end of children. Such a delicious body after all those children. And those two sweet little things . . ."

It would be a pleasure to kill him. But she'd have to work fast. She let him touch her bosom since he wanted to so much. Melinda was too tired to think how to kill him. She had even left the gun back at the monastery. Anyway, she couldn't kill him on the beach. Drown him? In the sea? Was he a good swimmer?

The sun was strong. Millefiori was talking to a minister. Maurice whispered into Melinda's ear, "There are usually at least five ministers around. Blamonche must be coming down in the world."

The cocktail had started a warm glow in her stomach. She fell asleep on the beach.

They woke her up later. It was nearly three o'clock and lunch was ready. She plunged into the water. It was almost too cold but the pain of it was refreshing. So was the color. As she dried herself, she still felt its tingle.

A waiter led her up some steps and into an elevator that was shafted straight up through the rock.

There were three buttons. The waiter flicked the top one.

"Are there several floors?"

"No, only one."

"What are the other two buttons for?"

"One's the winter garage for the boats. The sea gets rough here. The other one's an alarm bell."

"I see. I imagine it's not very pleasant to stop in the middle of this mountain."

"It's never happened, madam."

They had lunch outside, plagued by wasps and later by mosquitoes. Melinda showed off on water skis, and at eight o'clock she, Millefiori, and "the boys" went back to the monastery. Their motorboat was very fast. Night was falling and even Melinda was stunned at the beauty of the seascape. A fire blazed up on the mountains.

"Don't worry, that happens all the time."

"It looks like a big one."

"It's the shepherds burning the brush to make new grass grow. And when there's a drought like this and no rain for three months, that's what happens."

"Excuse me, madam," the Corsican sailor interrupted, "but it's the Pieds Noirs. They say it's us, but they're the ones who start the fires."

"Nonsense," Millefiori whispered to Melinda, "it's them, the Corsicans. Sometimes they set fire to the crops of the Pieds Noirs, just because they're enterprising and showing that Corsica can be cultivated after all. Then they say it's the Pieds Noirs. Or else it's the shepherds who are pyromaniacs."

"Doesn't anybody end up in jail?"

"Here the Silence is in power too. More often than not, everybody knows who it was, and sometimes the small farmers suffer enormous losses."

They were now in view of another valley; it, too, was vivid with fires.

"I'd love to be there," said Millefiori.

"What a horrible idea. I'm scared. It's dangerous."

"But the beauty of it, just imagine. And we could go and see our friends, the Reuxes. They live in that valley."

"They must have cut and run by now."

"Not at all. I know perfectly well they're sitting round drinking champagne and watching the fun."

From the monastery they could see the full extent of the fire. It must have been burning all day, because it covered a huge area and the wind was spreading it all the time. Behind the mountains explosions lit up the sky. It was Hell as Cecil B. De Mille would have filmed it for *The Divine Comedy*.

"We ought to warn the ministers," said Jin.

"Wouldn't that be teaching them their job?"

"But maybe they didn't see it from the villa."

"What could the ministers do about it, anyway?"

"They could call somebody, have some help sent. Put everybody in jail."

"If you ask me, all ministers are useless."

Only three of "the boys" wanted to come. The American photographer decided that fires were a bore. But Millefiori was avid for it. They arranged to meet the ministers and Blamonche at the village, on the road inland towards where the fire was raging.

Millefiori was aroused.

"You'll see, darling, it'll be a new world. Isn't Jin the worst driver? Watch the road."

The conflagration spread as far as the eye could see. Every bend in the road exposed another valley seized by the flames. It was a sublime spectacle. The sea reflected its reds and oranges and the moon disappeared in its intense glow.

"Look, Millefiori, over there, above the village."

"Good heavens, I bet it's the old castle that's gone. The Reuxes, poor devils, will be ashes by now."

There were two cars at the crossroads; an imposing black one with the ministers, some wives, and Maurice; in the other, an open MG, Blamonche sat alone.

"Come with me," he said to Melinda.

"Melinda stays with us."

"No, no, I wouldn't dream of it."

She sprang from one car to the other.

"Darling, I want to see the fire with you. I want to enjoy the thrill with you. Besides, if you go with Blamonche you won't see the fire. Or you might from the window of the hotel in the square."

"We'll meet at the Reuxes."

Melinda

"All right."

"Blamonche, will you promise to take me to the Reuxes?"

"And where do you expect me to take you, my frightened little darling?"

. . . if Maurice came . . . or Millefiori . . .

"Look, there's room for three of us. Come on, Millefiori."

Millefiori jumped in beside Melinda.

"You'll catch fire immediately, Millefiori," said Blamonche.

He had changed his clothes. He had on a blue blazer with gold buttons, a silk scarf at his throat, and white ducks. A caricature.

"Have the ministers phoned?"

"They want to make sure the situation is serious first."

A phrase she had heard before . . .

The black car had gone ahead. So had Jin's.

"We three are going to the square and have a brandy."

"No, we are going to watch the fire."

"My car will catch up with them fast enough."

"See, Melinda? If I weren't around, you'd stay right here."

"Does the fire make you nervous?" Melinda asked him.

It was just as well Blamonche was a bit drunk and Melinda had some alcohol inside her.

"Look how they loathe him," Millefiori whispered while Blamonche was at the bar. "They won't serve him. He's hated by everybody."

"Why do you see him then?"

"Habit, more than anything. And he's always trying to take my girls away."

"Don't worry about me."

"Then why did you get into his MG?"

"I was afraid of Jin's driving."

"You could have told me."

"I was afraid you'd drive instead."

"Why? Don't you trust me?"

"It's the idea that frightens me."

"What are the two girl friends saying?" Blamonche came back to the table with two bottles of cognac.

"Listen, Blamonche. We must hurry, or the fire will all be over."

"I've ordered a taxi for you, Millefiori."

"Why?"

"So that you can go on ahead without waiting for us while we have a drink."

"Delicate and full of tact, I must say."

Melinda took a bottle and got into the car. "We'll drink on the way."

They went up the hill: stench and smoke and flames. It was difficult to breathe.

"Let's put up the top, or our hair will catch fire."

"Millefiori's is already in flames."

Millefiori screamed. Of course it wasn't true.

"That would have delighted you, yes, Blamonche?"

The burning olive trees looked like human bodies. They burned from inside, and once in a while a trunk snapped and fell across the asphalt.

"It's dangerous."

There was fire on both sides of the road.

"I'm beginning to be afraid too."

"Melinda. Look how beautiful it is. The inferno. Over there: those red valleys. The sparks spraying up into the sky. The smoke bringing tears to your beautiful eyes that never cry. The bodies of burning martyrs praying to their God, their limbs stretching towards the sky. Look."

"Millefiori, please."

Blamonche was worried.

"I can't see the other cars."

"They'll have gone ahead to where the Reuxes are. If you hadn't been so stupid as to stop for that brandy . . . that reminds me, give me some."

All three drank some.

The other cars were at the crossroads. They didn't dare drive further inland on the dirt road leading to the Reuxes, for fear a timber would block the way back.

There was a family in tears. Maurice explained, choking back his laughter: "They came out this morning for a day in the country. They left their nice trailer . . ." He couldn't stop laughing. "They couldn't find so much as a wheel when they came back. Nothing!"

The little girls were crying and the ministers were trying to console them. They were dignified and concerned.

"I'm going to the Reuxes," announced Millefiori.

"I'm not," said Blamonche. "You'd better walk."

"Precisely what I'm going to do." Millefiori marched off with Maurice.

The air was thick with smoke and their eyes burned.

Half an hour passed. Then another quarter of an hour. The show was exquisite but they were beginning to be bored.

"We must go and see," Melinda said to Blamonche.

"I'm not coming," said Blamonche, who was holding a handkerchief over his eyes.

"Come on, come and show you're a man." She knew that would make him move.

"We'll go together."

They began walking.

"Nothing will happen, you'll see."

"What a ghastly idea to come here. I'm sure the Reuxes left hours ago. And if they're here they're charred to ashes and it's not worth it to go on."

They had been walking for twenty minutes.

"Where's the house?"

"Farther on, on that hillside."

There was no sign of Millefiori and Maurice.

"Watch out." A tree was falling. Melinda gave Blamonche a push away from it.

"Thanks, darling."

Now he would trust her.

"Will you lead the way?" said Melinda. It was a narrow path. In the distance they could see the hill where the villa was. To one side was a gentle slope dropping down to the fire.

Melinda extracted poor Nora's minuscule revolver from her shoe.

"Blamonche, don't turn round."

"No, darling, I'm still leading the way."

"Do you remember me, Blamonche?"

"Of course, Melinda."

"But do you remember when we met on Katerina Nubytch's stairway?"

Blamonche jumped. He hadn't expected that.

"Why did you kill Madame Nubytch? Why does Ostrovsky want to kill you? Tell me immediately, please."

She saw that Blamonche was bending his arm slightly, towards his own revolver. Another second and it would be too late. Melinda slipped the safety catch and the tiny trigger jumped under her forefinger. Blamonche fell instantly. Just in time: Melinda saw that Blamonche had managed to pull out his black pistol. Alive, he must have been an excellent shot. She fired a second shot into Blamonche's neck. She didn't want the poor man to burn alive.

Brandy over his suit, on his hair. She dragged him by the trousers. Nobody had heard a thing. The others were a long way off; the fire crackled noisily and then that revolver of Nora's was very silent. She sent Blamonche's already flaming body rolling down towards the sea of fire below. Farewell. What a lovely romantic death. In a Corsican forest. Nobody would ever find the body. Count de Blamonche disappears while carrying out his duty, trying to save . . . He couldn't have wished for anything better.

Melinda walked on. In the drawing room of the villa she found Maurice and Millefiori and the Reuxes drinking champagne.

"Is everybody all right?"

"Sure, we're fine."

"We were so worried!"

Melinda

"There's a wonderful view from here. Let me introduce you to Madame Reux—our famous Melinda here, like Brünnhilde, a prisoner of the ring of fire."

"And this is Monsieur Reux."

"May I offer you some iced champagne?"

"And how did you manage to get here?"

"I came in a rescue team with Blamonche. Then we split up."

"Did he make a pass at you?"

"Of course. Right in the middle of the fire. As if one could lie down anywhere. But he was drunk, so maybe he went back."

"Do you think we should go back to tell the others we're not dead?"

"No. It's so nice here." Melinda took a glass of champagne from Monsieur Reux. The idea was to give Blamonche enough time to burn through.

"Delicious, iced like this. Marvelous. Perfect. How clever of you."

"I think some music is called for."

"Shall we attend some music?"

"You mean listen."

"What sort of music?"

"There's no electricity."

"Have you got a transistor record player?"

"Of course. Sorry, I didn't think of it."

"What shall we have?"

"Bartók."

"My God, not Bartók. Either Wagner or Berlioz. The only decent ones for a fire."

"Berlioz then. We haven't got any Wagner."

"What Berlioz?"

"The Great Mass."

"For the Dead?"

"Yes."

"Perfect."

✦

The longer they stayed up at the villa, the better. Perhaps she would have been better off killing Blamonche with his own gun. But that was impossible. Would anybody have believed it was suicide?

It was three o'clock when they returned to the main road. All the other cars had gone, taking with them the trailer family. Only Blamonche's car remained.

"How nice of him."

"Can you drive it?"

"We can try."

"No, Millefiori, not you."

They laughed. They were all a bit drunk and in excellent spirits. Melinda was pleased. Now she could go back to England and marry Mark. The Reuxes had stayed behind in their villa. They were fine, they'd said. The ministers sent some airplanes that glided along the surface of the bay filling their holds with thousands of gallons of salt water. After two days the fire was controlled. The planes succeeded in destroying both fire and countryside.

Melinda stayed for those two days.

"Millefiori, I'm leaving tomorrow."

"Why, darling? Stay."

"I'm going to get married."

"You didn't tell us, darling. Who to?"

"I can't tell you yet. I don't think he'll marry me."

"Anybody would marry you, darling."

Millefiori kissed her passionately.

"Come back soon."

"Where's Blamonche?"

"He disappeared the night of the fire."

"Really?"

"He disappears from time to time, on business of some sort. But it's serious this time. He left his car behind. A man like him wouldn't do that."

"Where do you think he is?"

"In my opinion, that's something you know."

Melinda felt depressed: could she never kill anyone without someone's knowing?

Ostrovsky could hardly believe it. "How did you do it? But is it true? Impossible. You're a genius."

"Now then, let's have some explanations."

"Melinda, the less you know, the happier you'll be."

"It's time I had a little rest."

"Who with?"

"Listen, Ostrovsky. I've had a son that I've got to have sent on from Moscow and I haven't had much sleep, and I'd also like to see some friends of mine."

"Van Der Belt?"

"Precisely. If it's any of your business."

"May I just inform you that your relations with him are now a matter of public knowledge?"

"What about Mark?"

"I don't know. I imagine he's terrified. Or else he's so obtuse he hasn't noticed."

"What would you do, Ostrovsky, with somebody like . . ."

Already she regretted having begun the sentence. What affair of Ostrovsky's was her private life? "Oh, well. You always know where to find me. We must talk about a number of things. But leave me in peace for a while."

"Melinda, if I were a government, I'd give you a medal."

"Ostrovsky, you are a government, aren't you? And one day you'll tell me which one, won't you?"

"One day, my dear."

They said goodbye.

Rendezvous in the lobby.

"Shall we go in separate cars?"

"I've left mine just off Halkin Street."

A certain embarrassment. Melinda tried to act casual. Mark didn't look at her. Instead he kept rifling through one jacket pocket for his glasses. He always dressed impeccably. Apart from his shoes.

"How perfectly sweet, you're shy," he said once he'd found them.

The truth was that she was worried.

They arrived. Mark pushed open the gate: there was the garden of his London home. Trees, moon and stars, and lights in the distance. It was like being in the country. A servant appeared a couple of times.

"Don't worry," Mark said to Melinda, "it's a tomb. He's the sort of servant who'd let himself be drawn and quartered before he'd intrude." Mark was worried.

"Will anybody be coming here?"

"Who would come? Aglaia's in the country."

"Are you sure?"

He was sure, but very worried.

"I'm not too well."

"What's the matter?"

"Stomach ache, indigestion. I'm a bit tired. I'm going to take a bath."

More embarrassment. Oh God, had she come here for nothing? It was possible they would just sit and talk.

Melinda

"Go and have a bath then."

"You have a whisky while I put on some music, will you?"

There were a few records bought at random; some symphonies, opera excerpts.

Now Mark was going to leave her alone in the drawing room while he bathed, and she would pretend to leaf through magazines downstairs, finishing her drink, which Mark had absent-mindedly filled with soda.

"This is beautiful. Do you know it?" It was the *Unfinished.* "Do you mind if I have a bath?"

He disappeared.

Looks around the room. Leafs through some magazines. Wanders over to the mirror. Asks herself why she came. Enter the butler. Feigned embarrassment on both parts. Pours herself a whisky, this time without soda.

Shall I go? Mark will come back and find me gone. What will he think? But then I shall regret it. It would be like telling him to go to hell. Something I'd like to do, but another time perhaps. Ostrovsky's right.

Enter Mark in blue striped bathrobe, all clean. Nice.

"You look delicious, Melinda. All demure. You haven't even taken your coat off."

Actually she'd mechanically put it back on, intending to walk out.

"It's difficult to have a real relationship with anybody." (Was he talking about her? But in this case it wasn't her fault.) "The longer I live, the more I realize that human relationships are complicated and difficult."

What a remark. She must have heard the same remark a hundred times before, probably from him. What was it supposed to mean?

"But the more superficial a relationship is, the easier it is. Why don't you have a Fernet Branca?"

"Ah, that certainly." Was he accepting the idea or the Fernet?

Silence. What was he thinking about? What could Melinda say

to him? She leaned her head against his knees, barely covered by the bathrobe. Agonizing atmosphere.

"Your brother wrote to me."

The magic formula.

"Which brother?"

"William."

"I didn't know you knew him. Where did you meet him?"

"At dinner one night. At dinner one night. At dinner one night."

"Why do you say it like that?"

"That way I hope to . . . oh, forget it."

"What?"

"That I met him at dinner. I saw your son yesterday."

No, it was too easy. She must find something better. Mark took her arm.

"Come upstairs immediately. Walk quietly. Don't make a noise. On tiptoe."

Shhhhhh.

Silence. The door, ajar. The bedroom.

"Let's open the window." The light from a gas lamp shone yellow on the bed and on Mark's face.

"Now get undressed. It's ridiculous, me half naked and you fully dressed. Take my dressing gown from the bathroom." It was all soft and rather dark. It suited her hair.

"Your hair's too long, you know, you ought to cut it. Otherwise you look a bit of a whore. It falls all over your face. I need you, you know. Did you know that? Did I ever tell you? I need you."

"I need you too."

In a way that must be true, Melinda thought, if she'd come back to him again.

"That's less important. And do you know why I need you?"

"Why?"

"Guess."

"You tell me."

"No, you must guess. Anyway you'll realize why."

"I think I can guess." Humbert Humbert in person?

Melinda

"Everybody takes your intellectual qualities seriously. They admire your intelligence."

Absolutely not. Obviously he doesn't understand that everybody thinks I'm delicious because I've no intellectual qualities at all.

"I don't," he added. "I admire something else. You. All of you."

Was that the explanation? Probably.

"I like you naked."

He removed the dressing gown.

A cold draft came in through the window. Best leave it open. Melinda foresaw what a disaster the evening was going to be. Every night with Mark was a disaster.

"You're very healthy."

It was a compliment. Clearly she should take it as such. "I've never seen anybody healthier than you."

"I am, actually."

"I like being with you like this. Stand over by the light, I want to see you." Mark's mouth, exactly like Abraham's. It was like making love with an absent-minded version of her father. She buried her head on Mark's shoulder. The same warmth and the same odor of flesh no longer young, of sweat. They didn't kiss on the mouth. Neither of them liked it.

Maybe he still had a stomach ache despite the Fernet Branca. Maybe he was tired, his bath notwithstanding, and couldn't bring himself to make love to her.

"Let's just do this for a while. It's so nice . . ."

Why not. I shouldn't let myself be embarrassed that he brought me here to read magazines and listen to the *Unfinished Symphony*. Somehow she couldn't concentrate on Mark or her own body.

Mark rested his chin on her navel.

"Say something."

"You say something. I adore you talking on my tummy. Go on, talk."

"I had lunch with Drew—do you know him? Lord Drew. Used to be Minister of Aviation. We went to quite a good restaurant. Can't remember the name of it. He was telling me . . ."

Was it possible? Once again, complete detachment from whatever vestige of eroticism they had generated between them?

Melinda looked at the ceiling. "I love you," she said. She could see no other solution.

Mark's mouth was instantly on her face and his eyes were melting. Mark's hands, both of them, stroked her belly and thighs, gently, skillfully, entered to find her, with caution.

"God, that's lovely, Mark. Go on."

Again his face, his mouth, on her neck.

Now Mark was laughing.

"Why are you laughing?"

It was all over again.

"I don't know, just laughing."

"But you're always distracting me. It's impossible to make love with you."

His tongue passed through her teeth, his hand between her thighs. Now I'll think about him, only him. And I'll think only about that hand which isn't mine, which belongs to him and I love it. I love it. It's a beautiful moment and I must think only about him. It was impossible to do. Perhaps he'll start laughing again. What's he thinking about? Does he want me? Is he tired? He stopped.

Mark went into the bathroom and Melinda really came, under her own steam. Now she was satisfied, but it was cold. She pulled up the bedclothes. Mark got back into bed.

"I'm tired," he said.

"Go to sleep, darling."

"No, open your legs."

Always she got cramp in her right leg.

"Wait. Move over on the other side."

"No, I want to look at you."

She would have to suffer and put up with the cramp.

But it was nice having Mark inside her once again after all that time. For a moment his absent-mindedness contained within her. Then he turned her over. In some American states, like Iowa, she'd heard you could go to jail for making love this way. If only Mark wouldn't talk so much . . . He started up yet another conversation. He'd been reading the poems of T. S. Eliot . . . Enough, the evening was over.

She had come back into the room. She was wearing his dressing gown: it went well with her hair. Where was Aglaia? Perhaps she was sitting in front of the television in a bathrobe, or perhaps she was with friends. Melinda was different from her. Aglaia understood things because, in her own natural way, she took the trouble to listen and observe. Melinda on the other hand grasped things only if she happened to grasp them. But if she did grasp something it was in a flash.

"Your hair's too long, you know, you ought to cut it. Otherwise you look a bit of a whore. It falls all over your face."

Her hair *was* too long. And it was a pity people couldn't see her face. She had a beautiful face. More than beautiful, it was striking, full of expression and attentive.

I wonder what she thinks of me. If she thinks of me. Is she fond of me? A bit? A lot? In what way? An unusual way. Melinda is unusual, after all. Funny that she should have happened to me. She's good for me.

"I need you, you know," he said. "Did I ever tell you? I need you."

"I need you too," came the voice of Melinda.

Was it just something to say? Why didn't she have a better answer ready? Why was she surprised? The important thing, after all, was that it was Mark who needed her. It was a novelty for him.

"That's less important. And do you know why I need you?"

"Why?"

"Guess."

Can she guess? Why do I need her? Not even Mark really knew.
"You tell me."
"No, you must guess. Anyway you'll realize why."
"I think I can guess."
What can Melinda be thinking? I bet she never thinks. Is she
in love with me? If she weren't, why would she come after me or
let me come after her? She's intelligent. I'm pleased that she's
intelligent. She understands me at once. She understands about
my family; my moods.
"Everybody takes your intellectual qualities seriously. They
admire your intelligence. I don't. I admire something else." He
liked Melinda's body, liked the way she was made and how she
moved. He liked her soft, clean, young skin. "Something else.
You. All of you. I like you naked, Ag . . ." He was going to say
Aglaia. Fortunately Melinda hadn't heard. He took the dressing
gown off her. Lovely fresh air was coming in through the window,
clean, restful. He anticipated the delight of plunging into Melinda's body. Or rest . . . But he was tired and he'd had a headache. He would have liked to fall asleep, now, next to her, next
to that body. But Melinda—what would she think?
She had a lovely young body, healthy, bronzed.
"You're very healthy. I've never seen anybody healthier than
you."
"I am, actually." Melinda's voice had fallen to a whisper. She
was expecting to be made love to. Why do women always expect
to be made love to? He would have liked so much to lie down next
to her without feeling obliged . . .
"I like being with you like this. Stand over by the light, I want
to see you."
She was absolutely beautiful in the light from the street. Mark
thrust his body, his muscles on to her, heart pounding, his blood
throbbing in floods, swelling, driving, running towards her. He
dragged his head across Melinda's belly.
"Say something," he said.
Suddenly he didn't feel like taking that childish body and driv-

Melinda

ing himself into the moist warmth of her sex, her stomach, her thighs.

"Say something," he said.

"I love you," she said.

Was it true? Did she want him? Want him, Mark, an old man? She wanted him who adored her? She wanted to have . . .

Mark buried his face in Melinda's and thrust his tongue into her palate, against her teeth, touched her hair and then grasped her hips. When he touched her thighs, Melinda shuddered. Mark began to caress her, to touch the soft corners, the curves, the hollows, and with his fingers he penetrated Melinda and stroked her outside and in and out . . .

"God, that's lovely, Mark. Go on."

What a funny thing to say, thought Mark. Go on. Of course I'll go on, but I can't go on forever. He found himself laughing.

"Why are you laughing?"

"I don't know, just laughing."

"But you're always distracting me. It's impossible to make love with you."

He began to kiss and stroke her again. He felt the sweat gathering on her shoulders, he felt an immense pleasure, and he also felt that he must go and pee.

So I haven't got an erection, he thought.

He got up and went to the bathroom.

When he returned, Melinda was under the sheet, almost a mummy; all that showed of her was a little of her hair and the mounds of her breasts. She had a certain static, happy look.

"I'm tired."

"Go to sleep, darling."

She said it without resignation. It didn't matter to her if he went off to sleep without making love to her. What went through this girl's mind?

"No, open your legs."

With a slight effort, as if he'd asked her to do something absurd.

"Wait. Move over on the other side."

She liked unusual positions in love-making, dear Melinda, who knows whom she learned them from.

"No," he said, "I want to see your face."

He took her hips and thighs in his hands and pressed her body under his. Again he felt his loins tingle with pleasure at the warm contact with her. Melinda was something to be had. An apple, to be touched, bitten, sniffed, rubbed, licked.

Another tremor through Melinda: Mark's hands between her thighs.

Their lips were together and at intervals she sucked gently at the corner of his mouth.

Mark no longer felt fatigued. His erection was growing. But not enough.

Besides, the more he thought about it, the less he was gripped by violent desire.

"Melinda."

Again his hand between her thighs. She was moist and opened her legs again. With his tongue Mark sought her belly and then descended between her legs. Into a mysterious world of live flesh. It tasted like ham. It made his own desire ludicrous.

Inside, deep, still deeper. He substituted a finger for his tongue and felt it disappear into the flesh, sucked far away as if there were a hungry animal inside her body.

He felt the edges of her diaphragm.

The idea rather annoyed him that Melinda had taken precautions, that she'd anticipated his desire for her. On the other hand it was natural. Better that than having another child, another of those many fatherless children of Melinda's.

She moved round again. She took Mark's hands and brought them up to her soft, delicious bosom. Her shoulders were against Mark's chest, the soft roundness of her buttocks clung to Mark's stiffness which was growing again with the desire to take her. A hand on her breast . . . the other on her sex . . . Melinda was in ecstasy: she turned around suddenly, searching for his lips.

Then for some reason he started talking. But he was tired and

Melinda

the mental strain of making love was too great. He went on talking and Melinda burst out laughing.

They never did finish making love that night. But Melinda
seemed satisfied all the same and Mark fell happily asleep. When
he woke up, at five o'clock, Melinda had disappeared.

(To be filmed with television cameras)

Characters

MARK

MELINDA

VOICE OF A TAXI DRIVER

WAITERS

A HOTEL PORTER

TRAVELERS, AMERICAN SOLDIERS, PASSERS-BY

SCENE I

*Two o'clock in the afternoon. Outside Paddington Station
Hotel. Noises offstage include the chug and puff of trains pulling
out. People dressed for traveling hurry about the station and plat-
forms. The atmosphere is dominated by trains about to leave and
people about to miss them.*

Out of a taxi come:

MARK, *carrying a small suitcase of light brown leather; and*

MELINDA, *with several shoulder bags and carrying a raincoat.*

*Mark is about fifty and looks it. He is wearing a light wool
shirt with narrow green stripes, and a plain colored tie. His eyes
are very light, more gray than blue, and big and heavy: he has a
pointed nose and that rich look of one who has always lived well
and always been well fed. He is not very tall.*

His companion, Melinda, is slightly taller than he is. She is

*wearing a short tweed skirt that leaves her knees bare and clings
to her long thighs. A camel pullover, and a lot of necklaces, un-
matching, some pearl, some with pendants. She looks scarcely out
of her adolescence. She could even pass for a girl taken by her
father to the train back to school. But there is a self-assurance
about this girl evidenced by the way she moves, speaks, and walks
and it is clear Melinda must be nearer twenty-five than fifteen.
She has very long hair and is altogether striking. There is no
danger of not noticing her immediately.*

MARK: Have you got any money for the taxi? I've no change.
Melinda looks in her various bags and pays the driver.
VOICE OF TAXI DRIVER: Thanks.
MARK: I've booked a room in the name of J. Walter Wells.
MELINDA: And who am I?
MARK: Mrs. Wells.
MELINDA: What a good idea. And we've got to catch a train, I
suppose.
MARK: Yes, today. Late this afternoon. Now let's eat, though.
I'm hungry.

SCENE II

MARK
MELINDA
A HOTEL PORTER

*A hotel lobby, Edwardian and spottily redecorated. Broad stair-
cases, potted palms, and semi-abstract paintings.
Through the revolving door from the street come* MARK *and*
MELINDA.

MARK: Go straight in and get a table, otherwise we shan't get
anything to eat.
MELINDA: Do you want me to order for you as well? What
would you like?

Melinda

MARK: Order some wine straight away.

MELINDA: I must go to the loo first.

MARK: Be quick, or they'll close the restaurant.

MELINDA: Surely I can go to the loo, can't I?

SCENE III

MARK

THE HEAD PORTER IN LIVERY

MARK (*with that accent which brings out all the most servile instincts in the English*): My secretary booked a room in my name, for tonight. Wells. Mr. and Mrs. J. Walter Wells.

HEAD PORTER IN LIVERY: What name did you say?

MARK: Mr. and Mrs. Wells.

HEAD PORTER IN LIVERY: Would you like to sign the register? *Mark scribbles. One camera moves in. Close-up of Mark's worried face. The other camera follows Mark's hand as it fills the form. Hesitation before inventing address, telephone number, occupation.*

MARK: I've got a train to catch at six. Would you please have my bill ready in time. In the meantime my wife and I will have lunch.

Mark looks round. Nobody he recognizes. The lobby is empty except for a small group of American airmen and one or two gray-suited men.

The camera follows him as he walks towards the cloakroom and leaves his small case. He then moves towards the dining room.

SCENE IV

MARK *and* MELINDA

NEGRO WAITERS *and* VARIOUS PEOPLE WHO DON'T SPEAK

The dining room is vast and reminiscent of a drawing by Steinberg. It is full of people. The men sitting at the little tables all look identical and the waiters have the same sort of faces as the diners.

Camera dollies behind Mark. From behind the white stucco columns, the palm trees and the trays of hors d'oeuvre, emerges the head of Melinda. She is sitting at a table in the corner alone, studying the wine list, or at least pretending to study it to look busy.

MARK: Darling. Everything's arranged. Have you ordered?

MELINDA: Not yet. I've only just sat down. The loo—you've no idea. Enormous, all in pink, with horrible little bottles and a fitted carpet. A family of fifteen could live in there.

MARK: Let's eat fast. What do you want? Some salmon—it's good for you—and then . . .

MELINDA: Smoked salmon and then smoked salmon and then some salad and a coffee.

MARK: Two lots of salmon?

MELINDA: Yes, and on two plates. Otherwise I shall eat it all at once and I shan't know what to do while you're eating your second course.

MARK: Do you like Chianti? I never know what Italian wines will be like.

MELINDA: I think the white ones are the best by far. The red ones all taste the same and they bottle them badly, with certain rare exceptions but I couldn't tell you what the names of them are.

MARK (*to one of the waiters hovering round their table*): Number 123. A bottle, please. (*To Melinda*) Listen, I've got a book of poetry with me. I want to read it to you.

MELINDA (*dismayed*): All of it?

MARK: Some. Do you mind?

MELINDA (*whose face has changed from radiant to worried*): It sounds like a wonderful idea, darling.

A waiter arrives with a bottle of wine in a basket. He pours a few drops into Mark's glass, then half fills Melinda's.

Melinda drinks hers immediately.

Melinda

MELINDA: Darling, what a surprise. I was afraid you'd ordered Chianti. It's wonderful . . . let me see . . . (*Looking at the label*) . . . excellent, nothing better. Fantastic family, they do everything so well.

MARK: Shall we order another bottle?

MELINDA: Let's wait a bit and see how long this one lasts.

MARK: You see, the Rothschilds are rather like my family . . .

MELINDA: I'm sorry to tell you, but the Rothschilds are much better than your family.

MARK (*in close-up, with a cross expression*): Political power, taste—I don't see how they're better.

MELINDA: Much better taste and a desire for power that's stronger and more genuine than . . . Let's let it go, Mark, you don't like criticism, especially about your family.

MARK: You shouldn't say that, it's not true. Have you got any money? I might not have enough.

MELINDA: Sure. In any case, I can write a check.

MARK: That you really must not do.

Fade out on Mark and Melinda. From the palm trees on which the camera focuses, we can only hear various snatches of conversation.

Snatches of conversation: . . . That reminds me, I must phone my sister . . . She's a lost soul, my sister . . . Do you know my sister? Listen, why don't you buy up that weekly and make something really wonderful of it? And then would you write for it? No, I'd edit it . . . William and I . . . You know him . . . Your mother . . . if you leave me . . . if Aglaia found out . . . I'll leave you, I'll as much as divorce you . . . Aglaia must never know . . . I'll divorce you long before that . . . Aglaia knows . . . no . . . forgive me, that was nasty of me . . . I fill the gap . . . you fill the gap in my marriage . . . I don't want to fill any gap in your marriage . . . Melinda . . .

MARK (*to a waiter*): Coffee, please.

WAITER: At this time of day, coffee is served in the lounge.

MARK (*to* Melinda): Let's go have coffee.

MELINDA: Let's have it upstairs.

Scene IV

MARK and MELINDA (*in bed*)

The room is big and very impersonal. Square or rectangular furniture of polished wood, striped green and brown curtains, not quite drawn. Outside, the noise of trains. There are two armchairs and a small table. Lying open on the table is a large volume of poetry. There is a telephone and two dirty coffee cups on a tray.
Two small beds. One empty. In the other (on which the camera slowly closes in after close-ups of the various objects) Mark and Melinda are in each other's arms.
On the floor, their clothes in a pile.
A sound of sighing which is like the hissing of trains.

MELINDA: You've no idea how lovely it is, Mark. Ah, it's lovely. *Mark, lying alongside her legs, moves on top of her. With one hand he lifts off the bedclothes, and the camera, out of modesty, takes the two bodies only from the waist upwards. Melinda's body is hidden by Mark's torso. Melinda's hands slide down from Mark's shoulders to his legs, and her mouth, which is not visible, moves all over his face. There is a look of ecstasy on her face.*

MARK: Do you think I'm in love with you?

MELINDA: Yes.

MARK: I'm glad you know it.

Mark raises himself and looks at her.

MELINDA: Oh please, go on.

He looks at her, touches her breasts, moves away and regards her whole body.

MARK: I adore looking at you, Aglaia.

MELINDA: You really mustn't call me by your wife's name. Oh God, you've ruined everything now. No, come here, darling.

Melinda

She kisses his ears and catches hold of his shoulders.

There's no knowing when you'll say things like that. I'd better get used to it.

MARK: That's not true. I'll never say it again.

MELINDA: Would it upset you if, from tomorrow, say, we stopped seeing each other?

MARK: Very much so. I'd be rather, what shall I say, wounded. But there's no need. You shouldn't break up something that's valuable in its way.

MELINDA: What do you mean, valuable? What are you talking about? Darling, all of that's very well, but soon there's going to have to be a divorce.

MARK: I've never known anybody who wanted a divorce as often as you.

MELINDA: I do with my husbands, but with you it's more difficult.

MARK: You wouldn't want to marry me, by any chance?

MELINDA: Don't worry. I certainly don't want to marry you. I'm very well off as I am and all my marriages are casual and unpoetic.

MARK: Yes. Well, I wouldn't dream of it either.

MELINDA: That's quite clear without your saying it. And I don't see that you need to mention it while we're making love, more or less.

MARK: Darling, you're right.

Mark rolls on top of her; kisses her at the same time.

Now come, Melinda darling, come. I want you to come. I want us to come together. Scream out if you like, do what you like, please come, darling, Melinda . . .

The noise of trains. A few moments of silence. The camera trains on the faces of Mark and Melinda, which are touching.

MARK: Now I'm going to read to you.

MELINDA: We've made a mess.

MARK: On the sheets?

MELINDA: Yes.

MARK: It's bound to happen.
Mark gets up. He is naked. The camera photographs his shadow. Goes over to table, takes book, and lies down on the other bed. He opens the book.
First I'll read you this poem by Keats.
The camera cuts to Melinda's dumfounded face, while we faintly hear Mark's monotonous reading punctuated by the whistle and hooting of trains.

"This is Charles Baukwortly speaking to you from Brighton, the smiling English coastal resort where this year the Conservative Party are holding their annual conference. The large hall, containing four thousand people, Conservative delegates from all over the United Kingdom, is lit by searchlights and booming with loudspeakers. The atmosphere is at fever pitch. Before me are sitting Alec Douglas-Home, Reginald Maudling, Iain Macleod, Enoch Powell, Quintin Hogg. Listen now to the applause for Lady Douglas-Home, who has just entered, radiant in a yellow velvet hat. Just in front of me on the platform, the Prime Minister, the Right Honorable Anthony (static blots out the surname), has stood up to tremendous applause, in spite of the party's recent internal battles. Among the observers I can see Melinda Publishing, MP, sitting in the front row and already much photographed in her red-and-white checked dress, and next to her the ex-Conservative MP, Mark Van Der Belt, whose family has produced a number of politicians.

"Now we can get a good view of the famous 'star' of British politics, one of today's most curious characters. Certainly her brilliant career and her boldness and courage have stirred the British political scene. She is one of the most respected members of Parliament.

Melinda

"Now the Right Honorable Edward Heath is standing up to great applause. The television cameras are all trained on him. And the Honorable Melinda Publishing is also standing up. No, she is not going to speak. She is merely walking out, perhaps in protest. And she is followed by the former MP, Van Der Belt. All eyes in the hall are on her, and indeed one can't help noticing this highly colorful figure, with her long hair down to her waist. Now Ted Heath's starting his speech . . ."

"Darling, how boring."

"It was you who wanted to come."

"I never imagined it would be so hot, or that there'd be so many ugly people or such a lot of nonsense spoken in so short a time."

"But conferences are all like that."

"But one with you ought to be different."

"Without me . . ."

"In your company."

"How was Corsica?"

"Gloomy and full of odd people."

"You never tell me anything. Who did you see? Who did you stay with? Why did you go there? Was there a man?"

"Would you mind?"

"In a way, yes."

"What do you mean by 'in a way'?"

"Nothing, I suppose. It doesn't mean anything. Shall we go and eat?"

Mark hailed a taxi, which took them to their hotel. They went to the top floor.

"Do you want to stop in the room?"

"I don't need to."

On a covered terrace they ate the usual prawn cocktails with sweet tomato sauce.

"Listen, why won't you marry me?" said Melinda.

"I don't see why I should."

"Nobody said you should. But don't you want to?"

"No."

"Why? Wouldn't you like it?"

"You know I wouldn't like it. But why do you want to get married?"

"I just can't sleep alone."

"That's not a reason."

"It certainly is."

"I love Aglaia. I'm tied to her. She's my wife."

"Never mind. If you really don't want to marry me, it just means I shall marry somebody else."

"It's almost two o'clock. In the Metropole Hotel the members of the Conservative Party make last-minute arrangements before moving off towards the hall where the conference is being held. This is the power center, the place where the political decisions are taken, where men consult and decide the moves to be made, who will make the speeches.

"And here we see them all having coffee, some sitting in groups, others consulting with their secretaries.

"Melinda Publishing is here again, talking to the former MP, Van Der Belt. In an armchair beside her is the Prime Minister, and Melinda Publishing exchanges a few words with him.

"Miss Publishing, tell us, are you here as an observer? Have you any comments to make to our listeners?"

"No, no. No comments."

"What do you think of this conference?"

"Rather slow, don't you think? Not very productive."

"What are your plans?"

"I'm going abroad."

"For any particular reason?"

"To get married."

Melinda

"You plan to marry again? And would it be indiscreet if we asked who will be the lucky man?"

"Not yet, not yet, but why don't you talk to the Prime Minister? He has so many interesting things to say about the conference. I know very little about it."

"Thank you, Miss Publishing, thank you very much."

"He is the only person who could have saved the conference and reunited the party so swiftly with a balanced and highly skillful speech. Just listen to the applause. The party is united again . . . the delegates are charged with enthusiasm . . ."

"Switch it off."

"Melinda . . ."

"And now we see Melinda Publishing naked in bed in the Metropole Hotel, and lying beside her is the former Conservative MP, Mark Van Der Belt, who refuses to marry her, so that Miss Publishing will be compelled to marry somebody else."

"Please, don't marry again—it'll only end badly, like all the others."

"But my marriages don't end badly."

"They do end."

"Not badly, though."

"The fact that they end—that's bad."

"It depends on your point of view."

"That's my point of view."

"It's not mine."

"Look, we couldn't marry. I'm too old to get divorced and marry you and then divorce again."

"But I wouldn't get divorced from you."

"Of course you would."

"No, I wouldn't, I love you."

"It's not true."

"How do you know, anyway, when you're so vague?"

"I'm alert enough to understand that."

"You don't understand that."

"Anyway, it's impossible."

"Never mind."

"What do you want to do?"

"Let's talk."

"What about?"

"About your family."

"Do I often talk about my family?"

"Now we see the two of them, the ex-MP and the female member of the Opposition, embracing. They aren't talking any more, they're making love. The audience applauds. Can you hear? The audience applauds."

"Stop it, darling."

Mark gets up and slips on his jacket.

"You look funny like that."

"Let's go."

"Where?"

"To London."

The telephone.

"Will you make out my bill, please."

And then Melinda: "The hall porter? Can you tell me the times of the planes for Rome tomorrow afternoon? Yes, from London. Thank you."

The next day.

"Darling . . ."

"Ah, is that you?"

"Are you really leaving?"

Melinda

"Yes, I'm going tomorrow."

"Shall I see you before?"

"When?"

"This evening's out, so is lunch . . . tomorrow for tea."

"I shall be on the plane."

"What about lunch tomorrow?"

"I would miss the plane."

"What do you suggest?"

"Tonight, of course."

"But I shall be at home, with Aglaia. I can't."

"Well then, why did you ring me?"

"I wanted to talk to you. Aren't you pleased?"

"Yes, I'm quite pleased. What have you been doing today?"

"I went for a long walk and thought what I shall plant this winter. I was thinking maybe fruit trees in the meadow near the house, do you remember?"

"No."

"Anyway, lots of them, with flowers all round. Then I read the papers and I was in my study dictating letters to my secretary."

"What time did you wake up?"

"Are you interested?"

"Not really."

"So why did you ask me?"

"Because I couldn't think of anything else to say."

"I want you badly. I want to see you and make love to you."

"But when we're together, you never make love . . ."

"It doesn't matter."

"I suppose it doesn't."

"Where shall we meet?"

"When?"

"Sometime next month?"

"I thought you'd abandoned me."

"No, of course I haven't."

"Then I'm abandoning you."

"Why?"

"Because my father was right."

"What did Abraham say?"

"He said I shouldn't run after you."

"Why?"

"Because you're peculiar, because you won't look out for anybody but yourself."

"But that's not true."

"Maybe not, but you puzzle me."

"In what way?"

"I don't know, but I don't understand; you behave so oddly."

"But so do you."

"For me it's all right."

"And why not for me?"

"Because you exchange roles."

"What do you mean?"

"I mean that you're the one who should take care of me, cuddle me, love me, manage things for me, screw me, and grow fond of me."

"Instead of which, you do, I suppose?"

"Oh, I don't know. I haven't really thought about it. All I know is it seems a muddle and verging on the boring."

"Melinda, I'm very fond of you, you mustn't say that."

"Well then, marry me."

"Oh, don't talk nonsense."

"No, you're right. Don't marry me. I don't feel like marrying you, really."

"But will you really get married?"

"I think so, certainly."

"When shall I see you?"

"Soon, I expect. But let's not organize things this time. It'll be a nice surprise."

"You drop me badly."

"You're the one that's rather spoiled things. Anyway, bye. And love to Aglaia and your sister and your brothers, especially William, the one I met one evening at dinner."

Melinda

"Do you think you're being amusing?"

"I'm only trying to be nasty."

"Melinda, don't ring off on me. If I catch a train now . . ."

"Where are you?"

"In the country . . . I'll be with you in a couple of hours, and then we can talk."

"What about?"

"Just talk. What time is it now?"

"Two o'clock."

"Ah, I can't. I've got to have lunch out, with the family."

"I might have expected that."

"No, no, this time it's important. We've got to decide . . ."

"Listen, it doesn't interest me in the slightest."

"Will you write to me?"

"If I've got something to tell you, yes."

"Do you know that I love you in a way?"

"You've already said so."

"What about you?"

"On the phone—it's disgraceful. Aglaia's listening to every-thing."

"Don't try to be witty. What about you?"

"Of course I do, otherwise I wouldn't be talking to you now."

"But seriously?"

"Yes, yes. Are you pleased? Bye, darling. I've got to go out now. All the best."

"Who are you lunching with?"

"With my brother Medoro."

"I didn't know you had a brother."

"Yes, and he's very good-looking, but he'd fancy you too and maybe even ask you to marry him."

"Is he queer?"

"Brilliant deduction. Bye."

"Bye, darling."

"Thanks."

"Thank *you*. Have a good journey."

✦

That man, the bore, had taken up so much time and energy that she'd had no time to see Anthony. She was sorry. And she didn't dare write to ask him the things she really wanted to know. Letters could always fall into the hands of obnoxious private secretaries. Melinda had read in the papers about the escape of somebody who had taken part in the train robbery. Superb, a triumph of organization.

There was nobody to meet her at Rome airport. How could there be? She hadn't told anybody.

"Mrs. Publishing?"

Naturally and rightly, the usual treatment. A drink with the compliments of the air company, a blind eye from the customs, and a car waiting for her.

"I believe your father is here in Rome," said the Alitalia steward escorting her.

How humiliating to have to be told by a steward. She mustn't show it was a complete surprise.

"Oh yes, of course. When did he arrive?"

"A couple of days ago."

"Do you know where he's residing?"

What a word! Residing . . . But this was the language of hotels and airline officials.

"No. Is there anything you need, before you get into the car?"

"I'd like to make a couple of phone calls."

"Certainly. And where are you residing?"

There it was, "residing" again. But she'd started it.

"I don't know where I'm residing." She might as well wallow in it.

In the V.I.P. lounge the phones were white, of course.

"Amerigo?"

Melinda

"Who's speaking?"

"Melinda."

"Where are you?"

"At the airport."

"Which airport?"

The question was pardonable, but, after all, absurd.

"Rome, of course. Why does it always rain in this city?"

"Shall I come and collect you?"

"That would be nice, but I've got a car. I'll come to you."

"Where are you?"

"I told you: at the airport."

"No, I mean, where are you spending the night?"

After all, "residing" at least expressed the idea.

"At your place, of course."

"But there's no room here."

"Have you seen my father?"

"No, but I know he's in Rome."

"Have you any idea who he's staying with?"

"With an English friend of yours, I think."

"Who?"

"I don't know. How are you, anyway?"

"Well. Listen, I'll try to get hold of Abraham and then I'll be around. If you really can't put me up, perhaps you can ring Liz and tell her I'll come straight to her place."

"Why don't you do it?"

"Look, I haven't got time and I've no secretary with me."

"Oh, just listen how spoiled we've become."

"Please."

"Well then, come straight round here with your cases and I'll try to sort out something for you. If worse comes to worst, you can stay with me."

"Be with you soon, darling."

"Bye, Melinda."

It took hours to phone to London. Melinda had forgotten how badly the phones worked in Latin countries.

"Are you Mr. Publishing's secretary? I'm Melinda, his daughter. Where can I find my father in Rome? But what do you mean—a secret, my foot. I'm his daughter. Look, tell me straight away or I'll have you sacked. No, no, my father won't sack you for telling me. Ah, he's staying with Liz. I might have known. Oh well, I can't stay there then. What a bore. All right. Goodbye."

"Liz—listen, it's Melinda. Ah, Amerigo rang you then? Yes, I know Abraham's with you. Can I come and stay? To the other house? Yes, all the better. I'm all alone. How lovely. Can I speak to my father? When can I come? This evening to get the keys, all right? About seven. Abraham? God, how terrible, I didn't even know you were in town. What are you doing? Social intrigues or amorous-social intrigues or business-social intrigues? Don't ask me, please. Yes, I've seen him, of course. But never again. No, I'm not marrying him. Really, you're sorry about David? But you never met him. Listen, how's your son? Yes, I mean Medoro. What's he doing in Poland? Photographs? But there's no Royal Family in Poland. The usual, I suppose. Who gives him the money? Listen, I'll see you this evening. No, I'm certainly not coming to supper with you. Drinks with Liz at seven."

She was pleased to be in Rome again. The colored houses, the beautiful stone, the colorful, good-looking people. She wondered how long she would be able to resist them.

"Amerigo."

He was listening to a record of English madrigals, correcting the proofs of a book, finishing off two articles and beginning a novel. He had on a blue dressing gown and he'd put on some weight.

"You look well."

"Too fat."

"You were too thin before."

"Do you want some pâté? And what will you drink?"

"Champagne? No, thanks. Campari with ice. No, let's try Campari and Fernet Branca mixed with ice. Why not, after all?"

"I spoke to Liz."

Melinda

"Yes, so did I. Abraham's with her."

"Oh yes? That she didn't tell me."

"He's incognito. As if he ever could be. Just imagine, he'd absolutely loathe it. He must be having an affair."

"With whom?"

"I don't know. He disapproves of my affairs, and I've made up my mind to disapprove of his."

"Are you tired? Because tonight we could go to a little theater where they're doing an unimaginably stupid piece of music, but we can hear a bit of it and then leave halfway through. Before that, there's a dinner for Helen Mitchell, but we could leave after half an hour. Only you mightn't be up to it."

"What makes you think I'm tired? Why should I be? Helen here? There's not a single Italian in Rome. It's all fine, but at seven o'clock I've got to go to Liz's to get the keys to the other house and say hello to Abraham. Will you come with me?"

"We can go on from there. Fine. But you'll have to change right away."

Amerigo was pleased to see her, no doubt about that, and pleased to be going out with her and to be meeting Abraham. It had stopped raining and it was warm.

"Look, you see it's not always raining in Rome."

"What gets on my nerves is this myth that it never rains here."

Liz's house was delightful and completely nonsensical; one room inside another, private life impossible, and the look of a big cellar with ultra-modern pictures. Liz was paler and thinner than usual.

"She's undergoing a cure," her husband, Joseph, warned Melinda. "She sleeps twenty-three hours a day. Even if she's standing up. It's a bit of a bore, but there it is. Just say hello to her and leave it at that."

"Liz, how are you?"

She was asleep and didn't reply, but pointed towards sofas and chairs, and poured herself a big glass of gin.

"She shouldn't drink," volunteered Joseph.

"But what's the matter with her?"

"A form of colitis."

"Colitis is always nerves."

"It must be your fault. What are you going to give us to drink?"

"Sorry, Melinda darling." He moved over to the bar. "Abraham will be here soon. Here's the key. Watch out for the outside door —it gets stuck. Best to leave it open. There's a maid who comes in the morning at ten o'clock. Very Catholic. I mention that so you won't let her see any guests in pajamas."

"I'm on a chaste holiday."

"Is it true that you're getting married?"

"I think so."

"Who to?"

"I don't think he knows it, so I'd better not tell you."

"I adore you—God, how I adore you. There's only one Melinda."

"Thank God for that," said Abraham, coming in that moment wearing a dark green velvet dressing gown.

"Abraham, darling." Melinda put her arms round him.

"We don't see each other often enough, do we."

"You're right. Papa, do you know Amerigo Vespucci? He's a writer. You'll have to publish him."

"But are you any good?" Abraham asked Amerigo.

"Don't ask him that, Papa. My word's good enough."

"But you never read anything."

"That's true, but there are certain things one knows straight away."

"What sort of things?"

"Don't make fun of me. You've never read a book either."

Liz was asleep. The bell rang. Joseph went to open the door.

"This must be Elisabeth."

"Is she your flame?"

"Please, not in front of strangers."

"But Amerigo's not a stranger—he's a great friend."

"Do you mean you want to marry him?"

Abraham always knew these things.

Melinda

"What nonsense."

"It's not an experiment I would advise. There's not a single woman who has gone through it without neurosis, nervous breakdown, and one suicide at least, on one side or the other."

"Never mind about that—tell me about this lady of yours before she comes in."

"Dame Elisabeth. Very intelligent, fabulous family. She lives in a lovely house in England, she's very interested in animals and birds, but she makes a special study of insects. At the moment she's writing a thesis on crickets."

"On crickets? And you want to marry her?"

"I've been thinking about marriage for some time, you know. Sometimes I feel very lonely. After all, I'm an old man, and at times when all my guests have left, I find myself alone in the house with nobody to talk to or share my experiences with."

Liar, thought Melinda, she must be rich. But anyway, Abraham's got such a horror of marriage that he'll never marry her.

Dame Elisabeth was tall and younger than "Dame" might have suggested. She immediately began talking to Liz, but realizing that she was asleep, moved on to Melinda.

"How do you do? I'm Elisabeth Mallet-Smollet."

She put out a long, elegant hand, thin and not at all affectionate.

"Abraham, Joseph. Good evening to you both."

"Signor Vespucci." To Dame Elisabeth, Abraham indicated Amerigo, who was obviously enjoying the scene.

Melinda settled comfortably next to Dame Elisabeth.

"Where do you live?"

"I don't know yet," replied Melinda. "In Rome, I think, for the moment. I'd like to find a job. I haven't told Abraham yet, or Amerigo, but I'm hoping to meet some man tonight who'll offer me something."

"What a strange idea, wanting to live in Rome."

"I feel like a change of air. Just for a while. I'll probably be fed up after a couple of months. In the meantime I'd like to set up house. I've got a lot of children. I never see them, and if they don't come here I'll lose track of them completely. Already they hardly recognize me."

"I've never had children."

"Have you been married?"

"No, but what does that matter? I've always wanted some children."

"I know you have a beautiful house."

"Yes, I must say it is very beautiful. It's near Oxford."

"So you know . . ."

Yes, she knew everybody.

"But I try to see people as little as possible. I'm working."

"What on?"

"I'm making a study of the sexual life of crickets."

That Abraham hadn't gone into. Too amusing.

"And you'll publish it, will you, this study?"

"I don't know. I'm doing it for my own interest. Nobody's ever studied cricket sperm, and it's very interesting. And so are their sexual habits."

"Are you on holiday?"

"Not really. I'm collecting Mediterranean crickets. I imported the first four thousand from Greece. I had to hire a complete compartment of the train, to keep them in a warm and constant temperature right across Yugoslavia and France all the way to England. I have a special studio out in the country, with Mediterranean plants and a temperature that won't inhibit their sexual reactions."

"It must be madly expensive."

"Don't even mention it. I'm now converting one of the libraries into a laboratory, so as not to mix up the Greek crickets with the Italian ones."

She had a small delicate face and thin legs and she was dressed in black, with no concessions to fashion.

"If Liz goes on like that, she won't be able to come to supper with us," said Abraham.

"Melinda, why don't you come with us?" asked Joseph.

Melinda

"It's ridiculous, going out for an evening on the town with one's father. Besides, Amerigo and I have got the evening all worked out. In fact, we ought to be going now."

"Yes, we ought to go."

"Darling, I'll ring you tomorow. I'm staying in Rome for a couple more days. What about you?"

"I don't really know yet, Abraham."

"Don't forget then."

"Dame Elisabeth, good night."

On the way out they met eight more people arriving at Liz's house.

"Now I'll explain," Amerigo told her in the car. "We are going to Mario Esposito's—he runs a very important weekly. The dinner's for Helen Mitchell. There'll be a lot of people there, Italian journalists and writers. A few bores. The women are idiots and a bit common, except for one or two, and I'll introduce you to those—but you'll pick them out for yourself."

"Tell me about Esposito. What a name, for God's sake."

"Esposito comes from the south of Italy, it embarrasses him but that's life. He married a banker's daughter and in no time at all Esposito second-rate journalist becomes Esposito publisher of the biggest weekly in Italy."

"What's his paper like?"

"Well, not bad. Some good names, but a bit home-made, like all Italian papers. They have high standards, though, and decent political articles. But there's a lot of crap too and two or three stupid writers that Esposito loves because he thinks they're fashionable. You'll make a big impression on him."

"Does he know I'm coming?"

"Yes, I warned him. He was very pleased. Your picture was in the paper a couple of times."

"As an MP?"

"As a duchess."

"Ah, that sort of weekly. What's it called?"

"The *Inviato*."

"What a name."

"Now don't be difficult. Anyway, it's the only possible one."

"Do you write for it?"

"Certainly."

"But you write for everything."

"Have I told you about my trips?"

"LSD?"

"No. Eight countries in a month. And have I told you about the ball?"

"Yes, you told me about that."

"And about the sailors."

"You never tell me about your private life."

"No, I mean the sailors at the ball."

Esposito's house was in Parioli. A penthouse with a terrace. The furniture was partly English antique, partly fake English antique, in conventional-banal taste, without any imagination. Blaring music from a Parioli jazz trio. A mass of people wading into lasagne and stuffed eggplant.

"Mario, Lady Publishing."

Amerigo could not resist the temptation. Esposito, tall, dignified, inundated in cashmere and vicuña, padded with chamois leather trimmed with brass, was the man to give her a job, Melinda decided.

"I've heard so much about you."

"And I about you."

"Have you now? May I call you Melinda?"

"But of course. Really, you know, I have heard a lot about you. And good things."

"I can't believe it. Who's talked to you about me?"

How could she disillusion this man? She couldn't say, Amerigo, five minutes ago.

"A good reporter protects his sources."

She would have sworn she would never be reduced to a cliché like that.

"Shall we dance?"

Melinda

People were dancing between the eggplant and the lasagne. Esposito's hand slid languidly between Melinda's feathers.

"You like me then?"

He wasn't used to an unconventional approach.

"Will you come and see us?"

"I haven't met your wife yet."

"No, I meant at the paper."

"Why not? I'll come tomorrow."

"How long are you staying in Rome?"

"A couple of months, I think."

"How nice. You're staying with us for a bit. Why don't you write something for the *Inviato?*"

"I'd be very pleased to. It's an excellent paper."

"So you know it? Do you really like it? Have you seen this last issue?"

"No. I haven't seen it because I've been in Corsica."

"Interesting. What were you doing in Corsica?"

A pity I can't tell him the truth. That I went to kill a French count. But Esposito wouldn't have found it funny.

"Just a holiday. I was writing for a paper."

"But you're a professional then! What paper were you writing for?"

What would she invent?

"*The Observer.*"

She would have to send the editor a telegram immediately.

"Really? I've never seen your name in it."

"I write under a pseudonym."

"Perhaps you could write something for us on English Parliamentary life and your courageous decision to join up with the left."

"Gladly."

"Come tomorrow then."

"I will."

"I don't know if you know, but we've got with us one of the most famous American writers, Helen D. Mitchell. Mrs. Mitchell? May I—"

"Melindaaa!"

"Helen darling."

A long hug.

Melinda, Esposito decided, was the woman for the *Inviato*. What luck that she'd turned up at his house the very evening she arrived in Rome.

"What are you doing here, Helen?"

"Holiday. And there's a meeting at the Press Club. And you?"

"I'm not sure really. Did you know Abraham's here?"

"The wretched man, he hasn't been in touch."

"Why don't we have lunch together tomorrow?"

"Fine. Have you seen any more of Jacob?"

"No, we got divorced, you know. And then I married again."

"And where's your husband?"

"He's not my husband any more. Yes, yes. It's not so amusing to talk about."

"It amuses you, though."

Helen had the same sort of intuition as Abraham.

"And what are you doing with Amerigo?"

"Just spending the evening with him."

"I've heard that you're vaguely in love with each other."

Amerigo came up just then, holding a leaky vol-au-vent.

"Good evening, Helen. I shall have to take this wicked creature away before it gets too late. Otherwise we shall miss the concert. Come on. Wait a minute, let's go meet the Great Italian Writer."

"But isn't that you?"

"Not everybody realizes it. They think it's still him."

The Great Italian Writer seemed pleasant, but already Amerigo had given her an affectionate push, so Melinda was introduced, said goodbye, and thanked Esposito and his wife.

"See you tomorrow."

"Are you taking her off already, Amerigo?"

"We're going to a concert."

"You want to do too much in one evening."

"I work so hard during the day . . ."

Melinda

Amerigo took her hand.

"Perhaps we'll meet up later at the Piper."

"No, that's a place I never go to. It's horrible."

"Esposito doesn't understand a thing," Amerigo said in the lift, "but he's obsessed with the idea that he does. He liked you a lot."

"I did everything to make sure."

"What did he mean by 'see you tomorrow'?"

"I'm going to work for him."

"That's the most absurd idea I've ever heard. Do you need to work?"

"No, to tell the truth I'm very rich, but I'd like it. It would amuse me."

"Oh, all right, if you put it that way."

Ten minutes at the concert and fifteen of intermission, hand in hand.

Twenty minutes of prose and fifteen minutes of entr'acte, hand in hand.

"It's early yet to go to the Piper. Let's go and have a drink at Rosati's."

At Rosati's, there were still plenty of people around: the slutty painter, as Amerigo said, and the absurd set designer, the lost sisters, the writer in decline, the respected writer and his wife, the writer who appears in the magazines, the better writer who never appears in them.

After a few brief chats they went on to Canova's, which was closing.

Just then Abraham came in with Dame Elisabeth.

"What are you doing here?"

"What are you doing?"

"We're only here because Elisabeth wants to go to the loo."

"Helen's in town."

"Helen who?"

"Helen D. Mitchell. I said we'd lunch tomorrow, the four of us."

"The four of us—who?"

"Me, you, Amerigo, and her."

"All right, but don't tell Elisabeth."

"As if I talked to her every day on the phone. Anyway, why not? Is she likely to be jealous?"

"Never mind, I'm just asking you not to tell her."

"Fine."

"And what about this Amerigo?"

"What do you mean, what about him? He's a friend of mine. Tomorrow I start work."

"Who for?"

"For a paper."

"Which one?"

"The *Inviato*."

"Now I've heard everything. Why don't you work for me?"

"I want to stay away from London for a bit."

"Mark?"

"No, no. I want to have a change of air and get married."

"You couldn't manage it with Aglaia around, could you?"

"Listen, Abraham. If you go on like that, I'll get a divorce from you too."

"All right, all right. Ah, here's our grand lady coming back from the loo. Enjoy yourselves. Are you going to the American Embassy too?"

"No, we're going to the Piper."

"Why don't you come with us?"

Amerigo would have jumped at it if Melinda hadn't refused.

The Piper was an enormous and very noisy hall holding about a thousand people, half of them dancing, the others watching—everyone who hadn't been invited to the Embassy or to the Espositos'. Social life in Rome, Melinda knew without Amerigo having to explain, was limited.

Oh God, again those delicious fingers entwined with hers, and his face nestling on her hair, and Melinda . . . and Amerigo . . .

Of course she loved him. He was the best of them all.

Melinda

The house that Liz lent her had lots of little balconies and tubs of orange trees and long rooms, almost like corridors, which led in and out of the kitchen, the bathrooms and bedrooms, with no sort of pattern. Melinda woke very late every morning to the smell of coffee and orange leaves and looked around at the pink roofs, stretching herself and blessing Rome and her decision to come.

The first morning she woke fairly early to go to the *Inviato* office. It opened at ten o'clock and Melinda wanted to be punctual. But she arrived at eleven o'clock because the traffic was chaotic and she stopped to have an espresso at Rosati's, where she met a friend.

But at the *Inviato* the publisher hadn't turned up. Nor his assistant, nor any of the editors. All Melinda found was a couple of secretaries.

"It's always like that," explained the porter. "They come in a couple of hours late."

"This morning's an exception," Esposito told her in his office done in Danish furniture and Toulouse-Lautrec lithographs. "The party went on late last night. How did your evening go, by the way? Nice chap, Vespucci, don't you think? He's the best writer we've got in Italy, of his type. Where did you meet him?"

He told her about the paper. It was serious and alive. Above all, it was different.

"We've got eighteen suits against us just now, Melinda. So you'll have to share an office with Dantini, Serghetti, and Cobalto, our best men. We're trying you out. For the first week you'll watch what we do and absorb our style. Because the *Inviato* has its own style. Our writers have to get the hang of it."

Melinda spent the rest of the morning in the office with Dantini, Serghetti, and Cobalto, who gave her drinks and played dice.

At two o'clock Amerigo came to take her to lunch.

"So the two of you are going steady, are you?"

And two days later, in fact, Amerigo and Melinda got married at the town hall in Fiesso d'Artico, in the province of Padua.

Back in Rome, Melinda met Abraham, who was still there.

"You've made things very awkward for me, darling daughter. Dame Elisabeth is furious. Because of Helen."

"It's not my fault if you screwed her."

"Is that any way to speak to your father?"

"Isn't it so?"

"Yes, sure."

"How did she find out?"

"She just guessed—she's not at all stupid."

"Come on, she may not be stupid but she can't guess something if she doesn't know about it."

"She saw us together."

"Where?"

"At Helen's hotel."

"You could have told her you were collaborating on a book with her."

"But she saw us in bed."

"Do you mean to say she went into Helen's bedroom?"

"Yes, she's an old friend of hers."

"And you hadn't locked the door?"

"I suppose not."

"Well, it's your fault then. It's the man's job to think of these things."

"Have you decided how long you're going to stay in Rome? Because I'm leaving tomorrow with Elisabeth. I've calmed her down a bit now."

"I've decided to stay."

"For how long?"

"I'm working for the *Inviato*. And then I got married yesterday."

"You don't mean to tell me you've married that chap you were with the other evening."

"You are horrid!"

"I see, you married him then. You could have thought of something more brilliant, darling. But certainly nothing more original. I'll ring up Anthony."

"See that he doesn't mind too much. It always upsets him when I get married."

"Does anybody know?"

"Not yet."

"Can I break the news in England? I've no intention of giving you a wedding present. I'm fed up with it."

"You've never given me any."

"I did for your first marriage."

"You did indeed—a present for my first marriage. Some shares in your publishing house. Which I've never seen, by the way."

"But you're much richer than I am."

"You were the one who brought the subject up."

"What are we going to do with Medoro?"

"Don't you ever see him?"

"Very rarely. He's such a good-looking boy. I've an idea he's a bit lost. Why don't you adopt him?"

"I've got too many children already."

"They'll all turn out like Medoro, if you don't look after them."

"But I'm not at all like Medoro. And you never looked after me."

"I looked after you a bit too much, my dear Melinda, a bit too much . . ."

And they parted with the memory of their past loves.

She had a letter from Abraham the same afternoon: "Be careful, Elisabeth has put a curse on you. Her house is full of ghosts and I believe it. Write her a couple of lines."

He's old and silly, thought Melinda. What a pity.

The news of Melinda's latest marriage caused great excitement. Esposito asked her a lot of questions. Had they been planning it for a long time? Were they really in love? He really wanted to ask her if they went to bed together, but he didn't dare.

After their marriage, Amerigo and Melinda continued to lead their own lives. Melinda rented a place of her own and decided it would be better for Amerigo to go on living in his, which, after all, was so well organized. They exchanged visits from time to time. They decided to put off the honeymoon, because they were both working and Melinda was perfectly happy, as usual.

Esposito took her out to lunch and told her that one day they would go to bed together. Once again he was the Ezio Pinza–Latin lover she had met the first evening.

"You've got a hard face, Melinda. Calculating. What do you want from life?"

As if one could discuss certain things over lunch with complete strangers, a bit tipsy with wine, looking out, it must be said, over the divine panorama of Rome. As if one generally could talk about that kind of thing.

"Oh, do you think so?"

"You're a clever woman. And you know it. But what do you want from the future?"

"To be peaceful and contented."

A stupid question deserved a stupid answer.

"Are you happy about working with us?"

Really she hadn't worked very hard. She had written a few letters and learned to use the phone.

"Tomorrow will be the most interesting day of your first week. On Thursday, as soon as the new number's ready—before it really comes out—we all meet, from the editor-in-chief on down, and draft out the basis of the next number. New ideas are brought up, we discuss them in round table, then we decide who are the right writers for the various stories and which of our correspondents to feature."

"It sounds an excellent idea."

"Yes, I think it is. It's my idea, actually. And of course it ends up with me writing the whole paper."

In fact, Esposito did all the editing. He picked the photographs and the typography, he wrote the headlines, he read all the stories, and then he passed everything on to Dantini.

Dantini's function, after working on the *Inviato* for years at a meager salary, was to proofread the articles and reshape them. He added whole sentences and described people he had never seen. There was no doubt, though, that the articles in the *Inviato* acquired a clean, unified style.

"How much are you going to pay me?"

"Not much."

"How much?"

"Talk to the general manager about it."

"But the general manager says that you fix the salaries."

"He's right, in fact."

"So it must be up to you to decide my salary."

"Do you really want to be paid? Aren't you rich enough?"

"Rich I am, but it would be absurd to work and not be paid."

"But you haven't done a thing this week."

"No, but it was you who told me not to."

"We'll think about it, we'll think about it."

Melinda managed to keep Dantini under control, and her first article was not rewritten. She was paid 15,000 lire. It didn't seem much to her, but Esposito assured her that all Italian papers paid badly.

"No, look, what counts is the style, the homogeneous quality of the paper. You'll see, you'll see, at the meeting . . .

It took place in the editor's office at nine o'clock on Thursday morning. Esposito sat behind his desk and the others lounged in chairs and sofas.

"What we need for the big spread are new ideas. Ideas, dear gentlemen, ideas."

"Ava Gardner," said Cobalto.

"Who on earth wants to read about that bag?"

"But we could talk about sex, Ava Gardner's sex life."

"And she'll tell you all about it, will she, Cobalto?"

Gagliardi suggested Elizabeth Taylor.

"There's been too much on her already."

"Let's have a new face."

"Twiggy."

"For God's sake."

"Julie Christie's love life."

"No, that's not it. Let's ring and see what Roberta says."

Roberta was having tea.

"Yes, we're all here at the meeting. How are you? What's new? Roberta says there's an English sculptor who's done some interesting things and we ought to do something on him," said Esposito, turning back to the group.

"What did you say his name was? Mor? Henry Mor? Never heard of him. What about you chaps? No, they don't know him either. We've got somebody new, the duchess who married Vespucci, and she says that if it's Henry Moore, with double "o," she has heard of him. She says he's old hat, but it would be all right. We'll go for the Mor. Goodbye. Tell your mother hello. And work hard. Send everything along. What else is there? What are we going to do about the lead article?"

"But wasn't that it?"

"What, a lead article on a sculptor? Sex is what you need to sell copies. Sex."

"How about an exposé?"

"Excellent. Who said that?"

"Serghetti."

"Good for you, Serghetti."

"An exposé of sex in Italy."

"That's it. A marvelous idea."

"Sex among teenagers."

"Or sex among provincial women."

"We can do a series."

"The provincial homosexual."

"Female homosexuality in Italy."

"Marvelous."

"Let's start with sex and the average Italian teenager at school. You do that, Serghetti."

"What do you mean, me do it?"

"Go around to a few schools and ask some questions and read a couple of books."

"What books?"

"Well, you'll have to find them."

"But there aren't any books on the sexual life of the average adolescent Italian."

"Well then, read the ones on the American adolescent and have a look round yourself. Don't be so unimaginative. I want it in two days."

"All right, Mario."

"Now you, Melinda, you could do a piece on English political life."

"Again?"

"Different from the first one."

"Then I'll have to go see what's happening in London."

"You can't, because our correspondent will be put out."

"But it would be something else."

"He still wouldn't understand."

"All right, I could do something on the English aristocracy."

"Excellent idea. But from a left-wing angle—you know, disapproving. And a bit of sex in it."

"But then . . ."

"It's sex that sells copies."

"We need a piece on the Vietnam war."

"I'll look after that."

"No. The editor writes that."

"Let's send Gagliardi. You can leave tomorrow."

"There ought to be something on the Italian political crisis."

"But that never ends."

"And we go on writing about it."

"The fifth installment on the prostate gland of the aging male can go on page 12."

"And what about something on the secret meeting of these economists?"

"I'll make that one up."

The paper came out, full of sex, and since Melinda had been busy looking for a maid, Dantini had rewritten her article so that the ladies of the English aristocracy came out as nymphomaniacs—just as did adolescent girls in Italian schools. Irked with office routine, Melinda left the *Inviato* for a seaside holiday with her children.

Eyebrows close together. Elbows entwined. Close. Amerigo inside her mouth. Curved lips. Of her mouth—of his mouth. Goodbyes.

Amerigo and Melinda had dinner alone, not because they had anything to tell each other, or because they wanted to be alone, but because they hadn't found anybody that evening to come with them. Besides which, Roman girls disapproved of Melinda's habits, and Melinda didn't approve of Roman girls.

Melinda

They had dinner at nine. It was hot.

"What wouldn't I give for vichyssoise."

"Or iced soup."

"Or tongue in aspic."

"In a hot place like this you can never get anything cold to eat."

"I've left the *Inviato*."

"I thought you'd soon get fed up. What do you want to do now?"

"I'd like to write articles for some other paper. Will you help me?"

"No, leave it, leave it. For one thing you're not good at it."

"I also wanted to go down to the coast for a bit. I thought I might rent the little villa at Spencer's place."

"Have you been there before?"

"I stayed there once years ago, with Medoro, my brother. A writer lives there. Spencer. Do you know him?"

"No, but I've read some of him. He's ancient, isn't he?"

"Quite. He has an Irish niece who takes care of him. But it's a beautiful place, with the sea and the garden. I was thinking of taking the children down there for a bit. Would you like to have a child?"

Embarrassment.

"Would you be away from Rome for long?"

"There's no need to be embarrassed. If you want a child I can have one by somebody else. I haven't found out yet what sort of marriage you want."

"I'm happy as we are. And you've got so many children already. We could go and see Eleonora after dinner, and then on to the Piper. Unless you want to hip over and see that little opera they're doing at the Cometa."

"Yes, why not, even if we've missed a bit of it already. Anyway, listen, I'd like to go off tomorrow or the next day and you could come and spend a few weekends with us."

"But how long do you want to stay there?"

"A couple of months, I think. Then we ought to go to Ireland. A friend there invited me over ages ago."

"But did he invite me too?"

"He invited David. After all, a husband is a husband."

"I ought to finish these books and then I could do a series of articles from Ireland. La Spezia doesn't appeal to me."

"But you don't know what Spencer's like, or the house or the people that go there. Young boys just down from Oxford, and this Lily . . . anyway, I think you'd like it. And then there's old Spencer, who just won't die."

"We'll see. I might come."

"What about our honeymoon?"

"What about our honeymoon?"

"Where do you want to go?"

"Somewhere where we've got lots of friends who can take turns inviting us to their marvelous houses."

"I don't know anybody. You're the one with all the friends."

"We could go to the States. New York and Long Island and New Orleans and San Francisco. But perhaps I'd better go there alone."

"Listen, there's something I must tell you."

"What's that?"

"In a way I'm jealous."

"Of me?"

"Yes."

"How sweet of you."

"No, I'm serious."

"I expect you are, otherwise you wouldn't have said it."

"I wouldn't want you to go to bed with lots of others."

"There'll be a few. I might as well tell you straight out. And we can always get a divorce if it doesn't suit you."

"This Cobalto—is it true?"

"No, I haven't been to bed with Cobalto."

"That's what they're saying."

"I wouldn't worry. If that's what they're saying, it means it isn't true. But what about you? What about your love life? Have you got some boy friends?"

Amerigo was embarrassed: he didn't like talking about his private life. He did have a boy friend, but he didn't see him very often.

At the Cometa *Il matrimonio segreto* had started three-quarters of an hour late, so Amerigo and Melinda managed to see almost half of it. They saw the horse piece, which Melinda liked so much. Amerigo knew it all by heart. Joseph and Liz were sitting in front of them. Liz, of course, was asleep. Joseph, seeing all the empty seats, left her and sat down next to Melinda.

"Liz is still asleep."

"You should either stop with those medicines or leave her at home, poor woman."

"In her rare lucid moments she insists she should keep up her social life. And she oughtn't to drink—that's what makes her fall asleep. Have you heard about your father and Helen?"

"I've heard nothing."

"It seems that Dame Elisabeth found them in bed together."

"It sounds as though she invents things, this Dame. Can you imagine Abraham getting caught in bed?"

"But it was your father who told me, not Elisabeth."

"And Elisabeth, was she angry?"

"Very, because they're engaged to be married. What do you think? Will they really get married?"

"I never know what Abraham's going to do. Anything can happen. But she seemed rather fascinating."

"After the opera we're all invited to Eleonora's," interrupted Amerigo.

"What an awful idea."

"You could leave Liz at home."

"If she wakes up, she'll want to come too."

In fact she came.

Eleonora lived more or less with Vito, the Catholic journalist who was the son of the Christian-Democrat deputy and the female agitator of the Catholic masses, literary critic of *The New Belfry-man*, *The Cloistered Review of Literature*, originator of the television series "Father Paul's Altarside Answers," and literary director of the Italian Radio. Big white teeth and a little Elle-Bon-Magique dress, Eleonora was hopping and twittering mad. She greeted Melinda and Amerigo and showed them into a flat that boasted lithographs and reproductions, mock Swedish and real Swedish, sober-modern ceramics, white curtains. An inexhaustible fount of information was Carlotta, the Amazon ex-Communist, ex-pro-tector-of-the-weak, ex-literary-muse, and current bosom friend of Eleonora. Vito's parents, Carlotta told Melinda, divided their time between the Vatican and a village near Treviso. They bitterly disapproved of Vito's brother because his wife was not only riffraff but had given birth to six daughters. Vito's father, who was always elected by thundering majorities, spent his days in country inns putting his case to the electorate. He was reported as saying, "I am like the Communists, I don't believe in anything." A devout man, Vito's father, whom Melinda had found with Ostrovsky at a big ecclesiastical lunch; he was often on the telephone to His Eminence or His Holiness. But it was the Countess Amantide, Carlotta assured Melinda, with her round of orphanages and cocktail parties, who gathered the Catholic votes. They were a great Italian family, and Melinda saw that the doors to the world of television would open wide with Vito's help.

"Congratulations."

"On what?"

"Your new marriage."

How disapproving he was, and yet Melinda was only legalizing what all of them did on the sly. But she was pleased to see the Great Italian Writer again.

She sat at his feet. She liked his big nervous face, his jerky way of speaking, and his lovely luminous smile. He was the nicest of them all, she decided.

"I think you're very nice," he said to her.

"I think you're nice too. Very. Come and stay with me."

Melinda

"Where?"

"On the coast."

"Have you got a house there?"

"I've rented one for a couple of months."

"From when?"

"From tomorrow."

"And you're going straight away?"

"Tomorrow."

"And your marriage—how's it going?"

"Very well."

"But what do the two of you do together?"

"Nothing, nothing at all."

Cute of him, not being able to resist the question.

Vito came over to them. He couldn't resist stars.

"What are you two talking about?" He didn't have anything else to say.

Even Eleonora came hopping and trilling over with a flutter of Bon-Magique chiffon.

"Just watch me take Amerigo away from you."

"Go ahead, please do."

Disgraceful. Let her try.

Amerigo and Melinda went on to the 84 Club, which was packed; they had a steak. Then on to Rosati's, but it was closed. Then to Doney's on Via Veneto, then Rosati's on Via Veneto, which was just closing, and then to buy papers. Then to the Piper, and each home separately. Drrrrrrum. Brake. Screeeeeeek.

"What a noisy driver you are."

Amerigo took her face in his hands and touched her lips.

Why had she married him?

He touched her knees.

"Listen, it's late. I'm going to bed. Perhaps I'll ring you up tomorrow morning."

"Are you really going tomorrow?"

"Will you miss me?"

"A bit."

He hunched his shoulders and shrugged.

"Good night." Melinda kissed his sulking mouth.

There was a letter from Mark waiting for her. It had been slipped under the door and Melinda recognized the handwriting.

"Goddess Minerva, so you really did get married. Come, please, anywhere in the whole wide world, and spend a couple of days with me. I suggest Lausanne, for a weekend, the Bellevue Hotel. Reply soonest."

She had completely forgotten about Mark. She spent the rest of the night packing. Would she enjoy an amorous weekend with Mark? But organizing the thing, tickets . . . Mark would forget about it or turn up somewhere else, or be seized with a fit of faithfulness to his wife.

Goddess Minerva. What did that have to do with her? Mark didn't understand her at all. All the better.

She rang Amerigo, but he was still asleep and she didn't have him woken.

"Tell him his wife rang and that she sends him all the best."

Melinda stopped off in Florence. She didn't like that city of gray stone.

"Enoch, can I come and have lunch with you?" In Italy she knew only British and Americans.

"Darling, it's nearly one o'clock. Mother'll be a bit upset. You'll have to take pot luck. Good and wholesome. A family meal. Helen's coming to lunch."

Impossible. Melinda knew these lunches very well. Four courses, five or six footmen, the magnificent dining room, and Mother sliding drunk under the table at the end of the meal. The car took her right up the big, tree-lined drive; cypresses grew all the way along to the Renaissance palace, the garden was populated with white statues, little Baroque figures, semi-nude ephebes, Renaissance damozels. Everything a superb symphony of stone and greenery. The statue that suddenly walked towards Melinda was Enoch's aged and decrepit mother, with her white skin, white eyes, a white dress, and pink hair.

Melinda

"My dear Helen," she said, "it's been such a long time. Up in these hills one doesn't realize how the years pass."

She was already drunk and her fine Boston accent seemed to be exaggerated by the alcohol.

"How are you, Madame Soane?" (It was always "Madame," never "Mrs.")

"Such a charming book of yours, my dear Helen."

Melinda thought it wouldn't do to point out the confusion of names.

And yet Helen would have been furious to hear her book called "charming" and Melinda decided she had better warn her after all.

"Do you remember me? I'm Melinda Publishing, not Helen."

"Ah, the one who's always getting married? How nice. I could never do it. My marriage was so awful that when my dear husband died, forty years ago, it seemed like a gift from heaven to be able to live alone with my Enoch. But come along, the Cardinals and the Bishops should be here by now."

Enoch's house was red, velvety, and full of extremely fine things. Something between a museum and Citizen Kane's Xanadu.

"Melinda, my darling."

Enoch came towards her and kissed her on her lips. He was tall and elegant, with wise eyes.

"Have you met the Reverend Singult?"

"Father, I want to introduce a young American writer," said Madame Soane, leading Melinda by the hand. "She writes some very saucy little things! You'd like them."

"She forgets. Forgets everything, poor darling," Enoch said in a mournful voice as he looked with great tenderness at his mother's pink head.

"It's time for cocktails," his mother announced.

A servant brought out some Chinese tables, one large, one smaller, and another smaller still, each one sliding out from the other, like those Russian wooden dolls.

The martinis were very potent.

Helen arrived with His Eminence.

"Melinda, you turn up everywhere."

Madame Soane felt confused. If Melinda was Helen and Helen was Helen, how did things really stand? Who was called what?

"Father Singult is my confessor," she announced, having given up trying to sort it all out. "He was the one who made me put fig leaves over certain parts of the statues in the garden. But when the Nazi general came, they took all the leaves off. Heh, heh, heh."

A second round of martinis.

His Eminence was tall, with elegant long white hands; he was American.

"I believe we met in Tangier," he said to Melinda with a smile.

"I don't think so. I've never been to Tangier . . ."

"It must have been Marrakesh . . ."

"No."

"Monte Carlo then."

"Could be."

His Eminence turned away and didn't address another word to her.

"Another little martini for Helen?"

Helen and Melinda answered in chorus.

"No, thanks."

"Can't I speak for myself, Melinda?" Helen protested.

Too complicated to explain. In fact, Madame had meant the question for Melinda, which amazed Helen, who turned away and began talking to the Cardinal.

"As soon as we've eaten I must go and have my hair done," said Madame Soane, smoothing her china-white hand over the pink wool on her head.

"I'll take you if you like. I've got a car."

"It's much quicker by plane."

Melinda looked at her: perhaps she hadn't heard right.

"Into Florence, by plane?"

"No, no. My hairdresser's in Lausanne. You know, he's used to my hair by now—he's been doing it for years."

Melinda

"And you always go to Lausanne?"

"No, not always. Once a week. It's much cheaper than having him come here. I did it a couple of times and there's his journey, the time he spends here, and the time he could have given to other customers. Not only that, but he likes Florence and stays as long as possible."

"A Swiss hairdresser? That's absurd. They don't exist."

"Well, he may not be particularly good, but I've had him for so long . . . It's a question of habit."

"And you go to Lausanne every week?"

"Now don't go and put it in one of your books, Helen."

At the sixth round of martinis, Monsignor De Wrun arrived; he had blue eyes and a fast hand. At two o'clock they sat down to lunch.

"Ah, my dear, I can't seat you on my right because the Monsignor is considered a lady. You know, my dear, it's such a pity you're no longer a duchess. Ah, my dear, if only you'd come yesterday—the ex-Queen was here and the young Prince. Ah, my dear, Mother has already slipped under her chair. Fortunately Father Singult is going with her to Lausanne, so she'll be able to confess in the plane. Ah, my dear, haven't you been to I Tatti yet? Ah, my dear, it's so sad now. Ah, my dear—women professors who know all about Testa or some other minor artist and have bad breath. Ah, my dear, how lucky you are to be the age of love. What wouldn't I give, my dear, to be always in the age of love."

Helen must have been feeling a bit guilty, because of the business with Abraham, and she never glanced once at Melinda. She hadn't liked the mix-up over names or Melinda answering several times to the name of Helen.

"Helen dear," said Madame Soane to Melinda as she leaned on the butler, "the Reverend Singult and I must hurry off for our appointment. For my appointment, to be exact. Now don't forget, send me your latest novel."

Melinda arrived at the coast that evening and tried to have a bouquet of flowers sent to Madame Soane.

She found Spencer's house and, even worse, the villa she had rented in a state of fearful chaos, so she spent the first night in a hotel.

The first thing I'm doing tomorrow is find something to clean that house up and put something to sit on in it. Then I'm going straight to the beach without letting anybody know I'm here.

Who could come and stay? Whom could I ring at this hour?

"Anthony? Come and see me."

"But, darling, where are you?"

"In Italy, but come all the same. I'd love to see you."

"Don't put on that mournful voice. Find yourself a husband."

"I've got one, a new one, but he's not here."

"I read that you'd married, but I thought it was a joke in very bad taste."

"On whose part?"

"On your part. For giving out false information."

"I'd like to talk to you."

"So would I, but not on the phone. I'll send you a secretary."

"Don't send anybody."

"When are you coming back?"

"Soon, I expect."

"What are your plans?"

"A few weeks here at the seaside. And then I don't know."

"You're bored, in fact."

"A bit."

"We'll meet soon."

"Good night."

The best thing would be to go to bed and sleep. Which she did.

Melinda

It should be added that it took Melinda only a week to organize the house, or rather to find staff to organize it for her. She arranged for a few of her children to come down with nannies, she turned brown from the sun, invited Amerigo not to join her and had not answered Mark. Instead, she found Octavian.

Octavian's real name was Robin, but because of his good looks and youth (he wasn't yet eighteen), Melinda had rebaptized him with the name of the hero of *Der Rosenkavalier*. It especially amused her to play a role, so new to her, like that of the Marschallin. Lily had welcomed her with revolting warmth.

"Melinda! What luck you've come. I've got so much to do—if you only knew how hard I work. The old man refuses to die and he's so selfish. Fortunately we have Robin with us, who reads to him all afternoon and night. I never have any money. Everybody steals. And I mean all of them steal. You'll have to be careful. And I'm not at all well. Do you see? . . . my pyorrhea . . . look, it's getting worse."

These medical consultations meant violent and intimate views of her gums.

"And there's my stomach. I can't eat and I'm always having to go to the lavatory. Sometimes I even do it in my pants."

Physically Lily was the most unpleasant person Melinda had ever met. Sometimes she went down to the beach and lay in a tiny bikini which just hung on her skinny body.

"I've got a lovely French body. You can see I'm not English. Wouldn't you say? Ah, here come my children."

Bounding and barking came the dogs, pregnant and slavering, full of ticks.

Octavian was Melinda's only consolation. They swam together and kissed for hours out on a rock, exploring each other's bodies.

Octavian, who was exactly like Melinda, was fascinated by the number of people she knew.

"When I go back to London, will you introduce me to some of them?"

"Yes, Octavian." Said inside his mouth.

"I don't know anybody."

"We'll see about putting that right, Octavian."

In his first year at New College, Oxford, Octavian was obviously very successful and sought after in his small way. He was the editor of a satirical paper, he had a fellowship, he was well read, above all he was beautiful. But in spite of all their tumbling in the sea and on the rocks, Melinda and Octavian had never made love.

"We can't do it on the rocks. What if people saw us?"

"And who's going to see us?"

"What about your husband?"

"He's in Rome."

"What about Lily?"

"I don't give a damn about her."

"But I do."

"Come to my house this evening."

"But what about nannies and children?"

"We shan't make too much noise."

The usual trouble with English students. There was the added complication that Octavian's family life was difficult, parents divorced, remarried, never saw Octavian.

"You don't know what I'd like to do with your body if I could . . ."

If I could . . . if I could . . . Maybe he was impotent.

But he was golden and had beautiful hair and was handsome and smelled nice. In contrast to Lily.

The big villa had become, if possible, even more ramshackle. The beautiful Genoese lacquered furniture had been reduced to the wood by the dogs' urine; the curtains hanging at the windows (which were always shut now) looked like those medieval battle

Melinda

banners that are sometimes draped in cathedrals. Threads and tatters hanging miraculously together. Melinda found the aged Spencer considerably into second childhood.

"I'm Melinda Publishing."

"Who?"

"Melinda Publishing, Abraham's daughter."

Still that enchanting view from the windows, the gulf, the islands. But Spencer no longer sat on the terrace. He stayed in his room now, stretched out on his bed. There was a marble washbasin, a little table with medicines and the black box. Inside the box were the ashes of Lady Volumnia, his beloved wife, twenty years gone, she who'd had the farmers exterminate all the cicadas because the noise got on her nerves.

"Yes, yes. I think I remember. What's Abraham doing—is he dead?"

Why should Abraham be dead?

"No, no. He's very well. He was in Rome a few days ago."

Silence. They had nothing more to say to each other.

Spencer leaned his tired head back against a mountain of cushions stained with vermouth and medicines. The covers were a network of darns and ancient embroidery.

"Now I'm going to see the children," said Melinda, meaning her children and not the dogs.

"Come back soon and tell Lily not to come in. I can't stand her."

He wasn't so senile after all.

"How did you find him?" Lily asked her at once.

"Fairly well, I thought."

"That's the trouble. He just won't die. And as long as he lives I'm a slave. The Countess never gives me enough money. The old man sucks it all up. And I've had to turn a bathroom into a kitchen and a kitchen into a bathroom."

They were in Lily's room; the poodles were licking each other. As always, there were six or seven half-unpacked suitcases, and an iron which had not been turned off and had already left its mark previously on the rug and a table.

"Eros arrives tomorrow—at least he'll keep his uncle quiet with some music," Lily said.

Eros was coming with Delly, a sweet Italian girl whom he tutored, very rich. Eros, in a way, turned up too late, because his uncle was in no state to listen to music or receive people. Lily had left both windows in her uncle's room wide open overnight and the old man had developed bronchitis, to make his poor health worse.

Melinda, who went down to the beach early to take the morning sun, or to enjoy the golden-brown curves of Octavian's body, saw this girl Delly arrive around midday. Delly was all curls, curls fresh from the hairdresser, hair a peroxided frizz. Her eyes well painted. Pale lipstick. Bikini, handbag, shoes, ribbons, and a watch strap all matching in a blue flower print.

Straight away Delly began talking about Eros and Lily, making a strange sucking noise at the end of each phrase. Melinda prodded her on.

"It's a madhouse," she told her, "such chaos, a pigsty. I can't tell you what sort of room they've given me and the children. And the servants all steal. No wonder they steal, they're paid nearly nothing and nobody watches them."

"Is this the first time you've been here?"

"No, I come often; Eros and I are great friends. Eros gives me and the children English lessons. And you know how it is in Italy, a woman can never go out on her own, so Eros comes everywhere with me. Mind you, he can drive one mad. He's always trying to borrow money. Today Lily even handed me the butcher's bill."

"You mustn't pay it."

Delly patted her curls into place and ran the lipstick over her lips.

"Lily asked me to lend her two hundred pounds. Just as I walked in the door. What can you do? I gave it to her. I shall never see it again. And Eros suffers from Lily, you know. She's awful and overbearing."

"Really?" Delly was anxious to tell her something new.

She put on some more lipstick. Melinda thought of Eros's long, unappetizing face. Odd that there was any sex drive left in him, after years of Lily and dogs.

Just then Eros arrived, all spruced up. His hair was well cut, and he wore a red bathing slip. Even his nails were clean and with signs of a manicure.

"Lily's bought another refrigerator," he announced.

"What?" protested Delly. "Aren't there three in the house already?"

"Yes, but she's bought another one. With the money you lent her this morning."

"You see?" Delly turned to Melinda. "It's pure madness. And then she says she's no money to pay the servants or buy food or have an operation for pyorrhea."

"Yes, yes, we know," Eros snapped.

"How's Spencer?" Melinda asked.

"Bad. It looks as if he's dying."

"I'm not going to swim, or I shall have to go to the hairdresser's again," said Delly, putting on another touch of lipstick. Octavian had disappeared into some cave or other. No knowing what that beautiful creature was doing all alone.

"The De Marinos are coming over."

"Who are they?"

"You mean they're coming over here, to our beach?" whined Delly.

"He's the grocer. We owe him so much money we have to let him use the beach," said Eros, looking hopefully at Delly.

"I hope they don't start up last month's performance again," said Delly. "You couldn't get near the beach, it was so mobbed. The lawyer's family, the De Marinos' house guests, their acquaintances, everybody and his brother. So who am I to want to go to the beach? Really, I'm never setting foot in this house again."

"So tell Lily."

"So *you* tell Lily. Because if I don't give her money for the room or any more loans, where's she going to get her fifth refrigerator?"

All this was very embarrassing and Melinda dove into the water. Octavian had fallen asleep on the rocks just outside the bay. He was so handsome, a Botticelli, a marine ephebe. She shouldn't have woken him.

"Octavian, what will you do if Spencer dies?"

"What did you say?"

"You're on vacation, aren't you? You're not reading for anything?"

"No."

"Then let's go away together, this afternoon."

"No, the Countess is coming today. I want to meet her."

A little snob, that's what he was.

"But I'm better than the Countess."

"What's that got to do with it, Melinda? I'm just curious to meet her."

"And how do you know the Countess is coming?"

"Because Lily rang her to say her cousin is seriously ill. You know she's the heiress?"

"Not at all. She owns the place. She keeps them all."

"She keeps Lily and Eros?"

"Until Delly came into the picture, yes."

"Who's Delly?"

"Ah, haven't you seen her yet? A doll with pink lipstick who keeps Eros."

"His mistress?"

His mistress, Miss Tress. Me Stress. What garbage. What divine words.

"What do you think? If she keeps him and they live together and they dress up for each other, what conclusion do you reach?"

"You treat me like a fool."

"Darling, of course I don't treat you like a fool."

He was so handsome and he looked so much like her. Octavian

was warm from the sun. He was on top of her, rubbing against her thighs.

"I don't want to make love to a married woman. I swore I wouldn't."

"Who did you swear it to?"

"To myself. It's against my morals."

Ridiculous. And he'd got it all wrong. It is with married women that you do make love. Octavian tried vaguely to come into her, but perhaps he really was impotent. Melinda kissed him. Octavian was one of the few men she enjoyed kissing.

It was two o'clock and Eros and Delly had gone off. Her bikini dripping wet, Melinda climbed the steps and turned towards her house.

A black Flaminia, with gray curtains pulled across the windows and an impeccable chauffeur, passed on the lane that led to the big villa.

The Countess, thought Melinda.

Following the black Flaminia was an enormous red van bearing a gigantic refrigerator.

Lily suddenly dashed out.

"The Countess. The Countess is here. Did she see you in your bikini? Got up like that? Your hair all over the place?"

As if Lily's hair wasn't always a mess. Panic.

". . . the Countess. The house is in a bit of a mess. I shall have to get her some supper. I haven't got much in the house . . . Can you lend me something? A piece of meat? And some salad? And a bottle of whisky? Could you send a man to clean up the house a bit? And maybe your gardener could fix the legs on these three armchairs . . ."

"But, Lily, she's here now. Anyway, the place is a mess and there it is. There's no hiding it."

"Please . . . the meat . . . some salad . . . wine . . . Will you come and have supper with us?"

"Thank you."

"But not Delly. She's too ordinary. I've told Eros to take her out to dinner. There'll be just the three of us."

"How's Spencer?"

"Well, quite well. He talked a bit. I must go."

She rushed away into the dust thrown up by the Flaminia and the van.

Melinda sent over the food and drink and turned up for supper at eight o'clock.

"You'll have to excuse me," said the Countess, putting out a hard thin hand, "but I can't have dinner here. I've heard so much about you, so I decided to wait for you."

She was long, thin, and dressed in black.

"Thank you very much." The idea of having dinner alone with Lily filled Melinda with horror.

"I found my cousin in excellent form," said the Countess, casting a look of hatred towards the kitchen (once bathroom), where Lily had taken refuge to put the finishing touches on the meal. "Lily told me that Spencer was in a coma. In fact, my cousin entrusted me with a packet of very important documents."

"What sort of documents?"

"They're letters. From a literary point of view they are fascinating and extremely important."

"I'd love to see them."

"Lily's got them in there at the moment. She's reading them while she cooks, before I take them away with me."

"Are they letters from writers?"

"Yes, exchanging ideas."

Lily appeared, looking very glum.

"The meat is burnt," she said.

"Again?" said the Countess.

It struck Melinda that here was an excellent excuse not to eat with Lily.

"But I could do some scrambled eggs . . ."

"I don't understand, my dear Lily, all these servants and yet you insist on doing the cooking yourself," said the Countess.

Lily had always boasted of her culinary prowess.

"We could do an egg salad," said Lily, going back towards the kitchen (once bathroom).

This time there was a shriek of horror.

"What is it, Lily? Is the salad burnt too?"

"The letters . . ." Lily stammered.

The Countess stood up, with eyes blazing.

"What's happened to the letters?"

"They've fallen, fallen . . ."

"Where?"

"In the water."

The Countess disappeared into the kitchen.

"No, it can't be, it can't . . ." The letters were reduced to wet pulp. They must have fallen into boiling water. Full of disdain and elegant with hate, the Countess went down the stairs, stepped into the Flaminia, and disappeared into the night.

"Why don't you go and join Eros and Delly?" Melinda suggested to Lily. "Do you know where they've gone?"

"They're in a restaurant in town."

"What with one thing and another, I'd rather go to bed now." She omitted saying "with Octavian." "And if I were you . . ."

"But I can't leave Spencer alone. The nurse hasn't come yet."

"But there's Robin."

"No, Robin's gone with Eros and Delly."

The wretch.

"Then I'll go and join them," said Melinda.

She got into the car and fled.

She spent that night with Octavian; at least there was the comfort of a nice body sleeping beside her.

✦

Amerigo kept annoying her with phone calls.

"Why haven't you written?"

"There's nothing to tell."

"What are you doing?"

"I swim every day."

"How are you?"

"Well."

"Have you found somebody?"

"Yes, of course."

"I say 'somebody.' A man?"

"You're ridiculous with your jealousy."

Melinda hung up the receiver. Meanwhile at the villa: silence. The usual dog pee on the marble porch. Books and magazines strewn all over the sofa. Melinda went down to the rocks but Octavian wasn't there. She fell asleep.

"I'm sorry to wake you," said Delly. She was in a swimming costume, slippers, straw hat, and bag all matching in a violet flowered pattern. "Only I must talk to you. They've asked me for another loan."

"Incredible," said Melinda drowsily.

"And they didn't even introduce me to the Countess. As if I weren't the pillar of this house. Why should they be ashamed of me, anyway? As if I were Eros's mistress. For God's sake."

The usual sucking noise from her mouth.

"I've been to the masseuse. And I had my hair done. How does it look?"

"But didn't you go yesterday?"

"Yes, but I need to go every day. Otherwise: disaster. He gave me a new wave across the forehead. Do you like it?"

Melinda

Melinda fell asleep again: she hadn't slept much that night. It was Lily who next woke her.

"Melinda. Come quickly."

"What is it?"

"My uncle is dead."

For a brief moment Melinda felt vaguely sorry.

"When did it happen?"

"While we were having lunch."

"What time is it?"

It was two o'clock.

"When I left he was resting quietly, he was all right, he'd been talking. Then I went back and he'd stopped breathing. Come on up."

"What for?"

"You can't stay in your bathing costume when there's a dead man in the house."

And why not? But she didn't say so.

"We must dress him and do the room and the flowers and organize the wake. Can you stay tonight?"

"All night? By the corpse? Why?"

"That's what you do."

"Where?"

"In Ireland, where I come from. In the Catholic countries."

"Really?"

"Yes, of course."

"Listen, I'll help you with the flowers. But I've rather a horror of dead bodies. Besides, I'm neither Irish nor Catholic."

Melinda climbed the steps to the house, behind Lily. Suddenly that large villa had lost all its charm. With Spencer had died the ghosts of Lady Volumnia and the Countess and even Eros and Lily.

Melinda broke off some branches of bougainvillaea and got on the phone in search of a florist. She spoke to several, but none of them would agree to send flowers to the Spencer house unless they were paid in advance. That address rang bells to creditors.

Eros and Delly had just gone off on a trip and wouldn't be back for two days, Lily had told her. The Countess had said she would come to the funeral, but that it didn't seem necessary to go back to the villa.

"He's left a will," Lily sobbed. "I was so fond of him. What will I do without him? Where will I go? I've nowhere to live now. He was my uncle. I was the only one he had in the world, I was everything to him. I was with him when he was dying and he said, 'Lily, I'm going.' Yes, he knew what was happening right up to the last."

Already the versions of his death were increasing and growing more fanciful. The one told that afternoon, if Melinda could remember, was that Lily had found him in his room and that he had died while she was eating.

"He wanted to be cremated. As if that were an easy matter in Italy. He wanted his ashes mixed with Lady Volumnia's and scattered around the garden. And he wanted his wife's ring put on him. I've dressed him, all nice, and now he's in the bedroom all alone. He looks as if he's still alive. Go and keep him company."

She shoved Melinda towards Spencer's bedroom.

The windows were all open and Spencer was already laid out in the coffin and covered with a patched lace shroud. On the floor, at the foot of the coffin, was the box with the ashes of Lady Volumnia. The dogs trotted in and out, occasionally giving the box a quick lick. A clock struck every quarter hour and from outside came the hiss of the sea. On the walls were Victorian water colors, photographs of friends and of Spencer in his youth.

Spencer lay there, his face in repose, the same, just the same as when he was alive.

Melinda had a real horror of death.

She would have to leave as soon as possible.

The wind that night blew stronger and stronger. It came in through the windows, it sent newspapers billowing about the room, tore off tatters of curtain, and ruined the flower arrangement on the corpse. Melinda left the room. She was looking for Octavian. Instead she found a Protestant pastor who had arrived with his family in an enormous trailer which he had parked outside the front door of the villa. He was fixing up the bunks and making a cup of tea.

"Want a cup of tea?" he said in English.

How annoying: a corpse in the house, Octavian nowhere to be found, a wind getting up, and the main entrance blocked by a Protestant pastor's trailer.

"Who are you?" Melinda asked him sternly.

"Mrs. Lily told us to come here. At the camping site they kept bothering my daughters."

Melinda glanced at the daughters. Impossible.

"Bothering? In what way?"

"You know what Italians are like . . ."

"No, to tell you the truth I don't know many. How, in what way were they disturbing your daughters?"

"They kept following them and touching them . . ."

The embarrassing account was interrupted by the appearance of a little boy with glasses, hanging on to his mother. He must have been about five years old and Melinda thought with disapproval that he should have been in bed at that hour.

"How old's the little boy?"

"Eighteen," said the mother. She added with forlorn brightness, "He's a bit retarded. Do you know where Lily is?"

"She'll be watching over the corpse."

"Who's died?"

"Old Spencer."

"How awful," said the pastor. "I got here too late . . . so there was no spiritual solace . . ."

Poor Spencer would have had a less peaceful death, thought Melinda, if he had known about the pastor in a trailer outside his beloved house.

"He wasn't a religious man. Oh well, good night. I'm going to bed. There's going to be a storm tonight."

✦

When it broke, it was terrifying. Forked lightning struck at the trees and the thunder burst like bombs. The nannies were jumpy and the children woke up frightened; but Melinda slept like an angel and woke fresh and rested.

"Amerigo? Yes, he's dead. A pity . . . If you want to come . . . as you like . . . this evening?"

"Lily, darling, when are you going to organize this cremation and the funeral? I know it rained last night and cooled things off, you still have to hurry up. You sound tired. Do you want me to do it? You didn't sleep. Why not?"

She wants to keep the body, that's obvious. When the corpse is taken away she won't have anything more to do and she's no house to go to.

Melinda walked off towards the cliffs. She found Octavian there, wearing a red flannel shirt and shorts. Adorable. The storm was still building up over the gulf.

"Come over and see," said Octavian, taking her by the hand.

"Where were you last night?"

"I was out. But come and have a look."

"You could have told me. I felt lonely."

"Come on."

He led her into the cave that went into the rock and under the villa.

"Look, another bit's come down."

"Do you think the villa will fall into the sea?"

"Not for another couple of generations. But this sort of storm brings down tons of rocks."

"There'll be another one tonight."

"They said on the radio that the autostrada's flooded and nearly all the roads to Rome are blocked."

Melinda

"What a disagreeable journey Amerigo's going to have."

"Is your husband coming?"

"Yes, this evening, unless he gets swept off the road."

"Don't say things like that about your husband."

"Did you see the pastor and his idiot son?"

"Poor things, they couldn't sleep for the rain coming into their trailer."

"I slept very well. Did you spend the night with the body?"

"How did you guess?"

"Have you talked to Lily about the corpse?"

"No."

"Somebody will have to make the decisions."

"And what's it to you?"

"I can't stand the thought of the body staying in the villa."

"But you're not there."

"I just want to see it taken out of the house before it starts decomposing."

"But obviously that won't happen. Lily wants to keep the body."

He wasn't stupid, Octavian. The red shirt, in the cave; the water reflecting off his face, his fine brown legs in the water.

"Come here."

"No, listen, your husband's arriving this evening."

"What about it?"

"You won't want to go on, will you?"

"Go on with what?"

"Us two."

"But we've never started."

It was a way to humiliate him.

The dogs, their stink: Lily was coming.

"I'm so tired, I can't eat or sleep. If only there were a bit of sun! I feel like dying."

"Lily, have you rung up the crematorium?"

"No, the inspector hasn't come yet. I have to wait for the sanitary inspector to come first and inspect the body."

"But in the meantime you can arrange for a nice little hearse to come and collect the body."

"No, no, we must wait."

"When's Eros coming?" Octavian asked. Lily looked at him with surprise.

It struck her for the first time that between those two there might be something not quite all right.

"When does your husband arrive?" she asked Melinda.

"This evening."

Amerigo did turn up that evening, exhausted. Melinda was taking a walk with Octavian and she met him on the rocks.

"I didn't think you'd make it with the roads so bad. How do you feel? Tonight there'll be a hell of a storm. This is Robin, my husband."

"I must tell you. There was a little party at the Dantinis', deadly boring but so ridiculous it was worth being there. Esposito kept on talking about you, and Helen was furious because she said you were pretending to be her in Florence. I didn't really know what she was talking about . . ."

Later that night.

"Listen, there's nothing for it. We shall have to share a bed."

"Do you think it's right, that young boy and you, before my very eyes . . ."

"But you liked him too."

"Stop it."

"But you've been courting him. Did you see how embarrassed he was? Did you like the bier?"

"You shouldn't go on like this."

"It's no good you playing the Latin lover because I don't believe you."

"I told you. I'm jealous."

"And I told you that it's no good."

"Why do you stay in this ridiculous place? Anyway, the corpse is going to stay here for good, that's obvious."

Melinda

That night there was a cataclysm: explosions, blinding flashes, rumblings, eerie glimmerings. The next morning, at last the sun. Amerigo and Melinda went down in bathing costumes to the rocks.

Oh God, it looked like Aberfan, the almost destroyed family of the Protestant pastor.

"The atmosphere's pretty gloomy here," Amerigo said.

"We'll leave tomorrow," said Melinda. "In any case, we're expected in Ireland."

Eros and Delly and Octavian were sitting together; none of them was in bathing costume. Delly had fewer frills and bows than usual.

"How tragic," Eros kept saying, "how tragic."

"But you know the old man must have been pleased to die."

They pretended not to understand; and yet it was true.

"Eros, you must organize something for the funeral," Melinda suggested.

"We were just discussing that. My uncle wanted to be cremated and have his ashes mixed with Lady Volumnia's . . ."

"Yes, I know, but you can organize things."

"It's too complicated."

"It's tragic," Delly said again, running the lipstick over her lips.

"Some more of the cliff must have dropped off," said Octavian, but nobody paid any attention to him.

"There's a phone call for Melinda from London," called Lily's voice. "It's a Mr. Van Der Belt."

This time Octavian was as put out as Amerigo. Melinda ran off to the phone.

"How did you find out I was here?"

"I think it was your father, but I'm not sure. I saw him at a party the other evening. He told me you were having a wonderful time." (Bravo, Abraham!) "Why didn't you answer my letter?"

"I'm glad you've rung me."

His voice sounded far away, rather weak and anxious. But she was rather moved to hear that voice.

"Are you coming then?"

"Where?"

"To Lausanne."

"It could be managed. But why Lausanne? There are pleasanter places. Madrid, for instance, or Paris. And anyway, I shall have to be fairly discreet because this new husband of mine is jealous."

"I said Lausanne because I've got to go there to see my brother. He's staying at Château d'Oex."

He was still the same. He wanted to see her without putting himself out too much—and to combine it, of course, with the family.

"Which brother?" The words were out in spite of her. Almost a Pavlovian reaction. "Listen—no. I'm going to Ireland tomorrow."

"Go via Lausanne."

"That's unlikely."

"What are your plans then?"

"Not very definite. All sorts of plans." (Why should she have plans? Why did people want to know things in advance?)

"Are you in love with your husband?"

"No, but I'm in love with a new lover."

It wasn't true. She wasn't in love, nor did she have a lover.

Why did she feel an urge to annoy him? What was he to her, anyway?

"I must see you. I miss you a lot. Please come to Lausanne."

Yes, sure.

"Listen, I'll send you a cable from Ireland. I'll see."

"That makes me happy."

"And will you change your mind?"

"What are you saying? Me? Are you crazy?"

She was happy, radiant in fact. Octavian, with his flannel shirt and his impotent face, was suddenly terribly boring. He was a homosexual all right. Whatever had come over her? Oh well, never mind.

She decided to pack her cases immediately.

"Farewell, Lily, good luck with the corpse. Bye, Robin, good luck with your studies." She felt like a respectable matron.

A van set off with the luggage and Amerigo and Melinda followed in a car.

Beneath the sun, which had grown warmer, in the still, liquid air after the storm, there was a terrible noise. First a rumbling, then a brief silence. A few seconds later there was a hair-raising roar that went on for nearly a quarter of an hour.

Amerigo switched off the engine.

From the first bend in the road they looked back and saw what they had not dared to suspect: the cave had fallen in. The Spencer villa and its inhabitants had disappeared into the Mediterranean.

The first anniversary of their marriage—a month —they spent in Paris. Millefiori Cucchi was giving a big party for the opening of a Surrealist exhibition in the Rue du Bac. It was raining and Melinda found Paris unpleasant—especially as it was now, all cleaned up because of that ex-patient of Hochtensteil's (doubtless an effect of the analysis). She spent the days in boutiques: at Lanvin's, a tartan coat down to her feet, with red and green feathers; at Cardin's, a little skirt in tweed and leather; at Dior's, a lovely shimmering thing.

The exhibition was amusing, designed with imagination, one dim little room inside another, full of surprises. Black mirrors that, at the touch of a button, revealed glass display cases with mice on broken drums, and then pictures by Fuseli and Gustave Moreau, snatches of ideas, an arch supported by a wooden leg,

an enormous machine that uttered "Beep . . . Beep . . . Beep . . ."
Straight from the exhibition to the party. It was the anniversary of
Sade's death, as well as the anniversary of their marriage, and some
of the guests were in fancy dress.

"Millefiori, it's splendid . . ."

The flares, the Egyptian waiters stripped to the waist, the cats.
Towards two o'clock Sade himself made his grand entrance. He
wore a gray rubber face with glass eyes and a huge necklace of
crosses and tombs. The head of his scepter was a scarab of spiders'
webs; black gloves adorned with a cross on the back, chains,
instruments of torture—everything gray. From his chest hung an
enormous gray penis. And in place of his penis, a long chain. The
man looked tall and enormous in all that rubber.

"He must feel terribly hot."

"Poor André. We'll wait a minute before we free him. It's so
necrophilistically beautiful."

The next day they caught a plane to Belfast. It was
raining, of course. But Erikson Hoover had sent a car to meet
them at the airport.

"I can tell straight away that Ireland's exactly like Scotland,
and that it wasn't worth coming," Amerigo said scornfully.

"Wait a bit. You'll see Erikson and his entourage. It's rather
fantastic. And you'll also meet Medoro."

"What's he like?"

"Good-looking. You'll fall in love with him at first sight."

They went through the customs from Ulster into Ireland. The
chauffeur got out of the car in the rain and handed over some
documents to a policeman.

"Madam, I'd like to warn you not to choose a Sunday for your
return. The customs is closed."

Melinda

"What do you mean, closed?"

"Nobody can move from one part of the country to the other on a Sunday." People had warned her: Ireland was another world, where the most absurd things were normal.

They continued their journey. The fog had thinned but it was still raining.

"Whatever made us come here?"

"Tell me about Hoover."

"He's from Chicago, he's rich, and he's got this neo-Gothic castle with deer grazing, trout leaping in his rivers, and lots of rhododendrons. Just as it ought to be."

"And when did he buy this castle?"

"After the war, I think, but I'm not sure."

At Belfast airport Melinda had inquired about flights to Lausanne. But how could she send Amerigo to Milan? Divorce after a month of marriage didn't seem proper.

They passed through Londonderry: terrible. Towards Donegal, the country was prettier. Then, the sea. The cliffs were imposing and the sea black.

The private road that led to Holy Trinity castle wound through hills (groups of sheep grazing, deer scampering away, partridge in flight). A lake, romantic. On the lake, the reflected outline of Holy Trinity.

Amerigo and Melinda had separate rooms. Melinda's was upholstered in Scotch wool and looked on to the lake. Erikson was out shooting, Melinda learned from the maid who was unpacking her cases.

"Yes, I know, they were badly packed. In any case everything needs to be ironed."

"What will you wear this evening, madam?"

Melinda pointed out a dress.

"Otherwise Mr. Hoover gives his guests Tyrolean clothes to wear."

"Do you mean to say that people appear in dirndl?"

Melinda opted for a dress she had bought at Lanvin's.

A large Campari with ice and soda bottle appeared borne by a Celtic servant dressed in Austrian costume.

"Mr. Medoro Publishing would like to see you," he said with a strong Irish accent.

"Yes, immediately. Tell him to come in."

She brushed her hair and put on a dressing gown.

"Medooooooro!" They hadn't seen each other for a couple of years. He was vaguely changed, Melinda thought, he seemed smaller and neater and less handsome. She embraced him with the usual affection.

"Melinda darling . . ."

They all called her "Melinda darling." She wondered why. Medoro returned her embrace less warmly and intimately.

"Sit down and tell me everything."

Medoro looked round him. He was no longer used to this sort of feminine chaos, brassière on the table, stockings on the carpet, bottles of scent and jars of cream everywhere.

"What do you want me to tell you?" he said.

"But . . . what have you been doing, where have you been? And why, while we're on the subject, don't you ever write?"

"I never know where you are. But what about you? You're always getting married and I wouldn't even know what to write on the envelope."

"Now don't be funny."

"But I mean it. I learn about your marriages through the papers."

His voice had changed too. Intonations, words that hadn't been there before.

"Have I changed?"

Perhaps it was Melinda's expression that gave her away; certainly the thoughts going through her head always registered on her face.

"You have rather. What about me?"

"No, you're just the same, I must say. I've forgotten how old you are, but you still look your usual seventeen. I imagine you've changed in other ways . . ."

"In other ways? What do you mean?"

"More embittered or hysterical or cynical: anyway, not so gay as you used to be."

"Cynical? Me? Embittered? But I'm very happy. Never been happier in my life. I'd go so far as to say I don't know what unhappiness means. I'm sure people create it for themselves. I don't take offense, I don't get angry, I'm never gloomy. If people want to treat me badly, I avoid them or move on to others. Never worry about what other people do or think. The thing is to be attractive and enjoy yourself all the time."

She had never said so many words at a time.

"You see, I really need you," said Medoro. "I'm rather depressed."

"I can see that."

"You can?"

"You're still very handsome, but less ebullient. Is that the word?"

"Ebullient is just right."

"I saw Abraham in Rome."

"What was he doing?"

"Being the social butterfly, of course."

"There's another one with no worries."

"But you give him some."

"So do you."

"Me? Who to? Poor Melinda. I never bother anybody."

"That's what you say."

A hint of reproval. What did he want, this brother of hers?

"Come and tell me about it while I have a bath."

She took off her dressing gown and began rolling down her stockings.

"I don't know what you'll think of my husband," she said, looking at him and seeing a horrified expression on his face. "What is it? Do you mind? After all, we're brother and sister. It's not the first time you've seen me in the nude . . . Don't be scared, I don't want to seduce you, it's just that I'd like you to keep me company while I have a bath."

"I wouldn't dare tell you this if I weren't slightly drunk, Melinda, but you're a little bit monstrous."

"There you are, now he disapproves of me too. Anyway, look, some things happen because they have to happen. You get over them and start all over again. Once they're over, this sort of episode, they cease to exist."

"But not for everybody, Melinda."

"You aren't going to tell me that you became a homosexual because we made love a bit together? I've had enough of this rubbish . . . if you enjoy making love to boys, good for you, go ahead. But what's it got to do with me? Don't pull that horrified face. I didn't want to offend you, really I didn't. Come here and kiss me." She realized that she was almost naked. That night everything was going wrong.

Medoro would have liked to walk out of the room, but Melinda said things with a sort of innocence. He couldn't make himself be nasty to her. She would always win.

"What were we talking about?"

"About my husband," said Melinda, slipping into the bath full of scented water. "He's a homosexual too."

It must be grotesque living with her, he thought. "I don't know what you'll think of *my* husband," Medero said out loud. "He's half French and half Spanish."

"And the royal families, the photographs? And your boy friend? Does he adore you?"

"I think so. We've been together for some time."

"How old is he?"

"He's quite a bit older than me and you."

"What does he do?"

"He keeps me."

"Quite right."

"And your husband?"

Melinda

"I keep myself and he keeps himself. I don't know if that's how a marriage ought to be."

"But are you fond of each other?"

She looked at him in surprise. Fond of Amerigo?

"I think so. I don't know why you ask me these questions. Perhaps because you're my brother."

"Are you fond of somebody, though?"

Fond of somebody? She longed to see Anthony again, and she wanted to go to bed with Mark and perhaps see Abraham again.

"Oh listen, let's change the subject."

(No, she isn't fond of anybody, Medoro thought.)

". . . later on."

"What did you say?" He had missed something Melinda had said while he was thinking.

"I said I must get dressed and write a letter and that I'll see you later on."

Medoro left the room with a certain sadness. He's nice, Melinda thought, and he's got older.

Markdarling, Darlingmark, darling, darling, darling, darling, darling, dar, da, d . . . Come and meet me at the airport at twelve o'clock, flight BE 231. Write immediately or phone.

She took refuge in her Campari and her dressing gown. Again somebody at the door.

"Who is it?"

"Count Santa Cruz Jawlensky would like to see you in private, madam."

Santa Cruz Jawlensky, thought Melinda. I don't remember him. He must be a friend of my father's or of Millefiori's. A name like that I ought to remember.

She was right not to remember, though, because it was Ostrovsky, disguised in tweeds and a checked flannel shirt, who appeared in the doorway. She found him a little thinner.

"Ostrovsky!"

"If I'd known, my dear Melinda, that I'd find you in Hoover's house, I'd never have come."

"Thank you very much. Very kind of you."

"I want to avoid, seriously, Melinda, any words in public that could be linked with certain episodes."

"I met Count Santa Cruz Jawlensky in St. Moritz. All right?"

"Excellent. Is that all?"

"Do you want a drink?" She moved over to the tray.

"No, thanks. I must get out of here. What would I be doing in the bedroom of somebody I met vaguely in St. Moritz?"

"Everybody comes into my bedroom at one time or another, and besides, Ostrovsky, I've got to speak to you."

"That we can do another time."

"No, now." She moved over to the door and turned the key.

"I'm armed."

"So am I."

"What do you want?"

"I want some explanations, and some answers, and I want to ask you what I've got to do now and what my next mission is going to be."

"There won't be a next mission. Your work's done and you've been paid. Isn't that so?"

"Yes, but . . . but spies always go on working . . ."

"Not you."

"Aren't you pleased with me?"

"Completely satisfied."

"And who was I working for?"

"For me."

"But for what government?"

"You've read too much Ian Fleming."

"Don't treat me like a little girl. Why did Blamonche kill Madame Nubytch? And why did I have orders to kill Blamonche? And why did I get rid of those Pussygirls? And why did that man . . ."

"How absurd to be talking of such fantasies in Ireland, when we're here to enjoy the company of friends and go for walks and relax round the fire."

"Listen, relaxing round the fire and going for walks has never appealed to me, and I shall be going off in a few days and before I do I want to know everything. Do you understand?"

"And if not?"

"You might be sorry."

"Would you be thinking of going to the police?"

"Listen, Ostrovsky, don't let's argue. We've always got on well. Just explain things in a few brief words and I won't bother you any more."

"So it's pure curiosity."

"Certainly. I want to know who I was working for and why."

"But didn't you enjoy yourself?"

"Sure I enjoyed myself."

The door.

"That must be my husband or Medoro."

"About Medoro, by the way. I don't know if I told you . . ."

"Told me what?"

"That he's living with me."

"You see? I can blackmail you. I'll make him fall in love with me or with my husband and we'll take him away."

"How's your Van Der Belt?"

"That's over and has been for some time."

"While we're talking amorous blackmail, I know perfectly well it isn't over and that you wrote him a letter five minutes ago and that you're going to meet him in Lausanne."

"How do you know?"

"I always tip the servants."

To sum up, this Ostrovsky–Eluard Santa Cruz Jawlensky was beginning to be very tiresome.

"Tell me everything and we'll go our separate ways."

"I can't now. Open the door, please, and don't behave like a little girl. Besides, the door's locked and somebody's knocking. You make me behave stupidly. Tomorrow . . . in the afternoon.

'We'll meet in the garden and I'll take you on the first long walk you've had in your life."

The evening passed without surprises. Just what one would expect of an evening spent in the house of a rich American in the Irish hills. Long cocktails and hour-long conversations standing up.

Amerigo, as might have been expected, managed to sit near Medoro.

Eluard Santa Cruz Jawlensky had ignored Melinda after a kiss on the hand and an "Oh, how nice to see you here, my dear. Do you still ski?" and, terrified, he had gone over to make conversation with the Duchess. He liked duchesses, no doubt about it. Now and then he glanced over at the corner sofa at Amerigo and Medoro. Erikson Hoover, dressed in Tyrolean costume, was talking to Helen. But of course, Helen was there.

"You turn up everywhere."

"What about you?"

"What are you doing here?"

"I've been told you're a bit angry with me."

"No, no, it's not true. A lot of nonsense. Your father still behaves oddly."

"You're telling me."

"I suppose you know about the latest episode?"

"There's no use pretending. I do know. But about that lunch in Florence, you know, she thought I was you and I tried to explain I wasn't you, but I couldn't get through to her, so it seemed simpler to carry on. It's not that I wanted to take over your name . . ."

"Think no more about it. Listen, I've a splendid idea. I must tell you about it later on. Let's hope they seat us close to one another."

"They don't put two women next to each other at table, you know, when there are so many men."

"The sexes are so mixed up here, it wouldn't surprise me."

Sebastian, a tall young decorator with fawn's eyes, was talking to Andrew Mayfair.

Melinda

"You never come and stay with me. You only go to castles. It's been ages since you promised you'd come for a weekend."

"I was working on a job, the last time you asked me. You mustn't be offended."

"Did you know that Domenico bit off Ludwig's nose?"

"Of course, in a taxi. It was when he told him he was going to get married."

"What's the story, then?"

"There were four of them. Domenico and Ludwig were arguing and suddenly—unggh—he took a bite at him. The nose fell on the floor and one of the others picked it up and put it in his pocket and they went off to the hospital. The doctors knew perfectly well what had happened, but since there was a girl with them, they thought she had done it."

"And what then?"

"They sewed his nose back on. But at first there was a piece of nose they couldn't find and they thought they'd left it in the taxi. Then the other friend remembered and pulled it out of his pocket."

"How frightfully marvelous! But what about Ludwig?"

"He got married. His wife is Canadian, rolling in money."

"Good for him."

"Have you seen Lietta lately?"

"No, she's just gone off to Laos to search for buried treasure."

"She's mad."

"Has been for years."

"How did the shooting go today?" interrupted Erikson. "After dinner we'll make a big bonfire."

"What?" Melinda asked.

"Erikson fattens his partridge artificially," explained Andrew, "so there are thousands of them but they're not good to eat. Today we brought down about a thousand."

"But I'd love to eat them. I adore partridge, artificially fattened or not," said Melinda.

"Erikson burns them on the other side of the lake, to keep the stink away from the castle. The effect on the lake is marvelous."

"How disgusting," said Medoro, who came up then, abandoning Amerigo on the sofa.

"Dinner is served," said the butler in Tyrolean costume. And the group moved off towards the dining room.

It was vast, with red damask walls and high-backed chairs. Landseer pictures on the wall: bleeding stags, stags in the snow, eagles hovering in wait for a stag's death. The three women were separated. The Duchess on Erikson's right, Melinda on his left, and Helen at the head of the table. The Duchess, who was about sixty and had a passion for bridge (which she had already suggested as the culmination of the evening), began talking about dogs. How many she had, and all about the ones she'd adored and that were now dead.

"Do you know Holy Trinity well?" Sebastian asked Melinda.

"No—do you?"

"I come here every year, when Erikson comes over from New Orleans."

"I like it very much."

"Have you seen the lions?"

"The lions?" Melinda laughed.

"I'm serious. One area of the park is separated off by a deep trench. And since Erikson opened the house to the public, he reckons he has attracted more people by having the lions roaming more or less free."

"And don't they ever escape?"

"No, no. There's the trench."

"But don't they die of cold?"

"They have a heated den. But I believe it costs thousands."

"The village is suing Erikson because it seems the lions can, in fact, jump over the trench."

"My walks will be even rarer," said Melinda. But she was delighted. And the idea of pushing somebody into the lion pit? Ostrovsky?

After dinner Melinda was called to the phone.

Melinda

Instead of Mark, it was Anthony.

"There's somebody who wants to see you in Ireland."

"Who is it, you?"

"Not exactly. A friend."

"You're very mysterious."

"Don't you understand? He's part of the 'operation.'"

"Where is he?"

"In Letterkenny. You'll find him at two o'clock tomorrow in the local pub, the only one, it seems, and he'll say, 'What day is it today? Good morning, madam.' He doesn't know who you are. He must talk to you."

"All right."

"Bye for now."

"Is that all? Don't you want to talk for a bit?"

"Another time."

"All right, I'll go back to the drawing room."

The ladies, the real ones, were in the drawing room, and the men, the fake ones, were drinking port in the dining room.

"Look," Helen said to Melinda, "I've got a marvelous idea for the two of us."

"Really?"

"Have you got a little money?"

"Yes, enough."

"I'd like to open a shop, a boutique."

"That's what all women of good family want to do. I wouldn't touch it if I were you."

"No, this is different. For one thing, the boutique will be in Tangier."

"That's no good. Now that it's no longer a free port, nobody lives there."

"But plenty of people pass through. And I want to sell something that nobody else sells."

"What's that?"

"Male sperm."

"But what nonsense. Who would want it, anyway? Are you going to sell it in test tubes?"

"Certainly. For people who want high-quality sperm; we're the only ones who can get special sperm. I mean from very intelligent men, from famous writers, politicians, scientists, or strong handsome men, or else interesting and intelligent men. Or else snob sperm, Hapsburg sperm, Bourbon sperm."

"And would you find any customers?"

"Any number. I've already had inquiries. We could guarantee the product and the ladies would trust us. Instead of going into clinics where they don't even tell you who the test tube came from, women with impotent, well-off husbands will be our faithful customers for one gestation after another. And we could get the product without paying for it. Apart from transport and laboratory costs."

"It doesn't sound a bad idea."

"I knew you'd like it. For one thing, the job would mean a lot of traveling. We must have the seed of famous scientists, film stars in California, members of café society in Paris, London, New York, and Nobel Prize winners in Stockholm."

"How much do you reckon this enterprise would cost?"

"Not much. Not much."

"You're probably right. I'll ask my financial manager what he thinks."

"For God's sake, don't mention it to anybody. They could pinch the idea from us."

"Perhaps you're right."

"It'll be first-class. We'll send our discreet elegant brochures to women married to sterile husbands all over the world, and the choice of paternity will be just sublime."

"Let's do it, no question about it."

"Right, we'll talk about it."

The gentlemen came in. How could she get a divorce from Amerigo? In Italy, impossible. In England, without his consent, three years. Mexico, perhaps. Before going to bed, she went to look for him. He seemed to be expecting somebody, but not her.

"What do you want?"

"A brief preliminary talk. Would you give me a divorce, tomorrow?"

"What do you mean—tomorrow?"

"I'll ring my lawyer and we could do it in a hurry."

"But why?"

"I don't know. I'm not fond of you, I suppose."

"What nonsense. Let's go on trying. It would be ridiculous, after only a month. Don't we get on well together?"

He put his arms round her. Suddenly he was kissing her hands and hair.

They made love and forgot about the partridge barbecue on the lake. Melinda also forgot about divorce and pushing Ostrovsky into the lion pit. And while they lay together she thought about Helen's boutique and what a good idea it was.

In the morning she went with Amerigo to see Erikson's apartment. She had heard a lot about the famous round bathroom. It was a small room taken up entirely by the bath, with jets of water coming out from all sides. The tub was of Irish marble and the ceiling was mosaic. You entered by a little velvet-padded door and then went down a couple of steps into the water.

"This stone conceals a telephone; if I press this button I can speak to the servants. And this is for the music," he said, pointing to a little gadget, "but only Elgar and Wagner for me. Even when I'm having a bath."

There was a cupboard full of dressing gowns.

"Do you want to see the bath in my guest room?"

A metal-trimmed mahogany bathtub shaped like a cradle. Here, too, jets of water, controlled by handles, came out from all directions. A shower from above, from right and left, and from below waves of running water.

"Fantastic. It must be nice being your guest, Erikson." Octavian would have ended up there, one day, if he was still alive.

A short note:

Dear Melinda, Eluard and I have left. Eluard had some very important business and didn't give me time even to come and find you. Let me know where you are.

Love,
Medoro.

He had tricked her. That accursed Ostrovsky. He had tricked her wholesale. And he wasn't a gentleman, despite those false names. But she would find out everything for herself, she would go and look for him. She saw it all and knew for certain that she wouldn't be bored for the next few months. And she liked Helen's idea for a boutique.

But now she had to go and see this escaped prisoner. She found him straight away, rather well dressed. He spoke with a Cockney accent.

"Can you tell me what day it is today? Good morning, madam."

"Good morning. How are you? Shall we go for a walk?"

She suddenly felt as if she were taking part in a bad play, having to speak lines written by a second-rate author.

"Is something wrong?" Melinda asked.

"No, no. They got me out of jail a few weeks ago, all very well organized. And I'm loaded with money. But I need to establish an identity here and I need a job for a few months. I'd like you to help me get a job in Mr. Hoover's house."

"I could try."

"That would be fine. Nobody lives in that house for eleven months of the year."

"I could say that you worked for me in London. What can you do?"

"I can serve at table and drive a car."

"Perfect. Where do I get in touch with you?"

"Couldn't you phone straight away?"

Obviously he had nowhere to go.

(The only thing, Melinda thought rapidly, is that if he comes into Hoover's house the man will find out who I am. Well, if there's any trouble, so much the worse for him.) But she took another look and decided he was probably all right. Anyhow he'd said he was loaded with money. Besides, Anthony would never try to make problems for her.

She got on the phone with Hoover and explained that she'd just run into an old chauffeur of hers while she was wandering around; he'd worked for her a while ago (during David) in London, but now he was fed up with the city and wanted some fresh air. A stroke of luck he'd run into her, all the way over here in Ireland. Really a marvelous chauffeur, could do as a waiter as well. Would Hoover be a dear and take him on? "Sure, why not, one more won't sink the boat," said Hoover.

"It's all set," she said. "Just go see the housekeeper. Anybody will tell you how to get there." She didn't offer him a ride and hurried back to Holy Trinity.

She was expecting a call from Mark. It got on Melinda's nerves to have to wait. She didn't like it, but this time it was worth it. And she didn't want Amerigo to hear the name Van Der Belt again. Just to be in Lausanne, in the same room, with a few days to spend together, eating and making excursions, with no worries about wives or husbands. Perhaps it would also mean the end of the Mark myth. All the better. She would take him to Chamonix to see Mont Blanc. She was sure he had never seen it. And they would drink and make love in the afternoon and evening, and perhaps they would hold hands too. She would tell Amerigo she was stopping in Paris to see one of her ex-husbands about children and money. She would have to be careful; Amerigo was jealous.

"Amerigo," she said, giving him her arm while they strolled in the garden, "such a silly thing's turned up and I've got to go to Paris for a couple of days to see a husband or his lawyers. It'll be best if I catch a plane from Belfast tomorrow, or the day after at the latest. You could stay on here for a few days."

He was enthusiastic about the idea.

She rang up and made two bookings, a false one for Paris and a real one for Lausanne.

"Darling," said an express letter from Mark, which arrived after tea, "I'm sitting here in the study telling myself how I adore you and how I'm taken with you. But we can't meet. It's impossible. It wouldn't be fair to Aglaia. You understand me, I know. You're an understanding woman and one doesn't have to spell things out to you. We know each other well enough by now and I know you'll forgive me. You know that I love you but I shan't ever say or write these words again, although we shall meet again soon. Your Mark."

She rang up immediately to cancel both bookings. She would go to Rome instead and prepare to track down Ostrovsky.

"Amerigo, a lot of boring snags have cropped up. The lawyer can't see me, it seems, so it's not worth my while going to Paris. I'll go straight to Rome and then I'd like to go on to New York for a week or ten days."

"I thought I might go back with you. There's no point in my staying." Was he afraid of losing her? Melinda booked two seats on the plane to Rome.

That evening another dinner like the one before. Luckily Helen was there. Otherwise Melinda couldn't have got through it.

Helen was always well dressed, with lace dressing gowns, Ferragamo handbags, and Hermès shoes. And so neat with her gray bangs. She would make an excellent business partner. Melinda could see her already in a white coat, enjoying her role of spermatological expert.

After dinner there was nothing to do: one could only play bridge with the Duchess.

"I play badly."

"You never do anything badly, Melinda," said Erikson.

He had got her all wrong: she did everything, but badly. So

Melinda

she played bridge, more or less, forgetting which cards had been led, who had bid what, who had opened, and forgetting to watch her partner's discards.

"Who opened?"

"Did you open?"

"Me? Impossible—I haven't a card in my hand."

"You mustn't talk in bridge. You've already given a hint."

"But I didn't open."

Helen on the other hand was very good, though she hadn't played in years. Now she was the one who did everything well. Melinda began to love her. Fortunately the game was interrupted. It was a phone call for Melinda. It'll be Anthony, she thought, and took the call in her own room.

It was Mark.

"I can never pronounce your new name when I ring you," was the way the conversation began.

"It's no more difficult than Van Der Belt. Thanks for the express letter."

"So you got it?"

"Otherwise I wouldn't have mentioned it."

"When shall we meet?"

"For the moment, I can't see any chance."

"It was a mistake writing to you. Making you share my problems. Please come."

"Where?"

"To Lausanne."

"But, Mark, it's absolutely impossible. I've changed all my plans and I'm going to Rome tomorrow."

"No, come to Lausanne."

"No. This time it's no. I was even sad and depressed for ten minutes because of you."

"But, Melinda, it's what I want most."

"So much so that if I say yes, I shan't find you at the airport. And anyway, what would I do in Lausanne?"

"What time did that plane arrive—the one you had booked?"

"At eleven o'clock in the morning. It would also have meant a horribly early start for me and that poor chauffeur."

"I shall arrive early in the morning and go straight around to my brother's, and then I'll join you at the Hôtel Genève, where I've booked two rooms in my name."

"And what time would you turn up? No, no, you'd never turn up."

"Ring up and book another room in your name. The number is 56883. Otherwise there could be difficulties with passports."

"Just a minute while I get a pen . . . What was the number?"

"56883, and send ten dollars right away to hold the booking, even if it arrives later. Tell them you're sending it while you're on the phone."

"Listen, I can't come and besides I haven't any cash. And it's too late to go to the bank."

"Don't worry about that."

"And what if you don't come? Me, in Lausanne, with no money . . . No, I wouldn't dream of it. But thanks for the call and the thought."

"Trust me, I beg of you. We'll be together in the evening and then the next day I shall catch a plane back to London and you can go where you like."

"All that for just one day? No, Mark. I've got to go to New York."

"A whole day. I miss you so much and I think about you all the time. Really. You know that's true. Change your ticket."

"All right."

"I want to talk to you for hours."

"You can't. I must start to reorganize my trip and invent some plausible story."

"I know I shouldn't have written you that letter."

"Why did you do it?"

"I promise I'll never do it again."

"If I have occasion to see you again."

"So you're not coming then?"

Melinda

"What about you?"

"Yes, I swear to you. I swear to you."

"It wouldn't surprise me at all if I got there and you didn't turn up."

"Stay in the hotel and wait for me there."

"About what time will you arrive, if you come at all?"

"Stop it now. About three."

"Maybe you'll make a mistake and get off at another airport or go into the wrong room with a stranger and not realize it until the next day."

"If you don't stop it I'll have my own back tomorrow. Come on, look sharp. Change the ticket again. And wake up early tomorrow morning."

"Bye."

"Bye and thanks. Thanks."

Mark's voice. Perhaps it was a huge mistake, but never mind. If he didn't turn up in Lausanne, she would get by. But if Mark hadn't changed his mind by the next day, she would be delighted. It was worth it. She wasn't sure, though, whether it was worth getting up so early in the morning. The plane left at eight o'clock. She would have to be in Belfast by seven. So that meant leaving Holy Trinity at four o'clock in the morning. So that meant she wouldn't go to bed.

She rang up the airline again. She cancelled the booking for Rome and made another one for Lausanne, yes, the first one again, in fact. She was sorry about the muddle. She called the butler. The chauffeur must report at four o'clock in the morning. She asked Amerigo to come up for a moment. She had to go to Paris, after all. She hadn't been able to say no, because it had all been specially arranged and the lawyer was one of those who spend their lives going to and fro across the Atlantic.

Amerigo would come and meet her at Rome airport. "Thanks, darling," she said.

A bit complicated. She would have to study the timetable. She would have to send him a cable from Paris. She would find somebody she could phone to tell him to send the cable . . . God, a real intrigue—what a joy!

At eleven o'clock she was at Lausanne airport. Mark could have surprised her by being there, after all. It was raining and cold. The hotel, fortunately, was the best in Lausanne. From Mark anything could be expected: a hole in some youth hostel, because he mixed up names of hotels which just didn't exist.

"Good morning, madam."

"I'm Mrs. Publishing-Vespucci and I telephoned yesterday from Ireland to book a room."

"Mr. Van Der Belt rang up to cancel that booking. In its place he's booked three rooms in his name. He said he would join you early this afternoon."

She had had a shock when the name Van Der Belt was mentioned. She was never really sure what Mark was going to do.

A room with two single beds, a sitting room, a bathroom; another room with two single beds, another bathroom. What ostentation. Melinda slowly undressed and switched on the radio: there was some nice music. She had a shower and went out. She might as well take a walk. Instead she went to a hairdresser's. She had great difficulty finding one at all, and of course it was wretched. Whatever possessed her to have her hair done in Switzerland?

She fell asleep under the drier. She was tired. She had just enough money to pay for the shampoo and set, not including a tip. She went back to the hotel, studied the timetables, and rang up Jacques to tell him to ring Amerigo and say she would be arriving at two o'clock the following afternoon.

Jacques asked no questions. He was so nice and it was years since they had met.

"When I come to Paris, we must meet. How are you?"

"Well. I've put on a bit of weight."

"Have you a wife?"

"Yes, we've got three children."

"Well done."

As it should be. And she fell asleep.

Melinda

✦

SCENE I   *The stage is divided into five parts, so that the audience can follow what is going on in the room where Mark sleeps, in the bathroom, in the drawing room, in Melinda's bedroom, and in Melinda's bathroom, without the characters being able to see one another. As the curtain goes up, we see:*

MELINDA, *a young woman in her twenties, asleep in her room. She is scantily clad. A semi-transparent flowered petticoat. Footsteps.*

Through the door to the first room come six brown leather suitcases, followed by a porter who shoves them laboriously into a corner.

Then follows:

MARK, *wearing a tweed coat, rather rumpled, and looking as if it had been made twenty years before.*

The actor playing the part of Mark must pay careful attention to his character. For, while he is extremely vague and no longer young, he is gifted with unfailing charm, so that his every gesture, even the most awkward, is backed by an assurance born of having made it thousands of times before (for example, the act of giving a tip). The way Mark moves his eyes must be subtle, yet distinctive enough to tell the audience of the often total lack of attention and vagueness which could be mistaken for bad humor.

MARK (*to the porter*): I never know how much to give, in Switzerland. (*He puts some money in his hand.*)

THE ACTOR PLAYING THE PART OF MARK: No, that line's no good like that. If this Mark is so self-assured, he'll know very well what to give a porter.

THE PRODUCER (*coming in through the bathroom door*): Listen, you keep to the script. Don't you realize Mark's also absentminded? From anybody else that line would mean shyness, but from Mark it's vagueness. It's up to you to get that over. Say it again.

MARK: I never know how much to give in Switzerland.

THE PRODUCER (*reappearing from another door*): No, no, the intonation's completely wrong. And look the porter in the eye . . . Mark's not excusing himself, he's stating something to himself, complaining about Switzerland and about the fact that European countries don't use the pound sterling, they don't speak English, and they don't eat eggs and bacon for breakfast. Try again. Make your entry again.

MARK (*looking at the porter*): I never know how much to give, in Switzerland.

The porter exits.

VOICE OF THE PORTER (*as he exits*): Merci, monsieur.

Mark casts his eye over a bathroom, a little sitting room, another bathroom and finally comes into Melinda's room. In the meantime we have seen Melinda wake slowly out of a sleep which is very deep, unless she is pretending.

MARK: Darling?

Melinda pulls herself painfully out of bed, embraces him, and stretches.

MELINDA: You made it then. What time is it?

MARK: Five o'clock. I'm hungry. Do you want some tea?

MELINDA: No, I've had a whisky sour.

MARK: Your favorite drink.

MELINDA: No, no, I hardly ever have it.

THE ACTOR PLAYING THE PART OF MARK: Take this line—"Your favorite drink." Why should Mark say a banal thing like that at such a tender moment?

THE DIRECTOR (*who has come into the room, where the two are still embracing*): Look, we chose you because you look like the character Mark. Shall we get on with this rehearsal? It's obvious that Mark is being attentive and wants to register with Melinda something that he believes to be true, namely, that he's observed the drinks she has a liking for.

Melinda

(*Turning back to the actress playing Melinda*): Take it again, will you, from the last line.

MELINDA: No, no, I hardly ever have it.

THE PRODUCER: Now you must have a bored, cross expression, like a little girl who's been refused something. And stop hugging him. Never embrace him too enthusiastically.

MELINDA: No, no, I hardly ever have it.

MARK: Let's order a couple immediately. What's in it?

MELINDA: Not too much whisky, and lemon and sugar and a cherry. I don't know what else. Angostura, I think. I like it very much.

MARK (*sitting down on the bed*): Tired?

MELINDA: Not any more. What about you? What have you been doing?

MARK: I went to see my brother.

MELINDA: Don't ask me if I've ever met him.

MARK: But I know perfectly well that you met him one evening. In fact we talked about you. Why did you say that? Don't you like him?

MELINDA: What did the two of you say about me?

MARK: He told me the Prime Minister was going to make you a peer, to spare you some embarrassing election campaigns.

MELINDA: He told me that once in Parliament. But I didn't know if he meant it.

MARK: But would you even want to stand again at the election?

MELINDA: When is it?

MARK: Who's the vague one around here?

MELINDA: Let me ring for the whiskies. Come over here. Do you want to have a bath? Is your brother's place very far?

Melinda, attentive, gets up and goes to turn on the hot water in the bath.

(*On the phone*) Two whisky sours, please, in Room 83, or 84, or 85. By the way, darling (*raising her voice*), all these rooms, how theatrical, but not one double bed. As usual.

MARK (*from the other room, where he is taking off his shoes and socks*): That's not my fault. We're in Switzerland.

MELINDA (*still loudly*): And who is it who chooses these Puritanical countries to meet in?

MARK: Come here this instant.

Melinda comes up to him, still in her semi-transparent petticoat. She looks at Mark, who is now almost completely undressed.

MELINDA: What nice underpants.

MARK: Come close. (*He puts his arms around her again, running his hands through her hair and under her petticoat.*) If you only knew. I missed you. Above all, physically. I didn't sleep well. In fact, I didn't sleep at all, and I was jumpy and irritable all the time.

MELINDA: So that's why you came then. I'm a sort of sexual tranquilizer.

MARK (*musing*): It's almost like that.

He pushes her on to the bed. A noise at the door. It opens onto the room where the two have fallen into the first stage of loving stupor.

THE WAITER (*looking away and pretending not to notice*): Your two whisky sours, madam.

MARK: What sort of tip should I give him? I never know what to do about tips. Especially in Switzerland. Somebody always copes with them for me. What do you do, Melinda?

MELINDA: Women never tip.

MARK: You don't tip.

MELINDA: Not unless it's to buy people.

MARK (*drinking his whisky sour*): Delicious. Excellent idea. Let's order another. What do you want to do this evening?

MELINDA: Let's go for a walk . . . Have some supper. Do you know a good restaurant? I don't know Lausanne at all. There's a good one in the old part of the town, but I don't know what it's called.

MARK: We'll ask the porter.

MELINDA: Anyway, you don't mind what you eat.

MARK: For once you're quite right. It doesn't really matter very much to me. Does it to you?

MELINDA: Very much. It's one of the greatest pleasures in my life.

MARK: And what are the others?

MELINDA (*thoughtful*): The others? You, for the moment . . . and things to do, and, oh God, I must go and switch off the water.

THE ACTOR PLAYING THE PART OF MARK: Look, how do I go on now? I can't strip naked in front of the audience. The censor will cut out this scene anyway, so we might as well cut it ourselves.

THE DIRECTOR (*coming out of the drawing room*): If you do it with a certain delicacy, we won't see a thing. Use a towel and take off your underpants.

THE ACTOR: It's embarrassing.

THE DIRECTOR: Don't be childish. Get on with the scene. It wasn't going badly.

Mark goes into the bathroom, undresses, and gets into the bathtub.

MELINDA: Can I come in?

MARK: Yes, darling.

MELINDA: (*Enters.*) We could take a bath together.

MARK: But haven't you had one already?

MELINDA: That wasn't the idea. My intent was purely erotic.

Again the door. This time the waiter hovers outside.

(*Slipping on Mark's dressing gown*) Come in.

The same waiter appears with two more drinks.

Melinda begins drinking one, then slips a jumper over her petticoat, and looks at her watch. She switches on the radio.

Melinda pulls on a pair of stockings and begins doing her hair and putting on powder and eyeshadow.

The audience will see that in the bathroom Mark has stood up. He is draped in a large towel and now he moves towards Melinda. He puts his arms around her.

You're all wet.

MARK: What are you up to? Why did you get dressed?

MELINDA: Do you want the tranquilizer before the meal or after or both?

MARK: What nonsense you talk.

He pushes her on to the bed. From under the towel come flying nearly all Melinda's clothes.

Don't you ever wear a bra?

MELINDA: It depends. If I feel like it, yes. But I haven't much bosom.

MARK: Soft, delicious. Do you want to make love by yourself, darling?

MELINDA: No. I'd like to kiss your eyes.

MARK: You can't.

Mark's head has disappeared under the bathrobe.

THE ACTOR: This scene's indecent. We really have to change it.

THE DIRECTOR (*angrily coming out from behind a curtain*): Listen, I'm the one who says whether the thing's indecent or not. And it was going well. How dare you keep interrupting. Besides, this is a club: we can put on anything we like.

THE ACTOR: The police will close the club.

THE DIRECTOR: That's for the manager to worry about. Now that's enough. Anyway we're at the end of the scene. Go and take a rest while we change the sets.

"What do you think of this play?"

"I don't know, and I don't care. It pays well."

"I think it's awful. It's unnatural. Who could possibly act like that? Frankly I'm ashamed to prance around naked on the stage and practically make love in front of everybody. Aren't you?"

"Me, no—I'm used to it."

"I know why they chose this play. Do you know why?"

Melinda

"Why?"

"Because it's filthy. And people like seeing filth."

"Oh, I don't think so, you know."

"Anyway, they're two absurd characters. He's too vague and, really now, going all that way to make love to a woman who's not even in love with him and makes fun of him the whole time."

"But he's making fun of her."

"You see? You see? They've no relationship. Two people who meet and have nothing in common and talk about nothing. It's not like that, believe me, in serious plays."

"Maybe. I only play in cabarets."

"I see, striptease and that sort of thing. And me? Why did they ask me? I'm a serious actor, you know, not a cabaret turn."

"But I'm a professional too."

"That's something different, though. We have different goals in our work. Don't you see that?"

"I'm going to change."

"The next scene makes me sick, too!"

"Maybe . . ."

"It's vomit. And to think that for crap like this I gave up a part in that marvelous play by . . ." (*His voice drifts away.*)

SCENE II   *The scene is a typical Swiss mock-chalet restaurant, with mock fireplaces and mock burning logs, broad cartoon-like scenes painted on the walls, cuckoo clocks, spits in profusion, and fondue with kirsch on every table.*
Sitting at the other tables (only a few of which are occupied) are big painted papier-mâché dolls.
The papier-mâché dolls represent the typical moneyed Swiss who go out to dine in the evening. The women are dressed in gold or

sequins and wear heavy shoes from which their big toes poke out, showing their thick nylon stockings. The men wear cheap ties and lots of rings and cuff links which glint in the half light. Candles on the tables.

The table where Mark and Melinda are sitting is, naturally, upstage.

In the restaurant there is also an atrocious orchestra, though it cannot be seen. It plays songs like "When I'm calling you— oo—oo, and you answer to—oo—oo" and "Blue moon, here I am, standing alone, without a dream in my heart, without a love of my own."

Melinda, in a woolen jumper and an extremely short skirt, is visibly annoyed.

Mark, still in tweeds but wearing a green tie, is ordering a second bottle of wine.

MARK: How's it going?

MELINDA: Squalidly.

MARK: Don't be a bore. Is it my fault if the restaurant's only so-so?

MELINDA: Yes, it is. And anyway, it's not so-so, it's downright squalid. Do you mean to say there's nowhere else in the whole of Lausanne?

MARK: Wasn't it good?

MELINDA: What?

MARK: The caviar.

MELINDA: Sure it was good. It's the place that's so horrible. And it's hard not to notice, with that orchestra.

MARK (stopping a waiter and slipping two banknotes into his hand): Tell the orchestra not to play any more, please.

MELINDA: Well done. Those are the tips that count.

Mark puts out his hand. The waiter comes with the wine and in serving spills some on Mark's sleeve.

WAITER: I beg your pardon, sir.

MELINDA: You see, they serve badly too. You ought to give a tip and ask them to sack the waiters, find another cook, pull down the restaurant, and build another one.

MARK: Don't act so spoiled.

MELINDA: But I am.

MARK: Don't you like the wine?

MELINDA: It's excellent. You always pick good wines, since you discovered that the Rothschilds are better than the Van Der Belts.

MARK: I don't like you joking about my family.

MELINDA: But I was joking about you.

MARK: My sister says you're a sweet girl.

MELINDA: That's good of her. So your family talk about me, do they?

MARK: In a way, yes.

MELINDA: You know that everybody knows about us?

MARK (*panic on his face*): Don't be silly. You know that I'd die rather than humiliate Aglaia. She must never know. And who's your husband now? Doesn't he mind?

MELINDA: He's new. And he doesn't know yet. He hasn't had long enough to find out, apart from your name being bandied about on various phones from one country to another.

MARK: Do you know that my sister talked to me about you?

MELINDA: You've just told me.

THE ACTOR: Look. This exchange is absolutely ridiculous. Nobody would ask a question like that after such a short time, unless he was totally stupid. And if Mark is stupid, I refuse to play the part.

THE DIRECTOR (*coming from behind one of the tables, where he was seated, pretending to be a manikin. He rather looks like a Swiss and also a papier-mâché doll at that*): Listen, I applaud your undeniable interest in the lines and the way the play works out. But I won't tolerate these continual interruptions at a dress rehearsal. You should have thought about it first. If you've really got some objections, keep them in mind and tell me at the end of the scene.

THE ACTOR: Sorry. But look, since I've already interrupted. Tell me, don't you agree? This man wouldn't repeat such a question to a woman that he's presumably been making love to only a few minutes before. And then this Melinda ought to be more tender with her man, after making love.

THE DIRECTOR: Who says they've been making love? Before dinner?

THE ACTOR: It's obvious—the curtain comes down on the two of them naked under the bath towel.

THE DIRECTOR: That's the beauty of it. From this scene in the restaurant, an intelligent audience will realize these two haven't made love. Otherwise Melinda wouldn't be so irritable.

THE ACTOR: If I didn't realize it, how do you expect the audience to?

THE DIRECTOR: A good actor never understands anything, dear boy. Where you go wrong is in trying to understand too much. A good actor is a complete idiot.

THE ACTOR: That's not only a personal insult, but an insult to the profession. I demand an apology.

THE DIRECTOR: My apologies, to you and the profession, but not so many interruptions, okay? Let's go on. (*He goes back into his corner.*)

MELINDA: You've just told me.

MARK: She's a strange woman. A mixture of love and anguish. A very sad person. I'm very fond of her. I'm afraid she's like my daughter.

MELINDA (*with no interest*): And what's your daughter like?

MARK: Like my sister.

MELINDA: And I imagine your sister is like your daughter.

MARK: There are some things you don't understand. Your family are so scattered. But fascinating, I must say. How's that Medoro? People have often told me about him. It seems that he's rather handsome but not very interesting. Abraham scares me, but he's an intelligent man. Tell me about Abraham, what he does . . . I'd like to know a bit more about your family life. Mine, deep down, is a failure. You pay dearly for a divorce. Have I ever told you about my first wife?

Melinda

MELINDA: Once or twice. Do you really want me to tell you about my family and Abraham?

MARK: You know, the trouble with my first wife was that she was so stupid. A nice girl, but she didn't understand me and I didn't understand her. Conventional, she was, boring. I got too bored.

MELINDA: And don't you ever get bored with Aglaia?

MARK: Never ask me questions about Aglaia.

MELINDA: I thought you liked talking about your family.

MARK: I don't like it at all.

MELINDA: Well, why do you do it all the time, then?

The waiter arrives with the coffee.

MARK: Did you order coffee? Do you want it?

MELINDA: No, but it doesn't matter. Anyway it'll be lousy.

MARK: Do you know we're arguing and it's not worth it?

MELINDA: I'm not arguing. Darling . . . sorry . . . and I'm so fond of you and I wanted to see you all the time and I missed you so much.

She stretches her hand across the table and this time it is she who is burned by coffee that the waiter spills on her arm.

Now we could take a little walk and go along by the lake and not say it but just think how much we love each other and how lucky we are to be here together, and look at the stars.

MARK: But it's cloudy.

MELINDA (*sighing*): Yes, it is—it is cloudy.

The curtain falls.

"Forgive me if I dwell on this, but are you sure about this play? Who chose it?"

"We chose it together with the backer. And anyway I thought you liked it when you read it the first time."

"Reading it is one thing. But playing it . . . It doesn't hold up."

"But we've already had several rehearsals."

"Not a dress rehearsal, though."

"Anyway, you should have thought about that before. But what is it you find so impossible?"

"The two characters, of course, it's obvious."

"But the characters are fine. Can't you see they're the essence of all of us, that all . . .'"

"You're talking like a director."

"And you're talking like an actor."

"I'd like to know what the author would say if you insulted him with a phrase like 'the characters are the essence of all of us . . .' Those characters are individuals, they stand for a number of people but not everything and everybody."

"You like them, then."

"No. The trouble with these characters is that they have no connection with reality. People like Mark and Melinda don't exist."

"I utterly disagree with you. And the beauty of a play is that everybody sees it in a different way."

"No, no, as a director you should make the rest of us see it in your particular way."

"As a director I want to leave room for the imagination of the actor and the members of the audience. Come on, go and get changed."

"What am I supposed to change into? I'm naked in the next scene."

"You're not—you have pajamas on."

"Well, more or less naked."

"Go and put on your pajamas, then we can all go home early. The electrician's wife's expecting a baby any moment."

"I wonder what that poor chap thinks of this play."

"He says he likes it."

"He says that out of politeness to you."

Melinda

SCENE III   *The same suite of rooms as in* SCENE
ONE. *In the bedroom where we saw Melinda asleep, we now see,
in the same bed, Mark and Melinda. We can see Mark's arm in
the sleeve of some white pajamas, and part of Melinda's body.*
*It must be about six in the morning, because an opaque light
is leaking into the room through the curtained windows, to one
side of the stage.*
Mark's eyes open. He turns over a couple of times in bed.

MARK: Are you asleep?
Melinda turns over with her back to him.
MARK (*louder*): Are you asleep, darling?
MELINDA (*yawning*): I was.
MARK: What time do you think it is?
MELINDA: Early.
MARK: What time's your plane?
MELINDA: Twelve. Amerigo's coming to collect me at two o'clock
at Rome airport. Are you leaving before that or after?
MARK: A little before.
MELINDA: Typical. I shall have to wait alone.
MARK: I didn't arrange it on purpose.
MELINDA: I should hope not. How do you feel?
MARK: Did I snore?
MELINDA: I don't think so. But once I'm asleep I don't hear a
thing.
MARK: My brother snores much louder than I do and he always
protests when I grumble about it.
MELINDA: How's that, do you sleep together?
MARK: No, but it has sometimes happened. Our family demands
absolute perfection and absolute conformity. And, of course,

individually we're not a particularly conformist family. But we always take sides with the law, even if the law's wrong. If there's a divorce, they are on the side of the wife and against the divorce. When my mother had to defend her brother . . .

MELINDA: Let's stay in bed until we leave.

MARK: You weren't listening.

MELINDA: Sorry, darling. But I'm so sleepy.

MARK: Aglaia mustn't know about Lausanne.

MELINDA: I'll write her a letter immediately and recommend the restaurant we went to last night.

MARK: Don't joke about it.

MELINDA: In fact I'll write to the editor of *The Times*. I'll begin "Sir" and sign it "Your obedient servant." Amerigo mustn't have the slightest suspicion either. I sent him a cable from Paris. Or rather, one of my ex-husbands sent it. Can I touch you? I so much want to touch you.

Melinda strokes his face and arms. She kisses his ears. We see Mark's expression change. Delight and joy. He takes off his pajama jacket, which he throws out from under the sheet.

MARK: My only complaint is that you don't touch me enough.

Little by little the room gets brighter. But the daylight is opaque, almost white. Mark and Melinda are making love. This scene is left to the two actors, who must not indulge in exaggerated contortions but project an impression of joy and total abandon. In the distance can be heard the noises of the city: bells ringing, noises in the hotel, doors slamming in the corridors, breakfast trays clinking.

Do you want to make love by yourself?

MELINDA: Just as you like, darling.

MARK: If you do, wait for me.

They kiss again.

THE ACTOR: Listen, excuse me interrupting again . . .

In the semidarkness onstage, a light is switched on.

THE DIRECTOR (*coming out from behind the set, and with a tired, long-suffering note in his voice*): What do you want now?

Melinda

THE ACTOR: Forgive me, but look, at this point I just can't go on.

THE DIRECTOR: Look, I don't care any more. It isn't a long part and we can always find another actor. But anyway, what's wrong this time?

THE ACTOR: You see, I'm ashamed. Because really, if the scene's going to come off well, we shall have to make love properly.

THE DIRECTOR: Well then, do it.

THE ACTOR: How can I, in front of the audience? I mean, getting hold of this young lady like this—really, I'd like to see you . . .

THE DIRECTOR: Think about something else.

THE ACTOR: What, for instance?

THE DIRECTOR: About your children, your wife, something boring, a slice of boiled beef, your debts. How should I know what you find unpleasant to think about?

THE ACTOR: I have no children.

THE DIRECTOR: Then think about the misfortune of not having any.

THE ACTOR: But why is Mark suddenly so interested in making love?

THE DIRECTOR: Because he likes Melinda—very much. He's even vaguely in love with her, taken by her, fascinated by her. How do you see him, honey?

THE ACTRESS: Oh, I don't know. They make love. That's what they both came to the hotel for. It would be stupid of them not to.

THE DIRECTOR: Quite right—a piece of simple feminine reasoning. Let's go on, please. It was going well, it was working, I'd say it was excellent . . . just give me your objections after the rehearsal.

MARK: If you do, wait for me.

More bells, then the house phone rings. Melinda reaches for the phone.

MELINDA: Hello? Yes? Nine o'clock? Thank you. Send up two coffees and some orange juice, please. (*Turning to Mark*) Do you want an egg? (*Mark nods.*) And a fried egg.

Mark puts up two fingers.

Two, please.

Another sign from Mark.

. . . and some sausages. Thank you. Fine. How can you eat all that?

Melinda bends over him, puts her arms around him, takes the pajama jacket, puts it on, and gets out of bed. She goes over to the window and opens the curtains. View of Lausanne under a thick carpet of snow. It is snowing hard.

Melinda stands looking out for a few moments.

Look, darling, it's beautiful.

MARK: It is. It must have been snowing all night.

He puts on a dressing gown, gets out of bed, and goes to look at the view with Melinda.

Snow always makes me feel nostalgic: it reminds me of when I was a child, at home, and the park covered with snow . . .

MELINDA: My God!

She looks at Mark with terror, as if she is thinking of something dreadful.

MARK: What is it, darling?

MELINDA: The planes.

MARK: Let's ring straight down to the porter and the airport. I didn't think of it. Good God! I wonder if we'll be able to leave this morning.

MELINDA: But I absolutely must.

Mark picks up the phone.

MARK: Is that the porter's desk? Yes. The airport's closed? Oh well, I suppose so. You say there's a chance for later on . . . ? What about trains? Can you see whether there's a train to Milan this morning, and one for Paris and London? They're already booked up . . . Have a look will you, I'll pay anything . . . If it has to be this evening, a sleeping car, of course . . . Ring me back as soon as possible.

MELINDA: But I can't wait till this evening. Amerigo's going to collect me today in Rome at two o'clock. And I can't tell him

Melinda

I got snowbound in Lausanne. What would I be doing in Lausanne? It's the one place where I never go.

MARK: Don't worry. Something will turn up. We shall have to keep calm and think of an excuse. You'll get there tomorrow. I don't dislike the idea of staying with you a bit longer.

MELINDA: Yes, and knowing you, you'll find a train for London that's leaving in five minutes, while I shall have one tomorrow night that will be cancelled at the last minute and I'll find myself in Prague.

MARK (*taking her round the waist*): What a baby! Be good now. *Melinda leans her head on Mark's shoulder and looks out of the window at the snow.*

What do you think there is between us?

MELINDA: What do you mean?

MARK: Do you love me? Do you think I love you?

MELINDA: I never think about such things, but if I must, yes, certainly you must be rather fond of me, otherwise you wouldn't have come all this way to meet me . . .

MARK: I really came to Lausanne to see my brother . . .

MELINDA: There you go. You would have to say something like that.

MARK: But it's the truth.

MELINDA: Didn't that famous mother of yours ever teach you that the truth is something one never tells?

MARK: I believe we love each other and we ought to meet more often. More often, and be together like this.

MELINDA: But every time we're supposed to meet, you change your mind.

MARK: It's not true . . . I won't do it any more . . . When am I going to see you again?

MELINDA: I've got to go to New York. I don't know for how long, but I imagine for a couple of weeks.

MARK: What are you going to do in New York again?

MELINDA: I've got business there . . .

MARK: You're so mysterious. I don't really see you as a business woman. Tell me what you do.

MELINDA (*worried*): What do you want me to say . . . family affairs, the stock market—you must have the same sort of things, with all your money.

MARK: Yes, but we have an office that looks after them. From time to time we have to take a hand ourselves, of course. Where are you going to stay?

MELINDA: I was thinking of going back to the Plaza.

MARK: You're going to a hotel? Would you like to have my flat? It's empty. If you like, I'll tell the manager to give you the keys.

MELINDA: Where is it?

MARK: Park Avenue, Sixty-fifth Street.

MELINDA: Sounds perfect. Is it always empty?

MARK: Nearly always. Yes, I know, it's a waste of money. But I detest New York. What would I do in New York?
The phone rings.
What? That's absurd. Are you sure? All right, take those straight away. If there's any other possibility, let me know immediately.

Darling, it's crazy. There are no trains to Paris or to Milan. There's a strike. BEA have got one too. The only thing he's managed to find is a train tonight to Vienna, and two planes tomorrow morning, one to Rome and the other to London. A sleeping car—all quite comfortable. But he says it's been very difficult.

MELINDA: Oh well, never mind, there's nothing for it. It'll mean another divorce for me.
The curtain comes down on Mark and Melinda looking out at the snow, while a waiter has just come in carrying a tray with an enormous breakfast.
As the curtain comes down, the impression in the room is one of disorder and great luxury. The tray is silver and loaded with fruit, eggs, sausages. Melinda's negligee, which we now see in the full light, looks very light and filmy.

Melinda

THE DIRECTOR (*going over to the actor*): Now, let's talk seriously for five minutes. You must make up your mind at once whether you want to back out. I've rung up another actor who's willing to step right in. Of course we should have to have more rehearsals. But remember, you signed a contract and I'll tell you quite bluntly that you could find yourself in trouble.

THE ACTOR: No, no. That last scene went much better. The two characters have come together more now, they're more human.

THE DIRECTOR: I'm not particularly interested in what you think of that last scene. So: do you want to go on or not?

THE ACTOR: All right, all right.

THE DIRECTOR: But get rid of that martyred look. I suppose you know there are plenty of actors who want to work with me?

THE ACTOR: The next scene's the last one, if I'm not mistaken.

THE DIRECTOR: It is. No interruptions, understand?

SCENE IV   A *sleeping car. Night. The blinds are pulled down and on the little table are a bottle of mineral water and one of brandy.*
Mark and Melinda are sitting on the edge of the bed.
Their cases are all on the top bunk.

MELINDA: I enjoyed myself.

MARK: Did you enjoy running around?

MELINDA: There's something Russian about changing trains in the snow. And killing time in a nightclub makes you think of Hemingway.

MARK: Except that in Hemingway all the characters would have accidentally met in the nightclub . . . your husband, my wife, Abraham, my family . . .

MELINDA: Sometimes you do say intelligent things.

MARK: Very kind of you. Sometimes? And all the other times I talk rubbish, I suppose. What do you think of me, Melinda?

MELINDA: Don't ask such questions—I never know what to answer. I imagine that you're better than me and that you're fond of me. And besides I like making love with you.

The ticket inspector comes in.

THE INSPECTOR: Good evening. Tickets, please?

Mark looks in his overcoat pocket, then in his jacket; he gets more and more agitated, till he sees the tickets on the table by the bottles.

MARK: There they are.

THE INSPECTOR: Passports, please. We arrive at seven in the morning. What time do you want to be woken?

MARK: Let's say six.

MELINDA: Half past would do.

Mark and Melinda look for their passports.

THE INSPECTOR: Will you please fill in this form, sir? Your wife needn't do a separate one.

MARK: Well, actually . . .

THE INSPECTOR (*handing another form to Melinda*): Excuse me. In that case you had better fill one in too. What would you like in the morning?

MELINDA: Coffee and orange juice for two.

THE INSPECTOR: We don't serve breakfast. We only have Vichy water.

MARK: Nothing then. We'll breakfast in Vienna.

MELINDA: I haven't been to Vienna for years. The last time was with my father and Medoro, during the Occupation . . . I can remember the changing of the guard between Americans and the Russians. And the little Russian soldiers who didn't want to be photographed, and the operettas and the general squalor. Then I must have been back with Jacques or Lawrence, but I can't remember clearly. I remember we ate at Sacher's in the morning and the afternoon and we went twice to the opera.

THE INSPECTOR: Well, good night, sir, madam, I'll give you a knock at half past six.

MARK: Thank you.

MELINDA: Oh, good night. Thank you.

MARK: I've never been to Vienna. I don't travel much.

MELINDA: Rich as you are, and no work to do? I'd do nothing else, if I were you. Are you really very rich?

MARK: I've more money than I could possibly spend. What about you, are you rich?

MELINDA: Yes, but of course nothing compared to you. Still, I shan't have to do anything for the rest of my life and I can buy whatever I want.

MARK: Does your money come from your ex-husbands?

MELINDA: None of my husbands has ever given me a penny, because I'm always in such a hurry for a divorce . . .

MARK: So how is it you've got so much?

MELINDA (*looking straight at him*): I've made a lot.

MARK: Being a spy . . .

MELINDA: Good for you—how did you . . . ?

MARK: It does annoy me when you joke about things. How did you make your money?

MELINDA: Stealing.

MARK: All right, if you don't want to tell me, I shall have to assume that you were a prostitute.

MELINDA: Think what you like, and while you're thinking, get undressed, because I'm sleepy. I adore sleeping in trains.

MARK: I shan't let you sleep for long. Let's sleep together.

MELINDA: It's not a particularly wide berth, but we can try. I like sleeping with you.

MARK: Would you mind if I were unfaithful to you?

MELINDA: What?

MARK: If I went to bed with another woman.

MELINDA: But I hope you occasionally go to bed with Aglaia.

MARK: Of course, don't be silly. I mean, apart from Aglaia.

MELINDA: No, darling, it wouldn't bother me a bit. As long as you're always a little fond of me and not nasty when you see me. Why, have you another mistress?

MARK: No, of course I haven't. What do you expect, when I feel guilty enough with one. But aren't you really jealous?

MELINDA: I don't think I've ever been jealous. Does that upset you?

MARK: Yes, and heaven knows how many times you've done it.

MELINDA: Done what?

MARK: Been to bed with other men, since we first met. That boy down on the coast, for instance . . .

MELINDA: But you don't consider yourself my one and only official lover, I hope? We hardly ever see each other.

THE ACTRESS (*looking around her*): Director?

THE DIRECTOR: Are you going to interfere too?

THE ACTRESS: Look, these last lines—I mean, no woman would say such things to a man.

THE DIRECTOR: Very few would. And that, I imagine, is what the author is trying to get over: that Melinda is not like other women.

THE ACTRESS: Melinda's just told Mark that you have to tell lies . . .

THE DIRECTOR: Yes, but the rules don't apply to her. And anyway, doesn't it seem natural to you not to have any ties, not to feel jealous? Don't you think that's what this character is all about?

THE ACTRESS: Maybe . . . it's not that I want to criticize, but Melinda doesn't seem much of a character.

THE DIRECTOR: Listen, you've been very good so far. Please, just go on. Now get undressed, but nicely, not like a striptease in a cabaret—something more casual and easy-going.

Melinda quickly undresses and slips on a nightdress. Mark undresses too, taking off his tweed jacket and his waistcoat.

MELINDA: I like the way you dress.

MARK: Really? I like the way you dress.

Melinda

MELINDA: But do you ever notice?

MARK: Certainly.

MELINDA: What was I wearing tonight?

Mark looks round, then sees the clothes Melinda has hung on the wall.

MARK: No, I can't remember, but I noticed.

He gets into the narrow bed and pushes Melinda over to one side. They are both under the bedclothes.

Shall we open the window?

MELINDA: For God's sake, it's cold enough already.

MARK: You won't be cold much longer.

He kisses her hands and neck and dives on to her. The noise of the train gets louder and the curtain comes down.

THE DIRECTOR: Good. I'm very pleased. Tomorrow we'll rehearse the restaurant scene and take the next day off. Monday, we open. (*Moving away, towards the proscenium.*) That's it, then. (*To the actors*) Any problems?

THE ACTRESS: No, no. I just wish my wig weren't quite so thick. My hair keeps getting in my mouth when I speak.

THE DIRECTOR: See the make-up man. And you?

THE ACTOR: Are you sure this is the end?

THE DIRECTOR: Perfectly sure.

THE ACTOR: Isn't there some kind of finale to this comedy?

THE DIRECTOR: For one thing, it isn't a comedy.

THE ACTOR: It wouldn't be a tragedy, would it?

THE DIRECTOR: There's no word for it. But I don't see the need for an ending. The end is its continuity.

THE ACTOR: But there is no continuity: these two make love, they go to Vienna, have breakfast, and then catch planes, one of them to one place, the other to another. Melinda—if I've understood her correctly—will get a divorce and then go to New York. But we don't even know if Mark and Melinda are ever going to meet again.

THE DIRECTOR: That we shall never know. But it isn't important. The two characters are of no importance. It's the situation that matters. And the link between Mark and Melinda is only a pretext for saying other things.

THE ACTOR: But as an onlooker I've taken a liking to these two; I want to know more—about Mark, and about how things end up.

THE DIRECTOR: Perhaps you're right. Perhaps we should carry the novel on.

THE ACTOR: But what novel? We're talking here about the theater.

THE DIRECTOR: Don't worry about it—these things are up to the author.

THE ACTOR: And will the author carry on with the play? Don't we need to have more rehearsals before Monday?

THE DIRECTOR (*thoughtful*): No, no. Don't worry. The novel must go on . . .

The director goes off musing to himself and the actor nods to the actress as if to say that the director is mad.

This time the flight across the Atlantic seemed short and Melinda was pleased to have a flat of her own, instead of going to a hotel.

That phone call to Amerigo from Vienna hadn't been such a brilliant idea, and, thank heaven, they hadn't met in Rome.

She wouldn't forget the night in the train with Mark for a while. But she was through with Mark. The Van Der Belts' flat in New York was lovely, large, and it had two phones.

News had also reached her that she had been created a Baroness in the new Prime Minister's Honors List. Poor Anthony, only a shadow Prime Minister. He wasn't used to it. Perhaps he would have more time to himself now and they would see each other more often.

She had talked on the phone to Helen, who was already in Tangier. She had bought, she told Melinda, a nice boutique-laboratory near the Hotel Minzah and she was preparing a list of various sperms. Melinda would have to look after Slav sperm, because it was in great demand. It was in fashion, and with her Slavic languages she might be able to arrange for possibly a scientist or an astronaut, preferably a Nobel Prize winner. There was quite a demand for McLuhan seed, but for the moment the clients would have to wait.

Melinda had had a hundred thousand dollars transferred from a Swiss bank to one in Morocco in the name of Melinda Vespucci, and another hundred thousand to Tunisia in the name of M. Inchball.

For the moment she must deal with Gambaino III. She rang the office of the Sexyboy Club.

"I'd like to speak to Anthony G. Gambaino III's secretary, please. I'm Baroness Publishing." (It was worth using after all.) "I need to see him rather urgently. This evening, if possible."

Gambaino would take her to a party and then to supper. The secretary stressed that this was a special favor since Mr. Gambaino had had to cancel dinner and an after-dinner engagement in order to see her.

Melinda went out. She had forgotten it was nearly Christmas. The decorations were obscene, overwhelming.

What was the use of Christmas? To send Christmas cards with photos of your children to friends who will only say "poor little things, they're so like their father"? Or photos of country houses to inspire envy or respect? The trouble was that now she had to buy presents for her children. She had never done it before, but decided to make a start. She went into a big store. The heat was oppressive; she took off her baboon coat and looked for the cloakroom. Canned music, so many people, rude sales people. She gave up the idea of buying her children presents.

As she passed a counter she saw a nice handkerchief. Nobody was looking, so she slipped it into her bag along with a handful of other handkerchiefs that she didn't like at all.

Out into the city streets again. Fifth Avenue was the most amusing. New York didn't impress her much because Europe was so Americanized.

The women were decked out like birds, and the windows of the skyscrapers were lit up above her. She stopped in front of Tiffany's. The windows were elegant. She went in and got George Trilling to show her the best jewels. He was the manager, a great friend of Erikson's, elegant, flighty, and a gossip.

"Melinda, what are you doing in New York?"

"I've come to see Tiffany's and you, of course."

"Do you want to buy something?"

"I'd like to see some jewels. This evening I rather want to impress a certain gentleman."

"What sort of gentleman?"

"A vulgar oaf for whom money counts a lot. So I want some big chunky jewelry and not particularly nice."

"If you like, we could lend you a number of pieces—but you'd have to pay the insurance for the evening."

He took her up to the third floor, into a little department full of small glass cases. Inside were enormous necklaces, gigantic pins, great chunky earrings. There was also a ruby ring, particularly well designed, that moved like algae.

"I'll buy this, Trilling. The pin and the necklace I'll just wear this evening. I don't like them."

Melinda

The car that came to collect her did not contain Gambaino III. The chauffeur said that Gambaino sent his apologies and would join her at Mimi Triumph's place. Her apartment was between Fifth Avenue and Madison Avenue, and of course very luxurious. Everything was white—walls, carpets, curtains, leather sofas, tweed armchairs, and hostess.

Melinda went up to her.

"I'm Melinda Publishing, a guest of Mr. Gambaino's. Forgive me for turning up like this, but I hope you were warned I was coming."

"Good for Anthony. He's always bringing me surprises. And now this one! Very pleased to meet you. You're not American, are you? My name's Mimi Triumph. But forget my last name. Call me Mimi. Tell me, what do you do?"

"I'm in politics."

She instinctively lit on the best way to define herself at an American cocktail party.

"But how interesting. Are you a journalist?"

"No, I'm in politics. I was an MP and now I'm in the House of Lords."

"You wouldn't be the one who . . . oh, but what an honor, how marvelous! I thought I'd heard your name . . . And what are you interested in?"

"What do you mean, what am I interested in?"

"Do you like creative arts? I'd like to show you my collection—my husband, you know, paints and collects . . ."

"I see," said Melinda, looking round.

"That's our Miró," said Mimi Triumph, pointing to an obvious Miró, "and that's one of our two Renoirs" (one of the usual

horrible reddish late Renoirs) "and there's our Utrillo" (genuine
or not, it was ugly all the same). "Tell me, do you collect?"

The zenith of conventionality: collecting in America. And the
Impressionists were the zenith of zeniths.

"I have a few pictures in the country. But I haven't really a
house of my own. At least I never live in it."

"What sort of pictures?"

"A Guercino, some Salvator Rosas . . ."

"Who?"

"Salvator Rosa."

"Italian? Modern?"

"Not modern . . ."

Mimi Triumph lost interest.

"What can I give you to drink?"

"A gin and tonic."

It was the only way not to drink too much. Melinda had learned
that. The second glass would contain tonic water with no gin.
Otherwise, if her glass was empty, the hostess would be offended.

"And do you like art?"

She was always tempted to say no to that American-cocktail-
party question. But she pretended not to understand.

"Come over and let me introduce you to some friends."

"Jill, this is Baroness Publishing, a very interesting person. This
is Barbara . . . but there's Anthony . . ."

Gambaino came over and kissed her hand. The gesture was
admired.

"You never do that to me, Anthony," said Mimi, clapping him
on the shoulder.

"Baroness, forgive me for being late. Mimi, have you and the
Baroness met? How are you?"

Anthony G. Gambaino III had a smooth, damp look about him,
though he wasn't helped by the leather and rubber he usually wore.
He disappeared into the next room, greeting people as he went.
Obviously he knew everybody. Melinda had never been to this
sort of gathering, and hadn't met people like this before. She only

knew that in New York social groups never mixed. She went up
to a man who was already half drunk.

"You're beautiful. What's your name?" he asked her. "I've been
looking at you ever since you came in. What do you do? Where
do you come from?"

"Tell me, who's Mimi Triumph?"

"What, you don't know who Mimi Triumph is?"

"No, I haven't the slightest idea."

"Where do you live then?"

"I live in Europe . . ."

"Yes, but I mean to say, even in Europe?"

"But who is she?"

"She's a singer."

"Is she successful?"

"Enormously. What about dinner tonight?"

"I'm going out with Mr. Gambaino."

"I didn't know Gambaino had girl friends."

"That's his affair."

She got talking to a fashion designer. His name was Jasper. He
had black hair.

"What do you do?"

"Where do you come from?"

"Are you interested in . . .?"

The opening questions were always the same. They were regu-
lation. Jasper brought her another drink and got her to give him
her phone number. Melinda wrote his in a notebook.

"I never go to cocktail parties. It wasn't such a bad idea coming
to this one. You have some splendid jewelry . . ."

"Thank you."

"Are they from Tiffany's?"

"Do you recognize them?"

"I recognize the style. Are you very rich?"

"Very. What about you?"

"Not very. But I make a lot. Are you free tomorrow?"

"Yes, I am."

"What would you like to do?"

"Sightseeing. I don't know New York very well."

A fat girl snuggled up to a man who had begun playing the piano. She was extremely drunk and dressed in pink.

"Jasper," she warbled.

Suddenly she fell to the floor and burst into tears.

"Jasper, Jasper, Jasper."

Melinda decided to leave Jasper to the fat girl and joined a conversation between Barbara, another woman, and, presumably, Barbara's husband.

"This year shifts are all the rage."

"I bought one that's gorgeous."

"I remember that blue one you had on the other evening. Where did you buy it?"

"Do you like the pleated one?"

The husband was completely ignored.

"Jasper," the fat drunk girl kept calling out.

"Isn't it so, darling, the pink one, with the embroidery? It's his favorite," she told the woman friend.

"We could leave now," said Melinda, stopping Gambaino as he went by.

"Really? So soon?" Protests from Mimi. "The violinist is going to play now. He's so good—and maybe somebody will sing."

"I hope you'll sing, too, Mimi," said Gambaino.

"I'm tired now. But you will come to the taping of my TV spectacular, won't you?" she said to Melinda. "I'll ask Anthony for your address."

They went out into the evening air. Obviously Gambaino wasn't used to going out in the company of one person, especially a woman.

They went to a restaurant.

"I recommend the Alaska crab," said the headwaiter.

It was enormous and delicious. Gambaino was impressed by Melinda's appetite. She drank some Pouilly Fumé, alone, because Gambaino was a teetotaler.

Melinda

"Do you remember, Gambaino," said Melinda after some vague conversation about England, "the tragic episode that put an end to my career as a Pussy?"

"When those three . . ."

"When Robertapussy threw herself off the parapet and the other two died in the same horrible way, while I was inside. So far as you could, you people at the Sexyboy Club kept the press out of that affair. And now I'd like to have some information from you. Naturally, anything you tell me I shall keep very much to myself."

"What can I tell you?" said Gambaino with a certain surprise, wiping some beads of sweat off his forehead. He sweated all the time: it wasn't a sign of nervous tension.

"Roberta was an ex-Communist and a close friend of Burgess and Maclean. She worked for a foreign power, and the other two girls were both agents too. You people at the Sexyboy know this perfectly well, otherwise—let's be open about this—you wouldn't have helped fabricate a story for the police. And without that help some unpleasant information would have got into the papers. Who were the three Pussies working for? And who paid you, Gambaino?"

"I don't know what you're talking about, Baroness."

"How much do you make, Gambaino?"

"I do all right."

"Yes, that's what I thought, but I'd like to pay the bill this evening because you're really my guest."

"But I wouldn't dream of it, Baroness . . ."

Melinda brought a check for fifty thousand dollars out of her wallet; it bore the name of Anthony G. Gambaino III, but there was no signature.

"This is a very expensive restaurant . . ."

"It is expensive . . ." replied Gambaino, looking at Melinda's jewels. Suddenly he realized they were all genuine.

"Do you know Ostrovsky?" said Melinda.

"Yes."

"Don't worry. I repeat, nobody will know the source of the information you give me. Besides, I'm putting myself on the spot by admitting I was involved. You'll have a weapon which you could use against me. Did you know that the three Pussies were agents?"

"The Pussies came to the Club on the recommendation of Blamonche, and Ostrovsky was working for Blamonche."

Ostrovsky had worked for Blamonche . . . then Melinda, in Corsica, had killed the boss . . .

"All of a sudden there was friction between the two of them," Gambaino went on. "Blamonche was setting something up, because he wanted to transfer the three Pussies to a new Sexyboy Club that we were going to open in Berlin and that he was going to finance. Then Ostrovsky, who had turned against Blamonche, came to us in New York."

"And gave you money?"

"That too. But he also put us on our guard against Blamonche and the three girls. He told us they were dangerous and would have to be eliminated, and that he would see to it, but he asked me kindly to help him out."

"Did you know about me?"

"Only when the scandal broke. Then we understood."

"Who's we? You and who else?"

"Me and Metcalf. Ffeifer knows nothing."

"And you also knew, I suppose, that the girl who was in the Club, and who everybody thought was me, was another girl."

"Certainly. In fact, we found her. Remember that Metcalf was the chief witness."

"And where's Ostrovsky?"

"When he's not with your brother Medoro, traveling round Europe, he's in the country in England, at Enston."

"And it's from there that he operates his network. What *is* his network? Who does he work for?"

"That I don't know. I know that Blamonche was working on his own account, a sort of agency that gave its services to one country or another. Attached to the CIA, perhaps. But I don't think they started anything big. They were planning something big when they quarreled."

"Has Ostrovsky been around lately?"

"No, but we know where he is."

"Where?"

"At his health farm. He practices as an osteopath under the name of Doctor Piotr Dief. And he's got a shiny bald head."

"Is he well disguised?"

"So they tell me. I've never seen him with that make-up."

"In your opinion, Gambaino, does Ostrovsky do it for fun?"

"It's possible. He's certainly got plenty of money."

Melinda knew that the train robbery had made Ostrovsky a very rich man.

"But surely he's rich in his own right, isn't he? He was telling me about a castle in Poland, and I know he has a house in Grenoble and one in London, and then this health farm which must certainly make money . . ."

"Why do you ask me all these things? Who do you work for?"

"For myself, at the moment. Curiosity. Ostrovsky never chose to tell me a thing. And I'm very curious about certain things."

"What do you intend to do?"

"Nothing. I'm pleased I've found out a bit more. Did you know Madame Nubytch?"

"Nubytch? No, no, I don't think so. I've never heard the name."

"I believe I forgot to sign that check, Gambaino."

Anthony G. Gambaino III handed her the check. Melinda signed it.

"Perhaps you'll find it convenient," said Melinda, "to keep that money in a Swiss bank—it'll avoid taxes and other bothers for both of us."

"Excellent idea. Switzerland is my favorite country."

It was easy, thought Melinda as they went out. Not very bright of Ostrovsky to leave so many witnesses wandering around. Or perhaps he had a plan to get rid of Gambaino, Metcalf, and her too.

"Shall we walk a bit?"

It seemed an odd suggestion to Gambaino. They went through Times Square. A man with his shirt off was being thrown out of a cinema by two policemen. The Camel cigarette advertisement sent out puffs of smoke from a gigantic mouth.

"What do you think of Ostrovsky?"

"A strange man for a spy. One of a kind, really." Gambaino was beginning to get scared.

At this point Gambaino became dangerous, Melinda suddenly realized. He could now phone Ostrovsky and get money out of him for the information that Melinda now knew too much. He might begin to understand a great many things, if he started thinking about them, and he probably was thinking. She couldn't try to kill him that night. Too many people had seen them together. "Have you an apartment in New York?" she asked.

"I have a house on the river."

"How nice. Where?"

"On the East River."

"If you invite me, one day I'll come and see you. I just love seeing people's houses." She would have to get a move on, before Gambaino could deposit the check.

"Is this check good?" asked Gambaino, as if Melinda had spoken her thoughts out loud.

"What a question, Mr. Gambaino!"

"What about dinner, the day after tomorrow?"

By then he would have had plenty of time to make sure the check was valid.

"Lovely. The address?"

"452 East Fifty-second Street."

"What time, and who are you going to introduce me to?"

"Come at seven. I'll find some interesting people for you."

They left each other at half past eleven. Anthony G. Gambaino III saw her to her apartment. Melinda rang up Jasper.

"Good evening. What luck finding you at home."

"What shall we do?"

"Go out?"

"Now?"

"Precisely."

"I'll come and pick you up."

Melinda changed into a dress she could move about in, low-heeled shoes, gloves, and the little revolver.

"How nice, your calling me like that. No American girl would have done it."

"I wanted to see you straight away, I couldn't wait till to-morrow."

"Where shall we go? Why have you changed?"

"Let's go somewhere nice."

They went to a nightclub in the Village. People were dancing and there was a group singing.

"It's a sort of Harlem—Harlem as it was when you could still go there."

They danced, a fast dance at first. Then slowly, their arms wound round each other. He wasn't bad, actually, this Jasper.

"Shall we go somewhere else?"

"Don't you like it here?"

"Yes, very much. But I'd like to see something else."

They went somewhere more elegant.

"Hungry?"

They ordered and held hands.

"Jasper. I don't feel very well."

"Do you want to leave?"

"No. Wait for me a minute, I'm going to the loo. Excuse me. Now don't run away." She went to the ladies' room. Fine: it was one of those without an attendant. With a window. Now she had to be very quick. She dropped out the window and a taxi appeared almost as if it had been waiting.

"East Fifty-second Street, please."

It would be the peak of bad luck if Gambaino hadn't got back yet. She told the driver to leave her on the corner of First Avenue.

It was easy to get around at that time of night. Eight minutes. There was somebody coming along the street. It would be too lucky . . . Yes, it was he! She slipped the silencer on to poor Nora's revolver. It pleased her to think that the little object she was clutching had once belonged to that very clever and unfortunate agent. Melinda stopped. Was there anyone else about? Gambaino must have left his car in some garage. She would have to kill him outright so that he wouldn't scream. He was walking fast, coming towards her. She would have to be quick. A few more steps and he would be in range.

Now.

She took aim.

Gambaino III fell, with a bit of noise but without crying out.

Melinda flattened herself against the wall. She had to get back the check. She put on her gloves. She looked up and down the street. Nobody. The check was in his jacket pocket, where Gambaino had put it in the restaurant. She walked away, casually but fast. She hailed a taxi on First Avenue. Fifteen minutes later she was back through the window. She came out looking a bit pale, first having torn up the check; the little pieces were already down in the vast sewers of New York.

"Forgive me. I've been sick. Did I keep you waiting?"

"No. I was a bit worried, that's all. I was just coming to look for you . . . Shall we go?"

"No. I don't know why, but now I feel terrifically hungry. Let's have something to eat." Then they went home together to bed and made love. She couldn't avoid it after her phone call and all that fuss. And in a way she was grateful to him for providing her with an excellent alibi. The phone shrilled at half past six in the morning. Melinda was asleep with one tingling arm under Jasper's heavy back. She had to reach across to pick up the receiver.

"Is that you, darling? Are you in bed alone?"

"Yes, of course, Mark." She signaled to Jasper to keep quiet.

"What have you been doing?"

Melinda

How amusing it would have been to tell him she had killed a man that evening, and not be believed.

"I went to a cocktail party, then I had supper with somebody who was a bit boring, and then I went out with another man who took me to a nightclub."

"When are you coming back?"

She mustn't leave immediately.

"Next week."

"You won't find me if you come to London. I'm going on a trip."

"Where are you going?"

"I don't know. Have you written to me?"

"Not yet."

"Why?"

"I didn't have anything to tell you—and besides, I've only just arrived."

"Do you miss me?"

"Do you miss me?"

"Yes."

"Well then, come to New York straight away."

"What a stupid idea. They'd all know about it."

"I don't care—and anyway, I'm getting a divorce."

"But I'm not."

"Always the same story."

"You want to make me divorce, I suppose?"

"And why not?"

"Don't you want to get married again?"

"No."

"Can I ring you up again?"

"It's your apartment . . ."

"But do you want me to?"

"No."

"Why?"

"Because I want to fall in love."

"Why?"

"Because I want to get married."

"Again?"

"And why not?"

"You've met somebody . . ."

"Lots of people."

"No, I mean somebody who's been making up to you?"

"Yes, sure."

"I suppose you've already had some offers of marriage, or at least of bed."

"Not yet, to tell the truth. But I don't want to marry another American."

"And who do you want to marry?"

"I haven't the slightest idea."

"Will you write to me?"

"Probably."

"I'll ring you later."

"Just as you please."

"Bye."

"Bye."

Jasper was horrified by this conversation.

Melinda didn't talk to Mark again because that same day she took a train to Washington. Kay Kent had invited her to stay. And Melinda didn't leave her phone number behind in New York.

She bought the morning papers at the station but they said nothing about Gambaino. The evening ones gave his death some prominence. If Ostrovsky read it and knew that Melinda had been in New York, he would guess the rest.

       "What's Washington like?" Melinda asked the handsome senator.

"Boring for everybody except politicians. But don't tell anybody here that Washington's boring. You'll only make enemies. And don't say I said so."

Melinda

"I wonder why one has the idea that senators are always old and boring. You're very handsome."

"Really? You think I'm handsome?"

"What goes on in Washington?"

"It's the women who rule. We used to be ruled by the Kennedy dynasty; now it's a bit better, because the White House isn't so important socially any more. But if a woman isn't invited to the White House, she spreads the word that she's gone to Europe or that she's very ill."

"Is Washington that small?"

"Yes, and there aren't any interesting people. Outside of politics."

"What a pity. A sort of mock capital, with no theaters, no literary life."

"You're telling me . . ."

The handsome senator, though, felt duty-bound to make an anti-Communist speech to her. Communism, he said, was the great threat to America. A Communist was a special kind of being, a person to be feared and one who should at no cost be allowed to enter the country. He advised Melinda to visit the FBI building, to see how America defended herself against Communism.

In Washington she was denied the pleasure of walking about, since there was no city. The monument-tombs, the gardens, the embassies and museums were separated from one another by wide avenues stretching away for miles. It seemed to her a city invented at a moment's notice, and even Georgetown, the old and stylish part of the town, was so polished that it seemed false. There was the Negro quarter, very poor, and a mass of little houses. And, of course, there was the White House.

The handsome senator took Melinda to the White House. It turned out to be a rather modest place, with dull pictures on the walls, and a few pleasant-looking objects. And here you could have seen little Caroline playing . . . And this is the rose garden that Mrs. Johnson dedicated to Mrs. Kennedy; it's called the "Jackie Garden" . . .

"But aren't you fed up with the Kennedys?"

The senator was intelligent enough to find the Kennedy myth exaggerated, but he didn't appreciate a question like that from a tourist. After all, Kennedy was to Washington what St. Francis was to Assisi or St. Anthony to Padua.

"If you don't like the White House, come with me. I'll take you on the Canal."

"Which canal?"

"The Georgetown Canal."

They climbed into the black car; a couple of miles, as usual.

"But it's like Europe," complained Melinda after a look at the Canal and the little old-fashioned houses.

"What *can* I show you to please you?"

The senator was handsome, the house was near, and his wife was away. They had a late lunch, basically oysters and clams. Melinda had some difficulty eating, since the senator was squeezing her right hand between his.

"Is it true that you were the girl friend of the ex-Prime Minister?"

"No, it's not true."

"You're right to answer like that. And I'm right not to believe you."

Nobody ever believed the truth; Melinda should have realized that by now.

"He's an interesting man. I met him when he was on a visit to Washington."

"He's an intelligent man. And a dear friend."

"A dear friend?"

"One of those people that I believe I can always count on."

"But, Melinda, do you need to count on people? I'd have thought you were in a position where other people counted on you. If I weren't married, I'd immediately ask you to marry me."

"To tell the truth, I'm looking for a husband right now. But we couldn't get married, you and I. I don't want to live in Washington."

Melinda

"I can't really blame you for that."

They drank coffee in silence. Melinda was looking at the senator's shirt. The little buttons stuck on the collars of American shirts gave her real physical displeasure. If she had noticed them earlier, she wouldn't have gone to bed with the senator.

"All right, then, if it will really amuse you, I'll take you to the FBI."

"I'd love it."

"If people see us together, they'll know we are there for amusement."

"And why else should one go anywhere?"

A big, big, big building. A big, big letter signed by J. Edgar Hoover ". . . in understanding our responsibilities, we think that you, as individuals, will be able to give us important help in combatting crime and Communism."

Some of the departments were fascinating: the fingerprint department, for instance. "If they were placed one on top of the other, they would make a column higher than . . ."

"In fact, they have 176,906,876 at the moment."

"Thank you for the information, Senator."

"Here they analyze blood and body fluids and determine the date, hour, and minute with mathematical precision."

"You've been here before, tell the truth."

"On the second floor, there's the propaganda department: how to defend yourself against Communism."

"Let's have a look. Tell me, is the CIA part of the FBI?"

"Of course not."

On the second floor, there was Stalin, looking treacherous, and Khrushchev, very surly, and a series of photographs and statistics demonstrating that there is no greater curse in this world than Communism. A large iron statue—a clenched fist—symbolized the iron grip of the Soviet regime.

"I won't show you the ground floor."

"Why not?"

"Because it is too ridiculous."

"Let's go there right away."

Bang, bang, bang, at targets shaped like men. Some fell over.

Why had she come to Washington? And why had she gone to bed with the senator, an hour-long gymnastics that had bored her, and why didn't she go straight back to Europe, why didn't she ring up Mark, and Anthony, and Abraham, and why didn't she immediately join Helen to see how things were going, and why didn't she go and see Ostrovsky, and why . . . ? W-H-Y: what a strange word. Who ever could have invented it? Abraham would certainly have offered some pedantic explanation. It came from the Old English, and before that from Sanskrit, and it occurred in Hebrew and Hittite, or so it was thought . . . One could ask many whys. Instead of which, one should never ask oneself why.

Melinda rushed home and changed. Dining at the Russian Embassy that evening.

There were two choices: a simple dress with no jewelry or a baroque dress with immense earrings and elaborate hairdo. Naturally she chose the latter. She didn't particularly enjoy arriving by herself. She wasn't used to it. And she found herself in a big room filled with strange faces.

Obviously a buffet supper, something Melinda hadn't calculated on. Two big tables laid with bread rolls, jars of caviar, salad (not Russian, just ordinary salad, how unenterprising). A glass of vodka was immediately thrust into her hand. She didn't know where to put it, what with her handbag and a cigarette.

She walked over to a lady who looked like an ambassador's wife.

"I'm Melinda Publishing. Thank you so much for your invitation!"

The lady who shook hands with Melinda, but spoke little Russian, had no idea what invitation she was talking about. Of course, she was the wife of an American journalist.

"The trouble is that you look so much alike."

"Who?"

"You Americans and the Russians. I suppose it must be that Germanic look about you. Which one is the Ambassador?"

Melinda

Melinda repeated her little sentence about the invitation. The Ambassador thanked her and politely hinted that he had other things to do, other hands to shake.

A secretary came over.

"Help me, will you please? I don't know a soul."

"Boris Skolnikov."

"What a lovely name."

Rather pleasant face. Tall.

"You are Baroness Publishing."

"How do you know?"

"I arranged for you to be invited."

"And how did you know I was in Washington?"

"It was in the papers."

That wasn't good news. If Ostrovsky kept an eye on the papers, as Melinda suspected he might, he was sure to have understood.

"Tell me, what do you do?"

"First Secretary at the Embassy."

"What does that mean?"

"I do a bit of everything."

"Politics?"

"More or less."

He spoke English very well.

"Where do you come from?"

"From Georgia."

"Tiflis?"

"That's right."

"I've been there."

It was a dull conversation. But with another vodka, perhaps, it might get better.

"Let's go and eat, I'm hungry."

"The food in this room isn't worth it. Wait a little and I'll take you into the other room. It's better in there: real caviar."

"And this?"

"Not top quality. In there it's that greenish color, you know, the really good stuff."

"How long have you been here?"

"Three years."

"Do you like it?"

He didn't want to make any comments about Washington.

"I see, you don't like it. I agree, it's horrid. And do you ever go back to Russia?"

"I was there last week."

"Really? On holiday?"

"Work. I'm always traveling back and forth."

"And what do you do when you are in Moscow? Who do you see there?"

"The government, of course. And the Prime Minister . . ."

"Will you give him my regards when next you see him? We used to be friends. But maybe there's a new one now . . . let's see . . . how many years ago was it? Not all that long, in fact."

"Then there's a different one."

"And what is my friend doing?"

"He lives in a lovely little dacha outside Moscow, very quietly, with his wife. And he still eats a lot."

"And how does he spend his time?"

"He takes it easy. He's no longer young, you know. He's happy when he can cook mushrooms."

"Yes, I remember, we often used to talk about cooking."

"How long are you staying?"

"I think I'll leave tomorrow. I'm so bored here. Besides, I've got things to do."

There were lots of boys and girls in the room dressed in blue jeans, checked shirts, short skirts, and plenty of eye make-up.

"How can people turn up like that at an Embassy?"

"They're the Embassy children. A few months in this country and that's how they dress."

"It's not very pleasant to look at."

"Are you married?"

"Not for the moment. And you?"

"I'm a confirmed bachelor. Did you like Russia?"

"Very much. I shall go back very soon."

"And what do you think of this country?"

"Exactly the same as Russia, but with more money about."

"Seriously?"

"Yes, really. Exactly the same."

"Come and let me introduce you to a few people. Who would you like to meet?"

"I don't know who's here. But I don't want to meet any Americans or journalists."

"That cuts out eighty percent. Do you see that elderly man sitting in the armchair? He's an Albanian scientist. Nobel Prize. Do you want to meet him?"

Immediately. Dash to meet the Nobel Prize winner.

"I'd love to."

She held out a small, much-admired hand towards the large white hand of the Nobel scientist.

"Professor Mirko Sligovitz, Baroness Publishing."

"Why did they give you a Nobel Prize?"

He gave her a broad smile. He reminded her of Stephen Spender. Perhaps he was Stephen Spender and the Nobel Prize business was a joke.

But he replied in halting English.

"Come, come. Sit next to me, I'm so bored. These smart parties are not for me. I'm no longer accustomed to see so many people all together."

"And what do you invent?"

"Rockets that go to the moon."

"What fun. No, but seriously. What do you invent?"

"But it's the absolute truth. Rockets. And the next one we send up I shall name after you."

"Do you know what my name is?"

"No, but you are so beautiful. Your name must be beautiful too."

"It's Melinda. Really? Do you promise? I would love that. And then I'll come and launch it. With a bottle of champagne."

"That might be more difficult."

"Where do you live?"

"Depends. I have a flat in Moscow. And I travel sometimes."

"Where do you go? Do you ever come to London? Will you give me a ring?"

"No. I nearly always travel in the Soviet Union."

Jutting cheekbones and dark-pigmented skin. A bit of Robert Lowell about him as well as Spender. Excellent combination.

"But you don't look Albanian."

"My mother was Polish and my grandfather Russian. The rest of me is Albanian. But tell me something about yourself."

He was enjoying Melinda's company.

"I'm here and I'm bored. But now that I've met you, I'm no longer bored. I really want to see your rocket and I would like to go out with you."

"That would be a bit difficult for me. I don't speak English well and I'm only here for a few days. I've never been out alone in Washington."

"Where do you sleep?"

What a stroke of luck it would have been for Helen. Albanian-Polish-Russian scientist. Nobel Prize. The lot.

"At the Embassy, of course."

"Let's leave now."

"That would be an insult to the Ambassador. He was kind enough to invite us."

"All right, admit it, they don't let you go out alone."

"That's not true. But it would be simpler if we met somewhere else."

"Where?"

"Kharkov, for example."

"But that's such a long way to go. No, I can't. Why don't you come to Tangier with me?"

"Tangier? What for?"

"We'd be together. Then you could go back to Moscow."

Melinda

He was not the kind who would take her to bed. It wouldn't even have crossed his mind.

Too late. A group of deferential admirers were coming up to him.

"Professor Sligovitz. Please give me your address, then. I will come to see you there. Without fail."

They exchanged pieces of paper. Melinda had another vodka and decided to go to bed, even if it meant sleeping alone. She was happy enough just to have spoken with Mirko Sligovitz.

She had no idea how important that meeting was going to be for her.

Calf-length garbardine skirt, a flowery flannel shirt; under the shirt, a vast bosom pressing against a woolen undershirt, big cork-soled shoes, brown hair parted down the middle and gathered severely at the nape of her neck, a shabby watch on her wrist, gold rings in her ears, very thick silk stockings, shoulders a little rounded, and a stiff way of walking with violent movements of the arms.

The glasses were a little annoying because they pressed down on her ears.

She had tried out various disguises. This was the most plausible and the easiest to do. But she would have to move fast. The reason for the disguise was to play the part of Olivia MacIntyre, thirtyish, kidney stones, secretary in an insurance office in Charlotte Street, Edinburgh, with only one week to be cured in the famous Villa Felix Health Farm, owner Piotr Dief. She had made the reservation several weeks in advance, writing on Scottish Widows' Assurance Society stationery. In London she had not got in touch with anybody, not even Anthony or Abraham. Mark, of course, she would never see again. She had made up her mind about that after Lausanne. He had never suited her for one thing, and besides, he would never have married her. It was a waste of time. She had sincerely decided to devote herself to Helen's great project and to make a great deal of money and meet lots of new people. She would find a new man, less desirable than Mark because more attainable, but certainly more satisfying.

Melinda arrived in Enston by train and then she took a taxi. She carried a little white plastic suitcase and a shiny leather beige handbag. She had amused herself shopping in Oxford Street for an absolutely atrocious wardrobe: coffee-colored evening shoes and shiny satin blouses. In the daytime she would have to look like Olivia MacIntyre (horrid cotton printed skirts and heavy blouses) who presented herself every morning at the Scottish Widows' office. She had practiced long and hard in front of mirrors, trying on various disguises, pulling her skin about and talking with a slight Scottish accent. And now here she was.

The drive was long and gloomy, bordered by pines and rhododendron bushes now out of bloom. Then the great edifice of Villa Felix. This was where Ostrovsky lived: a red Victorian manor with red turrets.

From the elaborate portico an attendant came and took her luggage. Melinda paid the taxi and gave the driver such a tiny tip that he showed his disappointment. It was part of Olivia's character to be unsure of herself. With a shaky hand, she put six more pennies into the outstretched hand of the fuming driver.

"Mrs. or Miss?" asked the attendant at the reception desk. Olivia would have to blush.

"Miss," replied Melinda, hoping she was blushing violently.

"I suppose you're new, aren't you?"

In a voice that was scarcely a whisper, Melinda said, "It's the first time I've been here, if that's what you mean."

"The specialist nurse will take you round the health farm and will show you the daily routine. Villa Felix, as you know, is the best of its kind anywhere. I congratulate you on your choice, even though," he added, "I see you are only staying a week. That's not really long enough. I hope you realize that. It's a terribly short time."

"I have to be back at the office."

The attendant had a yellow face, not at all healthy-looking.

"You've got liver trouble, haven't you?" he asked her.

"Yes," Melinda tried to remember whether, in her letter, she had mentioned kidney stones or something else.

"As I expect you know, we believe in fasting as the cure for all disturbances and many illnesses. Some people come here to slim down, others just to convalesce. Among our clients we have actors, businessmen, professors, office workers like yourself . . . but not many, to tell the truth. You all live together for a time. I want to emphasize again that a week is a ridiculously short period for a satisfactory cure." The attendant looked Melinda up and down. "We should be obliged if you would pay a deposit. Shall we say forty pounds?"

Obviously the attendant had his doubts about Olivia Mac-Intyre's financial means. "It's expensive, but it's worth it," he went on. "You'll soon feel the benefits. Now just a moment while I call the nurse, Miss Alice."

He rang the bell and a nurse with her hair gathered up under a little white cap led her through a series of rooms. There wasn't a soul about. Little furniture and a great many television sets. They went out back of the building on to a lawn where a number of patients were enjoying the damp.

"Each patient has his own little chalet in the park. In the central building we have lounges, dining rooms, and, of course, equipment and treatment rooms."

Nurse Alice took Melinda into a minuscule one-room house. Melinda recognized her own luggage, which had been placed on the only chair.

"If you're cold you can use this heater. You have to put a coin in."

She caught Melinda's eyes looking desperately round for a second door.

"No, there's no bathroom. The clients go to the main building of Villa Felix, which is well equipped with them."

"And what about the morning?"

"Don't worry, everybody goes about in dressing gowns. Follow me, please." Melinda followed Nurse Alice, taking care to walk awkwardly. She had to concentrate on the part she was playing. But where was Ostrovsky?

"This is the park. There's croquet, if you like, and you can go for walks. But generally patients are too weak and spend their days sleeping. You'll see for yourself, when you start dieting you'll feel very tired."

A wonderful discovery, making people starve themselves, sleep in little huts, and charging them a lot of money for it, thought Melinda. Ostrovsky must be making a fortune out of it.

"All the food you eat at Villa Felix we grow ourselves, and we don't use chemical fertilizers. There's a kitchen garden, an orchard, and we have poultry and some cows."

"But then one really doesn't diet . . ."

"Oh yes, you have to diet; sometimes you eat nothing at all, other times you have a meal of one grapefruit or one orange."

"Is the grapefruit locally grown too?"

"Of course not," said Nurse Alice crossly.

"And the oranges?"

"No." She surveyed Melinda irritably. Olivia MacIntyre lowered her eyes.

"But in that case, who eats the stuff that grows here?"

"The visitors, we nurses, and the doctors. And our patients, too. After dieting for two weeks, they have to get used to normal food again before they go home, with a graduated diet of salad and tomatoes."

"Are those grown here?"

"Certainly. The routine is simple. You get up at half past seven. At eight o'clock, you're in the clinic for treatment, which varies, of course. Massage, cold baths, hot baths, cold-hot baths, high-pressure showers, osteopathic therapy, Turkish baths, facial

Melinda

massages, electric ovens, muscular treatment, group gymnastics. The doctor, who will examine you later, will decide on your treatment and the diet you'll have to follow. What is your complaint?"

"Me? I don't complain at all."

"I mean, why did you come here?"

Once again the joy of being able to tell the truth . . .

"Liver." (Or was it the kidneys?)

"I imagine you'll be put on a purgative diet and some bath treatment."

"And osteopathic treatment?"

"Not for liver trouble."

"But I've got muscular pains too."

"You might have told me sooner. Anyway, to go on: at 11:30 treatment ends and you go and freshen up. Then, at midday, there is the one meal of the day for those who are allowed to eat it. The others, those who cannot eat anything at all, drink just one glass of water. Our clients normally talk among themselves and towards one o'clock they go off to rest. Sleep is essential at our farm. In the afternoon, clients are free and can go to the village or to the cinema. But that's something we don't advise. There are many temptations and few patients manage to resist a glass of beer or a chocolate bar."

"And how do the clients go out?"

"They nearly all have their own cars, of course. If you'll follow me, I'll take you to the doctor who will examine you."

They went back to the main building; the curtains were dark red chintz with big flowers; the fitted carpet was also red—and there were flowers, as well as the television sets, and clocks everywhere. There wasn't a soul to be seen.

"They're all downstairs, having treatment," explained Nurse Alice.

"Downstairs?"

"In the cellars, which have been converted and fitted out as treatment rooms. We've got about forty patients. You were lucky to get a place. People book up even a year in advance."

"Really?"

"Who told you about Villa Felix?"

"I read about it somewhere in a newspaper. And it's just what I wanted: a rest, a good flushing out, strict diet and sleep."

"You'll see what a difference it makes. Even your skin will change," said Miss Alice, passing her hand over her own spotty face. Then she said, "Wait a moment."

She left Melinda in a large room with light coming in dimly through a single window looking on to the park. What if the doctor who was going to examine her discovered that her liver— or kidneys, for that matter—were perfectly sound? And would he notice the padding on her bosom and bottom? Besides which her stockings were lined inside with rubber and made her legs resemble shapeless sausages. She mustn't let herself be examined.

Alice came back.

"This way, please."

How many times a day did Miss Alice utter those words? What a dull job hers must be. They went down the stairs, towards the cellars. Steam and the noise of voices, machines and water. Through half-open doors Melinda saw Lazarus-like bodies wrapped in sheets, and nurses that all looked alike busying themselves over semi-naked bodies. A phantom passed near Melinda, hair hidden under the white towel, face streaked with sweat.

"That woman," said Miss Alice in a confidential tone, "is the famous stage star, Odette Redburn."

"Really?" said Melinda eagerly. Though Melinda had never heard the name before, Olivia would certainly have seen the woman on some provincial stage, and anyway she would have tut-tutted at her picture in some woman's magazine.

Alice knocked at a door and went in without waiting.

"Doctor, here's the new patient."

Alice walked out of the room without saying so much as good-bye. Olivia wasn't the sort of client to hand out fat tips at the end of her stay.

Pleased that she had made the right impression, Melinda

Melinda

whispered a very nervous "Good morning, I'm very pleased to meet you, doctor."

"MacIntyre?"

"That's right."

"First name?"

"Olivia."

"Age?"

"Thirty-two."

"Married?"

She lowered her eyes and pulled her legs together. "No— Miss . . ."

"What is your trouble?"

"My liver, kidneys, and some muscular pains."

"What sort of pains?"

"I think it's arthritis."

"Go behind that screen and get undressed."

Melinda didn't move: she went on looking down at her feet in terror.

"I asked you, Miss MacIntyre . . ."

"Doctor, I'm not used to undressing in front of a man . . ."

"You must have been to other doctors in your life . . ."

"They examined me with my clothes on."

The doctor rolled his eyes to the ceiling.

"Lie down, then."

Melinda lay on the white couch.

"What sort of trouble do you get from your liver?"

"Indigestion and bad breath. It's not serious, you know, doctor. But I know that here at Villa Felix rather than cure illnesses you ward them off before they come."

"Exactly."

The doctor took a pencil and began scribbling on a form.

"And the arthritis?"

"Well, muscular pains . . . when there's a change in the weather, so it's nearly all the time. You see, I work in an office, bending over my desk all the time. In my back . . . and sharp pains in my neck, and when it rains they come down into my back . . ."

"For this sort of thing we have the best osteopaths in the world."

The best osteopaths? Was there more than one? She must have Ostrovsky.

"Which one is the very best?"

"Our director is also an osteopath. He's the best of all, but he takes on very few patients and he charges considerably more than the others."

"What's his name?"

"Dief. But I would advise you, Miss MacIntyre, to choose one of the others. They don't cost so much, and in any case Doctor Dief is already very busy."

"If you don't mind, I'd rather have treatment from Doctor Dief. After all, I'm not staying long and I want to make sure I have the best."

"You'll have to pay in advance."

They were still fooled by her appearance. The disguise was working.

"All right, I'll give you a check."

"You will begin your treatment tomorrow morning. In the meantime here is your form and schedule. You can have a more or less normal meal today—a steak."

"But I don't want just a steak—I want potatoes, rice pudding . . ."

"I warn you that that is the only piece of meat you'll see at Villa Felix throughout your stay. From tomorrow you'll be on a diet. Two glasses of water a day and half a grapefruit. After the third day you'll have an apple instead of grapefruit. Every morning you will take a cold-hot bath, excellent for the liver . . ."

"What's a cold-hot bath?"

"The body in a bath of hot water and the feet in a tub of ice-cold water."

"Is it really good for you?" Such an anxious little voice . . .

"Certainly, miss, and I hope you'll trust us—otherwise it's useless your coming here."

Where the devil did this doctor come from? Perhaps he was an escaped convict, a delinquent, or a respectable little doctor

Melinda

who knew nothing about Ostrovsky and believed blindly in the effectiveness of Villa Felix. Maybe even Ostrovsky believed in it. A strict diet, fresh food grown without chemical fertilizers, no alcohol . . . Melinda wondered what the other guest-patients were like . . .

"I would advise you," said the doctor, "to pass the time till lunch unpacking your cases. A bell will ring for lunch. You can go for a walk or read these brochures—" he thrust a pound of printed paper into her hand, "—so you can get an idea of our rules and our beliefs. As you'll see, our clients are very nice people, with whom you might even strike up some lasting friendships."

Melinda's mouth moved in a faint smile.

"Cases where people met at Villa Felix and struck up warm friendships which even led to marriage," said the doctor, looking her in the face, "are not so rare."

What was really needed here was a vivid blush. But she couldn't manage it. She only managed to suppress a giggle.

Melinda bade the doctor a deferential goodbye and walked back across the damp grass to her chalet. She had some difficulty finding it. There were dozens of them, all identical. Luckily the form the doctor had given her had the chalet number (24) on it as well as a helpful list of Miss MacIntyre's complaints. She didn't change her clothes. She hid away her secret gadgets—poor Nora's revolver, a knife—in the suitcase with a false bottom. Then, afraid that they might take away her luggage, she cut open a bath sponge and pushed the revolver into the porous substance. She took a stroll in the park while waiting for the bell to ring for lunch. "Our treatments are based on biological principles, as in osteopathic and naturalistic philosophy . . . regeneration of the tissues . . . health of body and mind . . . dietetic, vitamin therapy, biochemical, hydrotherapeutic . . ." Ostrovsky described his principles with absurd terminology. Who could believe it?

Dong-dong-dong-dong-dong.

What a racket. Anything but a rest clinic. The cows jumped up and Melinda ran towards the main building.

The dining room, which looked on to the garden, was particularly grim and squalid. Waitress-nurses walked round with miserable trays containing half a piece of fruit and a pale glass of fountain water. Several little tables; groups of hungry patients sat round making scant conversation, others ate alone, ravenously swallowing down even the grapefruit seeds.

Melinda went and sat at a little table away from the rest. She was the only patient not wearing a dressing gown.

A waitress came up to her.

"You have to go up to the counter and turn in your form; you'll find a tray all ready for you."

Melinda stood up.

"My name's Olivia MacIntyre—I'm new," she said, handing over the form the doctor had given her after the examination.

"Please take table number 17."

Near the veranda, covered with a plastic tablecloth. The savory-smelling, triumphant arrival of the tray containing the steak. Suddenly, envy, hungry eyes everywhere on her.

She didn't dare look up. She would have laughed, and Olivia MacIntyre would never have dared do that.

She plunged her fork into the steak and cut into a juicy corner. She brought the fork up to her mouth.

Dozens of eyes traveled with that fork and reached her face.

Melinda raised her eyes. Slowly she looked round the dining room. It was locked in tense silence; there was only the sound of spoons against grapefruit skins now scraped bare and white. A table with two elderly gentlemen in slippers. A group of ageless women with weight problems. Several people sitting alone. A woman with a plastic hearing aid. Two others in curlers. A group of pathetic-looking souls who must have been on the starvation diet for several days, judging by the great dark circles round their eyes. A young man of about thirty with an old woman. Mark sitting alone at a table. Mark? Yes, no doubt about it! Definitely Mark and he was staring with a somewhat bored and distracted expression at her steak. He hadn't recognized her. He doesn't recognize me at all, thought Melinda, looking at him stupefied.

What was Mark doing at Villa Felix? Imagine Ostrovsky's ecstasy at seeing him arrive. Mark at the health farm . . . would he make things easier for her? Probably not. Mark's presence never made anything easier.

Melinda finished off the steak and got up. She walked past Mark, who was gazing miserably at his empty plate. Then he firmly picked up a newspaper and opened it, but without reading. Melinda walked by him again and this time deliberately dropped her handbag. Mark, of course, didn't stir. Melinda didn't move.

Certainly, Olivia MacIntyre would immediately have bent awkwardly to pick up the handbag and been embarrassed at having drawn unnecessary attention to herself. But this time she had to forget about Miss MacIntyre and behave like Melinda.

At last Mark's eyes focused on her with a sort of puzzled curiosity.

"Haven't we met before? You're a nanny with . . ."

What a temptation to say yes, they had indeed met before . . .

"I was waiting," she said, putting a slight Scottish lilt into her voice, "for you to pick up my handbag."

"Forgive me, I was reading. I didn't realize."

He bent laboriously down. He was tired and obviously hadn't eaten anything solid for days. He seemed older than usual. He picked up the little plastic bag almost with horror. Mark was accustomed only to touching beautiful things. Now he was going to start reading again, really reading this time.

"Could I sit down? I've only just arrived and I don't know anybody. Have you been here long?"

Mark made a little gesture that said neither yes nor no and Melinda sat down.

"Six days. Six days too long. I don't think I can stand it another week."

"Are you an actor?" Melinda asked shyly.

"No."

"I thought I'd seen your face before. Perhaps on television . . ."

"Unlikely."

"Perhaps you're a politician . . ." (She mustn't go too far, though.) "I think I've seen you on the news with a lady colleague. Could that be? I always watch television, you know, and when I go back to the office . . ."

He looked very distressed.

"Really? Were we filmed together? Were we on long?"

"I think so, otherwise I wouldn't remember your face so well. Don't you enjoy being a famous personality that people recognize?"

Mark looked at her for the first time. Not pleased at what he saw, he withdrew his eyes and gazed at the fleshless grapefruit peel.

"Mmmmmm."

"My name's Miss MacIntyre."

"I'm afraid it doesn't ring a bell with me." How rude.

"In fact it isn't meant to; it was an attempt at introducing myself. And you—what's your name?"

"Van Der Belt."

"One of the famous Van Der Belts?"

He was annoyed, but thinking about it later he would be pleased.

"Now you're a nanny with . . . ?"

"No, I'm a secretary."

"Why are you here?"

"Liver trouble. And you?"

"But isn't this place too expensive for you?"

"I gave up my summer holiday for it. I usually go on an organized tour, you know, to Tossa del Mar on the Costa Brava. It's such a lovely place, so picturesque. Spain . . . do you know it? But this year I decided to spend the money on my health. One's health is such a precious thing. Don't you think?" How well she managed the part of Olivia MacIntyre. And with Mark it was really a pleasure. Under those lowered eyelashes, Mark Van Der Belt despised her. Despised this lower-middle-class girl who had to earn money and hadn't even learned to spend it well. She was a nobody, there were thousands of Olivia MacIntyres in England, just that Mark had only seen them—and never had to speak to them.

"This is all a lot of nonsense, you know. I come here to slim down. But a month after I've left this torture chamber I'm back exactly the same as before."

"So why do you come then?"

"Out of habit. But this is the last time . . ." How Mark had changed.

"You wouldn't have a cigarette, by any chance?" A mischievous look, a sheepish smile, as if they were doing something sinful.

"You can't smoke here. Let's go out in the garden."

Mark was staying with her out of boredom and politeness. He went out first. Melinda followed him, looking awkward and embarrassed.

"Are you married?" she asked shyly, sucking the cigarette Mark had given her and holding it between two stiff fingers, almost as if she considered the act worldly and terribly wicked.

"Yes."

It wasn't easy. The conversation was forced to breaking point. Had Mark thought about her recently?

"Have you any children?"

"Yes, I have."

"What's new in the papers?"

"Nothing special. The usual rubbish. The papers get more boring every day."

Melinda had spotted some headlines about wars in Asia, revolutions in Africa, elections in Europe . . . Anyway.

"Really? Do you think so? But how interesting to hear that from you, Mr. Van Der Belt. I don't read the papers much, either. In fact, I don't read them at all. Do you read books?"

"When I come to these infernal places I bring some with me, but I'm so tired dieting all the time that after a few days I can't concentrate any more."

"Perhaps you could lend me one or two of your books . . . I'm sure you choose interesting ones . . ." How handsome Mark looked when he was embarrassed and bored. "Or maybe I could go into town and buy a few. What's the name of the nearest town?"

"Tring. And Enston."

"How long does it take to walk there?"

"Three hours."

The wretch. Not even offering to take her.

"Have you a car, Mr. Van Der Belt?"

"No. The best thing to do is call a taxi if you want to go to town. I'm going to have a nap now," Mark announced. He stood up.

"Who's your osteopath?" She wasn't letting him off that easily.

"I think it's Doctor Dief."

"He's mine too."

Of course. She would have sworn he would be. How Ostrovsky must be enjoying himself.

Mark was staying in chalet number 42. Melinda went back to hers to try to plan something, although Mark's presence at Villa Felix, there was no doubt about it, had muddled and amused her enormously.

She took a knife and cut the rubber padding around her legs, to make a place for the little revolver. Best not to leave it in the chalet, after all. At five o'clock she went over to Mark's chalet.

"Mr. Van Der Belt?"

He had gone into Tring without her. He wasn't there: Mark was running away from Olivia MacIntyre (as well as Melinda). She would have to hurry things along as fast as possible. She would die of boredom, otherwise, and of malnutrition.

The evening came on slowly. There were the television sets but, of course, no supper. Melinda walked from one to another; everybody was looking at the little flickering streaky screens, some managed to play cards at the same time, yawning and lolling at the tables. No sign of Mark; he just wasn't there. Chalet number 24: Melinda changed—a dressing gown over her naked body, off with the wig, oh her lovely hair tumbling down on to her shoulders. Nothing on her feet.

Melinda

CHALET NO. 42:

Knock   knock

Louder:

Knock   knock

"Who's there?"

Atto Primo	Act I
Scena Prima	*Scene I*
Notte. In fondo al palcoscenico si scorge lo chalet di Mark. All' alzarsi del sipario si vedrà Olivia MacIntyre avanzare nella penombra inciampando tra gli sterpi e bussare alla porta. Dopo breve indugio, odesi la voce di Mark che dice "Entra." Stupore sul volto di lui: i due si allanciano in amoroso abbraccio. "Non lo deve sapere nessuno. . ." dice lei in un sussurro. Mark si inginocchia davanti a lei e le prende le mani. "Grazie, grazie per avermi cercato." Stupore sul volto di lei, questa volta.	Night. Upstage, Mark's chalet. As the curtain rises we see Olivia Mac-Intyre advance, tripping through the gorse, and knock at the door. After a brief delay we hear Mark's voice: "Come in." Surprise on his face; the two throw themselves into an amorous embrace. "No one must know . . ." she says in a whisper. Mark kneels before her and clasps her hands: (*spoken*) "Thank you, thank you for coming to me." Surprise on her face this time.
I due si abbracciano di nuovo.	The two embrace again.
Che istanti. . . che momenti. . .	A memorable moment.
Dal podio, il direttore d'orchestra fa segno ai violini di attacare. Dolcemente i corni si uniscono agli archi.	From the podium, the conductor indicates the entrance of the violins. Softly the winds join the strings.

No. 1. *Recitativo*	No. 1. *Recitative*
MARK	MARK
Amor, dopo giorni di dieta e di noia dopo giorni d'arance e insalata ecco, alfino io ti ho ritrovata la mia gioia confine non ha.	My love, after days of diet and boredom, After days of oranges and salad, Here, at last, I have found you again. My joy has no bounds.

MELINDA
Finalmente ti ritrovo
vita mia. . .

MELINDA
At last I have found you again,
My life . . .

No. 2. Duetto

MELINDA, MARK
(andante con moto)
Mai piú, mai piú
ci lascerem.
Uniti sempre
sempre starem.
Che sorga bufera
Che sorga tempesta
la fiamma, ch'è vera,
d'amor resterà.

MELINDA
La fiamma, ch'è vera,
d'amor resterà.

MARK
Che sorga bufera
Che sorga tempesta
La fiamma, ch'è vera,
d'amor resterà.

No. 2. Duet

MELINDA, MARK
(andante con moto)
Never more, never more
Will we part.
Ever united
Forever we'll be.
Let blizzards blow;
Let tempests rage;
The flame, which is true,
Of our love will prevail.

MELINDA
The flame, which is true,
Of our love will prevail.

MARK
Let blizzards blow;
Let tempests rage;
The flame, which is true,
Of our love will prevail.

No. 3. Recitativo

MELINDA
Chiudi la porte a chiave
ché temo l'imprevisto
amor, mia vita, insisto,
mai piú ti lascerò.

MARK
Come tu voi, mia vita.
Stendi le membra tua
che Citerea ti diè.
(Slaccia la cintura della vestaglia
di Melinda)

No. 3 Recitative

MELINDA
Lock the door.
I fear the unforeseen.
My love, my life, I repeat:
Nevermore will I leave you.

MARK
Whatever you wish, my life.
Extend to me the limbs
Which Cytherea gave to you.
(Unties the belt of Melinda's
dressing gown)

No. 4 Aria

MARK
(andante)
L'amore che ha serto
di luce divina
la vita, che prima,
di torto riempí.

MELINDA
Di torto riempí.
MELINDA, MARK (assieme)
Di torto riempí.

No. 4. Aria

MARK
(andante)
Love has engarlanded
With light divine
My life, which before
Was filléd with gloom.

MELINDA
Filléd with gloom.
MELINDA, MARK (together)
Filléd with gloom.

Melinda

MARK
Vieni dunque.
Ti voglio sposare
e, amore, lasciare
la sposa che ognora
diletto non è.

MELINDA
Fuggire con teco!
Ovunque verria!
Gioisco, che pria
piangevo quaggiú.

MARK
Lasciar la consorte!
O sorte mia ria!
Piuttosto la morte
che perderti ancor!

No. 5. Duetto

MELINDA, MARK
(allegro con moto)
Doman ce ne andremo
lontani e soletti
paesi vedremo
che mai scorderem.
Amor ritrovato
affetto premiato
la gioia, il mio petto,
non può contener.

MELINDA
Ma pria, mio diletto
chiederti desio
il favor ch'ho nel petto.
Sparir da qui degg'io
domani mattina
da sola e meschina
a Tanger men vo.
Seguirmi tu devi,
la sposa lasciare,
oh! fonti di chiare
giornate sarà. . .
Sarà il tuo desio
di essermi accanto
non piú questo pianto
asciugare drovò.
Al tocco dimane,
Olivia sarà
partita, per mai piú,
mai piú ritornar.
Melinda ti aspetta
novella consorte

MARK
Come with me then.
I wish to marry you
And, my love, leave
The wife who no longer
Is my delight.

MELINDA
Flee with you!
Wherever you go!
I now rejoice, where before
I lamented here below.

MARK
Leave my wife!
O wicked fate!
Yet I would die
Rather than lose you!

No. 5. Duet

MELINDA, MARK
(allegro con moto)
Tomorrow will we leave.
Afar and alone will we go.
We will see countries
That we'll never forget.
Our love refound,
Our love rewarded,
My joy by my heart
Can never be bound.

MELINDA
Ere we go, my treasure,
I must ask you
The favor I have in my breast.
Flee here I must
Tomorrow in the morn;
Alone, miserable me,
I must off to Tangier.
You must follow me
And leave your wife.
Ah! there will be freshets
Of clear days before us . . .
It will be your desire
To be at my side.
Never again these tears
Will I have to dry.
At dawn tomorrow
Olivia will be
Gone forever,
Nevermore to return.
Melinda awaits you,
Your new wife to be.

oh! gioia! La sorte
benigna ci fu.

Ah! Joy! Fate
Has been kind to us.

Scena Seconda
  Fuori dallo chalet si sentono
voci, poi urla. L'orchestra attacca
il motivo de L'Incantesimo del
fuoco.

Scene II
  Outside the chalet are heard
voices, then shouts. The orchestra
plays The Enchantment of Fire
theme.

No. 6. *Coro*
(allegro molto)
Orror, orror.
Piú sorte non v'è!
Il fuoco bruciò,
bruciò lo chalet.
La povera giovane
che dentro abitava
a cener ridotta
dev'esser di già.

No. 6. *Chorus*
(allegro molto)
Horror, horror.
Worse could not be!
The fire has burned,
Has burned the chalet.
The poor young girl
Who livéd within
To ashes reduced
Must already be.

Scena Terza
  No. 7. *Recitativo ed aria*
MELINDA *(da una parte, mentre*
Mark è sulla porta dello chalet ed
ascolta il coro)
(andante con moto)
Han tentato di ammazzarmi,
me meschina, quale orror,
e col fuoco dilaniarmi
qual terror, qual terror.
Forse fu quel sciagurato
quell'Ostrovsky disgraziato
che alla mia vita attentò.
Forse fu, per mia disdetta
un'accesa sigaretta
che la foga dell'amore
obliare pria mi fe'.
Forse fu la sigaretta
forse fu quell'attentato
oh! qual caso sciagurato
domattina me ne andrò.

Scene III
  No. 7. *Recitative and aria*
MELINDA *(to one side, while Mark*
stands at the door listening to
the chorus)
(slowly with animation)
Someone has tried to kill me,
Poor me, how horrible,
And with fire tear me in pieces.
What terror, what terror.
Perhaps it was that scoundrel,
That wicked Ostrovsky,
Who tried to take my life away.
Perhaps it was, by my neglect,
A lit cigarette
Which the fire of my love
Before made me forget.
Perhaps it was a cigarette,
Perhaps it was an attempt:
Ah: Whatever caused the misfortune,
Tomorrow at dawn I shall go.

No 8. *Cabaletta*
(vivace con brio)
MELINDA
Ma l'ora mi aspetta
di grave vendetta.
l'Ostrovsky meschino
la fine vedrá.
Il braccio mio puro

No. 8. *Cabaletta*
(vivace con brio)
MELINDA
But the hour now awaits me
Of weighty vendetta.
Wicked Ostrovsky
His end will see.
This arm so pure

Melinda

deh! aita Signore!	—Come, God, give it strength!
punisca l'onore	Avenge my honor
offeso, sí. Sí!	Offended, without fail!
L'amor conquistato.	My love is conquered;
Novella vittoria!	A novel victory!
mi copra di gloria	It covers me with glory
e di fedeltà.	And with faithfulness.
Quell'esser reietto	That outcast being
sí, pria di perire	Will, before he dies,
svelarmi i segreti	Reveal to me his secrets.
dovrà, sí, dovrà.	He must, yes, he must.

Melinda si avvolge nella vestaglia che si gonfia di vento ed uscendo nella notte ululante, il capo eretto e le braccia conserte, ripete:
Dovrà, sí, dovrà.

Melinda wraps herself in her dressing gown, which flaps in the wind, and, exiting into the howling night, head erect and arms folded, repeats:
He must, yes, he must!

Da lontano si sente il coro che ripete:
CORO
La povera giovane
che dentro abitava
a cener ridotta
dev'esser di già.

From afar the chorus repeats:
CHORUS
The poor young girl
Who livéd within
To ashes reduced
Must already be.

MARK *(mentre canta il coro, da un lato, ripete):*
Lasciar la consorte!
O sorte mia ria!
Ma tosto la morte
che perderti ancor!

MARK *(at the same time, to one side, repeats):*
Leave my wife!
O wicked fate!
Yet I would die
Rather than lose you!

L'orchestra chiude con tre squilli di tromba mentre, dal proscenio, si sente di nuovo la voce di Melinda:
MELINDA
Vendetta, vendetta.

The orchestra closes with three trumpet notes while from offstage we hear Melinda:
MELINDA
Revenge, revenge!

Melinda had not realized that she would have to enter the bath nude. Her legs were too thin, and the wig was crooked. She had left the revolver in the wardrobe, and almost all of her Olivia clothes had been burned in the fire the night before.

The bath was agony. Boiling hot, and her feet were immersed in a bucket of icicles so sharp that Melinda had to be careful where she put them.

Had it been an attempt on her life? Had it been an accident? Surely it was an accident. Ostrovsky had not seen her yet and he couldn't have discovered her disguise in a matter of hours.

"Miss MacIntyre, would you like to put on your robe and follow me?" Miss Alice asked, handing her the robe.

"Should I dry?"

"You have to go to the Turkish bath for a few minutes. It's part of the treatment."

The wig . . . the wig . . . would it survive? Dief came towards her through the Stygian fumes. She would have recognized him anywhere in spite of his bald head and the mustache so carelessly glued under his nose. Only Mark was unobservant enough to have failed to recognize in Dief the Ostrovsky of the ball and the waiter in Venice.

"Miss MacIntyre, I am Piotr Dief."

What a relief. He hadn't recognized her. "A pleasure." She extended her hand uncertainly.

"I see from your chart that you are to be treated by me. Won't you step into my office? You ought to be just about ready."

Her head and shoulders bent, her step hesitant, Melinda entered Ostrovsky's office.

"How old are you?"

What had she said before? She couldn't remember. She'd have to be more careful about details.

"Thirty-one." (She hoped she guessed right.)

"Married?"

"No, single. I thought you had already asked these questions."

Piotr Dief smiled and came near. He touched her shoulder.

"Is the pain here?"

"No."

"Where?"

"Lower, I think."

"What, you think?"

"It's gone now."

"And just when do you have this pain?"

"When it rains."

"But in this country it rains all the time. My dear, in the first place, Olivia MacIntyre, plain little secretary in an Edinburgh office, does not come here unless she really does have excruciating pain. Furthermore, she doesn't let someone else pick up her bag, nor does she spend the night with Mark Van Der Belt, nor does she give false answers, nor does she mix up her ailments, nor does she wear a wig. You see, in the last analysis, Olivia MacIntyre wouldn't come here at all. It would be ruinously expensive for her. So many mistakes in such a short time, my dear Melinda. But a clever thought, nevertheless."

"Dear Ostrovsky. I knew you'd recognize me. Do you mind if I take off this ghastly wig?" She peeled the adhesive anchor from her forehead.

"What do you want of me, Melinda, and how did you find me?"

"A long time ago you mentioned a certain Dief in a rest home, an osteopath."

"I didn't tell you that I was Dief."

"Anthony told me you had a rest home in the vicinity—you remember the Melinda affair?—and I guessed."

"Don't play the fox with me, Melinda. In any case did you come for me or for Mark?"

"If I were foxy, I'd say I came to see you, Ostrovsky . . ."

"So you came for Van Der Belt. I couldn't believe my eyes when I saw him arrive. He usually spends a couple of weeks in a rival clinic. But what do you want of him?"

"I'd like to marry him, as usual. And we've decided to do just that."

"You made it, then."

"Don't be rude."

"What do you say, Miss MacIntyre?"

"Did you set fire to the chalet?"

"Yes, but I knew you were in Mark's chalet. I had you followed."

"Why then?"

"To warn you not to do anything foolish . . ."

"It cost you a chalet, that warning . . ."

"They're cardboard. And now you've lost that little pistol . . ."

"You even had my luggage searched. When did you realize I wasn't Miss MacIntyre?"

"When I saw Van Der Belt I knew you couldn't be far behind. I knew you'd come when I read of the death of the unfortunate Gambaino. And that letter from little Miss MacIntyre. Really! Secretaries don't come here. You must try to be better informed."

"But do you read all the letters that come?"

"Generally we know everyone who comes here, or they appear in the *Daily Express* gossip columns."

"Although I've got what I came for, I would, as you can imagine, like some information."

"And what did you come for?"

"Mark."

"Of course. And what information?"

"You know."

"I beg you, dear Melinda, don't push me. Forgive my impatient words. But remember that I am behaving so well only because you are Medoro's sister. Otherwise you'd have been in that chalet last night."

"You're a bastard—and a crook."

Melinda went out of the room as if she were going away. When she came back in, she had recovered her revolver.

"Here I am again."

"And just as curious."

"Just as curious," Melinda said, pointing the gun at Ostrovsky. "I have one, too."

"But not as handy. And not with a silencer, I'll bet. This was your friend Nora's. You, Piotr Dief, couldn't shoot a client in your own office. You wouldn't get away with it this time. And just think, now you have all that money, your little rest home,

Medoro, all's right with the world. Why risk prison or being killed by me? I'd get away with it. Only you know my true identity."

"And Van Der Belt."

"Mark is terribly vague. He wouldn't put two and two together. In any case, he'll be my husband."

"Leave Mark alone. He's a quiet sort. Don't ruin him."

"Just listen to the moralist. The Save Mark campaign is a new line for you. Listen, Ostrovsky, I'll be getting my things and disappearing this very morning. I'm going to Tangier. What you tell me is between the two of us. Blamonche was the chief . . . but of what?"

"What a bore you are!"

"Of what?" pushing the gun against Ostrovsky's chest. "Of what organization?"

"Of a partnership we founded together."

"What kind of a partnership?"

"A limited partnership. Blamonche and I shared the stock, though he had more than I did. I was not controlled by a major power. We were getting the wrinkles out so that we could offer our services at a very high price. We had to demonstrate our efficiency with a series of brilliantly accomplished missions and be able to offer a staff of first-class agents."

"And I was one of the agents?"

"You and Anthony, Nora, the Pussies, Madame Nubytch. Agents recruited from various strata of society."

"And then what happened?"

"Blamonche thought he could set up for himself and began looking for clients among the richer nations. I disagreed with him. As I was trying to stop Blamonche's approaches through our most trusted agents, I discovered that Blamonche intended to eliminate me. Some of the agents I had recruited, including the Pussies and Madame Nubytch, were already in touch with foreign emissaries and I had been cut out of the picture."

"How did you find out?"

"Madame Nubytch told me."

"That's why Blamonche killed her."

"Precisely."

"And why didn't you want to start some genuine espionage?"

"I didn't think the organization was ready yet. I told Blamonche we ought to wait. We had a violent fight and Blamonche ordered several people to get rid of me. I bought Gambaino, Metcalf, and, above all, you, Melinda—I approached you first—with Blamonche's money. I guess we rather divided up the agents."

"And you didn't need money any more with the clinic . . ."

"The rest home doesn't begin to cover the extravagances of my life, but, thanks to you, the money from the train robbery will provide for my future. I began to realize that the partnership with Blamonche was dangerous and that there were, after all, other ways of getting money. But all that interested Blamonche, who certainly didn't need money, was the idea of running an international espionage ring."

"So you had no further interest in the experiment, and that's how you used me?"

"Used you? How?"

"You had me kill Blamonche because he was serious about spying."

"We weren't ready yet. We weren't ready to get underway. We didn't have enough agents, and they weren't fully trained. Anyway, it was impossible to discuss things with Blamonche. Even Millefiori knew he wanted to kill me."

"Was Millefiori an agent too?"

"No, a friend. As you are, I hope, Melinda."

"Why should I be your friend? You made me kill Blamonche . . . you made me lose my one chance to be a real spy. And all this time wasted for nothing. Fool that I was, I thought I was working for a major power. You've made a fool of me, Ostrovsky, do you realize that?"

"You mean you are sorry that you were only playing at being a spy?"

"Don't you understand this is the greatest humiliation you

could have given me? I felt important, mysterious. I was influencing the deeds of several prime ministers . . . and instead, it was all a joke."

"But all the spies in the world are only play acting. You're an intelligent girl, you ought to know that. By now there are no secrets left, and spies survive only by spying on one another. The profession survives only because there are so many spies around the world. But no secrets, believe me, Melinda. You were as real a spy as all the others."

"No, I wasn't. You said I was working for a major power and it was all a joke."

"Pull yourself together, Baroness . . ."

Ostrovsky was frightened. He realized he had made a mistake in telling Melinda the truth. He had hurt her.

"I had a certain feeling for you, Ostrovsky, and respect as well. And when you penetrated my disguise, I liked you even more. Now I hate you. I wouldn't have dreamed of killing you before, but now I must. I simply can't forgive you." Ostrovsky looked out the window.

"Mark might see . . ."

A second. Melinda had turned and Ostrovsky kicked her wrist. The gun was on the floor, and her wrist was sore.

"Rat."

"My dear Baroness, you have placed me in an extremely awkward position. What will I do with you?" Ostrovsky wondered as he clutched the small revolver.

"You tell me."

"You're an enemy. You hate me because I didn't put you to work as a spy for the Chinese, or the Armenians, or the Belgians. If you hate me, you're dangerous. You killed the Pussies, Gambaino, Nora maybe, you might kill me too."

Melinda stepped back. Ostrovsky had a gun in his hand, pointed at her. Ostrovsky . . . might . . . now . . . Quick, out the door, into the Turkish bath. She heard Ostrovsky after her. The bucket . . . a sharp icicle, pointed as a rapier, sharp as a knife . . . In the

Turkish bath . . . there in the fumes . . . running back towards him.
She felt Ostrovsky's flesh yield to the frozen blade. And Ostrovsky's
hands on the weapon that was already dripping from the heat of
his body into a puddle of blood and ice water.

"Damn you . . . damn you, Melinda."

It was a very strange case indeed: Piotr Dief, director
of the Villa Felix Health Farm, found stabbed to death. Of the
scimitar, knife, sword, or whatever it was, no trace at all.

The police had looked everywhere. The only clue: a lady's wig.
the fact that Dief himself wore a wig and false mustache gave
the newspapers a field day for speculation, while Scotland Yard
began its investigation.

The police discovered that one of the guests—a certain Olivia
MacIntyre—had hastily left the Villa Felix the very day of the
crime. But there was no Olivia MacIntyre employed by the Scottish Widows' Assurance Society of Edinburgh.

A boring investigation . . . Mark, who had intended to go to
the country at once to discuss divorce with Aglaia (he couldn't
just write or telephone, he decided), had to stay. He was questioned at length.

Had he spoken to Miss MacIntyre? One of the nurses claimed
she had seen Miss MacIntyre enter Mr. Van Der Belt's chalet the
night before. Did he know anything of Miss MacIntyre's relationship with Doctor Dief? Embarrassing. The least Melinda could
have done was not to leave right after this revolting business. She
probably left without hearing anything about it . . .

Melinda

The dining car was half empty. Mark had taken the first train he could. One had to admit it, England was changing. These things wouldn't have happened before the war. One goes to a luxury rest home, pays for privacy, for some peace of mind, and one's name appears in all the papers.

There was a smell of cooking fat in the dining car, the smell of England. Mark was not very hungry. He was finishing his second bottle of Bordeaux, while the roast beef, cold and untouched, lay on the plate.

"Stilton?" the waiter asked.

Mark ordered a brandy. He was worried. He should have had word from Melinda. How else could he join her? And how could he begin to tell Aglaia? They talked so rarely . . . how could he come round to it . . . a walk . . . at dinner . . . No, they always had guests to dinner, and if they didn't have guests there were servants all over the place.

Wasn't it a mistake to marry Melinda? After all, Mark was over fifty . . . And could Melinda have been satisfied in the country, playing hostess, organizing weekends with amusing guests? Melinda was so full of life, had so many interests . . . She would never bore him. Of that he was sure. But Aglaia? Had she ever bored him? Actually, no.

Why had he decided to leave her then?

Mark finished his brandy and realized that he was drunk. He was sure of one thing: he hadn't the courage to talk to Aglaia.

The chauffeur was waiting at the station. He greeted Mark respectfully and took his bags. That kind of life . . . the organization that was indispensable to the success of a marriage.

"What a bore, darling," Aglaia embraced him. "You couldn't

have had worse luck. Those awful clinics and that doctor murdered . . ."

"Don't even speak of it. It was an awful nuisance. I hope no one is coming for the weekend."

"You told me to ask some friends. Actually, it's a full house."

"You could have sent them away."

"How was I to know that in the clinic you chose an osteopath was going to be murdered? Darling, they're all friends, Fiona and Edward with their leopard. The evening, you can't imagine. The servants are petrified . . . but the leopard is gorgeous. James is here, and Robert and his wife . . ."

"I'm tired now. Is there post for me?"

"There was a telegram from Melinda. Urgent. From Tangier. 'Expect you Tuesday. Book flight and wire.'"

Three days to tell Aglaia. No, less. Saturday was almost over. A tea and a dinner to finish that day. Sunday would be the papers, and Monday, alone with Aglaia . . . He looked at her sweet face, the clear skin. She was so dependent, Aglaia . . . those bright eyes so full of promises, and that voice, so musical and warm . . . She didn't have that young and innocent air of Melinda's nor that look of the eternal child-woman, but she was vulnerable.

Mark didn't answer Melinda's cable. He waited till Sunday.

"Shall we take the leopard for a walk?"

"Fiona'd better come, or he'll eat me alive," Edward said.

"He doesn't like Edward," James explained.

"He's called Lily, because we thought he was a she."

"But isn't he dangerous?"

"Once he bit a butler's leg."

"They can't keep servants," Robert explained. "They flee in terror."

"He bit the gardener too."

"That's not so. Lily only bites my husband."

Sunday at lunch they were twenty-three. Mark loved to see his table full of guests. He liked rapid, intelligent conversation.

The butler whispered in Mark's ear.

Melinda

"A gentleman to see you, sir."

"Tell him to wait."

"He says he can't. He says it's an urgent matter." Mark got up, vaguely excusing himself.

It was Anthony.

"Come in and have lunch. What a pleasure to see you. But why didn't you give your name? Aglaia will be livid. Come along, we're only on the second course."

"I can only stay a minute, and I've got to talk to you very seriously. Listen carefully."

"What is it?"

"First of all, tell no one that I've been here."

"Why?"

"Say that it was the gardener or some bloody nuisance . . ."

"Why?"

"Frankly, I don't want to be compromised."

"Compromised?"

"Mark. I know you're innocent. But the police suspect you. I shouldn't tell you this. Imagine the trouble I would be in if it ever came out that *I* had told you. The police suspect you of Piotr Dief's murder, a man you had already met before. But when the police questioned you, you said you'd never met him."

"Dief? They're mad. And when could I have met him?"

"At a ball in Paris, it seems, the night you first met Melinda. And again in Venice. The police are trying to get evidence against you. They think the motive was jealousy. And if they succeed in discovering anything about you and Melinda, or find your letters, that could be enough. I'm telling you all this, Mark, because I know you're innocent."

"I don't understand."

"I suppose you were seen with this Olivia who disappeared right after the crime. Olivia's chalet burned down that night. All very suspicious. I know that the Scottish secretary and Melinda are one and the same person, and so does the police . . ."

"And how do you know that, Anthony?"

"It's obvious. In any case, we all know about you and Melinda."

"What should I do?"

"If I were you, I'd disappear for a while. If you don't, there will be the most fearful scandal. You may be able to prove that you didn't murder Ostrovsky . . ."

"Who?"

"Don't you know that your osteopath's real name was Ostrovsky and not Dief?"

"How could I know that? He always said his name was Dief . . ."

"Your affair with Melinda would come out, in every detail, and that will also put Melinda in a dicy position."

"Must I leave?"

"If I were you, I'd leave at once."

"Where?"

"Abroad. Remember, Mark, not a word of this . . . And tell Melinda, if you see her in Tangier, to keep out of England for a long time . . ."

He took his hand with a certain warmth, conscious of the fact that he had done a good turn both to Melinda and to Mark.

What did Anthony know? . . . "Tell Melinda, if you see her in Tangier" . . . he knew a lot. Obviously there was no choice but to get out and leave Aglaia.

The police? Olivia? He still didn't understand. To see Melinda in a few hours? What effect did that have on him? He was happy. But the idea of leaving Aglaia didn't suit him at all.

She came out of the dining room, and he took her by the arm, leading her towards the garden. The last time they would take that walk . . . Mark talked vaguely about the trees that would have to be planted before summer. He put an arm around his wife's warm shoulders. He had already told the butler to pack his bags and his secretary to book a flight for Tangier.

"My dear Aglaia . . . one day you'll understand . . . or perhaps I ought to tell you myself . . ."

The swallows in the air, the blue woods in the distance, the hawthorns.

Melinda

"We must get a divorce and I must leave you. I'm leaving this afternoon. They're packing my bags. I'll telephone as soon as I get there. You can talk to the lawyers. I haven't time."

"Mark, it isn't because of Melinda . . ."

Even Aglaia knew. How was it possible?

"It's all rather complicated. I'll explain as soon as I can. I really wish I didn't have to go. I really wish I didn't."

Beneath the wall covered with wistaria, Fiona, all unawares, was bathing the leopard in the pool.

"Mark, Aglaia, come and see how happy Lily is."

Not an unpleasant flight. Melinda hadn't announced her arrival to Helen. She wanted to surprise her and to see how her money was being spent.

She avoided the papers. She did not want to read descriptions of Ostrovsky or theories about his murder. She was sorry he was dead. She was sorrier that he had ever lived to make a fool of her that way.

Tangier, a nasty little city, had the advantage of its climate and beaches on both the Mediterranean and the Atlantic, which, from Cape Spartel, went on for miles, dune after dune.

Melinda would look for a house on the Straits of Gibraltar and then send for the children. For a while she would have to keep away from England, and she must surround Mark with luxury, distractions, and love. What sort of pastimes could be found for Mark in Tangier, she couldn't even imagine. Melinda, though, would have her hands full if she was to be of any help to Helen.

The door to the clinic was small, discreet, and very elegant in carved wood. A brass bell and a shiny name plate: Mitchell–Publishing. Melinda rang. An Arab servant in livery opened the door and led her to a salon. Black and white Morocco carpets, black leather armchairs, white marble tables. A Gio Pomodoro statue suggested why the client had been brought to that room.

"May I help you?"

"Mrs. Mitchell, please."

"Your name, please?"

"Publishing."

"Have you an appointment?"

"No."

"She's busy at the moment. Would you have a mint tea while you wait?"

Splendid. Good work, Helen. How cleverly she had used her colors. No suggestion of infancy or mewling babies. A marvelous cross between clinic and drawing room.

She heard voices. Helen had finished with her client. There must be a second exit so that there would be the utmost privacy for the consultations.

A few minutes later, wearing a smock probably designed by Bohan and with her hair drawn behind her ears, Helen appeared in the doorway.

"Not to let me know! And no one to meet you at the airport!" She hugged her. She was glad to see her.

"It's marvelous, Helen. You're a genius. Let me see it all. Have you got clients? Are we making money? Everything is splendid—discretion, service, furnishings, colors, brass, leather."

Helen took her to see the laboratory.

"We even have a lady M.D. to give tone and professional seriousness to the place. She measures temperatures and blood pressure, checks the analyses and everything."

The lady M.D. was Swedish and greeted Melinda with icy cordiality.

"This is the consulting room."

A cozy atmosphere, various chairs, a sofa, a desk, Picasso lithographs, Piranesi engravings. Elegant banalities.

"Here we have to break through the client's embarrassment. She'll usually tell you right away that her husband is sterile, but when we get to the sperm catalogue, which is why she came to Tangier, after all, she goes all timid. You've got to get her talking about the theater, films, her tastes. If she is a sports fan, you very tactfully suggest an Olympic high-jump champion or a marksman. If it turns out in conversation that she loves the films, you delicately suggest, or even wait for it to pop into her mind, that her offspring might grow up with the blood of a famous actor. But the conversation is always chaste."

"And where do the clients sleep?"

"There are five rooms upstairs. But we're already full, and some of them have to stay at a hotel. They usually stay for a couple of weeks for treatment and to be sure they're pregnant. The sperm is kept in test tubes in a refrigerated room. But we've got to increase our stock. As I told you before, there is a great demand for Slav blood. The woman who was just here was asking for it."

"Can't you fake it?"

"Absolutely not. We'd get a terrible reputation. If they pay for Nobel Prize and we give them Belgian sperm, you can be sure the results won't be the same. We've got to see to it that the customer is always satisfied."

"And what if a Nobel Prize or an actor produces a Mongoloid or an imbecile?"

"We're insured."

"What about twins?"

"Our clients sign a document exonerating us from that kind of responsibility. But it's not a bad idea to find out if the men we select have twins in the family or red-headed relatives. No one likes red hair."

"Why is that?"

"It casts doubt on paternity."

"Where do you live?"

"I have a house by the sea. You can stay with me, if you like. I've lots of room."

"I'm being joined by my future husband."

"He can stay, too. Meanwhile I'll help you find a house. If you don't mind my asking, who is he?"

"Mark Van Der Belt."

"Good for you. At last. And you intend to live here?"

"For now."

"Listen, though, you'll have to leave at once to get me some Soviet sperm. This new client is rich and wants it."

"You mean to tell me that now that I'm here, I have to leave at once?"

"If you get organized, you can be back in a couple of days. Is your Russian visa still good?"

"I'll have to go to the consulate."

"Do you have someone in mind?"

"Mirko Sligovitz."

"The Nobel scientist? Perfect. How long will you need?"

"A week, I'd say."

"Where is Sligovitz?"

"Moscow."

"Do you think you can telephone?"

"I don't see why not."

"You could leave tomorrow."

"All right. But if Mark arrives, would you tell him to wait for me in Tangier? It won't make him happy not to find me here . . ."

"Those are the risks he must run if he really wants to marry you. What an idea, Melinda, getting married again. I thought you'd had enough."

"And you and Abraham? I thought you'd end up marrying."

"You know as well as I do that Abraham will never marry."

"I suppose you're right. But if we make a lot of money, just watch, he'll grab you up or ask for a partnership."

"I don't think so. After all, I've enough money, and Dame Elisabeth is loaded . . ."

That evening they dined in the Casbah. It was a bit got-up, the Tangier Casbah, but amusing all the same. In fact, the only reason one could go there alone at night was that it was a watered-down Casbah. To one side, the villa of an American heiress, to the other that of an English queer. And the people in the club were of the same kind.

"The food's quite good, you'll see."

Helen already knew several people. A Moroccan painter (queer), an English interior decorator (queer), and an American teenager (queer).

Leaning against piles of pillows, they had to wait for the end of the Dance of the Seven Veils as performed by a young Moroccan before ordering. The boy slowly uncovered himself to the sound of four prehistoric instruments whose monotonous assonances gave Melinda a headache.

"I've never had a weakness for Arabs," Melinda announced to Helen.

"You'll see, they grow on you. The music, too."

"Never. This Salome with painted eyes. He doesn't even make it funny."

"If he clowned around with the veils, the British wouldn't get excited any more and they'd stop coming and then the food would be awful."

Chicken with nuts and almonds and rice and heavy coconut pastries stuffed with jam and rich sugary syrups. It was divine.

"Tomorrow I'll show you the list of our clients. But you must resist temptation and be discreet. You have no idea how funny. Aristocratic ladies that want prizefighters' sons, nouvelles riches with perfectly fertile husbands that long for royal sperm. Then there are couples looking for new blood after their first children have turned out badly."

"What do people say about our clinic in Tangier?"

"Some kind of gynecological clinic. They're not interested. Jeweled ladies, so it brings money to town. Nobody really cares."

"What do you do in the evening?"

"Sometimes the temptation is strong to shoot myself. I come here fairly often or I dine with friends. During the day there's the sea and gallops along the dunes. You can fly to Marrakech in no time. It's worth it. And when you have a house, you can have friends to stay."

"Try to amuse Mark when he comes. He's already bored anyway. Maybe it would be better if he joined me in Moscow."

"That's absurd."

"See what sort of humor he's in, then."

The boy had finished his dance, the veils were on the floor, and he stood there naked. Rather tense and nervous applause from the other tables. The boy must have been about fifteen. Melinda smiled at him.

"If I offer him money," she asked Helen, "do you think he'd come with me?"

"He'd go with anyone and he wouldn't ask for much. But he'd tell all his chums and they'd tease you."

"I wouldn't care."

"But you've got something better."

"It would be amusing to pay someone to come to bed with me."

"There'll be plenty of time for that sort of thing. That's all you'll do when you're fifty—in one way or another."

"It must be very boring. How is it that you're so wise, Helen?"

"I'm not wise, I'm fifty."

"And do you pay?"

"I am a famous writer, and that's a very powerful aphrodisiac. But sometimes . . . well . . . little gifts . . ."

"I'll write a book then."

The Moroccan painter invited them to his table for some hashish. Melinda told them at once that she'd never taken it and they must be patient with her and teach her.

Mohammed Abib gave her a long blond wood pipe carved with more or less decorative motifs. He showed her how to clean it by removing the small bowl and the stem. He took a bit of the pungent fine green powder between his fingers.

"It's not like marijuana. You've got to smoke a great deal more, lock out the world and concentrate."

"A pipeful lasts a very short time. You must clean the pipe each time and refill it with hashish. Be careful not to pack it too tight or too loosely. Now you're on your own. We'll all be going into trance and you mustn't disturb anyone.

"Slowly a marvelous sense of peace and happiness and calm will descend. The eyes look into the infinite, your movements will become slow, and your sight will become magical. Everything you look at will glow with incredible colors. Think of nothing. Nothing except the smoke you draw into your lungs, withdraw from the world . . ."

She liked the initiation. It had something unmistakably sexual about it.

But could she manage to concentrate on the pipe and the green powder? She couldn't concentrate when making love, so how could she propped up on uncomfortable cushions with a wooden pipe in her mouth and ridiculous people all around her doing the same thing? She'd surely start laughing.

She started to think about Moscow, about Sligovitz and how she would seduce him. She had just received a telegram from Mark saying that he would be arriving the next day, only a few hours after her departure for Moscow. Finally. To have Mark, tour Europe with him, have his name, legally be his wife.

The second pipeful . . . She didn't manage to clean the wood properly, she drew in puffs of the powder that made her cough. If she packed the powder, the pipe wouldn't draw. The others were all smoking quietly with dreamy faces. Melinda felt nothing. She was convinced that, as in everything, one must concentrate seriously. To see Christ, to talk to a ghost, to make love, to smoke hashish—you need faith. And that was one thing that Melinda found exceedingly difficult.

Mark alone in Tangier. Was that a mistake? But then it would be too late for him to go back to Aglaia in England. He belonged to Melinda. There was, of course, the possibility that at the last moment Mark would not arrive. But then with Mark there had always been that chance.

Helen lit her fourth pipeful, if Melinda had counted right. She was a lovely woman with a face that made friends. And the clinic was a masterpiece of intelligence.

Was she seeing magical colors? Really, it was just as it always was. Helen was on her fifth. Melinda was getting very fed up and wanted another one of those pastries. Where had the waiter gone? Everyone was gazing into nothingness.

Melinda wanted to go to the lavatory.

She also wanted to talk to Helen, for she had to leave very early the next morning.

She had to sneeze.

She could resist no longer.

"Sorry, but I've really had enough of this. What a colossal bore."

"But did you really experience something?"

"I suppose it's partly self-induced, and then you have to inhale deeply."

"Please don't forget about Mark. He'll be arriving this afternoon. See that there's a car to meet him at the airport and get him a nice room."

"Don't worry."

"If there are any messages, cable or telephone. General Delivery, Moscow. As soon as I arrive I'll cable my address. But don't write care of Sligovitz. That might scare him off."

"Bon voyage! And don't overtire yourself."

"Look after Mark. He's such a dear."

In Paris she transferred to an Aeroflot plane. If she had had more notice she could have arranged to meet Mark at the Paris airport for lunch. But then he might have decided to go with her to Moscow, and then how would she have seduced Sligovitz?

Maybe Melinda would, after all, be able to launch a rocket.

Did Mark realize that she would have to give up a lot to marry

Melinda

him? Give up a life of adventure . . . at least for a while . . . maybe Mark could get used to her kind of life and follow her.

Suddenly the idea of marrying Mark was less appealing.

Mirko Sligovitz did not meet her at the airport but he sent a large black Volga for her. There was that same confusion at Moscow airport that had struck her before. Dozens of tractors hauling airplanes onto the runways, the crowds of people buying photographs of Western movie stars, Lana Turner, Gina Lollobrigida, Gary Cooper . . .

Where did she want to be taken?

"Actually I haven't booked anything," said Melinda, shivering. It was much colder than Paris. "I'd like to go to the National, but I know it's not always easy . . ."

"Just call Professor Sligovitz, and there'll be no trouble at all."

"We could drop my bags at the National then. Is the Professor at home?"

"He'll be in the laboratory until four and expects you at his flat at six. He told me to wait for you."

"I can get a taxi. Otherwise the Professor won't have the car."

"Don't worry. The Professor has several cars at his disposal. He is always accompanied."

The driver had a broad pink face and deep-set blue eyes.

Moscow seemed the same. The great outer fringe with huge crumbling mansions and new buildings going up by the hundreds. The lack of stores, the straight, identical streets everywhere. Just like the outskirts of Milan. She had forgotten the continual disintegration of the roads. The heavy-set laboring women mixing bitumen, cleaning the streets, and filling the holes with stones were part of the landscape.

She had no difficulty at the National. She was given a room with bath on the third floor with a view of the Kremlin.

How would Sligovitz receive her? Had she come specially for him? Had she come on other business, and taken the opportunity to look him up? The latter was the better story, but she couldn't think why one would make the trip from Tangier to Moscow.

Perhaps for shopping. That seemed a good idea to her. After all, people go to Paris or New York to do their Christmas shopping. Why couldn't Melinda do hers at GUM and go back with Ukrainian embroidered shirts, fur hats, sables, and pounds of green caviar?

Dressed in white, she arrived in Ulitza Začepa, where Sligovitz had an apartment, furnished with total lack of taste. A few souvenirs of his native Albania, a number of chairs without recognizable color or shape, and photographs on the walls. Outside a detective disguised as a passer-by.

"M'linda . . ." The tone of voice was so warm that there was no doubt he was glad to see her.

"Professor, how are you?"

"Call me Mirko, please. I called you M'linda. I hope you don't mind, but after your call from Tangier I took the liberty of making plans for the evening. But perhaps you've made other plans already. . ."

"None at all." She liked Mirko Sligovitz's wrinkled skin and old liquid eyes. Melinda wondered if she was developing a Lolita-complex in reverse—she found Sligovitz's antiquity positively attractive.

"I've got tickets for the Bolshoi, M'linda. I haven't been for a long time. They are singing *The Marriage of Figaro* in Russian. It won't be much, I'm afraid. You've surely seen marvelous performances. For your sake, M'linda, I wish they were giving a Russian opera. The Bolshoi is marvelous in *Boris* and *A Life for the Czar*. Of course, we're less strong on Mozart. But I have forgotten, do you like music?"

Here was a man who would have spoiled her. Not like Mark . . . Mirko was the kind of person who would remember what she liked and didn't like.

"Yes."

"Their *Boris* . . . hundreds in the chorus . . . in the second scene it's almost as if you were at a real coronation . . . our theater shakes with voices, the walls almost collapse . . ."

Melinda

He spoke with fierce pride about the Bolshoi. "We are," "Our theater."

"I've only seen *Boris* once, but it was a poor performance."

"Why have you come to Moscow, M'linda?"

"Shopping. I wanted to buy some furs and some Christmas presents. And then I wanted to see you. Remember? I promised."

"I never hoped you'd remember that promise, my dear."

"And you promised me something . . ."

"What? Your memory must be much better than mine, you're so young."

"You promised to name a rocket after me."

"Oh that, I hadn't forgotten that at all."

"Where is the rocket? May I launch it? Will it really be called Melinda?"

"Of course the 0043/ZB is not in Moscow, but I can tell you now that its launching will be one of the most important events of the twentieth century. That's all I can tell you. It's a state secret."

"But if it's called Melinda and I'm to launch it, you must tell me everything. You're not going to call it by that number . . . what was it?"

"0043/ZB. No. It will be called M'linda. We'll talk about it later. How long will you be staying in the Soviet Union?"

"I don't know yet. It depends . . ."

"On what?"

"On a lot of things."

"How awfully rude I am. I still haven't offered you anything to drink. What would you like? Actually, all we drink is vodka." He poured a long drink into a colored glass. "What a beautiful white dress," he continued. "White goes best with human skin. I'd love to give you a white fur coat."

Things were moving along very fast, Melinda realized, and Mirko was so charming. There was not going to be any need for a grand seduction scene after all.

The opera had been very modest indeed. They arrived late, just before the "Non so più cosa son, cosa faccio," which was sung in Russian by a Cherubino whose immense, unsuccessfully trussed bosom suggested anything but an adolescent page. Later the Contessa's aria "Dove son" was simply cut.

"I'm glad you noticed," Mirko whispered to her. He had caught her expression of shock even in the darkened theater. He was an attentive and affectionate companion.

As usual, the Bolshoi was full of delegation groups.

In the stalls there was a throng of husky youths, Negroes, mulattoes, and blonds, all of whom obviously belonged to the same delegation. Melinda and Mirko wondered what brought together all those muscles in the stalls of the Bolshoi—until, at the second intermission, they heard them speaking Portuguese. Mirko asked the detective who had followed them and was sitting in the row behind them. It was the Brazilian soccer team, in Moscow for the world championship.

They dined in a new restaurant. There was a queue, but Mirko had booked a table. And his name got immediate reaction, rare in Russia, as Melinda had had occasion to observe on her first trip there. The detective tried to pretend to be just another diner but there wasn't a table for him and Mirko refused to invite him to theirs.

"He's become positively ridiculous. He follows me all day, and sometimes I have to give him a lift. Otherwise he'd lose me."

"Poor thing, will he have to wait outside without eating?"

"He chose his job, didn't he?"

He sat down after she did.

"I'm sorry, M'linda, not a very brilliant evening."

He took her hand very tenderly. She squeezed Mirko's forcefully. She realized her gesture had been too comradely and had upset, if not disappointed, the professor's delicate romanticism.

"That's silly. It was a lovely evening, and the greatest pleasure was to spend it with you, Mirko."

The next day she telephoned Helen. It took all morning to get the call through.

Melinda

"Helen? What? . . . I can't hear you. I can't hear a thing. I'll send the phial this afternoon. I'll send it by refrigerator car and you'll have it Thursday morning. You'll have to send someone for it. Yes, I explained everything. Somewhat surprised . . . Fast? . . . What? . . . He's arrived? . . . How is he? . . . That's what I thought . . . All right, tell him to come here. I'm at the National Hotel. I thought I might move to Ulitza Začepa today, but I guess I'll have to do without. Anyhow I may be going away with him . . . No, the Professor. There's a gadget I'm to launch . . . No, he hasn't told me where; it's a state secret . . . Siberia, I think . . . Pleased? Tell your client it's on the way . . . Who? . . . He wants to speak to me? . . . He's with you now? You could have told me before. Tell him to shout, he always speaks so softly . . ."

A moment of silence, then Mark's voice. Melinda lit a cigarette.

"Mark? Speak up, for heaven's sake . . . You're bored? . . . I'll be back soon . . . You really want to come? I think it's mad, but do what you like . . . I'm launching a rocket, actually a space capsule, oh, I don't know what they're called. One of those things that goes up in the sky. They're calling it Melinda . . . Of course I have to. I've never done it before . . . When will you have the divorce? . . . What do you mean, ten years? Is Aglaia out of her mind? What does she think? . . . Dief? . . . Yes, I know he's dead. There were complications? . . . What did she say? . . . Who? . . . Anthony? . . . Why in the world? . . . All right. Don't send a telegram, just come and join me at the hotel . . . Darling, really? . . . You mustn't feel that way . . . We'll have our own house, our friends, and we'll be peaceful and happy, wherever you like. Forget England . . . We'll go back in a few years . . . the lawyers . . . But of course I love you . . . All right, now it's your turn to come after me and depend a bit on me . . . We could take a lovely trip. South America . . . Where? No, why Australia? Of all places! What ever gave you that idea? . . . Darling, even if I am rich, this call is costing a fortune. You can't really have a conversation . . . No, of course not, who could be listening in? These poor Russians, always accused of spying . . . What possible interest could the Russian government have in what we say to each other? . . . If you continue to be so anti-Russian they'll withdraw your visa . . . You haven't got one? . . . It'll take two days at the very least then, before you can come . . . How am I? Fine, darling, fine, as always . . . Happy? . . . And you? . . . I'm sorry . . . But aren't you happy with Helen in Tangier? . . . You don't think she's very interesting . . . Find something to do. Moscow is a fascinating city, you'll see. I'll leave messages for you every minute in the hotel, in case you arrive and I'm not there . . . I might be out, for example . . . Take care of yourself, don't worry, don't fret . . . You're not alone, believe me . . . Yes, I love you . . . Don't be silly . . . of course, I love you . . . Bye."

She combed her hair and went to Mirko's house.

Mark liked being alone, passing whole days at his desk, but he had to feel that there was someone in the house waiting for him.

The idea of Helen was not enough.

The idea of Melinda, though, would have given him great pleasure.

But would she stay home, or would she be off without a word on some mad adventure? He should have thought of that before. Why in the world had he compromised himself that way? It had been such a satisfactory situation, husband to Aglaia, lover to Melinda.

He found Tangier boring and hot. He hated traveling, and he hated any place that wasn't England.

He had been to the casino and lost a great deal of money. He hadn't played roulette for thirty years. Why waste one's time like that? Simple boredom.

Melinda's call . . . not like her calls in the past. A certain impatience. If it hadn't been for Anthony's visit . . . No, he loved Melinda. He had decided to live with her, that was the important thing. He would change her, make her more responsible. Perhaps she would bear him a child. Melinda was still so young. Mark could certainly change her, mould her, soften her, make her dependent and aware of certain duties.

Did Abraham know of their decision?

Aglaia wouldn't give him a divorce. She would wait until he came to his senses, she had said. As if one could undo certain things. What was Aglaia doing all by herself in the country? Walking the dogs through the woods, maybe unhappy . . .

To be in the country with her. In the morning, breakfast in their separate rooms with the papers. Then a walk through the woods, usually together, with the dogs. Then Aglaia's secretary would arrive at ten, his at ten-thirty.

And now? What kind of life would Melinda give him? He didn't want to go from one person to another, one city to another. Would she betray him? Was she betraying him now? But Melinda was in love with Mark . . . She had pursued him so insistently, so steadily. He shouldn't think like that. He loved her. He had done right to abandon everything for her. Otherwise what kind of sacrifice would it have been? It would be marvelous to meet in Moscow, just the two of them, and they would return together, in a sleeper . . . Melinda . . . what was she doing? He didn't quite understand about the clinic in Tangier. And she had gone to Moscow for medicines. She could have had them sent. She would have to drop Helen and that job. Mark wanted Melinda to make some sacrifices for him, too. She should be content with a married life—isolated and calm.

He realized he was speaking aloud in the streets of Tangier, as if he were in the country. People stopped to stare at him. He realized his clothes were absurd in that climate, but he'd forgotten to tell the butler to pack summer things. Perhaps it would be different in Moscow. How did people dress in Moscow? Later, gradually, he would have all his clothes sent on. The butler would stick by him; his wages came from Mark.

He telephoned his lawyer from Helen's house.

"Hello. Van Der Belt here. It wouldn't be a bad idea to talk to my wife . . . It's too hot here . . . No, I hate going abroad, I never liked it. And I'm certainly not here on holiday . . . What should you speak to her about? Who? . . . What? . . . With whom? . . . Oh, you didn't know? I've decided to divorce my wife but she doesn't want to hear about it for the moment . . . Desertion? . . . I was almost forced . . . It's a long story . . . With discretion, try to find out what she . . . And come see me about it next Saturday afternoon . . . All right, you may be very busy, but I'm very rich . . . Cable me . . . The director of a rest home was killed, I was in the rest home, it seems that I am suspected . . . I know it's completely absurd, you don't have to tell me . . . But the important thing is that my wife not be stubborn . . . I don't know . . . Make her understand . . . I can tell you? Yes, I want to marry someone else . . . Not see her, how can I? . . . Don't worry. After all, I'm very rich . . . I'm not making any false steps, all I do is walk along the Tangier seafront . . . No, I'm alone for the moment . . . In Russia . . . And why not? . . . Just imagine . . . We'll talk about it Saturday. Don't forget. I'll send someone to the airport for you. Will you stay a couple of days? Why don't you bring your wife? . . . You're not married? . . . Better still . . . Do you have to know? My confessor? . . . Yes . . . How did you guess? . . . Yes, her. Melinda Publishing . . . Are we compromised already? When? But we've always been very careful . . . I don't want my wife to be unhappy, I just want a divorce . . . The same to you. Goodbye."

The call had not cheered him. And the fact that everyone, absolutely everyone, including Aglaia, knew of his affair with Melinda annoyed him. Well then, why had no one ever said anything to him?

He would be seeing Melinda in a few hours and the bad humor, the insecurity, the nerves would disappear. Enough to touch her hair . . . kiss her mouth . . .

Melinda

Melinda was terribly sorry.

Mirko had insisted and there was nothing she could do. Either leave at once, follow him blindly and launch the gadget, or stay in Moscow and give it all up.

She left a note for Mark:

"Darling: I can't even ask you to join me, because I haven't any idea where I'll be in a few hours. If you wait in Moscow (go see the Tretiakov, the Pushkin Gallery, and the Kremlin), I'll be back as soon as I can. Hugs. Your Melinda. P.S. How far along are we on the divorce?"

They were taking off in a large airplane, three other people were with them. Sligovitz introduced them.

She recognized one of them. It was the detective, now disguised as a flight officer.

"First names only. Otherwise our poor M'linda will be altogether confused. Yevgeny, Mischa, and this is my assistant Nikolai."

"Later," Melinda told the waiter, who was pouring vodka. "It's too early for me."

The other three went off to the back of the plane for their drink. Melinda and Mirko remained sitting next to each other.

Neither had a paper or a book.

"I wouldn't want you to misunderstand, M'linda," said Mirko, "but the 0043/ZB which I have designed and which will be named after you has a great future—it will land on the moon. At first we had thought to send up two monkeys, but after several experiments we realized it could carry a human being. Just imagine, the first man on the moon . . ."

"The first moon rocket . . . named for me . . . How happy I

am, Mirko. What a wonderful present. When will the ceremony take place? And when will we tell the press?"

"In just a few days, after we have selected the astronaut."

"Where are we going?"

"You'll know when we get there."

"Will I meet the astronauts?"

"The one we select, of course."

"Will it be a man or a woman?"

"We believe that the female constitution can better survive the temperature changes."

"How long will the astronaut remain on the moon?"

"A few hours. He'll have to take photographs and stay in constant radio contact with us. He won't even get out of the 0043/ZB."

"Marvelous," said Melinda, with a yawn. Her eyes were full of headlines announcing the launching of the Melinda and the Melinda's success, and she fell asleep.

It was hot in the plane. Mirko drew down the flower-decorated nylon shades and asked Nicolai not to smoke.

"I told her," he said to his assistant.

"What does she think?"

"All I've told her is that the 0043/ZB will have a human passenger and land on the moon."

"You didn't tell her everything?"

"A bit at a time. The launching will be glorious. The Prime Minister, the television and the press. We'll release the photographs after the landing."

"It will so surely be a success that one could have direct coverage. Is she at all interested in publicity?"

"That's the only part that does interest her."

"I'll take care of it at once."

They had a second vodka. Melinda heard them whispering and barely woke up. She moved the curtain.

"Oh, we're over the Aral Sea," she mumbled through her yawns. "We're not going to Siberia."

Melinda

"Good for you, Melinda, you know your geography."

"I've already flown over here. I so hoped we were going to Siberia . . ." The lids lowered over those famous eyes, slightly clouded by sleep and fatigue.

He had to wait five days for his visa. He was furious. At the Moscow airport he settled in at the Intourist office. The girl on the other side of the wooden counter barely spoke English and did not understand a word Mark uttered.

"Where is the guide?"

"What?"

"My guide."

"You ull haf guide at hotel in few hours."

"I'd like one now, at once, to accompany me to the hotel."

"Vhat say?"

"I said that the guide must accompany me to my hotel."

"Who?"

"The guide."

"For dot is no need. Taking taxi."

"And if the taxi man tries to cheat me?"

"Repeat and please to speak slowly, sir."

"If he is dishonest he will take my money."

"Who?"

"The taxi driver."

"Soviet taxi drivers not cheat."

"Suppose he isn't Soviet."

"Cannot be but Russian nationality."

"He might be a White Russian, a cheating anti-Communist. Besides I don't know how to pay. I don't understand Russian money."

"Is easy, learn fast."

"It may be easy for you, you've lived here all your life. I'd like to see you handle pennies and shillings in England."

"Vhat you say?"

"Where is my guide?"

"As Intourist visitor first-class super de luxe, you have right to guide six hours a day and car vith drive four hours day."

"What? I don't understand a word you're saying. My dear young lady, you know you speak and pronounce English very badly indeed. It's almost unintelligible. You'd better get another girl who speaks better than you do, right away. I might need the guide for several hours. Then again, I may dismiss him right away."

"But you here in tourism, many thinks must see, learn hear important historic ideas."

"I hate touring. I get terribly bored."

"Vhy is having then first-class super de luxe tourist certificate?"

"It's much easier to get a visa that way."

"Not come to Moskva for working? No?"

"My very dear young lady, I have never in my life worked in England. Just imagine if I'm going to start here in Moscow. Where is my guide?" Mark had raised his voice considerably, assuming that his diction would be more readily understood. But he persisted in uttering idiomatic expressions in his rapid White's Club accent. At last the guide arrived. She led Mark to a taxi.

"Where are you going?"

"To the Hotel National."

"Have you booked?"

"My wife has booked."

"Her name is Van Der Belt?"

"Publishing. In England we always book in the wife's name."

"The Baroness is your wife?" with a note of respect and deference.

"Why? Have you heard of her? Do you know the name Van Der Belt? My family name?"

"No, only the Baroness's. That's all we hear since this morning . . ."

Melinda

Mark looked at the woman. He suddenly realized that if he were to lose the guide he wouldn't remember the color of her hair or what she looked like. Short and fat . . . She was one of those women born old. She would look like that all her life.

"What are those asphalt strips in the middle of the road for? So that no one will cross over? What are all these Communist flags for? What square is that? What are all those people in line for? What's that?"

"That's the Kremlin. Don't you recognize it?"

"And why should I? This is my first visit to Moscow. If you came to Maidenhead I'm sure you wouldn't recognize the main square. What's written on those signs? How amusing that your alphabet is different . . . just to make life harder for all of us. My mother knew Russian," he sighed.

"Really? And you?"

"I speak no language. I barely read English. My mother used to say that Russian was ugly and difficult, and that it was much nicer to read Tolstoy in German or French than in the original. In any case, she always impressed on us that he was a terrible writer. Do you read Dostoevsky?"

"Dostoevsky? We are advised not to by the authorities, but we read him anyhow, with reservations of course."

"I can't imagine what reservations. What about Pasternak?"

"Pasternak is not published in the Soviet Union."

"Why? How very peculiar. I thought he was Russian."

"We all know why. Political reasons, in part, and in part Western propaganda. Besides he wasn't a very good writer and not much of a poet."

"How very odd. It's the first time I've heard such remarks about Pasternak. Where is he living now?"

"Who?"

"Pasternak."

"He's dead."

"Poor fellow. When did it happen?"

"A few years ago."

"Really?"

"This is the National."

The driver took out the bags as Mark and the guide entered the hotel.

"You'll have to give me a hand. What's your name?"

"Anya."

"Come along, Anya, ask them where the Baroness is. If she's in her room, have them tell her that her husband has arrived."

Mark looked around. Art nouveau decor, velvet and gilt wood —it might have been the Ritz for that matter.

"As I expected," Anya said a few minutes later, "the Baroness isn't back yet. I checked with the hall porter."

"What? What do you mean, as you expected?"

"Everyone knows that the Baroness went to Alma Ata."

"How does everybody know? I didn't know, and I'm her husband. And what is she doing at Ata-Ata? What sort of place is it? A nightclub?"

The hall porter brought him an envelope. It was addressed to Mark in Melinda's handwriting.

"Darling: I can't even ask you to join me, because I haven't any idea where I'll be in a few hours. If you wait in Moscow (go see the Tretiakov, the Pushkin Gallery, and the Kremlin), I'll be back as soon as I can. Hugs. Your Melinda. P.S. How far along are we on the divorce?"

"What is my wife doing in Ata-Ata?" Mark again asked Anya. "Never mind, just telephone Professor Sligovitz's."

"What should I say?" Anya asked.

"That I want to speak to him."

The servant had answered, Anya told him, and said that the Professor was in Alma Ata, of course.

"What do you mean 'of course'? What do you mean 'servant'?" Mark asked. "You don't have servants in Russia, at least you shouldn't have. Everybody knows that."

"There are servants, but they're servants of the state."

"And does the state pay them?"

"Yes."

"And the masters?"

"They, in turn, pay the state."

"It's the same thing, just more complicated. Imagine the kind of complications I'd make for the state: I have nine servants at home."

"You wouldn't be entitled to nine servants if you lived in the Soviet Union."

"I don't and I wouldn't even dream of it. But who is entitled to have personal servants?"

"Scholars, scientists, dancers, politicians."

"It's the same thing. In England, aristocrats who still have money and rich men who have become aristocrats by being dancers, scholars, politicians, and so on. My dear Anya, we're right back where we started. I must find my wife. What do you suggest I do?"

"Don't you know that your wife is at Alma Ata to be launched into space in a rocket called Melinda that will land on the moon? The radio and television have been talking about it for hours . . . and the newspapers . . . all over the world."

"What? Are you sure you understood?"

"How is it you don't know?"

"My god. Where is this Ata-Ata? She'll have to change her mind at once. Miss, take me to Ata-Ata at once."

"That's impossible. It's very far away."

"Well then, take me to a travel agency and we'll get two tickets for Ata-Ata. Where is this place?"

"In Asia. Near Mongolia. It's called Alma Ata."

"Far?"

"Very. And do you have a permit?"

"For what?"

"To go to Alma Ata. I seem to remember that your visa allows you to go no farther than 300 kilometers from Moscow."

"I'll go with you."

"But I haven't a permit either. And I can't leave Moscow."

"I'm rich. I can buy a dozen return tickets."

"That's not the question. You need the permit in order to buy the ticket."

"We'll rent a plane then."

"There are no private planes to rent in Russia."

"I must go. I must see her. I must make her change her mind."

The hall porter whispered something to Anya. Mark's forehead was beaded with perspiration, his beautiful eyes were clouded over, and his shoulders were hunched. Mark rubbed his forehead as if he found some relief in the gesture.

Melinda . . . finished . . . gone again . . . left. She was going to the moon. She hadn't even telephoned . . . She left him all alone in that hotel, with his bags on the floor.

"Well, take my bags upstairs," he told the taxi driver and asked what sort of tip he should give him.

"The porter," Anya interrupted, "says that the Baroness left no instructions that anyone would be coming into her room. And he doubts that you are her husband, because word has just come that Mirko Sligovitz and Baroness Melinda Publishing were married in the town hall of Alma Ata with the Prime Minister and the President of the Soviet Republics as witnesses."

"I hardly think that news is reliable," Mark said wanly. "It must be some sort of publicity."

Anya looked at Mark Van Der Belt. Both hands were at his temples, and he seemed extremely tired.

"Let's go into the hall and look at the television," she said. "Perhaps we'll hear the news."

Anya took his arm. In the hour since she had first met Mark Van Der Belt, he seemed to have aged considerably.

"I've had your things taken to the Baroness's room," she said. "I'm sure she would have wanted that."

Mark sat down in a large brown velvet armchair. His body and his fatigue sank into a mass of springs that had lost their elasticity and sent up a cloud of dust.

A figure on the screen . . . it was speaking . . . it was a man. In

Melinda

the background a horrible apparatus. Suddenly a picture of
Melinda.

"What is the man saying?"

"They're speaking about her."

"About whom?"

"About Baroness Publishing."

"Translate."

"Just a minute, let me hear first."

"But you're my guide. I'm paying you to translate . . ."

"Baroness Publishing, who became Baroness Sligovitz this morning at the Alma Ata town hall, has been in space for three hours,
headed toward the moon in a rocket designed by our greatest
scientist. Here is a photo of the 0043/ZB, the Melinda, that for
nineteen hours will carry the Professor's wife. Melinda Sligovitz
will be not only the first woman but the first human being on the
moon. This morning the Baroness changed her nationality, adopt-
ing Soviet citizenship. Here is a photograph of the Baroness as a
child. This is the Baroness at the time of her first marriage . . .
This is a photograph of her father, Abraham, whom we inter-
viewed in London."

The quivering face of Abraham appeared on the screen.

"I am happy and proud to be the father of the first human
being on the moon. I am proud that my daughter was brave
enough to accept and that she has married Nobel Prize winner
Mirko Sligovitz. If he can hear me now, my dear seventh son-in-
law, congratulations and welcome to our family. I hope you will
last longer than the other six. My new son-in-law is older than I
am. We're all very excited here in London and I am giving a
party (maybe you can see it on your screens) for hundreds of
Melinda's friends. The party will continue as long as our darling's
in flight. Having a marvelous time, dancing and drinking. We'll
be with her throughout her adventure. And when she returns I
hope she will want to write her memoirs for her father describing
what she has seen in space . . ."

"It is calculated that the rocket will reach the moon," the commentator continued, "at seven tomorrow morning, Soviet time. Professor Sligovitz is in constant communication with his wife. Professor," the commentator asked a white face that had appeared on the screen, "when did you last speak to the Baroness?"

"About ten minutes ago."

"How was she?"

How could Melinda have married that old man, Mark wondered. If Abraham was younger than his son-in-law, Sligovitz must be almost seventy. And he had an ambiguous air about him. And how could Melinda have forgotten their plans for the future?

"She's fine," said Sligovitz with the voice of Anya, who continued to translate rapidly, "in marvelous spirits and in complete control. She was describing the color of the sky."

"How did you manage to teach her in such a short time?"

"Our rocket doesn't require special training. M'linda's remarkable intelligence will help us in this work. And now, if you'll excuse me, I must go back to talk to her . . ."

"In just a moment," the commentator continued in Anya's monotonous translation, "for the first time in history, we will hear an astronaut's voice on television as she speaks to her husband. Of course, we won't see her. Attention, we're in contact . . ."

Mark was excited. Melinda in outer space, at that very moment, and the whole world listening for her voice. Melinda, no longer his . . . A faint noise. Then "Hello, hello. Louder."

Melinda was speaking English.

"Darling," Anya was no longer translating. "Something's going wrong." A note of anguish in the voice. "The rocket isn't climbing. It's going around the earth, in an orbit of its own. What button should I press? Damn it. I don't want to spend the rest of my life in this coffin."

"We're linked up to television," thundered Sligovitz's voice.

"What the hell do I care? Something's wrong, terribly wrong . . ."

Melinda

Anya lept to her feet. She was the only one in the room besides Mark who understood what was happening. She rushed to the television set.

"Please . . ." said Mark.

"We are interrupting this program," Anya translated the words of the commentator, "because of technical difficulties."

"What news?" asked Dame Elisabeth, rubbing her eyes.

Silver and gold decorations hung wearily from the center of the ceiling. The rotating lights creating an effect of spinning comets and satellites on the walls had lost the brilliance they had had the first day.

"They've heard nothing for a couple of days," said Anthony, munching a vol-au-vent.

"I'd like to lie down for a few hours, but Abraham gets angry when I mention it."

"For two days he's been promising marvelous things to celebrate the culminating moment. Fireworks over London, a cascade of stars from the ceiling, gifts for everyone, an incredible buffet."

"I think something has gone wrong."

"When was Melinda to arrive?"

"More than twenty-four hours ago."

"What do they say on the radio?"

"They say there's no official communiqué."

Helen, who had come from Tangier for the occasion, had a space hairdo, with silver pins and stars. Dame Elisabeth tried to avoid her, but they ran into each other on the dance floor or at the buffet every half hour.

"I think it's Helen's fault," Dame Elisabeth whispered to Anthony.

371

"Fault? For what?"

"That Melinda decided to go to the moon."

"I don't see how Helen could have influenced her."

"You know they have this absurd partnership, a clinic or something. Hasn't Abraham told you?"

"Melinda mentioned something about it, but I thought it was going along very well."

"I haven't seen the Van Der Belts these past few evenings."

"Mark is in Moscow."

"Who told you that?"

"Helen. He went after Melinda. Colossal confusion."

"How wicked. And Aglaia?"

"I don't know, but she certainly didn't go to Moscow."

Abraham joined them. He was very tired but smiling.

"You ought to lie down for a while," Elisabeth suggested lovingly.

"Nonsense. We must be awake for the historic moment. Lawrence has come. I'm glad that Melinda's ex-husbands have come to the party." He disappeared into the crowd.

Many of the guests had already left. Some came back, but fewer and fewer. Even the newspapermen didn't know what to write after the first day.

"Why don't we call Mark? He'll probably have word."

"And where will we find him? Abraham ought to try something, but he's so busy making statements to the press and having his picture taken that he doesn't even know the time of day."

"Isn't he worried?"

"On the contrary. He told me he had already sold world rights to the first words his daughter utters when she returns to Europe. As well, of course, as selected passages from the book that Melinda is going to write for him."

"Abraham ought to be a little more self-contained."

"He's at the peak of his career. And his daughter's. Who can stop him?"

The orchestra played spatial and lunar music: "Blue Moon,"

Melinda

"Moon of Manakoora," "Devil Moon," "Stardust," "Shine on, Harvest Moon," and "Swinging from a Star." They were playing these tunes for the hundredth time in the Claridge's ballroom, rented for the occasion.

"In another minute I'll have to leave. I can't take any more," said Dame Elisabeth as she collapsed on a sofa.

"I'll go talk to Abraham for a minute. I'm really worried. I think something has happened."

Anthony looked round the room for Abraham. He saw him deep in conversation across the room.

"Abraham, I've got to talk to you for a minute."

"I can't just now, dear boy. The television people are here and want to interview me."

"Have you any news?" Anthony asked a little man who was busy with the camera.

"About what?"

"The rocket."

"I don't know nothing, guv. I'm a cameraman."

A man wearing dark glasses and with a pipe in his mouth came towards Anthony.

"Are you the brother or the ex-husband? We'd like to interview you, too, after her father. We could sit down and prepare the questions here in the corner. You must be precise, but brief. Three minutes maximum. If you make a mistake, don't worry. Don't be nervous. My name's Paul. You can tell us what Melinda was like, what you did together, what kind of personality . . ."

"Look, I'm not her brother, and I'm not an ex-husband."

"Funny, the director told me to talk to you . . ."

"He's the lover," offered another man wearing dark glasses and with a pipe in his mouth.

"That's her brother," said Anthony, pointing to Medoro, who was coming their way. Anthony had learned never to lose his temper with television people.

"Ah, you're her brother? You must tell us about Melinda, after your father. A short interview. We can prepare some questions here in the corner. You must be precise, but brief. Three minutes maximum. If you make a mistake, don't worry. Don't be nervous. My name's Paul. You can tell us what Melinda was like when you were children . . ."

Medoro was dressed in mourning. It had been a terrible shock to discover that Dief, the osteopath, Ostrovsky, and his aristocratic friend were one and the same person. The shock was even greater when he learned that his generous friend had left a vague will, not clearly in his favor.

"What news?" Medoro asked Anthony.

"I don't know a thing. It seems that no one does."

Suddenly a dozen blinding lights shone on the few tired couples that were still dancing in the center of the room.

The interviewer, with microphone hidden beneath his tie, smiled out at invisible millions.

"Good evening. Here we are at Claridge's, suddenly transformed by a team of decorators into a vision of outer space. And here is the father of our space heroine. Mr. Publishing"—the interviewer came up to Abraham's tired but beaming face—"what will you do after this tragic news?"

"What tragic news? Melinda's marriage? I think it's marvelous, an intellectual family like ours being joined to a Nobel Prize winner of Mirko Sligovitz's stature."

"Mr. Publishing, I am referring to the latest unofficial but certain reports we've had. We know that the 0043/ZB left its original route and has gone into orbit around the earth. It's been orbiting for several hours, and there's no chance of bringing it back. What do you think, Mr. Publishing, of this magnificent sacrifice your daughter has made for love of science?"

Abraham's face and smile had collapsed in ruin during the announcer's words. The wrinkles of age and fatigue were accentuated by the television lights.

"Ladies and gentlemen in the television audience. This is one of the most moving human tragedies. Obviously Baroness Publishing's father wasn't aware of the disaster. This is a tragic mo-

Melinda

ment in the life of a father, to lose a daughter in the prime of life and at the peak of her career . . ."

"But there may be some mistake. Unofficial reports, you said? There must be some other reason for the delay . . . A scientist like Sligovitz doesn't allow all this publicity at the launching of a rocket unless he's altogether sure of success . . . I can't believe . . ."

"And now, ladies and gentlemen, a word from the brother of our unfortunate Baroness. Mr. Medoro Publishing, you who spent your childhood with Melinda, tell us something about the personality of this generous creature who has won a permanent place in our hearts and whose name will go down in history."

"I didn't know Melinda very well . . . We didn't see much of each other . . . Do you really mean it, that she is orbiting the earth? That she won't be back? Around and around? Forever?"

"Yes, forever. That's the latest news. Space observers are managing to intercept radio messages that she is sending to her husband."

"What do they say?"

"Apparently they can't be, uh, repeated. The first message was transmitted on Russian television, before they knew of the tragic mistake. And aren't you proud, Mr. Medoro Publishing, to be the Baroness's brother?"

"I'm sorry I won't be seeing Melinda again . . . I'm sorry . . ."

"And now, ladies and gentlemen, a word from one of the Baroness's closest and most devoted friends, the former Prime Minister. Your Excellency, you knew of the tragedy?"

"No. I knew nothing until this very minute. I was concerned, of course, about the delay and the lack of news. I'd like to know more about it. One of us ought to go to Moscow."

"Mr. Van Der Belt is in Moscow following the tragic misfortunes of his poor friend. It would seem he is making diplomatic relations between Great Britain and the Soviet Union very difficult."

"Has the British Embassy done anything about Melinda?"

"Remember, the Baroness is now a Soviet citizen."

"And Melinda is orbiting around the earth."

"According to American experts, the 0043/ZB will continue to orbit forever."

"And Melinda, is she . . . still alive?"

"The Baroness continues to transmit, so we presume she is alive."

"How long can it last?"

"That we don't know. It depends how much food and oxygen she has aboard the 0043/ZB. But tell us, Your Excellency, what was your reaction to the news? The country is sad, and our television viewers want to know the reactions of this exceptional lady's friends."

"Of course, I'm distraught . . . I can't imagine Melinda alone in space . . . orbiting around the earth forever . . . She must be in agony, knowing what is happening . . . We could only know the full extent of her wrath at this misfortune by tying in to their messages, but I can tell you this: Melinda Publishing loved life . . ."

"Tell us, Your Excellency, about the Baroness's love of life."

"She was a very active woman, with an inquiring mind, adventurous. She is a great loss for the nation, and for all of us . . ."

"And now a word from the Duke of Brighton, the Baroness's second husband . . . Your Grace, tell our television viewers, what did you feel when you heard the terrible news?"

"It must be ghastly for Melinda up there, above us all, spinning around the earth. I wonder if she's thinking of her friends, wondering what we're doing, and how we're reacting to this news. Melinda was a gentle creature, terribly sweet, human, honest, generous. It was her generosity that proved fatal. She has sacrificed herself for humanity, for science. I feel sure that tomorrow *The Times* will run a touching obituary about the loss of this woman who could be at the same time a devoted wife and an important political figure and extremely able at—"

Melinda

"I know we are all moved by the words of Baroness Publishing's former husband, the Duke of Brighton.

"Ladies and gentlemen, our program direct from the ballroom of Claridge's is at an end.

"Good night."

DATE DUE